ESCAPE TO FRE

The sound of voices drew nearer. I seized the rest of the sheets of paper and threw them away. Nadya placed Magda, half-asleep, on my neck and lay on top of me herself. Despite the sound of shots and voices I could still hear Nadya's whisper: 'And do you promise to forget?'

'I promise to forget,' I whispered, moving forward with my load, oblivious to everything that was happening behind me. I slithered forward like a giant tortoise until I reached the fence, feverishly raised the lowest barbed wire with my bare hands, pushed Magda and then Nadya through the opening. Nadya held the wire for me; I felt it cutting into my back but I made it through . . .

Operation Parterre

GEORGE BLAGOWIDOW

SPHERE BOOKS LIMITED
30/32 Gray's Inn Road, London WC1X 8JL

First published in Great Britain by
Piatkus Books Ltd 1982 under the title
of *Border Crossing*

Published by Sphere Books Ltd 1982

TRADE
MARK

Set in Baskerville

Printed and bound in Great Britain by
Cox & Wyman Ltd, Reading

Prologue

Anton's Story

Vienna, June 24, 1939

It was an impossible task for me to keep dry while running through the streets and parks of Vienna during a downpour, particularly since I did not own an umbrella or a raincoat. And I had to rush because I did not want to miss a single word of the speech to be delivered by the head of our organisation, 'Freedom for Russia,' General of the White Guards Skoblin, at four o'clock that afternoon. He was to speak to us on 'The Coming War and the Liberation of Russia.'

Despite my efforts to keep close to the buildings or run under the trees, I arrived soaking wet at Nibelungengasse 11. The meeting was being held in a studio that belonged to a member of our group. The official programme had not yet begun; some fifty men and a handful of women were standing in small groups, talking in agitated voices.

'*Noo vot khorosho,*' Krugov, a former Tsarist officer and the owner of the studio, said on seeing me. 'It's good that you came.'

'We love to see you young people here,' said a plump middle-aged lady extending her hand to me.

I bowed deeply and kissed it, saying: 'Anton Illich Nizov.' Water dripped from my hair on to the sleeve of her dress.

'And people with brains like Anton Illich,' Krugov said.

Fortunately for me, other people came up. In that way I managed to escape further talk about me, something I've always loathed. After I had circled around the other groups, as far as the space allowed, I found myself safe in a corner. From there I could get a good look at the others. It was a typical Russian refugee gathering. All ages were represented. Some members had brought their children along. There were young people in their twenties, like myself. But most of the people seemed to be middle-aged, some were very old. The variation in attire was also typical: a few men were in tuxedos and two ladies wore long silk evening gowns; the majority of the men wore dark suits, some quite new and some very much worn; there were even a number in work clothes. I was pleased about the range of dress. My navy blue suit, threadbare and patched in places, would not attract attention.

All of us present had two things in common: we all spoke Russian and we all had one desire, to return to our homeland. Although I did not know everyone there by name, I was familiar with most of their faces, had heard about their life in Russia before the Revolution, and in some instances, knew their occupations in Vienna.

'The soil on our estate in Malinino was as black as could be,' a tall man in gold-rimmed pince-nez was saying. I knew that he was now a street cleaner since I had seen him a few times at his work. 'It yielded more than double what the average crop in Russia used to be.'

'In our area we could only grow rye,' said another man, small and squarish. 'But I tell you, Ivan Vasilievich, we had the best partridge shooting in the world.'

A few white roses were arranged around a large portrait of Nikolay the Second who looked approvingly at the gathering. Here no one spoke about the grim realities of our life but only about the past, when Nikolay was the monarch, and when a flag, white, navy blue and red, like the one over his portrait here, was displayed everywhere.

Against the opposite wall was a table bearing a large tray of Russian meat pies, pirozhki, from which emanated the delicate aroma of dill and freshly baked dough. It was the standard practice at these gatherings to sell pirozhki prepared by some of the lady members for the benefit of a charity. Since I had not eaten them or any Russian specialities for months, I had skipped lunch, saving my money to buy them.

In the meantime more people had arrived, including Olenin who like me was studying at the University of Vienna. He was accompanied by his wife and two children. When General Skoblin came in I recognised him at once from his pictures. He was a tall man with sparse grey hair, closely cut. Skoblin, led by Krugov, sat down apart from the rest of us; they talked in whispers for a long while. Judging by Krugov's gestures and the expression on his face I concluded that they were discussing very serious things.

By this time the sound of spirited conversation was very loud, but when the General had shaken Krugov's hand and risen to face us, everyone stopped talking. Now you could hear the summer shower beating against the windows and the sound of cars passing on the street below.

'There will be another world war,' the General began, 'in a few weeks or a few months at the latest. In the initial stages the war will be between Poland and Germany, soon to be joined by France and Great Britain on Poland's side, and Italy on the side of Germany. That will be the beginning. Other countries will be drawn into the struggle: Rumania, Bulgaria, Hungary, Turkey, Spain, the Scandinavian countries, other Balkan countries, and it will be difficult to restrict such a war to Europe. The United States and Japan will participate also. The Soviet Union will not be left out of this global conflict. . . .'

I noticed that most of the listeners were nodding their heads in agreement with the speaker.

'Hundreds of thousands of us Russians living in exile, unwelcome and unwanted,' he went on, 'millions of our brothers persecuted by the Red tyranny in our homeland . . . all are waiting for this moment.'

The General was right in describing the life of us emigrants from Russia as hard. In most countries we could not get work permits and without them we could not get jobs. Since most of the nations of Europe did not want to give us citizenship, we had no passports. For us, travelling between countries was practically impossible. We managed to survive by selling our few possessions or by taking menial jobs that the citizens of our host countries did not want.

'The coming war will make it possible for our nation to rise up against our oppressors,' the General said. 'And perhaps in only a few years or even months from now we will be back in our towns or villages, living among people who speak our language and share with us our love for our fatherland. And then, walking through our fields full of cornflowers and wild poppies, and along roads lined with birch trees, we will . . .'

Since I was a child I have been familiar with the image of those birch trees against the Russian landscape. My mother had described them to me, using the endearing form of the noun, Byeryozka, and I longed to see them. But most of all I yearned to be among Russians and to speak my native tongue. The

General's words moved all of us. I noticed that Olenin had tears in his eyes and his wife was trying to control her sobbing; even their children, who could not grasp the meaning of the words, still felt instinctively the emotion of the General's speech and clung more closely to their mother. It was difficult for me to contain my tears at the flicker of hope that the years of misery and aimless wandering might be nearing an end and I might live in my home town, Kazan on the Volga, as my forefathers had done. But I was even more moved by the sight of Olenin and his family. While he might have suffered the same disappointments as I, he was not alone. He had his loved ones to share with him the joys, and the sorrows of the émigré's life. I lived alone longing for the touch of a woman's hand, the sound of her voice. And when I dreamed about returning to Russia I hoped that it would also mean the end of my loneliness.

'Inevitably, in the future struggle,' the General said, 'the Third Reich will be fighting against the Soviet Union. While we cannot possibly accept the Nazi philosophy with its concept of the superiority of the Germanic race – Russia's greatness was built on tolerance and equality for all nationalities – it will be expedient for us to cooperate with the German military forces. . . .'

I saw that his listeners were again nodding their heads in agreement. As for me, the sight of the table with its pirozhki was making it hard for me to concentrate, and despite my interest in the General's speech I began to hope that he would finish soon so that I could satisfy my hunger.

'I am convinced that Germany will win the coming war,' Skoblin continued. 'I and my colleagues have concluded that Germany is years ahead of her potential adversaries – France, England, the Soviet Union – in the strategy of modern tank warfare. While the English rely on separate tank units, and the French and Soviets consider tanks a supporting weapon for infantry, the Germans believe in the coordination of all arms but with tanks being given a superior role. The perfect . . . shall we say . . . orchestration, of all German arms could easily overcome an enemy's substantial numerical superiority in men and armour, provided that that enemy does not develop a substantially superior tank.'

I could see that the children were getting restless, and some of the grown-ups were glancing at the laden table. But the General was not concerned about that; he went on extolling the German military power. At last he came to the end of his speech.

'In the future struggle we may call on all of you,' Skoblin said, 'and ask you to risk your lives in the cause. We know that our cause is just and with God's help we will win.'

A standing ovation followed the General's last words. The same plump lady who had greeted me at the entrance stood up.

'Vaseely Georgievich, we all cordially thank you for your visit here and for your words. As a token of our appreciation of your efforts and your struggle in our cause, we have prepared a short programme, in which our youngest patriots ...'

'Oh, God,' I said to myself. I knew those short programmes – endless declamation, endless reading and playing of instruments. And I was right. It started with Olenin's seven-year-old son reading Lermontov's poem, *Ships*, and went on with recitations by other children of verses by Pushkin, Nyekrasov, Nudson and Tiutchev, followed by a fourteen-year-old Grusha playing Tchaikovski's *First Piano Concerto* – a difficult piece for an accomplished artist, and little Grusha had not had much training. The short programme also included a number of Russian folk songs such as *Kalinka,* each performed by a different soloist, and ended up with the choir singing *Vecherny Zvon,* 'The Evening Bill.' 'We Russians,' I thought, 'have one great defect: we lack common sense. We organise a political meeting and mix in with it the sentimental outpouring of childish performances. We exaggerate everything: a minor upset becomes the source of deep soul searching and pain, and a flicker of good fortune is reason for supreme joy. The tears of our laughter mix easily with the tears of our suffering. We lack a sense of proportion and time means nothing to us. A meeting that should have ended a long time ago must drag on forever.'

Finally, when it was already eight o'clock in the evening, the opulent lady thanked the artist and invited us to join her at the 'buffet' with Russian specialities.

Immediately a long line formed at the table. Service did not start until the tea was ready twenty minutes later. From my position at the end of the queue, I saw the ones with triumphant smiles carrying away plates of pirozhki. As I went on watching the serving of the food, a tall, grey-haired man came up to me.

'I am Lepin, Alexey Nikolayevich,' he said. 'You may not remember me, but I visited you and your mother in Poland.'

I did not remember him. So many friends of my parents had visited us.

'I recognised you,' Lepin said, 'more because of your likeness to your father – the same long hands and legs, the same narrow face – than from my recollection of you when you were fifteen. It was 1930, I think.'

'Pleased to see you again,' I said as we moved with the line towards the table.

'I served with your father in General Wrangel's army. Your father was a real hero. We fought the Reds in Crimea in November of 1920, till the very last moment, allowing thousands of us to escape by ship to Turkey. He was killed in the last battle of our Civil War, giving his life so that we might live.'

I hardly remembered my father, since I was only four years old when we were preparing for our flight from our country. He came to say goodbye, and I still remember his last words to me: 'Antosha, when you grow up I hope that you will be a good human being.' Then he embraced me.

'Colonel Nizov was always full of *joie de vivre,*' Lepin continued, 'and he would not have been happy living here. What a life. I am an assistant clown, the guy who gets knocked down by the chief clown while the crowd roars with laughter. My home is in Berlin now. If you happen to be there, look me up.'

We shook hands.

There were still five men ahead of me in the line, when I heard the lady say, 'No more pirozhki left, no more food.'

'Too bad,' I thought. 'At least they made the others happy.'

As I was walking home I kept thinking of Skoblin's words, of the roads lined with the *beryozka* trees, of Russia, and of the general's call for our sacrifice.

PART I

The Summer

Chapter 1

Berlin, Sunday, June 25, 1939

It was the first Sunday of summer, the first warm and sunny day in many weeks. The ladies in their silk stockings, best summer dresses and colourful hats, accompanied by their husbands in dark vested suits or summer uniforms, filled the parks and crowded the outside cafes. These Berliners enjoyed the sight of flowers and trees, the taste of their Bären beer or the coffee with heavy whipped cream, *Kaffe mit Schlag.*

But there were exceptions. In the General Staff Officers' Club, located in a nineteenth-century building on Unter den Linden Allee, a group of officers oblivious to the blue skies and the aroma of the linden trees in bloom, were sitting in front of a map, playing *Kriegspiel,* the traditional exercise of German officers before the start of a real war. The game played that afternoon was a simulation of the Polish campaign. All the participants had received the booklet of instructions, a 47-page typescript, single-spaced, a week before the game. It had taken each participant several hours to read and understand the 73 rules established for the game, many of which were extended into several sub-rules.

The participants had been divided at random into groups of six players, three of whom played the German side, while the other three represented the Polish adversary. Each trio was given a separate room in which the players could discuss their moves in privacy. Once the players had reached a decision, it was communicated in writing to their opponents.

Under Rule 17b, the players on the Polish side were entitled to the first move. They were sitting in the reference library around an octagonal table under a chandelier of brass and crystal. A large oil painting of Frederick the Great, looking sternly down at them, dwarfed a photograph of the Führer, Adolf Hitler.

Captain von Dolnitz stood up and paced slowly towards the open window through which the sounds of a distant band, the voices of the people passing in the street, and the noise of motor cars, came in to disturb the silence of the room. After shutting the window he marched back to the table and remained standing, his tall, lean body rigid, his blue-grey eyes focused on the map.

'Why must I always play on the losing side?' Captain von Stahlberg asked. He was of medium height, muscular and squarish, with yellowish hair cut short. He was thirty, the same age as von Dolnitz, his friend and colleague at the War Academy. Not expecting to receive any answer, von Stahlberg lit a French cigarette, a Caporal. He was perhaps the only German intelligence officer smoking the cheap French brand.

Major Wurmlein, turning away his large meaty face from the cloud of the strong-smelling tobacco, poured himself a glass of Kirsch, his fifth since the trio had arrived in that room some fifteen minutes ago.

'Ja, ja . . .' Wurmlein said, putting the half empty bottle back on the side table. 'It seems that even before we start we've lost our hops and malt.'

Von Dolnitz frowned. He could hardly understand Wurmlein's Bavarian accent and his folksy expressions. Yet, von Dolnitz wanted to understand every word Wurmlein spoke. For many months von Dolnitz had waited for the opportunity to get acquainted with the major, an intelligence officer like himself, who had friends among the top political leaders of the Third Reich. And right now von Dolnitz would need Wurmlein's power and influence to put through his scheme for a spying mission in the Soviet Union.

'The Kriegspiel is so designed,' von Dolnitz said, turning to von Stahlberg, 'that both sides have equal chances to win. We need only 325 points to be the winners; our opponents would need 1,000 points. The game is supposed to simulate the real situation, but . . .'

'To me it's Wurstegal who wins,' Wurmlein said, drinking his Kirsch, 'as long as we have some fun playing. Though, I must confess I wouldn't mind letting a louse run over Colonel von Krumm's liver, making him really mad by our good moves.' To von Dolnitz's astonishment Wurmlein unbuttoned his tunic.

'Fine,' von Stahlberg said, holding his cigarette in his mouth, 'let's decide on the first move. We have only twenty minutes left.'

Von Dolnitz knew that his friend was rushing because he had a date that evening. Von Stahlberg, a bachelor like himself, had many dates. But the idea that his comrade was thinking of such a thing now, in the midst of the Kriegspiel, an almost sacred occupation, annoyed von Dolnitz.

'I suggest that we divide the front in three parts,' von Stahlberg continued. 'I will take the northern front, the Major will make the moves for the central area, and you, Otto, will direct the moves in the south.'

Wurmlein lifted his heavy body with difficulty, and peered through a pair of thick lenses at the map of Poland and East Germany with a superimposed net of hexagons, each numbered. The playing pieces, small flags, showing names and numbers of various divisions, and mounted on brass stands, had been put in place before the game started by a research officer; they represented the actual deployment of Polish and German troops.

'First we must agree on the general strategy of the game,' Wurmlein said, lighting a black Niemeyer cigar. 'We have Poland here like a ham in an Easter basket. Only a small part sticks out. The only way we can win is to mass our forces on the Vistula, shortening the front by two-thirds.'

'That would mean giving up two-thirds of Polish territory right from the start. The Poles would never do it.'

'Don't forget, Captain, that in this game we are in charge of their army,' Wurmlein said puffing on his cigar.

'In this game,' von Dolnitz said, 'it does not matter where we move the Polish divisions. What matters is how we strengthen them with additional armour. The rules of the game provide for the purchase of tanks from France and horses from Russia.'

'The delivery of the French tanks,' Wurmlein said, 'would take too long by the rules of the game – six moves. By that time we would be finished. And I don't see any military advantage in strengthening Polish cavalry divisions. As it is the Poles are relying on them too much.' The ashes of Wurmlein's cigar fell on the Kashan carpet. The major, seeing von Dolnitz's reaction in his eyes said, 'That only improves the carpet. No point in adding more horses.'

'In my opinion,' von Dolnitz said, 'the only possible winning strategy is to buy the tanks from the Soviet Union.'

'But that is not in the rules,' said von Stahlberg.

'Not directly,' von Dolnitz said. 'But there is rule 64K-(4).' Von Dolnitz opened the rule book and read: 'The player is permitted to modify the rules when, to his certain knowledge, an element exists that would influence the outcome of the game significantly.'

'I am aware of it,' von Stahlberg said, 'but the Russians have nothing but junk . . . and this idea of yours will stretch out the game *ad infinitum*.'

'The Russians have better tanks than you think,' von Dolnitz said. 'They had the best tanks of all the combatants in Spain. They are crazy about tanks.'

'They have over 15,000 tanks, more than all other nations of the world combined. But, despite their tanks –'

'Franco won,' von Dolnitz interrupted, 'because the Russians were not prepared to exploit their advantages.'

'Russian tanks on the Polish front!' Wurmlein said, pouring himself another Kirsch and gulping it down. 'That would be an element of surprise for our adversaries. That would be the way to salt their soup for them. I can see old von Krumm losing his monocle when he hears the news. Their side would probably call for arbitration.'

'I say the Russian tanks are good,' von Dolnitz said. 'And if they've made further progress their tanks might be superior to ours now. I spent two years in Russia in a tank school operated by our general staff. You remember that by the Treaty of Versailles we were prohibited from building our tanks here in Germany? So we built them in Russia and taught the Russians the rudiments of tank warfare. They were very good students, indeed, they learned very fast.'

Major Wurmlein was studying the map and seemed not to be listening.

'There is a time limit, my boys,' Wurmlein said. 'Let's buy the Russian tanks; let's put them on the Vistula; let's move the Polish infantry divisions to 3740, 3826, 3947. Let's keep the mountain division as it stands. The Second Cavalry Division would reinforce the tanks in Krakow.'

'On our first move,' said von Dolnitz, 'we would be able to use the Russian tanks. We could use them on the third move when they would be available on the Polish-Russian border, in the hexagons starting with 2461, 2632 and so on.'

In the next few minutes the players proceeded to write down the proposed moves on a special form, including the one about the purchase of 620 light tanks and 100 medium tanks, thus doubling the Polish arsenal of light tanks and adding the brand new types of medium tanks. When they had filled in the form, von Dolnitz rang and a sergeant picked up the envelope. Twenty-five minutes later, the same sergeant returned with the moves of the other side. At the bottom, in the column for 'Remarks', there was a note in Oberst von Krumm's handwriting: 'In need the old devil would even eat flies.' It was obviously a proverb that the colonel had heard from Major Wurmlein many times.

The next round took 15 minutes for each side. Von Krumm and his players were not prepared to handle the surprise element of the purchase of the Russian tanks by the Poles, and Wurmlein and his colleagues won the game after nine rounds. As soon as the game was over, von Stahlberg saluted and left for his rendezvous. The major poured himself the last drink.

Von Dolnitz had waited for this opportunity to be alone with the major. Stretching his body, he glanced at his white uniform tunic and was ready to speak, but Wurmlein anticipated him.

'Thanks to you,' he said, 'we did not throw our rifles into the wheat field before we had even started. The Soviet tanks were a good idea for this game. But in real life that's all nonsense, nothing but nonsense.'

'The Soviet T-28 is comparable to our Panzer kampfwagen.' When referring to tanks von Dolnitz never abbreviated, as was the custom by calling them Panzer. That way of speaking not only expressed the character and personality of a precise well-organised man; but it was a way of paying respect to tanks, to the study of which he had devoted his entire professional career as well as all his free time. His interest in tanks had begun in his childhood. He was only nine years old when in December of 1917 his mother was notified of the death of his father, Major Rudolf von Dolnitz, in the battle of Cambrai, the first major tank battle in history, the battle that decided the Great War in favour of the Allies. How often, later on, had he heard quoted the famous expression, 'Germany lost not to General Foch, but to General Tank.' During that war the German General Staff believed that wars were won by soldiers and superior morale and not by machines. That was why, in the last few months of the Great War, Germany had produced only 20 tanks compared to the Allies' production of 7,300. And now, before the next war, Captain Otto von Dolnitz, an intelligence officer in the *Fremde Heere Ost* (Foreign Armies East) was concerned that his Fatherland might commit the same error of underestimating the potential enemy in the East, the Soviet Union and its tanks.

'What is most significant is not the quality of their current tanks, Herr Major, but the Soviet capacity to produce enormous numbers of tanks. According to confirmed information, they are producing 200,000 tractors annually. It is easy to convert a tractor factory into a tank factory.'

The major did not seem to listen. He was contemplating the almost empty bottle of Kirsch. Finally, not being able to resist the sight of the transparent liquid, he seized the bottle, overturned it above his glass, and watched the last drops of the Kirsch fall into it; they filled a third of it. Wurmlein raised the glass.

'Prosit, Captain, to you and to your project.'

'Yes, Herr Major. I would like to propose, sir –'

'Tss ... tss ... not here. The walls have ears. Come to see me next Sunday, at seven in the evening, in my apartment at Weidenstrasse 27. It's unofficial, you understand.' Wurmlein rose from the chair, looking at the empty bottle with regret. He appeared older than his 55 years. After a brief salute, he marched out in full control of his body.

Von Dolnitz remained standing at attention, not relaxing his posture after saluting the major, and watched him depart. It was impossible for him to control a smile of elation. The feeling that he had achieved a breakthrough stayed with him while he reopened the window in the library and let in the air of the summer night, and during his walk home. The feeling persisted all the following week and was with him even as he approached Weidenstrasse 27 the next Sunday.

It left him only when he was sitting in the major's small office, facing his host across the desk under a large photograph of Adolf Hitler and Heinrich Himmler on the wall.

'I know about your project, Captain. And I ought to tell you that I was the one most responsible for turning it down.' Wurmlein appeared to be a different man from the jovial companion of the war game. He appeared now like a teacher displeased with a pupil who had bothered him by bringing up the subject of a failed exam. Von Dolnitz could not believe that this was the man who just a week ago had toasted his project.

'Your objectives are not well defined, Captain.'

'Necessarily, Herr Major. I am proposing to learn about possible new models of Soviet tanks, and progress might come simultaneously in design, increased armour, mobility, better suspension –'

'And you think that a bunch of fossilised White Russian émigrés would supply you with such information.'

'Many members of their organisation, "Freedom for Russia," are specialised engineers, former intelligence officers –'

'It also includes Soviet spies. It is heavily infiltrated by Reds.'

'Most of the members are patriots who hate the Soviet Union and would risk their lives to –'

'That's not the kind of man I would like to eat cherries with.'

'I realise the drawback, Herr Major. But do we have a choice in view of directive H-453-G4/73?'

The directive prohibited any new spying mission in the Soviet Union. The Third Reich was not prepared at this stage to antagonise the potential new allies, the Soviets, whose friendship it needed in a war against Poland, France and England.

'Since the end of the Spanish Civil War,' von Dolnitz said, 'the flow of information on the progress of Soviet tanks has been interrupted. We must look for the new –'

'It's forbidden, Captain.'

Wurmlein rose and von Dolnitz followed his example.

'May I have your permission, sir, to explore such a possibility for the future? These White Guards have been engaged in one or another spying project of their own. If we suggest some of the objectives to them, we might benefit from it. And if their spies are caught, the Soviets will blame them and not us.'

Wurmlein turned and paced a few steps.

'I am not one who would look for hair in every plate of soup. Go ahead, Captain, talk to them. There is no harm in finding out what they could do for us.'

Von Dolnitz sighed with relief. While he had not achieved a go-ahead for the Russian émigré spying mission as he had hoped, at least he could talk to them.

As soon as he left Wurmlein's apartment, he called Krugov and made an appointment to meet him in the Hotel Palace in Vienna. Krugov had been recommended by General Skoblin, head of 'Freedom for Russia,' when von Dolnitz made his initial investigations of that group.

When Krugov entered von Dolnitz's hotel room a week later, the Captain was surprised. Krugov looked more like a retired actor than a former Tsarist intelligence officer and the potential head of a spying organisation.

Krugov had brought along an émigré Russian newspaper that he placed on a small side table. He sat down in a chair and lit a cigarette.

Von Dolnitz read the headline: 'European Powers Double their Armaments Budgets.'

'I see you know Russian, Captain. Anyway the world is getting ready for war. It is easier to take the sword down from the wall than to put it back. They are spending most of their money for planes, hoping that their air forces will win their wars.'

'Tanks and only tanks,' Captain von Dolnitz said, 'will decide the outcome of the next war.'

'I think artillery –'

'Guns, yes, mounted on tanks,' von Dolnitz interrupted. 'This is 1939 and not 1914. The guns must move by motor power; the crew must be protected by armour. The country producing the fastest tanks with better guns and stronger armour plate, will win the next war.'

Captain von Dolnitz stood up, strode towards the window, and closed it. The sounds of traffic on the Mariahilferstrasse, Vienna's main business street, died down. He also lowered the blinds, cutting off the rays of the sun. They were in room 37 in the Hotel Palace, once one of the top luxury hotels, which although it had kept some of its former splendour, was turning seedy. The bright light of the sun showing all the wornout spots on the carpet must have disturbed the Captain.

'However, I did not come here, Herr Krugov, to discuss with you the aspects of modern warfare.'

'I shouldn't think so,' Krugov said, wiping away with a blue handkerchief the drops of sweat from his head, which was covered by sparse blond hair. He was a big, heavy man who perspired easily.

'You know the purpose of this meeting?'

'Yes, General Skoblin, the Head of our Organisation, informed me of it, Herr von Dolnitz.'

'I expected that.' Von Dolnitz returned to his seat, keeping his slim, narrow-shouldered body upright, not leaning against the back of the chair.

'General Skoblin has given me carte blanche to make any decisions in this matter.'

'I am pleased to hear it. So you know already, Herr Krugov, of this possibility. You and your associates in the Organisation "Freedom for Russia" might be . . .' von Dolnitz searched for the appropriate word, 'of a certain usefulness to the Third Reich.'

Krugov nodded.

'Our goals might become analogous to yours,' von Dolnitz said, observing his stiffly starched detachable cuffs. Each protruded exactly one centimetre and a half from the sleeves of his grey flannel suit, so he was satisfied.

'As you know, Herr Krugov, there will be a war, the war you and the other White Guard émigrés have been hoping for. Only a war and a German victory can end the yoke of the communists in your fatherland.'

'I understand that the communists might be sending a mission to Berlin,' Krugov said. 'Something to do with economic affairs. Relations between the Third Reich and the Soviet Union seem to have improved.'

'You are quite well informed!' von Dolnitz said. 'However, you must not forget that only a year ago our boys were fighting on the side of Franco and against the Spanish Reds and the Soviets.'

'Will you please tell me your specific proposal.'

'Let me finish, please, Herr Krugov! We fought in Spain until Franco's victory. Opposition to the communists is the basis of our philosophy. For practical reasons we may reach a temporary accommodation with them, but –'

'Let us return to the basic purpose of this visit.' Krugov opened his crumpled jacket, which was too big for him, then adjusted his steel-rimmed glasses, and looked at the German with his round blue eyes.

'Exactly, Herr Krugov. Since our relations with the Soviet Union are improving . . . a temporary lull . . . we would not want to cause any incident which might spoil it.'

'So, to put it bluntly,' Krugov said, 'you would like us to send out our spies. Should they be caught, we, the White Russians, would be blamed.'

'That's the general idea, Herr Krugov.'

'Herr von Dolnitz, do you know what are the chances of a spy's surviving in the Soviet Union? One in ten in the first six months, practically none in a year.'

'I lived in the Soviet Union, Herr Krugov. I trained the Soviets in tank warfare. I know what life is like there, and I know of the N.K.V.D. in the Soviet Union.'

'So you know the odds, Herr von Dolnitz.'

'The war might create unexpected and more favourable opportunities.'

'On the contrary. During the war there would be an even greater effort to catch the spies.'

'All I want from you now, Herr Krugov, is this: talk to some of your men, get an idea who would qualify, select a number of them for an eventual mission, but don't tell them anything as yet. We could assist you in some way – funds for instance.'

'Oh, no, no thank you, Herr von Dolnitz. We will be able to raise the money from contributions. Our men are patriots. They do not expect payment, only expenses.'

'Do you have the capability of acting at a moment's notice, Herr Krugov?'

'We have a number of trained and devoted men, and some younger ones also. They would be willing to risk their lives to free Russia from the communist oppressors, but first I would want to be sure of the value of such an operation to us.'

'Your only chance would be our victory.'

'You said so before, Herr von Dolnitz. All I can say is that I would hope so. I would want to evaluate the risks my men would be taking.'

'Well, Herr Krugov, this is only a preliminary talk. All I want is to find out the possibility of such an operation.' Von Dolnitz stood up. The meeting, as far as he was concerned, was over. 'I will be in touch with you, Herr Krugov, when the time comes. Do not forget your hat.'

Krugov took the elevator down, walked through a small lobby, and entered the busy Mariahilferstrasse. It was a warm, sunny day, but even the rays of the sun failed to remind him that he had forgotten to put his hat on. He was busy contemplating how he would ask his friends about their readiness to join a spy ring. When Krugov reached the Vienna Opera House, he smiled. 'I will simply ask them whether they would like to become spies,' he thought.

Chapter 2

Anton's Story

Vienna, July 17, 1939

My favourite spot in Vienna was the Rosengarten. Of course, I liked it especially in the spring when most of the roses were in full bloom and the air was permeated with their delicate aroma, but a visit in the summer had its rewards too. There were fewer people, the plantain and horse-chestnuts shaded the benches, and one could relax for hours without feeling guilty about taking a seat away from some elderly person.

I was a graduate student in engineering and often had an hour or two to kill; it used to take me only a few minutes to come here and wait out the time between lectures. Since I had very little money and could not afford a meal or even a snack in the inexpensive students' Mensa, a visit to the Rosengarten had the decisive advantage of costing nothing. It was a good place to read my textbooks before exams, novels or history books at other times. In those days I liked to spend the time solving chess problems, such as 'white to move and mate in two, three, or more moves.' I did not always carry a chess book with me, so often, for my amusement, I would design a problem myself. That took concentration, especially since I did not use pencil and paper but visualised mentally the position of the chess pieces and the sequence of moves.

That morning in July I was contemplating the move of the white king against a threat of two knights and a bishop, while hoping to mate the black king in the following move. Suddenly, Krugov appeared.

'Anton Illich, love troubles?' Krugov asked, placing his bulky body next to me.

Krugov was about forty-five, one of the friends of my widowed mother, a White Russian refugee like myself. Though I respected him and enjoyed talking to him, on that occasion I was annoyed at being interrupted in my game.

'But why love trouble?' I said.

'Only a man hopelessly in love or a gambler who had lost his last rouble would sit in a park with his head down for hours on end. Since I know you do not gamble -'

'I wish you were right, Alexander Ivanovich. I would like to be in love. The only trouble I've had was with a white queen. I just lost her to a black rook and a bishop. I don't even have anyone to play chess with ... My life is like still water.'

'*À la longue*, standing water becomes poisonous, Anton Illich.'

'I don't know what to do about changing it.'

'How about doing something dramatic and different? Why don't you become a spy?' He was looking at me intently through the thick lenses of his glasses.

His question stunned me. It was as unexpected as lightning from the cloudless sky of that July morning. At first I was sure that Krugov must be joking, but his fixed expression convinced me I was wrong.

'I see I have surprised you,' he said, taking a neatly folded blue handkerchief from his breast pocket and wiping away the drops of perspiration that had accumulated on his round face.

'But Alexander Ivanovich, you know me ... I am not -' I started to mumble.

Krugov and I belonged to the same organisation, 'Freedom for Russia.' Many of my mother's friends were members. When I was only seventeen years old my mother had suggested that I join, and I had. But I was not a very active member. I attended a few meetings, heard some lectures. I had never lived in Tsarist Russia - I was too young for that - but I knew the most minute details of life under the Tsars from having listened to the endless conversations among the Russian émigrés, discussing mostly the atrocities committed by the Bolsheviks. I knew that they had tortured and executed millions of people, and I had spoken with many escapees from the Soviet Union who had given me firsthand accounts of those horrors. I had always wanted to fight the cruel Soviet regime, but I had no military training.

'Au contraïre, mon cher,' Krugov said. Krugov liked to use French expressions, a habit he must have acquired during his ten years as a taxi driver in Paris, his first job as a White-Russian émigré lieutenant of the Tsarist army. 'You would be perfectly endowed, shall we say, for such an assignment. You know many languages, you have been to school in a number of countries, and you are very intelligent. It is true that you are quite young, only twenty-three, but the life of an émigré, you know, makes one mature earlier. Then you look quite young. I would not have guessed that you were older than eighteen.'

Krugov adjusted his glasses and inspected me. 'You are good looking, tall, rather slim, brown haired, with regular features. Yet you would not stand out too much. Also you have a most valuable asset for a spy - you are a loner; you have the ability to endure loneliness, and that's good. Mixing with people, making acquaintances and friends, that is dangerous. People aren't stupid. Eventually they question, and they pry, and they talk. It is always dangerous to get involved, but in your case that should not be a problem.'

Krugov was right. I lived alone in my attic. Nobody ever visited me. I began to realise that Krugov was really serious.

'But who would want me, I mean, who would offer me ...' Krugov smiled, showing a row of yellowish teeth. 'You like to get right to the middle of things, *in medias res,* so to speak, dearest Anton Illich.'

'I was asking the question theoretically. I would not -.'

'You won't deny that my question intrigues you, *n'est-ce pas*?' Krugov looked around the park, but there were only a few people sitting on the benches several metres away. The nearest was a grandmother, busily knitting, while her granddaughter of about five played with her doll.

'You must confess that you get a little tired of your two meals a day, of the German food which is mostly cabbage, of your uninhabitable room in the attic and your studies.' Krugov pulled a small cardboard box from his pocket and offered me a cigarette. We both started to smoke in silence.

Krugov was right. My life as a student of engineering was hard. I had to earn money by exposing lazy and indifferent

Oberschule boys to the charm of the French language. All they wanted was an '*ausreichend*,' just a passing grade, so that one day they could become officers of the German armed forces and be entitled to the shiny boots, aiguillettes, medals, and all the other rewards that such a position would entitle them to. I had to teach mornings and evenings, Saturdays and Sundays, to prevent hunger from torturing me too much and to supplement my widowed mother's meagre income. She was living in Limburg in Germany and teaching piano.

'An assignment as a spy would be dangerous,' Krugov said looking towards the statue of Grillparzer as if he wanted to get from that writer a nod of agreement.

'And with my inexperience.' I was thinking of my mother and what she would do without my support.

'A strong wind spares more green leaves than the brown ones, *mon cher*. Besides that might be the only way we could serve Russia.'

Since early childhood I had been brought up to believe that the liberation of Russia from communist tyranny was the only goal in life worth living for, and that to give one's life in that cause would be my duty. All that I had doubted.

'Yes, for Russia,' I said.

As with most political refugees, forced out of their native land and not able to return there, I had been brought up to cherish everything Russian. Since my mother hoped that one day we would be returning to Russia, many private tutors had taught me Russian and given me courses in Russian literature and history with old textbooks. There were the same courses I would have taken at my age had the Revolution not occurred. If the public schools in France, Germany, and Poland were often chauvinistic about their respective cultures, my Russian tutors had considered it their sacred duty to redress the balance.

A lot of time was spent in the study of the Russian Civil War and the reasons why the Whites had lost it: principally, an international conspiracy to destroy the most powerful nation, Imperial Russia. Among the villains abroad were the English, particularly Lord Curzon, a former viceroy of India, who feared that should the White Guards win, they would embark on the conquest of India in order to make the Russian people forget the Revolution. Thus the English had failed to deliver the promised arms. Then there was the German General Staff, which had allowed Lenin to travel to St Petersburg to foment the Revolution, helping to weaken Russia and eliminate her as an enemy. Non-Russians now held the crucial political posts in the Soviet Union: Stalin was a Georgian; Beria, the chief of the secret police, was also a Georgian; and he had been preceded by two Poles.

From my childhood I was taught that it would be my sacred duty to fight to liberate Russia from this cruel foreign tyranny, and to give my life would be the highest honour. But I had always imagined myself as an officer on the battlefield and not as a spy.

'My mother would be terribly upset if she learned about this conversation. She hates policemen, spies, that kind of people.'

Krugov smiled again. 'I imagine you would not tell her, "*Maman*, I, your only son, have decided to become an espionage agent. Will you give me your blessing?" There are ways of concealing the truth. An assignment such as this would require it.'

I noticed that the conversation, which had started with a discussion of the theoretical aspects of spying, was now turning to practicalities.

Still, the idea of lying to *Maman* bothered me a great deal. It interfered with any further speculation about my being a spy. I was ready to ask Krugov a number of questions when an elderly gentleman sat down at the far end of our bench with his *Wiener Zeitung*. We changed the subject immediately.

'Are you still on the *La Traviata* set?' I asked, knowing that Krugov had been working on it for the last three months. He was executing the design of his boss, Novikoff, one of the top stage designers for the Vienna Opera.

'Just the last few touches and this job will be finished. I should be getting back to my studio now.'

After Krugov left the park I did not return to the University but to my attic room. Krugov was right. I was not particularly happy with my life in Vienna. The study of engineering had no appeal for me. I spent most of my time at the University attending lectures on medieval art. Master Franche's paintings interested me a great deal, and so did Byzantine history. I had no friends; it was because I was always penniless. Also, since for me to make friends I had gone to secondary schools in Poland, France, and Germany, each time I came to a new country I had had to repeat classes. My new classmates made fun of me, of my foreign accent, of my shabby clothing. We lived in small cities such as Arles in France, Czestochowa in Poland, Ingolstadt in Germany. In those places there were few if any Russians of my age.

It was equally difficult with girls. When we lived in Arles I was in love with Yvonne. We were both fifteen years old. Picking her up for a date one spring day I stopped to admire the display of tulips in her garden. The May rain had just stopped and the sun emerging from the clouds seemed to make the flowers even more beautiful. Through the open window I heard the voice of Yvonne's mother: 'You must stop going out with Anton. He is a foreigner. This will lead to nothing good. You understand, these foreigners will never be able to work at decent jobs. They are irresponsible.'

Yvonne and I went out together, and I pretended not to have overheard that conversation.

That night I could not sleep. I cried a lot. When my mother saw the wet pillow in the morning she asked no questions. I think she guessed what had happened. After that I never saw Yvonne again.

Then, when we lived in Germany, Nazi propaganda began to emphasise the inferiority of the Jewish and Slavic races. Although I had many opportunities to go out with girls who seemed quite friendly despite this, I stayed away from them. I was just too afraid that I might again hear someone say: 'He is inferior.'

Yet I loved to be with people. I dreamt of living in some Utopia where everyone would treat me as an equal.

That evening, as I was summarising my life, I must confess that Krugov's suggestion appealed to me. For the next few days I kept thinking of our conversation, but then I returned to my normal life and the idea of being a spy retreated into the background.

Chapter 3

Berlin, Monday, August 28, 1939

Captain von Dolnitz always walked to his office at Kurfuerstendamm 27. The crowded S-Bahn or the U-Bahn did not appeal to him, since he felt uncomfortable at being jammed against the other passengers. He preferred the open spaces and the cool morning air.

As he turned the corner of Friedrichstrasse into the Unter den Linden, Berlin's main thoroughfare, he saw the columns of tanks and the men marching in formation. It was the Third Panzer Corps, moving east, destined for the Polish border and the new war. Von Dolnitz remembered how as a boy of six he had stood with his mother and cheered the German soldiers in the summer of 1914. The soldiers and the crowds were jubilant then; now few people stopped, and only for a moment, looking at the soldiers and the tanks, shaking their heads and moving on.

Von Dolnitz strode with a quickened step to his office and took the 23 steps two at a time to the first floor. In a large hall called the 'Strategy Planning Room,' filled now with clouds of tobacco smoke, several officers were working. The telephones were ringing, and the operators, in uniform, communicated the messages to a group of officers standing in front of a large map of Poland.

'Twenty-sixth Infantry Division moving west from Posen,' one operator said.

'Twenty-eighth Infantry assembling north of Kattowiz,' another reported. 'Third Cavalry Brigade grouping south-east of Allenstein.'

'You will be late at your desk, Captain,' von Stahlberg's voice came from behind him.

Von Dolnitz turned around and looked sternly at his colleague.

'To be precise,' von Stahlberg continued, 'you will be late two minutes and 38 seconds.'

Von Stahlberg had not shaved, his hair was dishevelled; dark rings had formed under his eyes. He lighted another Caporal from the stump of the previous one.

'While we here work days and nights,' von Stahlberg said, 'you gentlemen in the Russian sector have plenty of leisure.'

Von Stahlberg, in the French intelligence sector, was kept working constantly, since the General Staff anticipated the French declaration of war after the German invasion of Poland.

'Not as much leisure as you might expect. This Khalkin-Gol battle between the Soviet and the Japanese armies is the first major tank battle in world history.'

'That is why I came to see you, Otto. I want to find out whether the Soviets are using any of the Renault tanks they bought from France.'

'There is no evidence of that,' von Dolnitz said turning in the direction of his office, 'but join me. I expect further news this morning.'

Von Dolnitz's office was small. Two of the walls were covered by maps. On one was a map of Outer Mongolia and Manchukuo; the other wall displayed a map of the border area between those two countries.

Von Dolnitz stopped in front of the detailed area.

'You see, here the battle is being fought in most unusual terrain.' Von Dolnitz was pointing to the river on the map. 'It is a desert area, crossed by the river Halha, that forms an extended swamp. The Japanese crossed that river, establishing a bridgehead. That was some time in May of this year. In the last few weeks, the Soviets have been mounting a counter-attack. They are using the BT-7 and the T-28-M tanks. Our information comes to us via our own embassy in Tokyo. Most of the time it is incomplete. The Russian general in charge of the battle is named Georgyi Zhukov. I checked on his background in our files: he is a former Tzarist cavalry officer. If I am correctly interpreting the various contradictory messages, it seems to me that Zhukov has assembled a total of some 400 tanks in the north corner of the area shown on this map, and, if the Japanese are not careful, those tanks will cross the river and attack them in the rear.'

'So your Russian general seems to be using Fuller's classic battle scheme,' von Stahlberg said, lighting another cigarette, 'using a column of tanks to fall upon the rear of the enemy and then destroying them by a frontal attack carried out by the main force.'

'Let's find out whether we have received any message.'

Von Dolnitz rang, and a sergeant appeared with a large envelope stamped 'TOP SECRET.' Von Dolnitz opened the envelope and read the typewritten message. He replaced the sheet in the envelope, resealed it, and sat down.

'This message confirms what I expected. It seems that the Russians have achieved a complete victory.'

Von Dolnitz stood up, walked back to the map, and contemplated it for a few minutes in silence. Then walked to the window, looking at the trees beneath it.

'Everybody here, busy planning the Polish campaign, is failing to realise that the decisive battle of the next war is being fought and won right now before the war has even started - won by our future enemies.'

'Come, Otto, you are exaggerating,' von Stahlberg said. 'You and your Russian tanks. You are exaggerating as usual.'

'I do not think so,' von Dolnitz said, still standing in front of the window. 'After such a complete defeat - as it seems to be - the Japanese would never want to fight the Soviet Union. With this victory the Soviets assured themselves that in an eventual conflict with us they will not have war in the Far East.'

After von Stahlberg left, von Dolnitz re-read the message several times. Then he called Wurmlein, requesting an interview. He was told that this was impossible since Major Wurmlein was engaged and would not be available for several days.

But von Dolnitz did not give up, and he was able to catch Wurmlein as the major was leaving his office well after midnight of the following day. Wurmlein seemed tired and he was not pleased when the captain approached him.

'I must talk to you, Major,' von Dolnitz said.

'I have no time, Captain. A car is waiting and I am due for another meeting.' And Wurmlein started down the stairs.

'The Soviets have won a major battle against the Japanese. About 500 tanks were involved. It is a major victory.'

'Oh, that Outer Mongolia affair.' Wurmlein laughed, 'It's far away. We have other problems on our hands, more pressing and closer to our hearts.'

They both reached the door. A sentry saluted. A black Mercédès Benz limousine stood out front, its motor running, and a uniformed chauffeur was standing at attention and saluting.

'May I have five more minutes of your time, Major?'

Wurmlein nodded.

'I guess I can use a five-minute walk in the fresh air, if you can ever call Berlin air fresh,' Wurmlein said walking away from the car. The street was empty.

'We get very little information about the Soviet tanks. We need it, Major.'

'You would like to use your Russians – the White Guards?' Wurmlein said. 'As a matter of fact, the timing here might be right. I can tell you in the utmost confidence that we have an agreement with the Soviets that they will participate with us in the conquest of Poland and eventually occupy part of it.'

Captain von Dolnitz was stunned. He knew, as the whole world did, that the Soviets and the Third Reich had just signed a non-aggression treaty, but he did not know anything about this provision.

'I would not mind finding out what kind of toys the Reds will be using in that game. So, go ahead, Captain. I have not much time.' Wurmlein turned and was walking back to the car. 'But treat this matter like a raw egg. I hope those fellows won't embarrass us. Although I think the Reds will give them little opportunity to do so and will probably wipe them out in a matter of weeks.'

The German armies invaded Poland on September 1st. On the same day, in the afternoon, Captain von Dolnitz called Vienna from his office at Fremde Heere Ost to arrange a meeting with Krugov for ten o'clock that night at the entrance of St Stephan's Dom. Krugov agreed, and von Dolnitz took the plane a few hours later.

Krugov, who arrived first for the meeting, did not have to wait long; Captain von Dolnitz came up precisely at ten. After a short exchange of greeting they ambled away together.

'You no doubt know why I am here,' von Dolnitz interrupted their silence. 'The war will offer you the opportunity I mentioned to you.'

'I don't see how, Herr von Dolnitz. We don't have anything against the Poles.'

'Yes, I do understand your doubts.' The captain was wearing

civilian clothes again, and as he passed a lighted area he checked the pin in his tie.

'No, I am not surprised at all by your observation, Herr Krugov.' A few men came out of a Bierstude. They were singing, shouting and laughing. Von Dolnitz walked faster in order to pass them.

Then there were other people on the streets, so the two continued their walk in silence. Finally they reached the banks of the Danube and found that they were alone. Von Dolnitz halted.

'At least we can talk here without disturbance, Herr Krugov.' Krugov took out his handkerchief and pressed it against his forehead.

'Will you be able to mount an operation within a few days?'

'I still don't understand –'

'The war with Poland will be over soon,' von Dolnitz interrupted. 'Our tanks will soon be reaching the Vistula, and we will occupy a large part of Poland.'

Von Dolnitz looked around, making sure that there was no one in sight. 'The Eastern part of Poland will be occupied by the Soviet Union.'

'What?' Krugov exclaimed. 'It's unbelievable.' He adjusted his glasses and picked up his hat which he had just let drop, startled by von Dolnitz's words.

'It is so, Herr Krugov. There are now hundreds of thousands of Poles fleeing from our armies, running away to eastern Poland which will be occupied by the Russians – sorry, I mean the Soviets. It is a good time for placing our spies. Also, there will be thousands moving in both directions before this partition will have been accomplished. Initially the border can not be and will not be well guarded. What better time to place our agents?'

'The war might last a long time,' Krugov said. 'It is expected that both England and France will declare war within a few days.'

'We will finish the Poles, Herr Krugov, before either the French or the British will have fired a shot. I promise you that.'

Krugov turned and found the support of an iron railing, directly over the Danube.

'This is rather short notice, Captain.'

'As you know, all we want right now is to plant some "seedlings"; reliable people, who would be able to establish their roots in the territory to be occupied by the Soviets. Then, when we need them, we can call on their services.'

'Provided they are not yet exposed, Herr von Dolnitz.'

'How many men would you be able to find for such an operation?'

'They should speak fluent Polish or Ukrainian or both,' Krugov said. 'This requirement will limit the number of available men to between ten and twenty.'

'You would be able to instruct them briefly in how to collect and transmit the information?'

'Specifically, what information, Herr Captain?'

'Tanks.'

'Tanks, tanks. I am not surprised. The numbers, the types; we could do that. The current models, of course?'

Von Dolnitz nodded.

Then he asked, 'Do you have a name for this operation?'

'Yes,' Krugov replied. 'It will be called *Operation Parterre*.'

'I like the idea. The ground floor and in French. The Reds might assume it is a French mission.'

'That's not the reason, Herr von Dolnitz. It's the name of a solitaire game.'

Von Dolnitz laughed briefly. 'I see your point. Solitaire in Russian also means patience. All of us are engaged in a game of patience, particularly with our seedlings.'

'That's still not the reason, but it's immaterial.'

Krugov looked at the water reflecting the moonlight. He adjusted his glasses and glanced at the captain.

'The name of the operation,' Krugov said, 'is all I want you to know about it.'

'Yes, but we will transport your men in our military vehicles. They can wear our uniforms for their protection, then change to civilian clothes at their destinations.'

Krugov walked a few steps away, as if wanting to be alone with his thoughts for a moment. Then he turned back.

'I don't like it, Herr von Dolnitz. I don't trust you.'

'But this is the opportunity –'

'I still don't like it. Your Government has betrayed us often. You sent us Lenin in 1917. A few years ago you collaborated with Stalin and revealed the generals' plot to him. Real or unreal. That does not matter.'

'I don't want the names of the participants or any other details. The soldiers transporting your men will only be told that your men are performing some secret mission against the Poles.'

'I want your word, Herr von Dolnitz. No files in your drawers, no notes on these talks, nothing.'

'You have it, Herr Krugov.'

'Also you must understand that we will decide what information we will pass on to you.'

Von Dolnitz pulled at his starched cuffs, which were shining now in the moonlight. 'What do you mean, Herr Krugov?'

'When we obtain information, we will evaluate it. If we decide that such information will contribute to the liberation of Russia, we will pass it on to you.'

'But Herr Krugov –'

'Let's not discuss that subject now.'

'All right, Herr Krugov. You can inform me in the next few days how many trucks you will need.'

'And where,' Krugov said.

'Yes, you may select any location within the Third Reich and in occupied Poland. Do you have any other questions?'

Von Dolnitz looked at his watch.

'Before we part, I would like to repeat my earlier question, Captain. What do you estimate the chances of survival to be under these circumstances?'

Von Dolnitz stood silent.

'Let's say within six months?' Krugov asked.

'The odds should be significantly better than before, what with millions of refugees moving around. Still, N.K.V.D. has files on many, if not all, of your men. They will use all their resources to search out your agents. And they will assume that such a ring of agents is operating.'

Von Dolnitz took Krugov's hand and shook it.

'About half of them should survive a period of six months. That's not many, but do we have an alternative? Good luck, Herr Krugov.'

Walking home, Krugov heard the voice of the radio broadcaster: 'Many Polish towns taken, Polish front broken.' Other people listening applauded, but Krugov pulled his hat brim lower and rushed home.

Chapter 4
Anton's Story

Vienna, September 2, 1939
I hadn't seen Krugov until the second day of the war, September 2, 1939. He was waiting for me in front of my house on Schopenhauerstrasse. I was returning from a cafe where I had listened to a radio broadcast about the German progress in the Polish campaign.

'It is important that I talk to you,' he said. 'I have been waiting here for several hours.'

'Well finally, after so much talk, they've started the war.'

'That's not what I came to discuss with you. I know of a little garden here in the neighbourhood, a former cemetery where the remains of Schubert and Beethoven were buried before being transferred to another place.'

We walked in silence. I thought that Krugov wanted to talk to me again about becoming a spy. It turned out that I was right.

As soon as we sat down on a concrete bench in the little square, and Krugov had reassured himself that there were no other people around, he spoke: 'Do you remember our conversation about this spy business?' Without waiting for an answer he added: 'Do you want to do it, Anton Illich? I can offer you that assignment now.'

'I did not think - I would -' I said.

'There is no time to think. There is . . . how should I put it . . . a deadline. You will have to decide now.'

I hesitated. From an open window I heard the monotonous voice of a radio announcer. Somebody else, maybe a student, was playing a violin, and on the first floor a family was drinking coffee. The aroma of freshly brewed coffee reached me. I felt hypnotised, unable to utter a word. I could not think.

'I would like to add something which I did not tell you before,

Anton. You will be spying in the Soviet Union, you will be living among the Bolsheviks.'

Krugov did not need to explain. In my crib I had learned those names: Bolsheviks, Soviets, Revolutionaries, Reds, Communists. I had learned to associate these names with absolute evil, long before God or Devil entered my vocabulary. As a child I had listened to thousands of conversations among the White Guard officers, friends of my mother, discussing the civil war in Russia and the atrocities committed by the Reds. When I grew older and became a student, I never wanted to hear or read anything about the Soviet Union. If any reference to the Soviets appeared in a newspaper or magazine, I would quickly turn the page. Although I read all the classic Russian authors, Gogol, Pushkin, Lermontov, Tolstoy, Chekhov, Goncharov, Turgenev, Dostoyevsky, and many others, I never read any of the Soviet writers.

'Your father was killed by the Bolsheviks,' he reminded me. 'The other time we talked about dangers . . . yes, the assignment is dangerous, and not only for you. If they learn who you are, everybody, all your friends, even the people you buy your bread from, will be subject to arrest, torture, death.' Krugov stood up. He was excited. 'We must do it. Somebody has to do it. Damn Reds. Somebody has to put an end to these criminals.'

I stood up. A military march was being played on the radio, but the violinist still played Mozart, and the aroma of coffee continued to fill the evening air.

'Alexander Ivanovich, yes. I will be honoured,' I said, and my own words surprised me.

'Your mother will be proud of you.'

'But she –'

'I told Varvara Sergeyevna personally. Well, not exactly everything. She understands. I will keep in touch with her.'

A few days later Krugov asked me to come to his studio on Nibelungengasse 11. Under the bright skylight, Krugov appeared ten years older than his forty-five years. Immediately after my arrival he began to give me the cram course on tanks that he must have given to other members of our mission; since we were not supposed to meet, he had to teach all of us separately.

Krugov turned out to be a good teacher. Knowing my interest

in history, he began by describing the first 'tanks', the chariots in the Kingdom of Ur used in battle some six thousand years ago: small vehicles operated by one warrior, resting on two solid wooden wheels and protected by leather, sufficient defence against arrows. As the arms and armour improved, man attempted to design and build an armoured military vehicle. The best brains worked on that idea. Leonardo da Vinci designed one that was never used.

The modern tank originated because of the need to break the stalemate on the Western front in 1915. At that time both the Germans and their enemies, the British and French, had dug themselves into trenches. The intricate system of canals, particularly in Flanders, was ruined and the battlefield turned into a swamp, making any travel or movement of wheeled vehicles impossible. A British team of engineers began to work on the problem of creating a tracked vehicle that was armoured and that would be able to cross swamps and trenches; since they wanted to keep the project a secret, they adopted a code name, 'tank'. Krugov said, 'It was a most appropriate word. While at the time it meant only a container, it had come into English from the French *etaing*, meaning pool, swamp.' They succeeded, and several months later, hundreds of tanks on the Allied side won the war for them.

In the 'twenties little progress was made with tanks, but in the 'thirties a major effort was mounted in order to build new models for the coming war. The Germans, having seen the Soviet tanks' performance in the Spanish Civil War, were concerned with their own progress. Krugov opened a large folder and began to show me photographs of Soviet tanks. In the beginning the various types looked identical to me, but by concentrating I began to recognise the differences. According to Krugov the tanks were divided into three major categories: first, the light vehicles with total weights of up to fifteen tons; most of the tanks now in existence fell into this grouping, but as the Spanish Civil War battles had shown, such tanks are vulnerable to guns and would probably be of little value in the war that had just begun. The tanks in the second category of medium size, between fifteen and forty tons, would probably be crucial. That was where most of the research was being concentrated and most of the improvements were being made, since those tanks combined high speeds and effective guns, and could be well armoured. The heavy tanks, the last category, can be used only in special combat situations, where heavy armour rather than speed is a great importance.

When I was leaving Krugov's studio, all this information appeared too complicated, and I was afraid that I would mix up the T-28 with the Bt-7 models when I submitted my reports through 'Nina.' A woman vendor of religious objects - calendars, prints of ikons, etc. would open her stall the first Sunday of every month in front of the 'sabor', the Russian Orthodox cathedral; there would be a charity box into which I would slip my message in the form of a shopping list. The different kinds of food representing various types of tanks.

A few days later Krugov told me that we would be leaving with a unit of the German Army, an S.S. unit. For our own protection we would be wearing S.S. uniforms. The idea of working with the Germans did not surprise or appal me. The Russian émigré officers had been treated better by the Germans than by other nationalities. Those Germans who had fought against Russians in the war of 1914-18 respected the Russian officer corps. When the Russians had had to leave their country after the revolution, the Germans had tried to help them. Also, many Germans liked Russian music, both popular and classic, and Russian ballet and opera. In Berlin there were several Russian cabarets frequented by the Germans; Russian émigré singers and dancers had performed to sold-out houses.

But I did not relish the idea of wearing an S.S. uniform. In my mind this organisation did not stand for the Germany that we émigrés so admired. Yet I nodded my head in agreement.

I received a set of Polish papers under the name of Slavski, and in Pruzhany I was to register in the last year of the local gymnasium, the high school.

'As you can see,' Krugov said, 'your first name remains the same: Anton. Your family name will be Slavski. Don't use the patronymic Illich; it is very Russian. Use Kazimirovich. That sounds Polish. Remember also, your documents show that you are a Roman Catholic. Be sure never to attend a Russian Orthodox church, or any other non-Catholic service. That is prohibited to Catholics. Again when you cross yourself, be sure to touch first the left and then the right. And now -' Krugov looked at me.

'There is a possibility that you might be caught . . . by them. I am not giving you a poison capsule. It is against our religion to commit suicide. During the interrogations you may tell them anything. By then they would have learned about me anyway. Talk a lot, no matter about what. It is easier that way. The spy is executed there soon after he is caught, always by firing squad. They are good at that, for they have had much experience. Now to other matters. When the time comes somebody will contact you. He will use a code word. Do you remember the short rhyme attributed to Pushkin? A friend stopped the poet saying:

> *"Stop dvoyka, tooz idiet."*
> (Stop two, the ace is coming)

Reputedly Pushkin's answer was:

> *"Kozyrnaya dvoyka tooza byot."*
> (A trump two takes the ace.)

'Your code will be the modification of this rhyme. Your contact will say: "Stop three, the king is coming," and your answer will be "A trump three takes the king." '

I was to be ready for the departure of September 10, later on postponed to the 13th. On that date Krugov and I travelled by train to Breslau where we were picked up at the railroad station by a driver in S.S. uniform, who drove us to a country estate, where we changed from our civilian clothing to uniforms. As we crossed the former Polish frontier I began to notice the ravages of war: destroyed houses, thousands of Polish prisoners of war marching west, thousands of wounded - both Poles and Germans being transported to hospitals. Tens of thousands of civilians walked along the roads carrying their possessions in bundles.

After three days of driving we reached the front line. We were stopped several times to wait until the fighting was over. On the sides of the road were scattered dead bodies of officers, soldiers, civilians, and horses. Among them the wounded were calling for help. I was deeply moved and wanted to help, but the driver shook his head. 'Orders,' he said and drove on.

At one of the forced stops, I left the car and looked around.

There had been about a hundred civilians killed just hours ago by low-flying Stukas which had mown down defenceless people. Why? I asked myself. Under a birch tree I saw the body of a little girl, still holding a doll, as if she had wanted to protect it from the bullets. I was so shaken that I stood in front of that child and was ready to cry. *'Komm!'* the driver shouted, and I had to rejoin them.

That night we parted from the driver, and Krugov sat behind the wheel. After a four hours' drive on dirt roads, he stopped the car and we both got out.

'It is only about twenty kilometres to Pruzhany.' Krugov's whisper was hardly audible. 'It is due east of here.'

Krugov nervously adjusted his steel-rimmed glasses, which were useless anyway in the pitch darkness.

'You must start changing now, Anton Illich,' Krugov's whisper went on. 'In just thirty minutes there will be light.'

The two of us were standing in the middle of a country road. It was quiet, which was a great relief from the noise of the guns, the explosion of shells, the shouting of commands, and the screams of the wounded and dying I had heard in the last few days.

I handed the black beret with the S.S. Totenkopf to Krugov, then unbuttoned the black jacket and the black pants.

'*Mach schnell*!' We always spoke Russian, but Krugov, probably in deference to the Nazi uniform, now changed to German. 'I want to get back to the German positions before the morning light.'

He handed me the uniform of the Polish Lyceum student, navy blue suit with dark red seams on the trousers and a shield with the number 326 on the right sleeve of the jacket. I dressed quickly despite the darkness. I was used to it. I had trained for this masquerade during the few preceding nights. It was not very cool on this morning of September 17, 1939, but I shivered.

'You are scared Panie Slavski.' This was not a question but a statement of fact.

'No I'm not. I don't think so.' I inhaled the soft moist air. 'Alexander Ivanovich, I don't know why I should become a spy – a spy for the Germans.'

'Why the doubts now?' Krugov's whisper changed to a full basso. 'It is too late. Do you remember all I taught you about the T-28, Bt-7 and others?'

I nodded.

'I could use a smoke, Alexander Ivanovich,' I said.

'Not now. Here are your rucksack and overcoat. You have there 200 Mewa Polish cigarettes.' Krugov hesitated a moment. The silence was interrupted by the distant barking of a dog, the one sign of life in these swamps. The air was permeated by moisture that carried a smell of water and fish.

'The Bolsheviks should arrive in Pruzhany by this evening or maybe tomorrow.' Then he added, 'Don't get involved with people there. Remember that, Anton Illich!' He shook my hand, turned around and went back to the half-track. In a few moments I heard the engine, but I did not look around. I started to walk east.

In the beginning I could not see much, but soon the first rays of sun began to dispel the darkness. After a while I could just make out the swamps and the outline of the road to Pruzhany.

When I had been walking for about an hour, I saw in the distance a group of Polish soldiers on horseback and two civilians. They must have seen me before, since they were looking in my direction. This would be my first encounter in my new role. My head began to pound.

As I approached the group I noticed that one of the three cavalry men had been wounded; his right hand was in a sling. All of them were unshaven and looked tired.

'Where are you coming from?' the moustached sergeant asked me.

'From Bialowieza.' That was the last town I remembered.

'Any Germans on the way?' the sergeant continued.

I had not spoken Polish for a number of years and I knew I had a strong Russian accent. The best way to conceal it was to answer all his questions as briefly as possible.

'You must be a Kresowiak' (a Pole from Eastern Poland). A tall man in his early thirties, partly bald, asked the question. 'Your accent is typical of Eastern Poland.'

I nodded. The sergeant lighted two cigarettes and pushed one in the mouth of the wounded soldier.

'Maybe you could show us the way to Pruzhany?'

'It is straight east from here.' I pointed in that direction and I noticed that my hand shook slightly. 'About fifteen kilometres.'

'So maybe we can reach it before the fucking Bolsheviks get there.' The sergeant spat out the cigarette. 'We must get to the hospital. The Soviets are a few kilometres away on one side, the

Krauts only just behind your ass. This fucking war. Our own officers disappeared. Oh, hell, let's go.' He waved to the soldiers and the three of them rode slowly away.

'Damn it!' the balding man said. 'As soon as there is trouble, they bitch about our officers. His own commanding officer probably died fighting while all these fellows were bitching.'

The other man, younger and with glasses, did not appear to be listening. He wore a black civilian suit which showed signs of long wear. In the sunshine his narrow face appeared sick and he looked undernourished. His thick black hair needed the attention of a barber. He hesitated a moment and said, 'My name is Kuper and this gentleman is Pan Bendarski. We met only last night. We almost drowned in these swamps, running away from a German military vehicle.'

I wondered whether that was the same half-track in which I had been a passenger. We started walking. Kuper told us that he was a student at the University of Cracow. He had finished only two years of study but he had had many interruptions. His wife was with his daughter now in Pruzhany, and he hoped to rejoin them. Bendarski was an engineer and worked in Torun in the municipal waterworks. His family was in Baranowicze, farther east, where they were spending their summer vacation. He was worried about their safety.

During the conversation I also learned that both of my companions had not eaten for the last 24 hours. I had a loaf of bread in my rucksack and proposed to share it with them.

We sat down in the middle of the road, choosing a spot which seemed to be less soggy than the rest of the marshy pass. I took out the bread and some butter.

'This may be the last piece of bread we'll eat in Poland,' Bendarski said. 'The next meal will be under the Tovariches, for sure.'

'That suits me,' Kuper interjected. 'No regrets here. I will not mourn the passing of the fine gentlemen from Warsaw.'

'We are still fighting there,' Bendarski said.

'Not for long,' Kuper said. 'Our elegant officers excel in the art of consorting with perfumed ladies, but not in modern warfare.'

'You speak like a Commie, my friend.'

'Sure enough. I am one,' Kuper said, obviously shaking up his companion. 'I spent two years in a Polish concentration camp right here in this area, in Bereza Kartuska. And why? Because I gave shelter to a worker who had killed a policeman. He was hungry and was asking for bread; the police started to shoot. Well, he grabbed one of their guns!'

I had never before met anybody who even called himself a socialist. I felt uneasy.

'They released me when I was half dead. A girl in Pruzhany, a nurse, took good care of me. She is now my wife. Just before the war she came back here to visit her father.'

'Well, I haven't had such a sweet life myself,' Bendarski said. 'But I still believe that we could best solve our problems without the Communists.' He looked at Kuper. 'Then you must know Pruzhany?'

'Oh, sure. It's the lousiest town in the whole world. Right in the middle of nowhere, just swamps around. The nearest town of any size is a few hundred kilometres away. Not even a railroad, just a spur line, narrow gauge tracks. Very poor population, mostly Jewish, some priests, and a few Polish policemen and administrators.'

We finished our meagre meal and started to walk. It took us four or five hours to reach our destination.

As we entered Pruzhany, I saw a scattering of small one-storey wooden houses, most of them with straw roofs. It looked more like a village than a town. The street was deserted. The first person we met was a young Jew with a yarmulke and a growth of red hair shaping into a budding beard.

After we had exchanged greetings in Polish, I asked, 'Where is the *gmina*?' (the city hall).

'What do you want there?' he replied in heavily accented Polish. 'They might have left. Who knows!'

'Well, we or rather Pan Bendarski wants to know how to get to Baranowicze.'

He spread his hands. 'The mob is now in charge.'

As we approached the centre of the town I saw groups of young people, all of them with red ribbons, awaiting the arrival of Soviet troops. It was already early afternoon.

'Quite a large group of converts,' Kuper smiled. 'We had better rush. My father-in-law works as a clerk in the city hall. I don't know where they live now. They moved recently.'

As we turned the corner, I noticed two young men walking in the middle of the road, holding the large brims of their black hats and repeating: *'Idzie sie, idzie sie.'* (We are walking, we are walking.)

'What is going on?' I asked.

'In all these towns here,' Kuper said smiling, 'there is no sewerage or plumbing. The people here are used to emptying their chamber pots out of the windows. These two fellows are trying to keep from getting it on their heads.'

I was shocked.

'Pruzhany is a backward place,' Kuper continued. 'Only a few houses have electricity, from time to time. Most of the houses use kerosene lamps to get some light. And that is very necessary here. The steady fog and drizzle lasts for months and turns day into night.'

I looked ahead. I saw a stretch of a dirt road with thatch roofed huts scattered at random on both sides of it. The wind blew dust in our faces.

'You are seeing Pruzhany in its splendour,' Kuper said. 'In a few weeks these roads will turn to mud, knee deep in places. Pruzhany will be isolated from the rest of the world, except for a narrow gauge railroad. One train a day, if it works.'

'So it is best to wait until everything freezes,' I said. 'Then one could travel.'

'Don't ever do it on your own,' Kuper said, 'there are quagmires around this place that don't freeze in the winter. If you step into one of those, it will swallow you in seconds.'

We went faster but were stopped by the crowds of people. They were watching a convoy. It was a series of horsedrawn open carriages. In each carriage, on the hay, were lying what appeared to be corpses. All were men with white faces, horribly emaciated. A number of men who looked almost as bad, were walking alongside, holding onto the carriages for support. The convoy halted. At the sight of the sick and dying the onlookers became silent. The leader of the convoy, a tall man in his twenties, in a white shirt, boots and breeches, turned to the crowd and said in German, *'Bitte, Wasser.'* (Please, water.)

'These are Germans,' whispered somebody in the crowd. 'They were interned by Poles in Bereza Kartuska because they lived close to the German-Polish border. They're just peasants.'

For a moment nobody in the crowd moved.

Then a middle-aged Jewish woman in a black sweater and

long black skirt shouted, 'My God! Poor people, dying of thirst. Let's get them water!'

A tall man, obviously one of the local farmers, said 'Hey, why bother? They are Germans. They killed our people.'

But the Jewish woman disregarded this remark. In a few minutes she brought water and a loaf of bread. Other Jewish men and women were bringing more food and water. The sick began to smile and they repeated, '*Danke, danke.*' (Thanks, thanks.)

Among the people helping the dying was a blonde girl. I was unable to see her features well. I was standing too far away for that, but what attracted me about her was the grace of her movements, which were natural and elegant. As I followed her with my eyes, she approached a middle-aged lady, her mother, I assumed, talked to her for a moment, then turned back. I saw later how her slim silhouette disappeared into the crowd. For a while we continued to watch the Germans. The two ladies I had just observed appeared better educated than the rest of the people. It occurred to me that I should look for a room here, and I might just as well ask them the way to a hotel or a rooming house. I waited for a few moments, but the girl did not return. I approached the lady.

'Pardon me, Madame,' I said bowing. 'I am a stranger here. Would you advise me where I could rent a room?' The lady, in a lilac hat and wearing white cotton gloves, made a welcoming gesture. 'Very glad to oblige, very glad.' She spoke Polish with a strong Russian accent. 'It would be an honour to lodge you in our house. But unfortunately, since the Revolution, we have had to move into a veritable shack and this after we had occupied a large mansion with twenty rooms. My husband, Pyotr Vladimirovich, speaking five languages fluently, had to earn money by selling ice cream from door to door, not an appropriate occupation for a former cavalry captain. And now he is in an area occupied by the Germans and I don't even know whether he is still alive.' She looked at me with curiosity. 'And you find yourself in an unknown town, and what a town!'

As she had continued her monologue, her Polish turned progressively into Russian.

'What a tragedy! And now that the Reds are coming, who knows what they will do with us? Do you understand Russian?'

'I understand it,' I said in Russian, 'and I speak it.'

'That's wonderful. I should have known right away that you are a Russian; from your looks, your slanting eyes.'

I realised that I should not have spoken Russian or admitted any knowledge of it.

'But I am Polish. My name is Anton Kazimirovich Slavski.'

'Well. Still, I would be glad to help you,' she said. I felt a certain weakening of her enthusiasm.

'I would be grateful if there is a hotel somewhere ...'

'Oh, no hotel here; there is none. Have you come from far away? Where is your home?'

'I lived in Czestochowa, escaping the Germans.'

'I know a place where you could have a room, Avram's. He rents clean rooms, not too expensive. But if you don't have money . . .'

'I do.'

'It is the third street after you pass the city hall to your left. Everyone here knows his house. Just ask. And if you need any help, my name is Olga Carlovna Gromov. And Avram could easily direct you to our house.'

She stretched out her hand. I took it, and kissed it, forgetting that it was gloved. 'Thank you, Madame.'

I rejoined my travelling companions who were still watching the convoy.

Despite their hunger the Germans waited until the leader of the convoy had divided the bread equally among all those who were still capable of eating. Then he gave them the signal to begin eating.

I was deeply moved by the scene. So were my companions.

'If I live long enough to write the story of this war, these people feeding their hungry enemies will be the heroes,' said Bendarski.

'Believe me, they all know how the Germans are treating their brothers and sisters,' Kuper said. 'This is the happiest moment I have had in a long time. It restores my faith in humanity. Let's go, before they close the town hall.'

We moved away from the convoy, walking in front of a Catholic church and then a Russian Orthodox church. We also passed a synagogue.

I was thinking that it was worth taking all the risks and facing all the problems to have witnessed this one event. Would I ever be able to help someone? Perhaps an enemy, even a communist! Would I have the courage to act as humanely as these men and women I had just observed? Could an unimportant spy allow himself the luxury of being humane?

When we arrived at the city hall, the only two-storey brick structure I had seen in Pruzhany, crowds of people were gathered there. Most of them were young; all of them wore red ribbons. The brick stairs led to the front door where some men were standing. Bendarski and Kuper started up the steps. I followed them. As the two reached the top of the stairs I got separated from them because some of the men who had been waiting to enter the building now crowded between us.

At the same time a number of young men were pushing their way out of the building. All of them were peasants who had hoped that the war would mean adventure and glory, but now that prospect was over. They had not seen blood yet, and they felt the need to take part in some sort of violence. Their faces were ugly with hate. They had come here to take revenge on a few underpaid Polish bureaucrats who had barely made their escape.

When they saw Bendarski and Kuper they stopped short. 'Who the hell are you?' one shouted. 'Polish officer,' somebody else shouted even louder. 'Pany,' (gentlemen) cried the crowd. Kuper was trying to say something but with all the shouting and exclamations of hatred nobody could hear him. At that moment I saw a tall young man strike Kuper with a big stick. Then someone else was hitting Bendarski. I saw blood. I started to shout, 'Not officers, good people.'

A hand, dirty with soil, full of wrinkles, covered my mouth. 'You will be killed, too! Shut up!'

Stricken, I watched the beatings continue. Blood blotted out the features of my two companions. Then to the cheers of the crowd their dead bodies were thrown from the stairs. Somebody shouted that more Polish officers were to be found at the station. Spurred by the prospect of additional victims the crowd pressed towards the station.

The man behind me relinquished his grip on my arm. I turned around. He was a man of about sixty. The outdoor life, the sun and frost had deeply etched his face. He looked straight into my eyes. 'Get away from here,' he said brusquely.

A remnant of the crowd gathered around the dead bodies. I was unable to move. My reaction was to go to them, to help them in some way. I started to move towards them, but the man who had covered my mouth must have expected such a move.

'Don't you dare,' he said, pushing me away from them. 'They are dead. You cannot help.' Then, seeing my hesitation, he pointed in the direction of the bodies. 'They will kill you. Get away from here!'

I felt numb. I walked away.

I went some distance, not knowing where I was going. I felt guilty at leaving the dead men on the pavement. I knew that I could not help them, and yet, without knowing why, I wondered whether I was responsible for their deaths. I had just met them, shared bread with them, and they had been unnecessarily and unjustly killed. Was I responsible? Would I bring death and suffering to others who chanced to cross my path? Recalling what I had just seen, I could not contain my tears.

It took me a while before I could control myself enough to ask for directions to Avram's house; that question was answered by the first passerby.

It was a one-storey wooden structure with a straw roof. Avram himself was seated on a bench in front of the house. His white beard was long; he was a small, thin man of about seventy, dressed in a shiny black overcoat, and on his head he had a black yarmulke. Seeing me, he stood up and bowed.

'Mrs Gromov recommended you.'

In silence Avram showed me my room. There were two beds, a table, a wash basin, a couple of chairs. Through a small window I could see the street. Avram asked me whether I was hungry, but I was too tired to eat. Despite my fatigue I could not sleep. Thinking of what I had witnessed a little while ago, I bitterly regretted having accepted this assignment. Was I suited for this role? I started to undress. Just as I took off my shoes there was a knock at my door.

In the half-opened door I saw a face resembling that of Napoleon III, except that the pointed beard and the trimmed moustache were white.

'Carl Vasilievich Utapoff, hm . . . the father of Olga Carlovna, the lady you met this afternoon.' I opened the door and Carl Vasilievich marched in. He looked around my room with the imperiousness of a general inspecting his soldiers' barracks. I half expected him to utter the command, 'At ease!'

'Despite my first name "Carl," I am not a German. My late mother, Zinoeda Feodorovna, bless her departed soul, was taking the cure at Carlsbad when I was born. That is why I was named Carl, you see, but my mother was of Russian, pure, purest Russian stock, née Schtschukina, her mother née Meshakova. Her grandmother's maiden name was Troitzina. All good Russian names.'

This monologue was taking place while we stood in the middle of my room. I asked my guest to sit down and I started to put my shoes on.

'For instance, the name Meshakov really could be a noble.'

'What can I do for you,' I asked him, assuming that he had not come to lecture me about his family tree.

'Oh, yes, yes, a very important matter, dear Anton Kazimirovich.'

The old man stroked his beard. In the meagre light of the kerosene lamp I saw that his trousers, once black, shone like a mirror, and patches kept the worn-out material together.

'Olga Carlovna, my daughter, was enormously impressed with you. After only a short meeting with you she told us, "Anton Kazimirovich seems such an unusual young man. What bearing! What manners! Really as if he had just been graduated from the Pashevski Corps." Oh yes, Olga Carlovna knows people well. She has a sort of sixth sense. Once we were hiring a maid, and you know, dearest Anton Kazimirovich, Olga Carlovna immediately spotted her as a thief just like that.' To emphasise his words he snapped his fingers.

I was very tired after two sleepness nights and the tragic events of the afternoon. I wanted to ask him what he wanted, but was afraid that the new question would produce a discourse on some other subject.

'The maid eventually stole us blind. She had a paramour, you understand.' He winked with his left eye. 'A local man, a watercarrier, hm . . . not a bad fellow. Married too, but a former soldier. When I walked into the kitchen he always stood up, saluted, and reported in his basso, "I have the honour to greet you, Your Highness." I would really have qualified for that form of salute, but it was the last war, you understand, then the revolution. My papers had even been signed.' Carl Vasilievich coughed, 'By the way, I know an officer, a captain in our division with the same first name and patronymic as yours, Anton Kazimirovich Sokolov. A good looking chap, and his successes with the ladies ... I went one day, it was 1915 or 1916, and you know ...'

My eyes were closing and to keep awake I started to tap the table with my fingers. Finally, I gathered all the energy and courage I could muster to say, 'Excuse me Carl Vasilievich, I am very tired. I have travelled a long way. What is it you wish to see me about?'

'The matter is a very pressing one. It must be attended to right away.' Carl hesitated a moment. 'You see, I was invited to a dinner with our Tsar Nikolay II. After the dinner we were allowed to take with us the china and the silverware we had used. The china is decorated with the two-headed eagle and the initials of the Tsar. So is the silverware.' He lowered his voice. 'The Bolsheviks are coming and if they find it, hm ... you know.' He made a gesture with his hand on his neck indicating that he would be hanged.

'We must hide it. Dig a hole in the garden. And, see, I am too old. Olga Carlovna is a lady, the weaker sex. My granddaughter Nadya has asthma. Will you help us?'

Immediately Krugov's warning about not getting involved came to my mind. I wanted to refuse, but one glance at Carl told me that I would not. He looked too tired, too feeble.

'Fine,' I said, cursing myself for my weakness.

He lived only a few minutes away. The door of the house opened directly into a room in which a large table took up most of the space. In the corner of the room were a number of ikons. All the wall space was taken by pictures, plates, medals, old maps, and photographs. The girl I had seen with Olga was sitting at the table. Her blonde hair was arranged in two long braids. She was working with paints by the light of a kerosene lamp, colouring an ikon.

'This is Nadiezhda Petrovna, my granddaughter, Nadya for short, our true hope.' Carl used an old cliché, Nadiezhda, meaning hope in Russian. The girl stood up and smiled at me with her large blue eyes.

'Nadya, darling, as you can see the war has some redeeming

features,' Carl continued. 'One does meet such nice people as Anton Kazimirovich.'

We shook hands. Nadya smiled, her white skin reddening a little.

'Nadya is a law student in Vilna University,' Carl said looking with pride at his granddaughter. 'What a mind. She could outsmart any man. Too bad Nadya is a woman!' Carl sighed, 'Otherwise she could become a general, a real general in the Imperial Army.'

Nadya, apparently used to her grandfather's stories, sat down and resumed her painting of the ikon.

'You see, Anton Kazimirovich, the Russian generals were the best in the world. Take Suvorov for instance; he beat all of Russia's enemies everywhere – Switzerland, Germany, Poland, the Crimea. Or take Kutuzov. He, he, he, Napoleon was just a cadet in comparison. I myself am not yet a general, but during the Civil War,' Carl said lowering his voice, 'despite those English traitors who kept delivering the wrong ammunition for the gold we paid them and by the way our so-called French friends and allies were not any better but anyway we still kept winning and I too made my contribution in leading attack with the bayonet – *l'arme blanche*, you know.' He looked again at Nadya. 'Thus you see, dearest Anton Kazimirovich, as we say the apple does not fall far from the apple tree; our Nadya, I could tell you.'

'Excuse me, Grandpapa!' Nadya interjected, 'our guest might want a glass of tea.'

'Oh, yes, I will go to the kitchen and we will have some tea first,' Carl said, 'and then I will finish the story.'

I sat down in a chair at the table. Nadya went on with her painting. With a narrow brush she was applying paint to a wooden surface.

'Do you plan to spend a long time here?' she asked.

'During the war one does not know.'

'Maman told us that you are alone. It must feel terrible, especially in times like these.'

'I am used to being alone.'

Nadya changed her brush and mixed some fresh paint. I noticed that she was wheezing.

'I am sorry that I must work on this now, but I promised Father Yacov to have it ready by tomorrow morning.' Nadya looked up and for a moment observed me with curiosity.

'What are you painting?' I asked.

'The ikon of St Andrew, the Fool.'

'Oh, I remember. He is the Byzantine Saint, a slave who had visions. He was locked in an asylum, then released. Oh yes, he was venerated in times of great crisis. It was the year 1000 in Byzantium when everyone expected the world to end. Then in Russia in the late 15th century, which was by one form of reckoning the year 7000.'

'For a Catholic and a Pole you seem to know a lot of our church history, Anton Kazimirovich.' There was a touch of irony in her voice.

'I suppose Father Yacov wants to have the ikon for the arrival of the Bolsheviks, right?'

'Oh, no, Father Yacov had a parishioner who just died yesterday. His name was Andrew, and the ikon will be buried with him.'

What an impossible situation, I thought. At a time of looting and murder, when the Bolsheviks were coming, this girl went on serenely with her futile task. The ikon would be buried with the dead man and Nadya's work would be lost forever. She breathed with difficulty because of an allergy to paint, I thought.

'The Soviets may close the church,' I said. 'They have closed many in Russia.'

'Who knows?' After a moment of silence, she added, 'I guess the only way is to carry on. Are you afraid of them?'

'I don't know. Times have changed since the revolution.'

'This morning when we heard the news we wanted to run away to the west. Some other Russian families tried it, too, but it was impossible. We even packed our belongings. But we just could not do it.'

I could hear the voices of Olga Carlovna and Carl from the kitchen. Also from the kitchen came the aroma of pickled mushrooms and of pear preserves. My feeling of anxiety began to disappear. I looked at Nadya. She reminded me of someone. Yes, she looked like the Madonna in Master Franche's Nativity scene, a beautiful young woman emanating calmness, serenity, and harmony. I felt a sense of warmth and safety here, in her presence.

Olga Carlovna appeared carrying a tray with pirozhki and

preserves. Carl followed with the tea pot.

'I knew the instant I saw you, Anton Kazimirovich, that you would help us,' Olga said. She wore a colourful apron. 'What a blessing that I met you.'

'I am very pleased to be of service to you.'

My drowsiness was gone completely. I felt happy to be with them. The food was good, and I enjoyed the pear preserves which I was tasting now for the first time in years. At the table the conversation revolved about the coming of the Bolsheviks and what they might do to us. Olga Carlovna was the one who was most concerned. She kept referring to them as striped devils. Only Nadya maintained her calm. Occasionally the talk wandered to more mundane matters such as the supply of food in the pantry. This was an important matter, since the stores were closed and we did not know how soon they would reopen or at what prices the merchandise would be sold when it was available.

I was surprised to find that Nadya knew more about housekeeping than her mother. Nadya remembered everything that had been bought, where, and at what price. In some way I felt sorry for her. At her age she not only contributed to the family earnings, but also was thoroughly involved in the running of this household. And this despite her asthma.

After the tea, Carl produced a small bottle of Kvass, a fermented drink made with bread which Nadya used for mixing her paints. Then he found a wooden box and we started to pack. First the china went into the box, and next the silverware. Then we packed a gold pocket watch with a two-headed eagle engraved on it, and a silver cigarette case with a similar gold eagle and the diamond studded symbol, N 11. The books went on top: four volumes of *General of the White Guards*, Wrangel's *Memoirs*, and Dostoyevsky's *The Possessed* in a two-volume edition. On the very top we put the ikon of the Virgin Mary, and we covered everything with hay for protection.

Eventually I carried the box into the garden to a pre-selected spot. The digging had to be done quietly in order not to arouse any neighbour's suspicions. I was not used to working with a spade. The ground was hard. It took me a few hours to dig a hole big enough to satisfy Carl. All the time he whispered directions and offered encouragement by repeating how well I was doing.

'When you want to hide the sausage from the dog you must hang it high, Anton Kazimirovich. In this case we must dig a deep hole, to hide these things from those devils.'

I sighed with relief after we had lowered the box into the hole. When the box was covered with soil I transplanted some chrysanthemums to camouflage the location of the box. I thought how sad it was that these people had to bury the last of their cherished possessions, their last link with what must seem like a glorious past compared to their present miserable existence.

When we went inside the house Nadya was still at work. She looked tired. If I had known how to paint I would gladly have taken her place so that she might go to bed.

I wanted to return to my place, it was three o'clock in the morning. But Olga Carlovna categorically stated: 'We will not allow it. You must have some tea before you go.' So I had the tea.

After the second cup, when I was almost ready to leave, there was a knock at the door. Carl opened it. A Russian Orthodox Priest entered, dressed in the usual black cassock, and wearing a cross on a silver chain. He was middle-aged, tall and bony, with long greying hair and a full beard. After the customary greeting, during which each of us kissed his hand as he made the sign of the cross over our heads, he said, 'I saw the light in your house, Carl Vasilievich, so I dared to disturb you. But I also came to tell you that I heard you digging in the garden.'

Carl reddened. 'Yes, Father Yacov, we had to put some things away.' He coughed. 'With the Bolsheviks coming, you know.'

'Oh, I understand. Yes, I understand, but the problem is that I saw that old fellow Gavrilo, watching you.'

'Oh, my God!' Olga exclaimed.

'But I think he can be trusted,' Carl said.

'Yes, now, but when they come . . . Oh, no, no, no,' Olga said.

'But, what can we do?' Carl said. 'It is possible that Gavrilo did not know what we were doing. Maybe he was drunk as usual.'

'Exactly. One cannot rely on people who drink,' Father Yacov said. 'Even if they are well intentioned, they may blabber.' Father Yacov paced nervously back and forth in the small space. He looked at the ikons.

'But you do not bury the Most Holy Madonna ikon?' he asked. Seeing Carl redden, he went on, 'But the ikon could protect you.'

I knew that this decided the issue. Both Olga and Carl looked at me.

It was easier to dig up the box, a task which I performed alone. When I returned Father Yacov was still there. Nadya had just finished painting the ikon and was cleaning her brushes. I looked at the finished work. She had used as a model the ikon by the follower of Dionysius, the saint deeply disturbed, with toga blowing as if it were in the midst of a hurricane. What struck me was the face of the Saint. She had used me as a model for the ikon of Andrew the Fool.

With the help of Father Yacov we hung the ikon back in the corner. There remained the task of destroying various items. First Carl and I broke the china with a hammer. We removed the gold eagles and hid them in the earth of the potted geranium plant, this against Father Yacov's advice. Removing the engraved eagles from the silverware took us much longer. We had only one instrument, and we alternated in using it.

Then came the books. The Wrangel *Memoirs* came first; they were torn in pieces and burned in the stove. When it came to burning *The Possessed*, I objected. I told them that I would take the risk and hide it under my mattress.

Carl protested: 'You know, Dostoyevsky's works are strictly prohibited in the Soviet Union. It is a most damaging piece of literature, a prophetic work, a critique of communism. If they find it –' Carl again made a sign meaning that I would be hanged.

'Let me have it, please,' I said. 'I will take care. If there is any danger I will destroy it. I promise.'

I said goodnight, which was not accurate, since it was already morning. I shook hands with everyone. When I shook hands with Nadya, she said, 'I hope I'll see you again soon.'

I wished I could have told her that I was not allowed to see her again. It was difficult for me to imagine that this must be the last time I was to see any of them. I would have to avoid them in this small town. I walked away saddened. I was thinking of Nadya, her ikon and her life. How much I would give if I could help to make her life happier, to bring her some joy! To help get her to a sanatorium in Bavaria or Austria where the benefit of the good mountain air would help her recover from her asthma. Before undressing I looked briefly at *The Possessed*, bound in brown cloth with an art nouveau gold design, a 1911 edition. I put it carefully under the mattress.

Despite my fatigue I was unable to fall asleep. The images of the last several hours came to my mind. Most of all it was Nadya's face, like the Madonna of Master Franche's Nativity altar.

I woke in the early afternoon. I still felt tired. I had not slept too well. I had been haunted by nightmares. Most of the time it was the round face of Krugov warning me to keep away from people. Sometimes he smiled. Then he shouted, 'Don't!'

I heard some voices on the stairs, then a knock at the door. It was Avram. He had come to tell me that the Soviets were expected any minute. Somebody had seen them a few kilometres east of Pruzhany. I decided to watch their entry and dressed quickly.

In front of the house Avram was talking to a stranger. 'You, too, are going to see them?' Avram asked. 'Take this.'

He handed me a red ribbon and a safety pin. I felt awkward. Me, Anton, a White émigré with a bright red ribbon on the lapel of my suit? Not wanting to offend Avram, I thanked him and pinned it on. As soon as I was out of his sight, though, I removed it and threw it into the gutter.

The main street was lined with hundreds of people, all wearing ribbons: some girls carried bouquets of flowers. The crowd was cheerful. Here and there a group of young people started to sing the Communist *Internationale*. Then somebody shouted in Polish, 'They're coming!' I heard cheers from the crowd farther down the road. Then I saw them. It was a truck with soldiers in their battle outfits. The people raised their clenched fists and then applauded. I was unable to move. But I felt like running away.

The soldiers smiled at the crowd. On the second truck a soldier was playing an accordion. It was a waltz. A tank passed. Five or six soldiers were singing, waving at the crowd.

The soldiers wore a variety of uniforms. Each wore a different head-dress – steel helmet, fur cap, side cap or forage cap. Most of the soldiers wore a pullover tunic, a gimnastiorka. The others wore leather jackets or woollen overcoats. Most had rifles with bayonets attached.

After the trucks had passed, the tanks began to roll by.

Watching these steel monsters, I felt dwarfed and powerless. The roaring of the engines and the sound of the steel tracks hitting the cobblestones filled the crowded streets and echoed far beyond into the swamps.

The people around me, who were shouting and cheering moments before, must have felt as I did at that moment, for they fell silent.

At first, I was so overwhelmed by the noise and by the sight of those steel giants that I forgot my assignment. They seemed all alike to me.

But then I began to remember Krugov's lessons, and to compare the tanks with the photographs I had seen in his studio. The tanks before me were the BT-7 models with the cylindrical turret. I was pleased about my ability to recognise them, and I began to count: nine BT-7-1's: each turret had an aerial. A few minutes later three BT-7-2's, with conical turrets passed; then I recognised two T-28 medium tanks and six T-26 models. During my trip through Poland I had never seen as big a concentration of German tanks as I was seeing here in Pruzhany of Soviet tanks.

As soon as I returned to my room, I began to draft my first report. I wrote it in Polish in the form of a letter that I dated before the war. In the body of the letter I mentioned that I had collected nine sacks of *papierowki* (an early maturing variety of apples) and three sacks of delicious. I imagined that an expert would recognise that the letter was a coded message, but most people would not suspect that there was anything unusual about that message. When I had finished writing I nailed the letter to the underside of my table.

I was pleased with myself. I had fulfilled my duty. But after a while doubts began to creep into my mind. I thought of Nadya. Would she approve of what I was doing? Would she think my assignment honourable?

PART II

The Autumn

Chapter 5
Anton's Story

Pruzhany, Sunday, October 1, 1939

Since the arrival of the Soviets in Pruzhany the town had changed its appearance. All the buildings and most of the private homes were decorated with Red flags. On the few public buildings there appeared portraits, many times life-size, of Stalin, Lenin, Marx and Engels. In the square they were exhibited, in addition to the members of the Politbureau: Andryev, Berya, Kaganovich, Voroshilov, Molotov, and others. Every available wall was plastered with illustrated posters, carrying slogans such as: 'Soviet fighters liberate their brothers from the yoke of Polish Gentlemen,' and 'Freedom to the Proletariat, death to the Polish Gentlemen.' *Polskye Pany* (Polish Gentlemen) were apparently the villains of the new order, the bad boys, probably as bad as the White Guard capitalists: they were named exploiters of the people, bloodsuckers, profiteers.

The streets were filled with soldiers, or since that word was prohibited, its etymology was derived from the Latin for mercenary, 'troops-fighters' in the same way, they were led by 'commanders' instead of 'officers'. For the first time I saw women in military uniforms, and they made up at least twenty percent of the invaders. Many civilians mingled with them, often starting conversations and asking for cigarettes or tobacco, since these things had immediately disappeared from the market. Most of the Soviets were sympathetic to such requests and pulled out of their pockets a page of *Pravda, Izvestia,* or some such newspaper, carefully tore off a piece of it, handing it over with a fistful of coarse tobacco, then showing how to make a tube of it so as to smoke it.

It was a sunny day, but cool. Some of the leaves on the birch and apple trees had turned yellow, confirming that the autumn had really started.

I had not forgotten that it was the first Sunday of the month. Keeping my hand in my pocket and holding there my first message, I was making my way towards the cathedral. The mass, as I knew, had started at ten in the morning and should be over around noon. This was the time when many people leaving the church would be stopping at the stalls, and my presence there would not be as conspicuous as during the service when hardly anybody would be around. From afar I noticed three stalls set up at the foot of the steps to the cathedral, all of them attended by women in their babushkas. Groups of people were looking at the objects displayed on those tables, a strange mélange of beeswax candles, booklets, calendars, prints of ikons and Byzantine crosses. Some of the Soviets looked on with curiosity but did not seem to be buying anything.

I recognised 'Nina' right away – the photograph that I had seen in Krugov's studio was a good likeness. She was talking to a fat, bearded man, telling him that most of her items would not be available again after these were sold. To my surprise she spoke Russian with a distinct Polish accent. At one end of the table was a cardboard box, probably a shoe box once, with a hole in the middle, and a sign reading, 'For war widows and orphans.' I looked at her once more, but she did not pay any attention to me. Quickly I put my message and a few Groshen into the box. Once more I glanced at her. She did not appear to have noticed my contribution and she went on talking to her customer, telling him that most of the booklets and calendars had been printed in Warsaw before the war. I turned away and in a few moments I was lost among the people on the street.

I looked at the warm, smiling faces of the Soviets and began to feel a sort of friendship for them. I had an urge to talk to them but I suppressed it. A thought about the destiny of my message occurred to me, perhaps in a couple of days my figures would reach Berlin, where a serious, monocled German officer would read them, evaluating the tanks and proposing to build better ones in Germany. Then the German tanks would come here. I was starting to feel guilty when I reached the square and I was forced to see the repulsive posters of Stalin, Beria and company. These monsters were responsible for killing millions of innocent people and putting more millions into death camps.

That thought helped to relieve my guilt feelings.

Although it was a Sunday, since the arrival of the Soviets the stores were opened, and a crowd gathered in front of each. Among the people waiting at the grocery store was Nadya. For a split second I wanted to turn back, but she had already noticed me.

'I am not surprised you have avoided us, Anton Kazimirovich. I, too, would avoid anyone who put me to such hard labour – and on the first visit.'

I blushed, feeling awkward. In the full daylight she seemed more mature than on the night I had seen her last. Her skin appeared to be paler and she had dark rings under her eyes. The rays of sunlight outlined her narrow face with its delicate features. Her beauty stood out among the other women in the crowd.

'Will you come to see us again,' Nadya went on 'if I solemnly promise that you will not be forced to dig holes in our garden?'

The people in the crowd stood waiting their turn. Among them were many Red Army soldiers. They joined every queue formed anywhere in the town and they were buying everything in sight, particularly clothing. The Polish zloty had been made equal to the rouble. Before the war, four roubles had been worth one zloty, so the exchange was now favourable for them. Before long however, the prices had gone up fourfold and more. Nevertheless, the Soviets were buying. They stood patiently in long queues waiting their chance to buy anything. These items, still in the shops in the small impoverished town of Pruzhany, had not been available in Minsk, Kiev or Moscow.

I looked at Nadya. It was cool and she wore a black sweater over a white blouse. Both her sweater and the skirt were well worn. Some skilful mending helped to keep her clothing neat.

I joined the line although I did not intend to buy anything. Previously I had made arrangements to buy everything through Avram, who managed to purchase food at lower prices than those in the stores.

'Oh, I will come. Soon.'

'We are back to our routine. Grandfather reads aloud after dinner – mostly Chekhov's short stories. We laugh.' Then she became serious. 'Still no word from my father. You know, we are still frightened at what may happen to us, 'Nadya said. 'But for the time being nothing has changed. Even the churches are still open, but who knows? Maman cannot sleep.'

'Worrying won't help,' I said.

'I heard today that one Russian family, the Zubrovs, left town. He told Maman that now in all the confusion, it's still possible to cross over to the German side of Poland.'

Then we started to talk about our studies. Nadya, because of her sickness, had skipped the last year. She still had two years to go in order to finish her courses. She told me that she had heard that the college would re-open in Pruzhany. 'Perhaps we will be classmates. As you can see, you cannot possibly escape me.'

'Oh, that would be wonderful. I would see you every day.' I started to think that if we were to go to the same school and something happened – the Soviets discovered my true identity and the reason for my presence – they could not possibly kill off the whole class. I felt close to Nadya, as if I had known her for centuries. I had a great desire to tell her everything about myself: my life in Vienna, Krugov, why I was here. I wanted to tell her about Yvonne, my disappointment, my loneliness.

Eventually we reached the counter. Nadya was greeted by a middle-aged, roundish woman in a red wig.

'It's lucky that you have company,' she said, eyeing me with curiosity. 'The parcel is rather heavy.' Her black satin frock vanished with its owner, but within seconds she reappeared carrying a package wrapped in newspaper that she turned over to me. She was right. The package was heavy, even for me. I wondered how Nadya would have managed by herself.

As we walked away from the store the fresh autumn wind blew hard in our faces, carrying dust and some of the already fallen yellowish leaves. At the first corner I turned right in the direction of Nadya's house but she stopped.

'I must deliver this package to a friend,' she said. 'Maybe I could manage it by myself.' But I did not let her take it from me.

The house, surrounded by a high wooden fence, was outside the town. The windows were covered by shutters painted green. In front of a small gate, Nadya took the package and asked me to wait for her. When she rang the bell one of the shutters opened a bit. Then the doors were opened and Nadya disappeared. When she came back, she had the smile of a person who had just accomplished a major feat. I was curious but did not dare ask her about it.

While we were strolling back towards the centre of Pruzhany, Nadya picked up a brownish, partly ruined, tennis ball. 'What a find!' she exclaimed. 'Now you must catch me.' And she started to run. I did not like the idea, since adults draw attention to themselves if they run, but I followed her. She had not gone more than fifty metres when she stopped. Standing in the middle of the street, she was trying to catch her breath, stretching out her hand in search of support. I was sure that she was going to faint.

'Hold me, hold,' she murmured.

I took hold of her elbows with a firm grip, but still keeping a distance between our bodies. She was still struggling to regain her breath; a few drops of perspiration appeared on her forehead.

'Sorry. So sorry.'

'You shouldn't run, Nadiezhda Petrovna.'

'I know, I know.'

We remained standing for a few moments. Nadya opened her eyes and smiled. I felt the warmth of her body. I was sorry for her. For a moment I had an urge to draw her closer, but I was able to control my feelings.

'We cannot stand like this,' I said. 'People will see us.' I was afraid to be seen with her for her sake. 'You must be careful about your health.'

'I know I was silly, but I had such an urge to run. I never had a ball as a child. Actually I never was a child. I had always been an adult living among adults. My first reading book was Gogol's *Dead Souls*. I learned the alphabet from that book.'

I knew what Nadya was saying. Émigré parents would never allow their children to play with the local children for fear they might pick up bad manners or bad habits. Since there were no other Russian children around, Nadya, like myself, had spent her childhood among Tsarist officers and their families.

When we reached her home she asked me in. I should have liked to have tea with her family and listen to Carl Vasilievich reading, but, collecting my strength, I declined.

When I arrived at my lodging, I started to regret my decision. It would have been so nice to spend the evening with that family, listening to Carl Vasilievich reading Chekhov. Nadya would be there. Maybe she would not paint this evening, and she would have more time to talk to me.

Then I started to imagine her visiting Vienna. I would take her to the Prater, the great amusement park. Or we would go for a trip into the mountains to breathe the good air with the aroma of pine trees.

A loud knock at my door woke me up. Someone switched on the light. I had difficulty in focusing my eyes. Two young men, both in Soviet uniforms, were in my room. One was a tall, strong fellow who with his brawny shoulders looked like a weight lifter or a champion wrestler. The other was a small man, squarish, but thin, with thick, light-blond hair.

At the doorstep stood Avram.

'I am sorry. Very sorry,' Avram said bending deeply. 'These gospoda, gentlemen, you know – '

Both uniformed men laughed. The big fellow in a deep basso interrupted, 'No "gentlemen". That's gone forever in our country.'

'Officers, then.' Avram tried to correct himself.

Both of them laughed even louder. 'Sorry, but that's even worse than gentlemen.' The smaller man said, 'It is amusing, but we have not heard those words for a long time. Nobody ever called us "sir". And we are not officers but commanders.'

'So these two gentlemen – pardon me, "commanders", have been billeted here,' Avram said.

Both commanders were looking curiously at me, at Avram, and at my clothing on the chair. For them the place and the conversation must have appeared as strange as if they had arrived on Mars and were inspecting two Martians for the first time.

'Well, why all this formality?' said the smaller man. 'I am Boris Lugov and this is my friend Gleb, Gleb Senko. We are both lieutenants in the army.'

'We were assigned this room by the Komandaturs. We didn't know that it was occupied,' Gleb said.

'You could sleep in the corridor, Panie Slavski,' said Avram.

I sat up in my blue-striped pajamas. Again the lieutenants of the Soviet Army regarded me curiously. They looked as if they wanted to ask me a question.

'*Khorosho*, that's fine with me. I am Anton Kazimirovich.'

They came over and shook hands with me.

'Why should we disturb Anton, yes, Anton Kazimirovich?' Gleb said. 'I could sleep in the corridor.'

I wanted to object, but Boris stopped me with a gesture. 'It's just as well, Gleb snores so loud that the walls shake.' Then, looking at Avram, he added: 'We have been travelling for the last fifteen hours. Bring us some hot water – we'll have tea.'

The newcomers began to unpack their bags. The fright of being awakened unexpectedly started to disappear. It was now my turn to observe them with curiosity. Gleb pulled a newspaper out of his pocket and covered the table with it. Then he found a large loaf of bread, some sausage, butter, and large lumps of sugar in a form I had never seen before. He set out two spoons, two knives and two tea glasses. There was also a jar of preserves. Both of them were apparently used to this kind of impromptu meal.

Since there were only two chairs in the room, I removed my clothes from one of them. I looked at my watch, it was two o'clock in the morning.

'You must be a Polish pilot?' Boris said.

'No, why?' I was surprised.

'This,' he pointed to my outer clothing.

'Oh, no. This is a uniform of a secondary school student.'

'May I touch it?' Gleb said. I nodded. 'It is of very good material,' Gleb said, inspecting my jacket. Boris joined him too.

Avram came in with a kettle of boiling water. The two Soviets moved the table over to my bed, motioning me to join them.

I knew it would be impossible to refuse. When we were all seated at the table, Gleb took a bottle from his pocket and divided its contents equally among the tea glasses. Boris offered the toast, 'To our friendship!' Both my companions tossed off their vodka at one gulp as if it were water. When I tried to imitate them I choked. It was very strong vodka.

They observed my handling of the drink closely, as if they were scientists conducting a final and world-shaking experiment. I was sure that if one of them were a journalist he would have composed a front-page headline: 'A Pole in the West Unable to Gulp Our Vodka!'

I was glad that the next fluid poured into my glass was nothing stronger than tea, although it was very hot. During the next few minutes we talked about our families. I learned that Gleb was not married and that he came from Putilovka, a village in the Ukraine. His older brother had died and his sister-in-law lived with her two small children at his parents' home. His hobby was soccer. Boris, I found out, came from Ulianovsk, a city on the Volga, where his father was an architect. He was single, too, and he had a younger sister named Sonia.

Soon our conversation turned to the subject of girls. They wanted to know how easy or difficult it was here in the 'West' to have sex. Of course they considered Pruzhany a small town lost in the centre of the swamps of the 'West'. Unfortunately, I could hardly enlighten them about the morés of Pruzhany. When I asked the same question about their own towns, they responded with various facial expressions which I construed, I think correctly, as meaning that there might be great difficulty, at least for my new friends, to have sex in the Soviet Union.

They wanted to know about prostitution in the West. I mentioned that there was legalised prostitution in some places, Vienna for instance.

'One evening, returning from a concert, I was approached by a girl standing in front of a door with a red lantern,' I told them. 'She even opened the door and I saw inside a few women in various stages of undress.'

My new companions wanted to know all the details of this encounter: the girl's dress, her stockings, her shoes, and even her hat. They asked me several times to repeat what I had said, and not because they had not understood. It must have been fun for them to hear it again. They both admitted that they had never before heard of such a thing at first hand, and they very much appreciated this authentic account. The only knowledge they had of this subject had come from reading Kuprin's *The Pit*. And they both anticipated an interesting continuation of my story.

'So what next?' asked Boris, lighting a cigarette and offering both of us his box. I took a cigarette; the tobacco was light and aromatic; the paper was of a cheap, heavy sort. I noticed the name *Kertch*.

'Well, when in the light of the open door the girl saw my shabby clothing, she told me to get lost.'

They were visibly disappointed in the sudden ending of my adventure.

'Tell me, ' Gleb said, 'if you really wanted –' Gleb used two words I did not understand. I asked him what they meant. My question produced a roar of laughter. They discovered that I did not know some of the common words of the Russian language.

Having learned Russian from my mother and others of her generation, or from reading Tolstoy, Pushkin, Turgenev, and other classics, I had not been exposed to an important part of the vocabulary. Of course I knew these words in a number of other languages, but not in Russian.

Boris and Gleb hastened to instruct me in what appeared to be a feature part of Russian vocabulary that was rich in nuances.

When we were ready to go to our beds, Gleb lowered his voice and asked me, 'Could you get us a picture of Hitler?' Maybe a clipping from a Polish newspaper or a magazine?' He noticed my surprise. 'In our papers we see plenty of photos of our people, but never of foreigners.'

I had seen a pile of newspapers in Nadya's home. 'Sure, I can get that.'

'And maybe of King George and Mussolini as well?' Boris added.

I thought of the huge portraits of communist leaders, many times life-size, displayed on every corner of Pruzhany: the ikons of the new religion. The communists did not believe in displaying the ikons of other beliefs.

The next morning, when I woke up, Boris was gone. On the table, at the place where I had eaten the previous night, there was now a piece of bread, a package of Kertch cigarettes, some butter and a large lump of sugar. They had also left a tea glass half-full of vodka. There was a little note attached: 'To your health and for practice.'

Strangely, I missed their laughter and their jokes. I wanted to tell them more about my life. I assumed I would see them again, but when I asked Avram he told me that they had moved out because he did not have a bed big enough for Gleb. 'They said they will visit us again,' he added.

A few days later I decided to visit Nadya to get the clippings from their newspapers and magazines before she, or someone in her family, discarded them.

Nadya opened the door with a smile. 'You forgave us? You must have. The promise I made you at our last meeting still holds.' She wore an old dress which she had outgrown. By current styles, it was too short: it showed her knees and was so tight that it seemed to burst at the seams. The fabric had huge lilac flowers which looked like chrysanthemums. It was quite dark in the room. The kerosene lamp was turned down and lighted only a small area around it. It was drizzling outside, but in here it was warm and there was an aroma of borscht and dill.

Nadya motioned me to the same seat I had occupied during my last visit. She turned up the lamp. 'Maman and my grandfather are out visiting a friend. They will come back soon. Then we can have tea.'

'Thank you, but really I came here because . . .' I was feeling awkward again. I felt ridiculous asking for the clippings. I hesitated.

'Let me guess. You came to brighten this sad, rainy afternoon.'

I told Nadya about my strange meeting with the Bolsheviks, relating our conversation which I bowlderised by omitting the tale of my encounter with the prostitute. She was very amused to hear about our meal and most particularly about the Bolshevik's request for the pictures of Hitler and the others. She took up a large pile of old magazines and newspapers. I sat next to her and looked for the best pictures, and then Nadya cut them out.

'Here comes another picture of the monster,' Nadya said. This was her usual way of referring to Hitler. 'Too bad that the world's two greatest monsters are never photographed together.' I looked questioningly at her. 'The other monster, tovarich, you know whom I mean.'

'Nadiezhda Petrovna, you must be more careful. You never know! Of course you can trust me, but the others!' I was terribly concerned. If she were overheard calling Stalin a monster, she would be in mortal danger. I feared for her safety.

'Anton Kazimirovich, I like this photograph showing the great Führer. And this one of the illustrious Commissar for Foreign Affairs, Molotov, representing our beloved leader and father of our country, Yossip Vysarinovich Stalin. Is that better?'

'You are a good student. And you must admit it's safer.' Our elbows touched and I noticed that at the neck of her dress one of the seams was torn, showing just a little of her white skin. She exuded a faint aroma of soap and roses.

' I have not seen you shopping,' I said.

'There is nothing to buy now. There is certainly no more buckwheat, and that is terrible for my grandfather. He says, "Borscht without buckwheat is like a kiss without a beard and moustache." ' Nadya stood up and smiled. I stood up, too, and then, propelled by some force I could not control, I kissed her on the mouth. She did not open her mouth as Yvonne had, but she returned my kiss. Her white skin turned red. We remained standing in silence.

I felt happy and wanted to caress her hands, touch her, kiss her once more. Then for a moment I thought about the wrongness of my act.

'I shouldn't have,' I mumbled.

'Oh, my God, you certainly shouldn't feel guilty. I challenged you. I am the real Eve. And I was so afraid that you would not kiss me.'

We sat down, the newspapers and magazines still spread in front of us on the table. She took my hand.

'I know that one day soon you will leave. We won't see each other again, ever.' She looked at me. 'But I want to remember you in that special way.'

She closed her eyes for a moment. 'You know, Antosha, I have had asthma since I was fifteen. That made me miss parties, friendships, boyfriends. I was afraid I would choke to death without ever having been kissed. But I should not really talk such nonsense. Let's cut out some more pictures for your friends.'

'I think we have enough for them. I want you to tell me about yourself.'

'There is very little to tell and I think you know everything about me.'

She was right. I knew a lot about her from my glimpses of her family. I knew how hopeless life here must have been for this sick girl. I could imagine her dreaming of getting away from this small town. And her future? I asked myself what was going to happen to her?

I heard the voices of Olga and Carl outside the door. We both got up to greet them.

That evening I stayed with them. Because of the shortages, there was very little to eat at dinner – there was no bread. Afterwards Carl read aloud Chekhov's short story, *The Last Mohican Woman*, which had nothing to do with Indians. It was about a big, tall, domineering woman who henpecked her small, frightened husband. When Carl finished Nadya said, 'That was an excellent selection. I am a budding last Mohican woman.'

When I left the house it was drizzling outside, but I did not feel the cold and dampness. I still felt Nadya's lips on mine.

Avram was standing in the corridor. When he saw me he said, 'They say that there may be some bread the day after tomorrow. Maybe. Who knows?'

That reminded me that I was very hungry. There may be some bread the day after tomorrow, I thought, and went upstairs.

The bread did not become available until a week later. In the meantime most of my nourishment consisted of potato pancakes and vegetable soup. I still had most of my money, the 500 zlotys, but it was impossible to buy anything. When Krugov handed me that money, I had assumed that it would last forever. At the time my mother and I were living in Poland, we used to manage on 60 zlotys a month. Krugov had told me, and made a big point of it, that the money came from the contributions of émigrés. I knew how hard many of them had worked for that money, and I began to feel guilty that I was not doing enough for the people who had entrusted me with the mission of getting information about the Soviet tanks so that one day they might return to their homes.

Propelled by such thoughts I decided I would go out and make another effort to look for new models of tanks or even minor changes in known ones. I would be able to send my next message on Sunday, November 5 and I wanted to supply some facts of significance. Since most of the time I kept thinking of Nadya and not about my assignment, I felt like a traitor to the cause, guilty of neglect. Such feelings strengthened my determination to succeed.

But that wasn't easy, since after their initial entry the tanks had disappeared from the town of Pruzhany. After five days of fruitless walks, however, I was rewarded. On the main road, just at the edge of town, a T-28 tank was parked.

Two crewmen were sitting on the grass, one of them playing a small accordion. Others of the crew were apparently working on the tank and repairing it. From the open turret I could hear their voices. I stopped to look. The T-28 had one main and two subsidiary turrets. The main turret was fitted with a 76.2 mm gun and the subsidiary turrets with machine guns. The vehicle, the first *stredni* (medium) tank to be built in the Soviet Union, was designed to break through well-fortified enemy positions. It had firing capability on all sides. The tank I saw had a gun on its right subsidiary turret that was perhaps of 40 mm or more, in place of the standard machine gun. I was pleased with that discovery and was going on with my inspection when I heard the voice of the accordion-playing crewman: 'Hey you, move on!' I turned back, pleased that I would be able to include this discovery in my next report.

In the next few days I continued to stroll around on the streets of Pruzhany but was rewarded only by the sight of two BT-7 tanks that I might have seen before. There was nothing unusual about them.

In the same period, following Krugov's advice, I registered at the local college. A spy without any occupation, as Krugov had said, 'is as easily recognisable as even a small hill on the plain.'

Since the only teachers available were Poles, the lectures were given in Polish. Most of the students were either Jewish or Polish. During intermissions students of the same nationality tended to group together, and since I was masquerading as a Pole I joined the circle of Poles. Most of our conversations centred about our new conquerors and their ignorance of civilised life.

Someone told how the Soviet women bought nightgowns, and assuming that they were evening dresses, wore them at dances. Another student told about a Soviet soldier seeing a flush toilet for the first time, who used it as a source of drinking water. These and similar stories evoked peals of laughter from the group. And they were followed by more anecdotes. But from time to time I observed the Polish students engaged in serious conversations conducted in whispers. When I attempted to join such conversations, the speakers stopped in the middle of a sentence and deliberately changed the subject.

The apparent leader of the Poles was Franek, a tall student with wavy black hair, and Krystyna, an attractive blonde girl, always well-groomed and well-dressed. I tried to talk to both of them a number of times, but while both were very polite, they remained aloof.

Every day I saw Nadya, who during the intermissions sat alone, most of the time reading a book or writing some notes. I tried to avoid her and she knew it and accepted it, assuming that it would be natural for a Pole to keep away from her. One day we bumped into each other accidentally in the school corridor, and in her surprise Nadya, blushing, dropped her books and notes.

When I began to collect them she apologised. I suffered from this self-imposed isolation: I wanted to be with her all the time, to talk to her, to hear her voice and laughter. Sometimes when I could not stand it any longer, I would approach her, starting a conversation, talking about the prices of bread or soap, while in reality I wanted to tell her how much I missed her. She blushed, appearing happy even with this little attention, but then I would cut the conversation short and rejoin the Poles.

At night, alone in my room and not able to read, to relieve my agony I would try to design chess problems. Since I was unable to buy a chess set, I built one myself from plywood and drew a chess board on a piece of paper. I created a series of problems, when white moves and the only way it can win is to sacrifice the white queen.

Usually, I went to bed well after midnight. Unable to fall asleep, I would think of Nadya, now possibly painting an ikon and imagine myself sitting across the table from her, watching her fingers moving, following every change of expression in her face. These fantasies about Nadya were followed by dreams in which I would rescue her from bombs, labour camps, quagmires. Awakening was a disappointment, for with the morning I had to face a new day and attempt to get new information about the tanks. I decided to cultivate the Poles because, as local residents, they knew the area intimately, and they might know where the tanks were parked and other facts that might be helpful to me.

The opportunity arose one night when I noticed Franek and Krystyna ambling before me. As I caught up with them, I greeted them and asked if I might join them.

'Of course, very pleased,' Krystyna said, 'dear Czestochowiak.' (native of Czestochowa). The tone of her voice was friendly.

I knew how she had learned my domicile. Just two days ago we had had to fill out a questionnaire in school, stating our religion, nationality, permanent address, father's occupation, and other details. I followed Krugov's instructions, putting down my nationality as Polish, religion as Roman Catholic, residence as Czestochowa. Krystyna had collected these forms, and I remembered how she had glanced at mine.

'Do you know Czestochowa?' I asked.

'No,' Franek said, 'but my cousin Zosia Bialek went to

gimnazjum there. You must know her?'

I hesitated for a moment.

'No, I don't recall her, though the name seems familiar.'

'Oh, I am pretty sure that you would recognise her if you saw her. She knows every *gimnazjum* student in Czestochowa.'

Krystyna said, 'We didn't know that you were Polish.'

The three of us walked on the cobblestones of the main street. The wind blew in our faces. It was getting dark.

I shrugged my shoulders.

'Yes,' Krystyna said, 'you always speak Russian with that Gromov girl, so we assumed you were a Moskal.' (A pejorative term for a Russian).

'How did you learn to speak Russian so well?' Franek said.

'My mother speaks it fluently, even better than Polish,' I said. 'She was deported to Siberia as a child. She used to speak Russian with me.' I was pleased with myself and at the same time felt guilty about my ability to lie so easily.

'Well, anyway,' Krystyna said, 'we are having a little gathering of Polish girls and young men. It is tomorrow night at nine at my house, Ulica Pulawskiego 17.'

'Your knowledge of Russian might be useful,' Franek said.

'If it's not wasted,' Krystyna added. 'You could fully understand all this propaganda. The other day I overheard somebody asking a Soviet soldier whether they had lemons in the Soviet Union. "Sure," he said, "four huge factories." '

Since that encounter, Krystyna and Franek were very friendly to me. Three days later Krystyna stopped me after a lecture and invited me to her home 'for a little friendly get-together' with Polish friends. For a moment I wanted to ask her whether I could bring Nadya along, but Krystyna, as if she had guessed my thought, added, 'Don't bring that Gromov girl. She is Russian. You could come tomorrow after school with Franek. He'll show you the way.'

As we walked together the next evening, Franek told me his theories about Poland's defeat. He seemed to be disappointed, even bitter, that the French, having superiority in arms, had not attacked the Germans while all German forces were engaged in the Polish campaign. As we reached the house, I recognised it immediately. It was the one with the high wooden fence and the green shutters where Nadya had delivered her package. Why would Nadya have anything to do with Krystyna? It was strange, but on the other hand she might have been returning some food she had borrowed from her. Was that likely? I doubted it. Anyway, I decided not to ask Krystyna about it.

Krystyna opened the door for us. She was wearing a white dress, and I noticed that she used make-up on her face. She looked attractive. Immediately I had to think about Nadya who never used even a touch of lipstick. Yet Nadya was a beauty. There were a number of other girls and some young men in the living room. It smelled of perfume, cigarette smoke, and some unfamiliar aroma of food cooking in the kitchen. The walls were covered with a purple and orange wallpaper which, fortunately, was covered with prints of hunting scenes. A portrait of Marshal Pilsudski hung in the place of honour under a white and red Polish flag.

I knew some of the people there.Others I remembered having seen at one time or another at school.

Franek and I joined Stach, one of our school mates. Stach was small and slim, with freckles and reddish hair.

Franek said, 'Had our "Slavic brothers" not stabbed us in the back, we would still have had a chance. We could have stabilised the front against the Germans.'

'It would have been difficult,' Stach interjected. 'Our armour –'

'Our cavalry was superior,' Franek said, 'and we won several battles. We had a better spirit. We were fighting off the aggressor.'

'And now we will have to fight both the Soviet Union and the Third Reich.'

'Don't worry. The English and the French will take care of both of them. I am looking forward with pleasure to the time when they will take away the tovariches' toys – of course I mean tanks and guns – and send them home to their farms where they belong.'

I said, 'There might be a war between the Germans and the Soviets first. Many Soviet soldiers say they came here to fight the Germans.'

'That would not help us,' Franek said.

Krystyna came up. 'We will be starting soon,' she said. Franek nodded. I assumed that she would be serving a meal and began to regret that I had not brought anything with me to contribute to the party.

'Please let me have your attention.' She sat down in a red plush chair. Everyone stopped talking. 'We Poles have gathered here tonight to discuss forming our first resistance cell.'

I was standing in a corner. I nearly fainted. I had come here expecting a social gathering. Now I realised that the purpose of this meeting was to form a Polish political group. I should have known better, but it was too late. I could not possibly leave now.

Krystyna went on, 'Within a short time we will be in touch with the Resistance Directorate in Warsaw. They in turn will be working with our Government in exile.'

Stach asked, 'Shouldn't we wait until they have established the organisation in Warsaw?'

A smallish girl with dark brown braids tied with ribbons and wearing horn-rimmed glasses, said, 'I would have to ask my parents' permission.'

Everybody laughed.

Franek, who stood next to Krystyna, waved his hands to ask for silence. 'First, to answer the question of colleague Stach,' Franek said, 'we should start working so that we can be ready when we are needed. Polish resistance cells have been formed in other towns and Pruzhany should not be left out of this movement. And I would like to mention to colleague Halinka that nobody who is not in this room should be consulted about or informed of our activities.'

'But what activities?' Stach asked. 'What can we do?'

Krystyna said, 'I must ask you not to interrupt us with your questions. You will be welcome to participate later. Now we should hear from Franek. He has prepared a report.'

I was getting concerned that my involvement with this Polish group would jeopardise my mission.

Franek pulled out a few sheets of paper and began to speak. He did not refer to his notes, apparently he knew their contents by heart. His long wavy hair kept falling over his face and he threw it back with frequent jerks of his head.

'We will, as I propose, form the following units:

'One. Military resistance unit, combat-ready to fight the enemy.

'Two. Propaganda unit, to disseminate the news of the Allied victories and the heroic exploits of our own resistance groups.

'Three. Military intelligence unit, to find out the military strength of the enemy and his movements of troops and armour.

'Four. Archive section to keep records of treasonous acts against Poland and against the Polish people.'

A blond man with a moustache asked, what would be considered a treasonous act?

'Working in any Soviet organisations,' Franek said, 'having any relations with Soviet citizens, visiting the enemy's theatre, movies, or any political or social gathering, except under orders and in the interest of our organisation.'

'I would go further, and include any friendships with non-Poles,' Krystyna said.

I could not help knowing that she glanced at me, but I pretended not to have noticed it. A few of the people in the room appeared to me to have some misgivings about the programme, but the majority were visibly enthusiastic. I remembered learning when I attended school in Poland that a part of Polish history dealt with the conspiracy against the three powers who had partitioned the country in the late 18th century. These resistance activities and uprisings created many national heroes. This group, I thought, was ready to take on that struggle. The whole affair seemed to me to be naive. I knew that many, if not all of them, would pay with their lives. Yet I must confess that I was impressed by their patriotism and their ability to organise. The Russian émigré circles were always tragically disorganised, they could never agree on anything.

Everyone was asked which of the units he or she would like to join, and Franek wrote down each name on a slip of paper.

I was wondering which unit I should register for. Eventually I decided on the Archive Section, hoping that this would involve me less than participating in any of the other units, but when my turn came, before I could open my mouth, Krystyna said, 'You will not be assigned to any specific unit. You will be on call as a translator.'

I nodded.

'Colleague Slavski,' Franek said, 'you don't seem to be enthusiastic about our project. Do you have any objections?'

I shook my head.

'Any suggestions?' he asked.

I gathered up all my courage.

'I think, colleague Franek, I think that you should not keep any notes. Nothing should be put down in writing.'

'But surely – don't you trust me?'

'It isn't you I distrust. I mean that the Soviets could stop you after this gathering and search you. All of us would be arrested and executed.'

'They would not –'

'Antoni is right.' 'Slavski is right.' 'The fellow knows what he is talking about.' These were the comments I heard.

'What else would you recommend?' I heard Stach's voice from behind me.

'Well, I think we should use other names.' I remembered how my name got changed from Nizov to Slavski. 'We should use code names.'

'That's a good idea,' Krystyna said. 'I will call myself "Partisan Eagle." In history books the underground fighters always had code names.'

Everyone came up with code names in no time. Except for Halinka, she said, 'Too bad that I am not allowed to ask my father.' Eventually she became a 'Partisan Nightingale,' Stach a 'Fox,' Franek a 'Wolf,' and I became a 'Partisan Camel.'

Everyone seemed to enjoy this part of the meeting. A few people asked me whether I had any further suggestions. 'We should never meet again in such a large group. We should forget the people who were here. Let's play some music so that if we are ever questioned about this gathering, we can say that it was a party to celebrate our liberation by our Slavic Brothers.'

I was pleased with my unexpected position as an advisor. 'We could put on some music,' Krystyna said, 'but we were planning to offer you some food first. Fortunately for us the Russians don't eat flaki and I was able to buy some.' She was right. The Russians do not eat tripe, but the Poles love it. I never had eaten any and now I was afraid to admit it. I thought that my non-Polish origin would be discovered because of my inability to eat tripe. When I had lived in Poland before, I used to see the sign on restaurant doors, '*Dzis Flaki*' (Tripes Today). I was only a child then. I asked my mother whether we could try them. 'What?' she said, 'That horrible stuff! The Poles eat it, but no Russian would ever touch it.' Since that time I had wanted to try them.

I saw how Krystyna, assisted by Halinka, was passing soup plates with some white stuff in them. I was horrified. I wanted to run. I began to sweat.

My turn came and I was handed a plate. I looked around. No one seemed to watch me. I closed my eyes and slowly put a spoon with a bit of the tripe into my mouth. It did not taste bad. I was hungry and I started to eat it.

Krystyna came by with a pot. 'Some more?'

I nodded. She refilled my plate. Next to me stood Franek. 'You did not have any yet?' Krystyna said.

'Sorry,' Franek said, 'but I never touch the stuff.'

And then he asked her a question: 'Any news from your father, Krystyna?'

'They deported him on the second day after their arrival,' Krystyna said, looking at me. 'He was a policeman. Every now and then he used to arrest a few men for stealing chickens. Now he is a great criminal. Locked up somewhere. We have no news. We don't even know whether he is still alive.'

'It is better to have some hope left,' Stach said. 'My parents were both killed the first day. Their crime was that they owned an estate, one that had been in the family for generations.'

'Let's talk about something less sad, like the future,' Franek said.

But it proved impossible to revive the conversation, and some of us began to leave.

I found myself walking with Franek.

'You had bad luck here,' he said, 'falling into the Soviet hands.'

'The Germans do not treat us better, do they?' I asked.

'We fought them, yet they have arrested fewer people than the Soviets. Only prominent politicians so far. Despite the ravages of war, they have restored order. The stores are open here. The prices rose, but did not skyrocket. You can get anything. But here it's the red hell, there it's the brown hell – a tough choice.'

We walked in silence.

Franek went on, 'The only thing in which the Soviets are superior to any other nation is their secret police.'

When I had returned to my room, I was still thinking about Franek's last words. 'Was he right? Will they discover me?' I wondered.

Chapter 6

Volki, a village near Smolensk, September 19, 1939

Commissar Oleg Vashin strode alone in the twilight on the dusty country road. He could discern the outlines of the first houses in the village on the horizon. Only a couple of kilometres more and he would be in Volki. He transferred the package from his right hand to his left and began to whistle the Katiusha song. He also speeded up his pace. Oleg knew every tree along this road, every stone here. The clump of birch trees told him that he was only a kilometre away from the village. A pile of stones some hundred metres from the road, all that remained of a house on the Barski estate, meant only five hundred metres more to his destination.

It was getting dark when Vashin opened the wooden door of the third hut on the left. It was dark in the one-room cottage he knew so well. It had the familiar odours of cabbage, cooked beets, and dill.

His mother rushed to embrace him. 'Oh, Oleg, *synok,* my little son.' She contined to call him *synok,* despite his age of 34, his broad shoulders, the first few grey streaks in his bushy, brown hair. 'What a wonderful surprise!'

'I managed to get away for a few hours between trains,' Oleg said.

'What a pity, only a few hours.'

'Yes, I must take the train around midnight in Smolensk.'

'You must be hungry, *synok.*' His mother always worried about his stomach. He was the youngest child of five, but the only boy in the family. She started to busy herself lighting the kerosene lamp.

'I've missed your cooking.'

He unwrapped the package and took out a loaf of bread, a dry sausage, and a jar of gooseberry preserves. He put these things on the table.

'Thank you, Oleg, but you'd better take the food with you. You'll get hungry during your trip.'

'Don't worry, mother. I also brought you this.'

With a look of triumph on his face, Oleg unwrapped the copy of *Pravda* he had used for packaging his present.

'Soap!' his mother exclaimed. 'And such a large piece. It must be at least two pounds. I have been out of soap for three weeks now. How thoughtful of you!'

She took the soap in her hands and admired it for a moment in the light of the kerosene lamp. 'The borscht is cold,' she said, 'but I will put it back on the stove. But I must rush,' she went on.

She put a few lengths of dry birch in the stove and kindled a fire. Oleg took a kitchen knife, cut off a piece of soap, poured water into the copper basin and began to wash his hands. It was a familiar noise that he enjoyed, and he took his time. He looked around. Nothing had changed here that he could remember. There was a Madonna ikon in the corner of the room. After he had joined the party and was working as an atheist propagandist in the villages of Siberia, he had asked his mother to take the ikon down. Her reply had been so vehement that he had never dared mention the matter again.

When he had finished washing his hands, his mother handed him a white linen towel that she had taken out of a wooden box.

'You have only a little water left in the barrel,' he said, picking up a wooden pail and going outside. When he visited his mother, he always refilled the barrel. The water had to be brought up from a stream a hundred metres away, and his mother, now in her seventies, was too weak to do it. His sister Olga, the only one still living in the village, had three small children and was pregnant again. Her husband Ivan was supposed to carry the water, but he was a drunkard and lazy and often neglected the task.

It took Oleg several trips to fill the barrel. When he finished the borscht was on the table.

He sat down. His mother sat next to him, pushing the plate with the steaming buckwheat nearer to his soup plate.

'Where are you going now, *synok*?'

'Moscow.' He looked at her face. She had aged in the six months since his last visit. Her blue-grey eyes were still lively, however. He wondered how this frail woman could live by herself.

'You are working so hard, *synok*. Never a vacation, never any time for yourself.'

'I don't mind it.'

Oleg took a spoonful of the buckwheat immersed in the soup, blew on it and then ate it slowly.

'It would be good for you to get married. A man without a wife is like a church without a bell. I would want to meet your woman before . . . '

'No time, mother.'

'Your father always hoped that you would get married early and have a son. You are now the only Vashin.'

'I haven't found the right girl.'

'Oh, Oleg. There are so many good girls around.'

Eating in silence he looked about at the room in which he had been born and had lived until he was sixteen, when he joined the army. There were two large beds; his parents had slept in one and the four girls in the other. He had slept on the floor near the stove on a bag filled with straw. In the spring and summer he and the girls slept on hay in the barn.

'The people say there will be a war,' his mother said. 'Everyone rushed and bought everything there was to buy. There isn't a grain of salt to be had.'

'Don't worry. We are only occupying part of Poland. Recovering our territories, liberating our people.'

'This is just a beginning, *synok*.'

'And Olga, how is she?' Oleg asked.

'She would love to see you.'

'I won't have time this visit. Next time.'

'I will give her the sausage and the piece of soap from you. That will make her happy.'

Before he left, his mother packed him a few pears and apples. She also gave him the towel he had just used, as a present. He did not want to take it, but eventually he accepted it with thanks.

'When will you come again?'

'You know that I'll come as soon as I can.'

'And then you'll stay, *synok*, for a few weeks?'

'Yes, mother, I will try to get a vacation.'

'And don't forget to find a girl, to be the right wife for you.'

When Oleg closed the door and began walking away he knew a feeling of sadness. He always hated to leave home, to leave his mother alone.

Oleg could have arranged for a car to drive him here and then back to the station. However, that would involve notifying the local N.K.V.D., getting permission, signing papers. His visit would be recorded and filed in his dossier. He preferred it this way. Even if they found out about this visit to his mother, they would not bother to make a record of it. He was a high official of the N.K.V.D., but still he wanted to avoid the slightest trouble.

Oleg had taken an express train in Minsk early that morning. If he had stayed aboard he would have been in Moscow by this time. He could have slept and been fresh for the meeting tomorrow. Visiting his mother meant taking the local train, possibly standing most of the way to Moscow, and arriving there just in time for the meeting. Oleg did not mind. He was glad to have had the opportunity to visit his mother; he did not mind the 10 kilometre walk to Smolensk.

Oleg passed the ruins of the Barski estate. He looked at the pile of stones, sharply delineated in the moonlight. He remembered, how, when he had been a kid, he used to watch the people there. They were so different from the people in the village. They dressed, spoke and even laughed in a different manner from the folks in the village. Pavel Barski, the owner of the estate, wore expensive fur coats; he drove in sleds drawn by four horses. He was a widower, father of two teenage daughters, Nina and Sophie. The young ladies, accompanied on their walks by their French governess, always wore wide brimmed hats and white gloves. They would laugh and joke with the stern madame. The girls seemed beautiful to Oleg. He never forgot their delicate profiles, their narrow faces, thin legs and arms. They were so different from the sturdy maidens in the village.

When the girls were passing, Oleg was so overwhelmed by their nearness that he felt weak in his knees and had to sit down. Later on, a long time after they had disappeared, he would still smell the aroma of their expensive perfume, hear the foreign words they used and the sound of their polite laughter.

Many years later, during the Revolution, the villagers killed Barski, and looted and burned his estate. The girls, who were away at the time, apparently survived, and he heard that they were now living abroad.

The laughter of those girls was still ringing in his ears when he entered the drab railway station in Smolensk. The train was two hours late, but once he reached an overcrowded compartment and was able to get a seat between a heavy matron and a teenager, he slept for most of the journey. Vashin arrived in Moscow on September 27, a significant date in the history of his country, for on that day the agreement between the U.S.S.R. and the Third Reich to divide Poland was concluded.

On the evening of the same day, on the tables in the Grand Hall of the Kremlin, a great variety of the best foods to be found in the world waited for the beginning of the banquet. This was the second reception in honour of the Nazi Foreign Minister von Ribbentrop and his colleagues.

Herr von Ribbentrop arrived on time and proceeded to greet Joseph Stalin and other Soviet dignitaries. For Herr von Ribbentrop greeting was a very special and ceremonial performance. First he shook hands, then retreated a step, quickly lowering his hand to raise it again in the Nazi salute, and cried 'Heil Hitler.'

When a few years back Herr von Ribbentrop had been Ambassador to Great Britain and had thus greeted King George the Sixth, he had been declared persona non grata. He returned to Berlin to be promoted to the post of Minister of Foreign Affairs.

Here in the Kremlin, however, his hosts enjoyed his way of delivering a greeting. 'Heil Hitler' was welcomed here. Stalin raised his glass to toast the health of Adolf Hitler. 'I have heard that the German people love their Führer,' said Stalin. 'I drink to his health.'

Tovarich Stalin had good reasons to offer toasts, drink, and be merry. Practically without firing a shot he had obtained Latvia, Estonia, and the Eastern part of Poland as the result of the treaty concluded late in August. Now, he had negotiated the occupation of Lithuania in exchange for a Polish district. He also signed an agreement stating that 'both Germany and the Soviet Union will not tolerate any Polish agitation affecting the territory of the other partner, and they will consult each other concerning suitable measures to that end.'

While the banquet was in progress, Vashin worked with his staff in his office. The territorial changes required revisions of data. They also required changes in policies and programmes.

The discussion of the security measures for the newly

occupied territories was held on September 30 in the Kremlin. The meeting was attended by some twenty-five officials and presided over by General Brodilo, Chief of Counter Intelligence for Eastern Poland, a heavy-set man with a bald head. Colonel Senin, chief political commissar for that area reported: 'The western Ukraine and Bielorussia were inhabited by some 12 million people. Hundreds of thousands of refugees from Western Poland have increased this number; it is impossible to estimate how many there are since most of them are still on the move.'

Senin, a small man with a moon face and a moustache like Stalin's spoke in a thin voice, reading from his notes. It was the custom that each participating speaker, with the exception of Brodilo, stand while he spoke.

'According to the Polish statistics, there are living in that area five million Poles, three million Ukrainians, and two and a half million Bielorussians, one and a half million Jews. I want to add that the Polish statistics exaggerate –'

'You stated the source of these figures,' Brodilo interrupted. 'Continue with the breakdown of the nationalities.'

'350,000 Russians, 150,000 Germans, 100,000 Lithuanians. There are about 50,000 Gypsies, 10,000 Karaimes, a few thousand each of Rumanians, Hungarians and other nationalities.'

'How precise is the number of Germans in those statistics?' Brodilo asked.

'The number is underestimated,' Senin answered.

Zekhlis, the chief political commissar of the Third Army, raised his hand. Brodilo nodded in his direction and Zekhlis stood up. 'Tovarich Brodilo,' Zekhlis said, 'there are all kinds of Germans.'

'You mean,' Brodilo laughed, 'the good ones and the bad ones.' Everyone in the audience assumed a broad smile, including Vashin, showing fully his two, white metal-capped front teeth.

'I am sorry,' Zekhlis said, adjusting his glasses. He was a thin man with a receding hairline. 'I meant that there are German citizens of the Third Reich, and others who were German nationals but have taken Polish citizenship. There are others of German descent who have been living in that territory for generations, like the settlement near Stanislavov. There are – '

'For me a German is a German,' Brodilo interrupted. 'We will let all of them go back to their Third Reich; we signed an agreement to send them to their Fatherland and we will.' He looked around, lighting his cigarette with a match. 'And for good measure we will also return some of the escaped communists, German communists.'

Brodilo watched his audience. Immediately smiles began to appear on their faces. Everyone knew that the communists who had fled Germany to seek asylum in the Soviet Union after Hitler's coming to power would be executed or imprisoned in concentration camps after their forcible return.

Brodilo turned to Senin. 'How do you propose to go about securing this area?'

Senin stood up. 'Polish officers and anyone working in the former Polish administration are now being "evacuated." We shall complete this task within the next few months. This goes for Ukrainian nationalists. We will also resettle to Siberia any families living within five to seven kilometres of the new Soviet-German border. Most of the Russians are former White Guard officers. We will "evacuate" them and their families.' Senin stopped to regain his breath.

'I am listening,' Brodilo said.

'Then,' Senin continued, 'we will arrest the members of the Polish communist party.'

'The Polish communist party ceased to exist in 1937,' Brodilo said. 'We closed it.'

'Former members of – '

'Your priorities are wrong,' Brodilo said. 'These former Polish communists must go first.'

'The White Guards will make trouble,' Senin said. 'They are naturally opposed to – '

'It is our intention to quickly establish communism, our administration,' Brodilo interrupted again. 'How can you arrange that with all these Polish communist troublemakers? You must arrest them first.'

'But the White – '

'I have instructions from Tovarich Stalin. The émigrés will not jeopardise the security of our state, not for the moment. Any comments?' The group remained silent.

'How many people do you propose to "evacuate"?'

'Two million, eventually,' Senin answered.

'"Eventually" is not a precise word,' Brodilo said.

'Two years.'

'I believe,' Brodilo said, 'that even with the White Guards around, that area might be safer, will be safer than Leningrad and Moscow with our own officers acting as spies. Tovarich Zekhlis, do you anticipate any espionage activities on a large scale?'

'Not for long, Tovarich Brodilo,' Zekhlis said. 'I assure you, Tovarich Brodilo, they won't get anything.'

'And you, Tovarich Vashin, you are in charge of military counter-intelligence White Guard activities for this area?' Brodilo said, closing his slanting eyes.

'Yes, Tovarich Brodilo,' Major Vashin said, standing up.

'Are there any White Guard spy rings?'

'No evidence yet,' Vashin said. 'They have not tried any spying for four years. It is probable that they might take advantage of the situation to plant some seedlings.'

'Well, Tovarich Vashin,' Brodilo said, 'you will be able to uproot them. Weed them out!'

'I will dig them out.' Vashin smiled again showing his metal caps. 'I promise.'

'There, Tovarich Senin,' Brodilo said, 'As you see, we don't have to worry about the White Guards. I always maintain that it is not worth rushing to build a high bridge over shallow water! By the way, Vashin, watch out for the Poles! They are the true trouble makers and the most dedicated spies.'

'I will keep it in mind, Tovarich Brodilo.'

'Put out your nets carefully and be sure that there are no holes in them. There is no use to spit on them after the eel has escaped. As soon as you learn about some White Guards spying, let me know.'

The meeting was over, and Vashin went to his office where he began to organise the file of refugee White Guard Officers who had been known to reside in Eastern Poland. Vashin sent out copies of these files to the local N.K.V.D. offices which were still in the process of being established.

After three weeks he received a report about a double agent working for the Russian émigrés. Vashin called on Brodilo immediately.

'They are calling it "Operation Parterre",' Vashin said after a short greeting.

Brodilo smiled, 'They like to use fancy names like that. Their previous operation was called "Talisman." Those guards have lots of imagination about names.'

'That's where it ends,' Vashin said.

'What is the name of our agent?' Brodilo asked.

'Savilov. An ex-guard,' Vashin said. 'Lived in Berlin. He was a member of "Freedom for Russia". He is reliable.'

'Where did they send him?'

'He was placed in Lvov. That is where he made contact with our office.'

'Any facts, Tovarich Vashin?'

'Not many. He is supposed to be a seedling. Waiting for instructions. They will get in touch with him. He does not know how many more are taking part in this ring. I told him to stay put, and wait to make his contact.'

'Nothing more specific?' Brodilo took a cigarette and lighted it. The smoke filled the small office, with walls painted white and portraits of Lenin, Marx, and Engels and a larger one of Stalin.

'Nothing,' Vashin said.

Brodilo said, inhaling the smoke, 'I am sure that they will try to learn our progress in tank design. They are obviously working for the Germans. The Polish campaign has demonstrated that in this war the tanks and nothing else will decide the outcome. The Germans used tank formations in Poland, like Pavlov in Esquivas in 1936 and near Guadalajara during the Spanish Civil War. Although Pavlov failed then, because he lacked the supplies and the infantry support, the Germans learned their lesson.'

'Zhukov won a big victory,' said Vashin, smiling, 'just a few months ago, using such independent tank action at Khalkin Gol.'

'But the Germans do not know the details.' Brodilo said. 'Their Japanese friends did not rush to inform them about the strategy which defeated them.'

'That will scare the Japanese.'

'And when we get the new tank,' Brodilo said, 'that will certainly keep them out of any war with us.'

'Do you mean the projected T-34? There are no reports from our own intelligence in Berlin that they have got wind of that project.'

'Of course not,' Brodilo said. 'The final plans have not yet been approved. Yet they may get some information, they may learn of the great breakthrough in adapting the diesel engine for this tank. What an improvement over the gasoline engine everyone else is now using, including the Germans. Less danger of burning when the tank is hit.'

'I understand the tank will be faster than any German tank, it will manoeuvre better, Tovarich Brodilo.'

'Anyway, our agent has nothing to say, Tovarich Vashin?'

'Nothing, but I researched the name "Parterre." It means ground floor in French: it also stands for a game of solitaire.'

'How interesting,' Brodilo said, putting out his cigarette and lighting another one. 'I will get in touch with our intelligence in Berlin. Let's find out what's cooking with the guards there. I will put in a request to check on the "Freedom for Russia" members who disappeared there. Maybe we can find them here. I hope you will enjoy the solitaire.'

After the meeting Vashin went to the library. Tatiana Mikhailovna, a buxom lady in her forties sat at a table, reading a book of Chekhov's short stories. 'What can I do for you?' Tatiana said, not moving her eyes from the page of the book.

'I don't mind,' Vashin said. 'Finish your story.'

'It doesn't matter, I know the ending.'

Tatiana closed the book and put it aside.

'Which one did you read?'

'Oh, you know the one about the general who has a toothache. Everyone tries to remember the name of a miracle man who can cure it.'

'Have you got a toothache, Tatiana Mikhailovna?'

'I tried to help it,' Tatiana said, 'by reading the story. It didn't help.'

'I am sorry,' Vashin said. 'I came here to ask for your help. I need a description of a solitaire game called "Parterre." Then I have a second request.' He looked at her hardly daring to mention it. 'I also need a deck of cards.'

Tatiana took two blank pieces of paper, and taking her time she wrote both requests down twice on separate sheets. 'We will try. Your first request should be possible.' Her voice was very deep. It sounded as if it had come out of a barrel.

'But the deck of cards, Tovarich Vashin, that is impossible. This is a library, not a bourgeois gaming establishment?'

'Do you know where I could get the cards?' Vashin asked.

'You know that cards are prohibited in the Soviet Union, Tovarich Vashin. Of course,' Tatiana smiled, forgetting her toothache, 'there might be some people still keeping the cards from the pre-revolutionary times, despite many searches by your colleagues.'

'So no one – '

'Maybe you could try the gypsies,' Tatiana said. 'They might have hidden some. You could also ask in the foreign embassies. The Germans may have them.'

'Do you have a book showing the cards, describing them? It seems that I may need just an ordinary deck of cards.'

'We will try, Tovarich Vashin, in a pre-revolutionary book or a foreign book.'

Again Tatiana wrote down the requests, handed him the copies and asked him to sign both of them.

Tatiana lowered her voice to a whisper. 'When you are through with those cards, don't throw them away. I want to use them.' She blinked her left eye. 'I would try to learn about my fortune.'

The material he had requested was delivered to Vashin next morning. The information came from a French book and the translation was attached.

Vashin opened the book showing the deck of 52 cards necessary for 'Parterre' solitaire. He pulled out of his drawer a pair of scissors, a sheet of paper and began to cut it in 52 pieces of 3 by 5 centimetres. After that task had been completed he designed each card with coloured pencils, following the illustrations in the book. This took him the whole day.

In the evening he began to study the instructions for playing parterre solitaire. First he had to shuffle the cards. Since the cards were made of paper and not of cardboard it was almost impossible to do it. For a moment Vashin thought of trying to get some cardboard. He decided against it, since it would take him several days to obtain some for which he would have to sign several requests and get the signatures of a multitude of officials.

He mixed the pieces of paper as well as he could and then began placing them according to the instructions; six groups of cards lying face up. The remaining sixteen cards were placed below the cards arranged in groups, hence the name Parterre. The purpose of this game was to take out all the cards in order. One could discard only the cards on the right side of each group, or any card from partners.

Vashin tried several times, but it did not work out; the solitaire did not succeed. It was only towards morning that he was able to complete a game. Before leaving his offices he wrote a note to Brodilo.

'The name "parterre" might indicate an organisational structure in units of six. There could be a reservoir of members which could be called upon when they would be needed. The groups of six could be contracted or expanded according to necessity. The members in the reservoir could also be called upon to perform independent tasks.'

Before leaving his office, he washed his hands thoroughly, and enjoyed every moment of it.

Vashin went straight from his office to get some breakfast. It was a dreadful morning in Moscow. Cold wind and rain hit his face and drenched his overcoat.

Two days later Vashin was summoned to Brodilo's office. He expected to be questioned about his report, but Brodilo, who was in a good mood, said, 'In a week I am going to Berlin as a member of our Economic Mission. I know that place. I was attached once to our embassy there, made a few friends, ha, ha. They might help us by giving us some facts about the "Parterre" gentlemen.'

Chapter 7
Anton's Story

Pruzhany, October 17, 1939
The few sunny days in October were followed by several days of rain which turned the town into a big puddle. Since I owned only one pair of shoes of the non-waterproof variety, my feet were wet and cold. Despite the mud, knee-deep in places, and the continuing heavy downpour of cold rain, I went out to watch for the tanks. Since the Soviet soldiers and the indigenous population stayed home most of the time, leaving the streets and roads empty, I began to venture a few kilometres outside of Pruzhany, but the only reward of these expeditions was the sight of dripping birch trees along the roads and my drenched clothing, not to speak of my overflowing, muddy shoes.

Returning from these tours I would pass with envy the newly-established *stolowka* (canteen), where through the half-opened doors came the sound of loud voices and the aroma of dill and cooked buckwheat; or a new library, where through the lighted window I could see books and a healthy, big-breasted woman librarian with two thick brown braids handing out books.

Returning home, I felt disappointed. Only a few weeks remained until the date for my next report and, besides a note about the unusual gun on the right subsidiary turret of the T-28 tank, I had learned nothing. I realised that with my method of walking around I had reached, at least for the time being, a dead end. The Poles in their naiveté, I thought, could only mean trouble. I must contact someone more important, someone in power such as a communist, who might obtain useful information from travelling or from official reports. I did not know any communists and it was not likely that I could approach one without arousing his or her suspicions.

One day as I passed in front of the former City Hall, now N.K.V.D. headquarters, I was reminded of Kuper's and Bendarski's death. Kuper was a communist, and his widow was a communist living in Pruzhany. I decided to find her and call on her.

Pruzhany being a small town where everyone knew everyone else, I learned Mrs Kuper's address from the first shopkeeper I asked. The same evening I knocked at the door of her house, which on the outside did not look any different from Nadya's. A tall, thin woman in a white nurse's coat opened the door.

'Pani Kuper?' I asked. She nodded.

'I travelled with your late husband. I was the last one to talk to him.'

For a moment she did not seem to understand, but then her expression changed to something resembling a smile.

'Come in, please come in.'

Inside a small girl with brown wavy hair was sitting in the lap of an old, grey-haired man who wore a shabby overcoat. The white-washed walls were bare; the only furnishings were a single wooden chair, an old table in the middle of the room and a bench. There was no floor. I was standing directly on hard clay and it was cold.

'This is my father, Zurek,' Mrs Kuper said. 'I am Wanda Kuper and this is my daughter Magda.'

I introduced myself, shaking hands with each of them.

'Did you know him well?' Mrs Kuper asked, as I sat down on the edge of the bench,

'I met him only that morning. We travelled together.'

'Mama, who is this man, who is he?' Magda asked.

'He is tata's friend.'

'So tata will come soon too, yes soon.' The little girl smiled.

Mrs Kuper took her daughter on her knee and asked me to go ahead. I told her slowly, with as many details as I could remember, how I had encountered her husband and how we had walked together. She listened without interrupting.

Only the girl said often, 'Tata will come soon.' A blanket covered Magda's short dress. Mrs Kuper must have noticed my expression of curiosity. 'We lost most of our belongings on the train,' she said. Mrs Kuper did not seem to want to hear any more. Possibly she could not bear to hear the end.

'Your husband was a communist. Now ... you know ... they

should ... I mean you will get any priority.'

She frowned, trying to catch the meaning of my words. Then she smiled. 'Oh, that does not entitle us to any preference.'

Her hands were small and well taken care of, like those of a nurse. 'I too am a communist. I am the one who introduced my husband into the party.' Then, looking at her father, she said, 'My father before me participated in the revolution of 1905.'

'Did you join the party because you believed it would bring about a better system?'

'There was no other hope.'

'By that she means for the proletariat,' her father added. Magda uncovered herself, but the old man carefully replaced the blanket. 'I had tried everything, studied at home, learned languages, and I was a doorman at the city hall of Pruzhany! Is that a career?'

'You'll see that that will all change now,' Mrs Kuper said. 'There will be a future, opportunities for everyone. A lot has to be sacrificed, but then there will be equality and a good life for the masses.' She looked at me. 'We need people like you: you could help us to build this future, to destroy the vestiges of the oppression by landlords, officers and capitalists.'

When she spoke on the subject of communism she was a different woman. Her eyes had fire. She must have been an effective propagandist. I was not surprised that Kuper, recovering from two years in a Polish concentration camp, had joined the communist party. But I felt that she was wrong, that there was something illogical in her statements. Slogans about the good life for the masses sounded fine. Such slogans had been used before, but when tested by practical experience the idea might not seem as valid. Not willing to get into a discussion of these subjects, though, I took my leave shortly.

At the door Magda ran over to me and took my hand with all her strength. 'Stay, stay here, stay.'

'I cannot stay, I must return to my own home.'

'Please stay, stay here,' she repeated.

'I will come back.'

'Come back! Soon, soon!'

That night I could not get my thoughts about the little fatherless girl and Nadya out of my mind. I felt such a yearning to do something for them, to help make their lives happier. For a long time I could not sleep for thinking about them.

The next day I met Gleb and Boris walking on the street. 'I have the pictures,' I whispered. 'Let's go home. I will give them to you.'

When they saw the result of Nadya's and my work they were as excited as children unwrapping their presents under the Christmas tree.

'Believe me, my friends,' Gleb said, 'in Kazan, at headquarters, those guys there will have to offer me a shot of vodka; oh, yes.' Gleb was holding a picture of Adolf Hitler addressing a crowd.

'When I show them this their eyeballs will stick a *vierst* out of their heads,' Boris added.

'Thank you, thank you,' Gleb repeated. 'Where did you get these treasures?'

'Oh, at an acquaintance of mine,' I said.

They looked at me. 'Your face got red. You must be in love with this so-called acquaintance of yours,' Boris said.

'Is she pretty?' Gleb asked. 'She must be. A girl in love is always beautiful.'

'It is unfair that you have kept your love a secret,' Boris said. 'There will be a dance in celebration of the twenty-second anniversary of our October Revolution. It will be on November 7. You both must come. Dancing is an ally of lovers, but in the meantime we are curious and nothing will stop us from visiting her with you.'

'We would like to meet her, Anton,' Gleb said.

I had no choice. After a few more jokes about my being secretly in love, all of us went to pay a visit to Nadya's house. I feared the reaction of Carl Vasilievich to the two visitors, but at least I would have another opportunity to see Nadya.

When we reached her home the family was at the table drinking tea. Carl got up, looked at my friends' military caps with a red star in the middle of each and a gold hammer and sickle on the star. A split second elapsed before he decided what to say.

'Come in, please.' He turned around, looked at the ikons. 'Take off your caps.'

There was a moment of silence. We sat at the table.

'I love your house, Olga Carlovna. It is like my grandmother's house.'

That statement broke the ice. We asked questions about life in the Soviet Union and in turn replied to questions about everything here. Boris noticed an open book on the table. It was a collection of short stories by Chekhov.

'May I read you one, please?' Boris said.

'Don't let him,' Gleb said. 'He will never stop.'

'That is my hobby,' Boris protested. 'I appeared on radio. I even got some prizes for reading poetry. May I?'

Boris took the volume and selected the one-act monologue, 'On the Dangers of Tobacco Smoking'. He did not have to look at the pages, since he knew the piece by heart. And it was not just a reading. It was an outstanding performance, one whose like I had never heard before. Boris was an accomplished actor.

All of us followed each word in silence. I was sitting across the table from Nadya, who kept her eyes on me, following every reaction on my face.

I knew the story well, as did everyone else at the table. But during the reading the piece acquired new dimensions for me. When Boris finished, we applauded and asked him to read some more. He consented and read the poems of Marshak, a Soviet author. This was a series of amusing verses, and we all laughed, including Nadya.

It was quite late when we decided to leave. To my surprise Nadya asked whether she might accompany us. The evening was cold and I noticed how Nadya shivered in her short overcoat, which was only as long as a jacket. After a half-hour's promenade, Boris and Gleb left for their house.

As soon as we were alone, Nadya took my hand.

'What have you done with me, Anton Kazimirovich?' We were walking through a street lined with horse-chestnut trees. Some of the leaves were already on the ground, forming a sort of carpet and dampening the noise of our steps. 'Since I met you my life has changed. I live as if I were suspended in the sky along with those angels on the ikons I paint.'

'I feel the same way, Nadya.'

Someone was passing us, a young man.

'Yes, Antosha, but for me it is the first time. The very first time.' Her grip on my hand tightened. 'And if this . . . this kind of feeling gets to you so late in life as in my case . . . you know, then it hits with the force of lightning.'

'I am even older than you.'

'But you must have kissed girls before, Antosha?'

'That was a long time ago, in France. I went out with a girl named Yvonne.'

'She must have loved you. Didn't she?'

'We went out together a few times.'

The smell of wet leaves on the ground filled the air. We continued to amble along the street.

'And then you left her, your Yvonne?'

'I overheard her mother telling her to stop seeing me because I was a foreigner not worthy of her, and then I never wanted to go out with her.'

'Oh, Antosha, just because of that. Did you ask her how she felt about you?'

'No, I did not, but you don't understand what life is like for an émigré.'

'So if you hear my mother or my grandfather say something about you, you will stop seeing me?'

'No, no, that's different.'

'But why didn't you ask her? You could have argued with her mother, even have fought with her.'

'I just couldn't.'

'Will you promise not to leave me like that? Tell me first, please, please.'

It was difficult for me to make promises. I really wanted to tell her that I could not continue to see her because of the danger my friendship might create for her. I was not free to tell her the truth.

'Do you promise me, Antosha?'

'Yes, I will. But we are in the midst of a war.'

'War or peace, what difference does it make? We still can be together as long as the circumstances will allow us.'

'Yes, yes Nadienka.'

The street was empty now. We were standing under a horse-chestnut tree. She came into my arms. Our cheeks touched. We remained standing like that for a while. Then we kissed.

When I returned home that evening, I still felt the same way as Nadya. The angels were singing and one of the angels had the likeness of Nadya. We were close together and I was holding her hand. The yellow leaves were falling around us.

From those dreams I awoke with guilty feelings about my

performance as a spy. I began to reproach myself that I was not using my brains, mostly because my mental energy was being spent in dreaming about Nadya.

Although the idea of getting information from a communist had not worked out, I should be able to come up with something else. It occurred to me that I should do some research in the Soviet library; reading their newest books and periodicals might help me. By reading between the lines, one might come up with some significant facts that one might be able to confirm through observation. The library was only accessible to the military. I thought of asking Boris or Gleb, but I decided against it. The best way to get access to the library would be to meet the attractive librarian. Then I could visit her at the library as a friend. It might be that the dance would provide a good opportunity for getting acquainted with her. While I could not dance, at least I would be able to introduce myself.

At our next encounter, I mentioned to Boris that I would love to go with them to a party, and he told me that a dance would be taking place in celebration of the twenty-second anniversary of the October Revolution on November 7. I was disappointed to hear about that delay, but there was nothing I could do about it. In the meantime I tried to learn as much as possible about Soviet military activities from my observation and my contacts with the underground.

In the next few days I learned by talking with my new Polish friends that the Soviets were levelling a large area outside Pruzhany where they had assembled a collection of huge tractors. According to them it might be a new airfield. I was glad to have this additional fact for my report.

Since my visit with Boris and Gleb at Nadya's home I was unable to restrain from seeing Nadya at her home and walking with her whenever we could be alone. Despite the rain, the cold and the mud we would go out often, holding hands, talking about love and kissing when nobody was around.

Early in November, Nadya heard from her father, who was now living in Warsaw. The family discussed the possibility of fleeing there, but because of their limited resources they decided to wait. In any case, there were rumours that the Germans would occupy the rest of Poland, and that there would be a war between the Third Reich and the Soviet Union.

On Sunday, November 6, it was drizzling and there were hardly any people shopping at the stalls in front of the cathedral. No one seemed to notice me as I put my message into the box. When I returned home, Boris and Gleb were sitting in my room waiting for me.

'So we'll dance tomorrow night,' Boris said, winking at Gleb. 'You and Nadya are coming along to our party, arranged by the Air Force Brigade.'

Both of them had not taken off their caps or overcoats. They sat on my bed, watching my reaction.

'I'll come,' I said, 'but I don't know how to dance. I never had the chance to learn.'

'Let the weaker sex decide,' Gleb said in his bass voice. 'Let's ask Nadya.'

'Besides, I could teach you tonight.' Boris said. 'But let's go and talk over the situation with Nadya.'

On the way to Nadya's home, Boris imitated Carl's famous monologue about his name. I found it funny, and the three of us roared with laughter. Just around the corner I noticed a tall man standing alone. As we approached, I recognised him. It was Franek. He seemed to be as embarrassed as I was and he walked away.

After the usual effusive greetings, Boris presented to Nadya the prospect of attending his party.

'I am not a good dancer,' Nadya said. 'But I am burning to go.' The hope of holding Nadya in my arms appealed to me. Besides I knew it would be impossible to refuse. Carl, observing us, could not restrain himself from saying: 'Remember, Anton Kazimirovich, that one judges a woman at the spinning wheel and not by the way she dances.'

'Since I don't know how to operate a spinning wheel,' Nadya said, 'I have no chance.'

'I don't expect you to know how to spin,' I said.

'What do you expect? What characteristics would your ideal lady have?'

I hesitated.

'Your answer must be spontaneous to be worth anything,' Nadya said. 'Quick, quick, I want to hear your answer.'

'It is unfair, Nadya,' Boris said. 'You should ask such questions without witnesses. Now Anton is blushing.'

'A good idea,' Nadya said. 'Anton should whisper one of his ideal lady's qualifications into my ear after first saying one aloud.'

Everyone was watching me.

'She should be able to inspire me to do the impossible,' I said. I was thinking that it best expressed what Nadya meant to me. Because of my love for her I would be capable of doing things far beyond my ordinary capabilities. I would become another man.

'It is beautiful,' Nadya said. 'I like that. We will have the first trial of my ability to inspire you on the dancing floor. And now, the whisper, please.'

I came close to her. For a split second our cheeks touched and I felt how hers were burning.

'Her name must be Nadya,' I whispered.

'Thank you, Anton,' she said. 'I will always remember it.'

In the meantime Olga had brought glasses, and she put one in front of each of the men. Boris raised his glass, 'Let's drink to a happy evening tomorrow.'

After dinner the two chairs on one side of the table were removed and my dancing lesson began. There was no music so we agreed that Carl, Olga, and Boris would sing. I was supposed to learn the steps of a tango. They all knew the Soviet tango called 'The Heart'. Boris interrupted his singing to give me instructions. The whole thing did not seem to go very well because Nadya was also inexperienced. I stepped on her shoes. Then Boris became my partner; he was able to avoid my attacks. Eventually I could make a couple of movements of that tango without damaging my partner's shoes. My clumsiness had always been a source of chagrin to me. The boys laughed at me. At the Polish schools my nickname was 'Niezdara,' Clumsy. In France the other boys used to call me The Pig: years after I had left, I used to hear my school fellows chanting in unison, 'Anton Cochon, Anton Cochon.' Here, despite my clumsiness, I felt happy. I enjoyed the laughter of the others and joined them in the fun of that evening. I knew all of them wished me well.

After my lesson we had tea. We talked about dancing, movies, books and poets. Nadya and her mother favoured Lermontov. I sided with Boris, who considered Pushkin the poet who had contributed most to Russian literature. For a moment I recalled the short rhyme attributed to him and I froze. I hoped that Boris was not involved in this Krugov business. The memory of my assignment upset me for a few minutes.

That evening Boris walked me home. I knew that there was something on his mind. He confessed after ten minutes that he wanted to read me a poem. It was a monologue of a Soviet patriot appealing to the court in a case in which he was accused of killing a woman, a traitor who favoured the White Guards during the revolution. His voice vibrated with emotion. The long recital was a love poem to the woman the man had killed. It was a very sentimental piece, interrupted by songs while the accused told the court how his lady love sang them to the guitar.

It was quite late, but I enjoyed listening to it. Later on I began to wonder why Boris had selected this particular poem to read to me.

The next day Boris picked up Nadya and me, and we went to the party laughing and joking about my coming debut as a dancer. The affair took place in the auditorium of our Gymnasium. As we walked in, I saw hundreds of uniformed people dancing to the music provided by a seven-man orchestra. Since there were fewer girls than men, many of the soldiers danced together. I saw also some girls dancing together. The place was crowded and very noisy. I could hear laughter and singing.

Boris said, 'It is time for you to practise what you learned yesterday.'

Although nobody paid any attention to us, I felt awkward and uneasy. Yet I took Nadya in my arms and we began to dance.

I was so overwhelmed by Nadya's closeness that I could not hear any music or see anyone around us.

I forgot everything I had learned last night, and from time to time, stepped on Nadya's toes, blushing and then apologising. When the music stopped we rejoined Boris, who waited for us standing near the wall. The orchestra played again, and Boris invited Nadya to the next dance.

It was hot in the room and I was perspiring from my attempts to dance. I went to the men's room, where several uniformed men stood drinking vodka from small, flat bottles.

Noticing that I did not drink, one young soldier with his round head covered with short brushlike hair, asked, 'Do you want a drink?' Without waiting for my answer he handed me a half-full bottle, 'Finish it. I'll get another.' Trying not to offend him, I took the bottle and began to drink. The vodka was very strong and I could only manage small gulps. My generous host observed my difficulties, looking at me with his round eyes expressing both curiosity and pleasure.

'You don't know how to drink vodka,' my new friend said. He took a bottle out of another soldier's hand and drank it off in one gulp. 'That's the way,' he said. 'You'll learn to do it one day.'

The others offered me their bottles, wishing to contribute to my education in drinking vodka, but I declined. I returned to the hall. My head was spinning and I had difficulty keeping my balance. I was looking for Nadya, but in the crowd I could not find her.

Next to the wall where Nadya had been, two girls in uniform were talking. I immediately recognised one as the librarian. As I approached her I saw her slanting brown eyes smiling. They must have been enjoying themselves since they broke up in a frequent roars of laughter. The librarian with the thick brown braids and big breasts, noticed me. 'Look at him,' she laughed, pointing me out to her companion. 'He is so funny. He walks like a crane.' They both laughed. 'You must be a philosopher,' she said turning to me, 'looking for eternal truth. You seem so serious.'

'I'm not that serious,' I said.

She said, 'Then smile to prove it. Oh, well, you look a bit better, but your smile is forced. It is a kind of Jesuit smile, not sincere.'

'I am looking for my girl. We came here together.'

The orchestra played.

'Come! I'll help you find her. Dancing, we'll find her sooner than walking.'

'I am not a good –'

'I'll teach you.'

We began to dance. 'What is your name?' she asked.

'Anton Kazimirovich.'

'Why so formal?' she asked. 'You are Anton and I am Masha. I work as a librarian in the soldiers' library. And you?'

'I am a student,' I said.

She danced well. I was aware of her breasts touching me. I felt guilty to be away from Nadya, but I tried to exculpate myself by telling myself that I could not offend Masha by refusing to dance with her.

'You told me that you couldn't dance,' she said, 'but you have talent.'

'Thanks to you, the expert dancer.'

'Chivalry and compliments,' Masha laughed. 'A proof of your western education. I don't mind it.'

As we were turning, I saw Nadya standing in the corner. She was talking with Boris. Masha also noticed her. 'Is that your girl? She is a beauty and very aristocratic looking. Let's go! I would like to meet her.'

'Here is your knight errant,' Masha said to Nadya as we approached them. 'You will forgive me for snatching him for a moment. He looked so lost without you.'

Nadya smiled and blushed. A tall uniformed man approached our group and invited Nadya to dance. For a moment she hesitated. 'I promised this dance to Anton,' she said. The man then invited Masha.

'I am the second choice,' Masha said, looking at me. 'That's my destiny.'

Nadya and I moved to the centre of the floor and began to dance. 'You don't feel too unhappy being here?' she asked.

My head was still spinning. I felt the touch of Nadya's fingers on my left hand. I smelled the faint aroma of roses emanating from her. 'I am happy. Very happy,' I said.

Nadya looked at me doubtfully. 'Even among us Russians?' she asked. 'Among the Reds and the Whites?'

I regretted at that moment not being able to tell her that I was Russian and of the same variety as she: White. 'When I am with you, you make me forget these differences, Nadya.'

'That's your Polish gallantry.'

'And you? Do you dislike the Poles?' I asked.

'I always did. They made our lives miserable here before the war,' she said. At that moment I stumbled and stepped hard on her foot. 'You are trying to get even for my last statement.'

'Could you love someone who is a Pole and a Catholic?' I asked.

The orchestra was playing a tango.

'Before I didn't think I would ever be able to do that.'

'And now?' I asked.

'You know my answer. You shouldn't ask.'

After a while she asked, 'And you?'

'I could, certainly.'

'Even the Red variety?' Nadya asked, smiling. I was about to answer, but Nadya said, 'I don't want to hear your answer.'

It was hot and the air was bad. I began to notice how Nadya was trying to conceal the trouble she had in breathing. I suggested that we go home and Nadya agreed.

We held hands while walking in the street. We talked about her new project, an ikon of St Nicholas. We kissed and I went home elated, my head still turning. While I was undressing I sang the tunes I had danced to that night.

I had trouble falling asleep, and when I did I had a strange dream of Nadya in a white ball gown and Masha in uniform. In my dream I made love to Masha in a library. She was still in uniform and on her breast, on her uniform tunic, there was a large red star. I woke up feeling guilty, but then I fell asleep again, only to have new nightmares – this time about being Polish and Nadya refusing to go out with me, and Krystyna and Franek prohibiting me from seeing Nadya ever again.

Next morning I decided to visit Magda and take her for a walk. I still had a headache from last night's party, and some of the tunes of the dances were stuck in my head. I went out whistling Katiusha, a melody the orchestra had played several times last night.

'*Dzien dobry*, good morning.' I heard Franek's voice suddenly as I was turning the corner. 'I tried to meet with you in the last few days. You always had some people around you.'

It was a cold foggy morning.

'I saw you last night,' I said. 'I didn't know you wanted to speak to me.'

'I did not want to call on you at your place. That's why I waited for you in the street. We have an assignment for you, for tonight, Antoni.'

'Yes?' My knees had a rubbery feeling.

'As you know,' Franek said looking around, 'a meeting is being held tonight to select the delegates to the congress. Everyone can go.'

I knew what Franek was talking about. For the last two weeks, huge posters had been announcing a meeting for November 18 at nine in the evening. The posters also showed the candidates' faces and names: Fyodr Katshak and Anna Polkina.

'We want you to go and report later about the meeting.'

'But not in writing?' I asked.

'No, you can tell us,' Franek smiled. 'We don't expect to learn much, but we must have a record of such a meeting, for our archives.'

'Your archives, Franek, will get all of us in trouble.'

'You will report about the mock elections at our meeting.'

I nodded. We shook hands. I did not like the idea of attending the Soviet communist show, but Franek gave me no choice.

I was still preoccupied with my obligation for that evening when I was calling on Magda. She was pale and thin.

'We'll take a walk together,' I said to her, 'if your mama will allow you.'

Her mother was pleased. 'The child needs the fresh air,' she said. 'Since his death I don't like to go out. Everything reminds me how happy he would have been to see the red flags here in Pruzhany. It's still hard for me.'

I remembered my own mother's insistence on taking me for a long walk when I was a child. She always felt that fresh air was the key to health. Knowing that Magda always stayed in their cold, poorly-ventilated shack, I wanted to take her out with me.

Magda did not have an overcoat, but her mother dressed her in a sweater and gave her a shawl.

'Where are we going?' she asked.

'Just for a walk.'

'Will we see something nice?'

'Quite possibly, but you must keep your eyes wide open.'

I saw Magda open her eyes wide, but we were only passing a few dilapidated huts.

'Maybe we could go to the market,' I suggested.

'Market, market. That would be fun. Are you going to buy things, candy?'

'I will try.'

'But not too much. Too much is expensive.'

Since most of the stores were closed now, the open air market was the only place where some exchanges still took place. The farmers came in their carts and sold vegetables and fruit. They usually preferred not to take money, but one could still get perishable foods by paying cash. I bought some pears, lettuce, cucumbers and rutabaga for two roubles. Magda observed my dealings with great interest. Several times she asked me about the prices I had paid.

'Are you going to cook all of it?' she asked.

'Some of it,' I said. 'The rest I will bring to your Mama so that she may cook it for you.'

'My mama could cook it for you, too,' Magda said.

'Yes, that would be nice sometimes.'

'Why not now?' Magda asked. 'You could stay and sleep with us.'

'Well, you see, I have a room of my own in town. I must study there.'

'It would be quiet, very quiet. You could study in my house.'

I did not know how to deal with this invitation. I knew that Magda was fond of me. A little girl who had lost her father so tragically must be attracted to men. She needed a man's presence and attention.

'I promise to visit you often,' I said. One of the farmers had some homemade candy made of poppy seeds and honey, and I bought it. We both started to eat it. Magda began to laugh.

'What is it?' I asked.

'You look so different, ha, ha, ha, with hair over your mouth. Like the man in the big pictures.'

Some poppy seeds covered my upper lip. I began to laugh too. It was funny to think that I resembled Stalin. It began to rain and we rushed home still laughing.

At two, as usual, I went to school. That evening I walked Nadya home. We talked about last night. Nadya did not feel well. We had to walk slowly. Besides not feeling well, Nadya was freezing in her short coat. We had to stop a few times for her to catch her breath.

Nadya invited me to come to her home, but I declined, telling her that she needed to rest after last night. I felt guilty at not telling her about my plans for that evening.

The meeting was held in the school auditorium, the only hall in town where a few hundred people could assemble. I entered the place well in advance of the starting time and it was already half full. The walls were decorated with huge portraits of the members of the Politburo: Andreev Voroshilov, Kaganovich,

Bernia, Molotov and others. There was a much larger portrait of Stalin. There was a sign in large letters hanging over the stage: 'Let's raise higher the banner of Marx, Engels, Lenin, and Stalin.' The room had no ventilation. It was warm and the air was bad. It smelled of wet outer clothing.

To my surprise I saw Masha's smiling face.

She said, 'I hope that at least one of the seats next to yours has not been reserved.'

I stood up.

'You are blushing,' she giggled. 'Where is the beautiful Nadya?'

'She did not feel well,' I said.

'I am sorry to hear it.' She sat down next to me. 'I hope it's nothing serious?'

'Oh, no.'

'Then I can enjoy having you all to myself. At least for tonight.'

The hall soon filled, all the seats were occupied and there were a few hundred people standing. It was hot, but everyone kept his coat on for fear that it might be stolen. I looked at my watch. The meeting was supposed to have started a half hour ago.

'Where are you rushing?' Masha said.

'The meeting was supposed – '

'It takes usually an hour, or sometimes two to get going,' Masha said. 'Who cares?'

'I do, Masha. I am used to punctuality.'

'Is it so important? I would like the programme to start late. That way I'll have the opportunity to talk to you. Were you always happy among these punctual people?'

'No, Masha. Most of the time I was unhappy despite the punctuality of the people. Living in foreign countries, I felt lonely most of the time.'

'Perhaps you were lonely because you chose to be.'

'Oh, no. I always tried to meet people. In a train, on a bus, or on the street a girl would look at me. She would smile and I would talk to her – and then she would discover that I was a refugee. "*C'est triste, Monsieur,*" she would say, continuing to smile, but the spark of interest in her eyes would be gone, and we would part forever.'

'You can be lonely while living in your own country, among people you like. The feeling of loneliness comes when you yearn to be in love and you aren't. It is like having a valuable present one wants to give someone, and there is no one to receive it, a present of one's own feelings and complete sacrifice.'

Masha's eyes became misty as she looked far away beyond the posters, the stage, and the people who now began to appear there.

'I was the only child,' I said, 'so I was used to being alone most of my life, but you – '

'I was raised on a farm near Iver. My father is a labourer in a Kolkhoz. I am the third child in a family of eight children; I love all of them. The younger ones I raised myself since my mother worked hard in the fields. I used to take care of them, feed them, change their nappies and read books to them. Everyone in the village was my friend and yet as I became a teenager the feeling of loneliness stole upon me.'

The people on the stage, wearing a variety of uniforms or civilian clothing, were talking to each other without paying any attention to the audience.

'You read too many books, Masha. You were influenced too much by Russian authors. You were formed by them.'

'You are right, Anton. I was an avid reader. That is why I became a librarian and I like it. I love to give people advice about what to read. But you are wrong in saying that the books formed me. Books are like mirrors. In them you can see yourself, you can discover yourself. They are not always regular flat mirrors but sometimes convex or concave, magnifying some traits and concealing others.'

'An irregular mirror distorts reality.'

'Not so much reality. Objectivity perhaps. But you stand before the irregular mirror to magnify the characteristic that is dearest to your heart, giving it a new dimension, reaching deeper into your soul. You also gain an understanding of other people.'

'This is why you are looking at me with such amusement, Masha. You must see me as a caricature, a reflection of me in a concave mirror.'

'This is why I called you a *tsaplya*, a crane – serious, eyes filled with anxiety and wonderment at the world around you,' Masha said laughing.

A big, heavy man came forward on the stage. The audience began to quieten down.

'That is how I see you with my eyes,' Masha whispered. 'But

my heart tells me that you are a unique, lonely human being,' her whisper became almost inaudible, 'with an enormous hunger to be understood and loved.'

The speaker began his talk by referring to the friendship of the two Great Powers, the Soviet Union and Germany, and how the cooperation of these two countries made possible the liberation of Western Bielorussia from Polish subjugation and slavery. He talked also about the Great Revolution and the Bolsheviks and how they liberated the people of Russia. This seemed to be a standard speech that he must have delivered hundreds of times. He spoke of the freedom of the proletariat, the happy lives of peasants in the Soviet Union, and the extermination of those enemies of the people, the capitalists, the clergy and the White Guards. Frequent applause interrupted this speech.

At one point the speaker stopped in the middle of his sentence, walked to the back of the stage and conversed with one of the men seated there. The audience sat quietly, awaiting the continuation of the speech. He came back, finished his sentence, and continued to exalt life in the Soviet Union and its great leader Yossip Vysarinovich Stalin. After the first speaker had finished, another stood up and delivered an almost identical talk, receiving similar applause. Then a third. Again no change of content. The three speeches were not only identical in content, but delivered in a similar way. They reminded me of preaching. That's exactly what they were doing, preaching the new faith under the ikon of the new god, Stalin, and his saints, members of the Politburo.

Too bad I could not share this thought with Masha, who sat quietly with an expression of *déjà vu* on her face.

Now, what will follow, will be the selection of angels, the new congressman and the congresswoman, I thought. I was right.

The first speaker came forward, introduced the two candidates, giving briefly their curricula vitae. They were indistinguishable.

Both came from poor proletarian families, both had become communists early in their youth. They had suffered persecutions that were not specified; they believed in Stalin. The speaker proudly stressed the point that in the Soviet Union only people with such proletarian backgrounds could participate in governing the country. It came to my mind that Karl Marx, the son of an industrialist and a rich woman, would not qualify for this sort of heaven. Nor would his having inherited a fortune and married a baroness improve his status here.

It was now the turn of the candidates to speak. First Tovarich Katshak came forward. A square-faced man in his fifties, he kept his hat on. He accompanied each word he spoke with wide movements of his arms.

'The Great Soviet Union, a world power, came here,' he began his speech, 'to liberate us from the Great Power of Germany, who also fought a Great Power, Poland, who earlier had fought the Great Soviet Union.' The audience applauded, but the first speaker appeared displeased.

'The Great Power, The Soviet Union will destroy the Great Power, Germany in order to liberate –'

'It's not necessary, Tovarich Katshak,' the first speaker said. 'All these Great Powers. Let them alone for the time being.'

Katshak, dressed in a sheepskin coat, nodded. 'I am not a learned person,' he said blushing. 'Just from my peasant's mind, you see. But Tovarich Stalin I like – with all my soul.' He made a gesture showing an embrace.

The first speaker nodded.

'Who is that guy?' I asked Masha.

'Commissar Lobin,' she whispered. 'You can see he has a red star on his left sleeve. That means he is a commissar.'

Lobin stood up with obvious relief and recommended that Tovarich Katshak be recommended by acclamation to be the delegate of the congress. The audience applauded. In a similar fashion Tovarich Polkina was elected.

The whole proceedings lasted about four hours, until well after midnight. When the formal meeting was over, the orchestra began playing dance music.

'Won't you stay for a dance with me?' Masha asked.

'I would rather – '

'Oh, come on!' she said, looking into my eyes. 'Just for a short while. You will be forgiven.'

So we danced. Since there was no place to leave our overcoats, we kept them on, leaving them unbuttoned.

'You could dance a little closer,' Masha said. 'I won't bite. I promise.' She laughed. 'You are blushing again! How wonderful!'

Masha did not wear a bra. When her breasts touched my body I felt as if I had been touched by a live electric wire.

'Anton, say something nice to me.'

'You dance very well,' I said. 'I like dancing with you.'

The orchestra switched from a tango to a foxtrot. We went on dancing. She asked me about my life in Poland before the war. When I told her that we had lived by selling various family treasures, she was amused. 'That would not be possible in the Soviet Union,' she said.

At the door sat a man who asked those leaving to register. I was used to these procedures and quickly filled in the form with my name, address, nationality. Behind the table stood Commissar Lobin, the first speaker of the evening. As soon as I put my form on the table he picked it up and read it.

'Antoni Slavski, Polyak, a Pole? How very nice of you to attend.'

I knew I must have been the only Pole to take part in that idiotic affair – and a false one to boot.

'*Preeyatno, preeyatno,* that's nice,' he said as we were shaking hands.

I was angry at Franek for giving me this assignment, and angry at Masha for keeping me there so long. Had I left earlier I would have escaped the need for registering.

It was already three o'clock in the morning. In contrast to the overheated hall, it was cold outdoors. I wanted to hurry but Masha ambled. The cold wind blew brown leaves in our faces.

'I feel bad about you, Anton. I know you are in love with another girl and I am holding you up.'

We walked in silence through the deserted and muddy streets.

'You remind me of the heroes in novels. Oblomov or Vronski, or Nikolay in *War and Peace*. They spoke and behaved as you do. Forgive me.'

At the door of her home we shook hands.

'There is nothing to forgive,' I said. 'I enjoyed being with you. Nadya will understand.'

'We can still be good friends,' she said.

I went home thirsty and tired. What stood out in my mind from the whole meeting was Tovarich Katshak's speech. He was the only one who expressed any thought of his own, his concern how the two powers, Germany and the Soviet Union, could co-exist. But that part of his speech has been squashed. In his clumsy way Katshak had expressed what was in everybody's mind. Would Hitler attack the Soviet Union one day? Will the war come here? Will the great steel tanks shoot live ammunition and the aeroplanes now flying over Pruzhany drop bombs? The thoughts made me uneasy and despite the fatigue I could not fall asleep for a long time.

Chapter 8

Berlin, November 27, 1939

A strong easterly wind blew so hard that the assembled delegation of the Third Reich, in their dress uniforms with the full complement of Nazi regalia, had to hold down their caps while waiting on the platform of the Friedrichstrasse railway station for the arrival of the train.

The wind made the flags snap, half of them with black swastikas and the others with hammer and sickle, displayed here to greet the Soviet Economic Mission about to arrive from Moscow. Colonel General Udet, second-in-command of the German Luftwaffe, stood in front of the other generals and the city officials. Standing well behind these high ranking officers and other dignitaries were Captain von Dolnitz and his superior, Major Wurmlein.

'Are you ready to receive our guests?' Wurmlein asked.

'Every word spoken by them will be recorded, every meeting registered.'

'Do you trust our officers and their memories?'

'I think I can, Major, they are – '

The noise of the locomotive interrupted von Dolnitz's sentence. When the train had stopped and the doors had opened, men in uniform of civilian clothing filled the platform. The military band began to play the *Internationale*, the anthem of the Soviet Union. Both guests and hosts stood at attention looking silently at the swastikas and the hammers and sickles above them.

In the next few days the guests visited factories producing aeroplanes, guns and tanks. On one such visit, General Udet, after he had invited the head of the Soviet delegation, Tevosian, to join him on the flight, piloted a Storch plane, after which Udet gave the plane to his guest as a gift.

In the evening the guests were fêted at many receptions given in their honour. The purchase by the Soviets of war material in exchange for raw materials was discussed in an atmosphere of 'mutual friendship and understanding' as the Berlin newspapers reported.

During one of these occasions in the Hotel Adlon, while hosts and guests were exchanging toasts in honour of their leaders, Wurmlein retired to the lobby where he was joined by von Dolnitz.

'I read your report, Captain,' Wurmlein said, carefully easing his bulky body into the depth of a red plush chair. 'They seem to be protesting too much that we are showing them old stuff.'

'And this despite the fact that we are showing them everything we have, including the newest tanks, Major.'

Wurmlein motioned the captain to sit down.

'The Soviet General Gusiev was uncivil. He almost called Udet a liar,' von Dolnitz said, sitting down on the edge of a stool.

A stranger appeared in a navy blue, double-breasted suit, two sizes too big for his bulky body. He hesitated for a moment, then approached them.

'I am being called Brodilo,' the newcomer said in heavily accented German.

The two Germans rose.

'It is very agreeable for me to meet you, Major Wurmlein, and you, Captain von Dolnitz,' Brodilo said shaking hands with his hosts.

Von Dolnitz was unable to control his expression of surprise that a member of the Soviet Delegation should know their names.

Brodilo noticed von Dolnitz's surprise. He explained, 'As we say in our country, "an angler recognises another angler from afar". Do you agree?'

'I hope that you find our capital city less irritating than I do,'

Wurmlein said. 'I miss the mountains of my native Bavaria.'

'Mountains, yes – not beer?' Brodilo asked, laughing aloud.

'We can bring our Bavarian beer here,' Wurmlein said, 'but not our mountains.'

'Yes. We have a saying in Russia: "a mountain will not get together with another mountain, but a man with another man will get together!" ' Brodilo, exhausted by that translation into German, lighted a cigarette. 'I think,' he continued, 'that one day we might get together. We might need each other.'

Von Dolnitz frowned, trying to determine the meaning behind Brodilo's words.

'Who knows, there might be sometimes a . . . ' Brodilo searched for the right word. 'A desperate situation.'

'A desperate situation!' Wurmlein said, smiling. 'I hope it will only happen when Pentecost falls on Easter Sunday.'

Brodilo did not understand. He tried to guess the meaning of Wurmlein's statement, helping himself in the effort by rubbing his hand over his bald head. Finally it dawned on him what Wurmlein had meant. 'Oh, yes, yes, we have a saying in our country for that: "when the lobster will whistle and the pike will sing." '

Brodilo inhaled deeply on his cigarette. Von Dolnitz felt awkward and wished that the guest would go away. The three of them stood in silence while Brodilo lighted another cigarette from the stump of the last one he had smoked.

'It is necessary for me to go back,' Brodilo said with a forced smile. 'It was nice to meet other anglers. Ha, ha, ha. And remember what I said: mountain with mountain – no, but with man, yes, yes.'

'A typical N.K.V.D. man,' von Dolnitz said as soon as Brodilo's bulky body had disappeared behind the glass doors of the dining room.

'And of a high position! Otherwise he would not be here,' Wurmlein said.

'Or he would not be free to refer to a "desperate situation",' von Dolnitz said. 'I wonder what he wants.'

'Obviously an exchange of information.'

'We would never, Major. Never.'

'Don't say "never",' Wurmlein said. 'In our line of work there are cases when there might be an advantage to both parties.

Anyway we should go now. I expect to learn something tonight that I would like to discuss with you in my office at eight tomorrow morning.'

Von Dolnitz was curious about Wurmlein's last statement, and could hardly wait for the meeting at eight the next morning: Wurmlein was an hour and fifteen minutes late.

'The same business kept me all this time. My apologies,' Wurmlein said, sitting down behind the desk in his office. Von Dolnitz could not fail to remark on the size of the portraits of Hitler and Himmler in Wurmlein's office. They were even larger than those he had seen in Wurmlein's home.

'The Soviet designers are working on something hot, a medium tank,' Wurmlein said, looking with disgust at the wet window spattered by a drizzle. Von Dolnitz assumed that Wurmlein had probably got his news from one of the Soviet delegates who was a spy for the Third Reich. As the major did not volunteer any information, however, von Dolnitz could not ask him. 'It seems that the Reds, having lost many of their tanks in Spain because their armour was too thin, are trying to build new models with much heavier plates. We must find out the specifications of these plates.'

'How about your well-informed friend, Major?'

'He does not think he could find out anything new. His job is being shifted to another sector of industry.'

'They would be testing such models,' von Dolnitz said. 'We might find out.'

'Might is not good enough,' Wurmlein said, leaning back. 'These gentlemen are keen to find out for sure.' He pointed to the portraits of Hitler and Himmler. 'My friend thinks the Soviets might test the tanks in the swamps of former Eastern Poland.'

Von Dolnitz was aware that since the tanks were originally developed for warfare in the swamps of Flanders, it would be natural for them to be tested in similar terrain.

'But why Eastern Poland?' von Dolnitz asked.

'The Russians have plenty of marshes in their country as in the neighbourhood of Leningrad. But the tanks are to be ready in a matter of weeks, and the swamps of Eastern Poland do not freeze as deeply, and they provide the right kind of test conditions. Besides, the Soviets have assembled some of our own tanks in the area near Kobryn, or Pruzhany. By the way, do you know where in hell those towns are?'

'About halfway between Berlin and Moscow, Herr Major.'

'Do we have any of our own men there?' Wurmlein asked.

'No, we don't, but the "Operation Parterre" spies might be in that area. We could use – '

'Use anybody, even the devil himself, but get those facts.'

'*Jawohl*, Herr Major.'

Von Dolnitz was capable of dealing with the assignment. The same day he bought six tickets for the performance of the Viennese Opera three days later, sent one ticket to Krugov, kept one, and destroyed the rest. There was no doubt in his mind that Krugov would be able to guess who had sent him the ticket and would appear in the lounge. Von Dolnitz arrived during the first intermission.

'The friendship between your country and the Soviet Union is in full bloom,' Krugov said, getting up from a small stool in an enclosed private sitting area behind the lounge.

'Yes, but – ' von Dolnitz said.

'Quite a reception for your red friends,' Krugov continued. 'Red flags waving in the station, orchestra, speeches. They were housed at the Adlon! The best hotel in Berlin.'

'I chose to meet you, Herr Krugov, during an "intermission." Let that word be the symbol of the situation. I hope you have enjoyed the voice of Maria Cebotari. Great voice. Only Italians are able to sing with such feeling.'

'As it happens, Herr von Dolnitz, Maria Cebotari is Russian. Her real name is Tshebotarieff. Your last statement needs to be corrected: only Russians are able to sing with such feeling.'

Von Dolnitz was tapping the arm of his red leather chair. 'New developments in Moscow,' von Dolnitz said. 'On the 21st Stalin abolished their Panzer Corps.'

'What . . . is this kind of . . . I don't believe it.' Krugov rose to his feet, almost hitting the low ceiling with his head.

'I could not believe it myself, Herr Krugov. They don't try to keep it a secret. The tanks will be assigned to various infantry divisions.'

'He did it after what you Germans demonstrated in Poland. After you showed what a Panzer division can accomplish. My God! That's insane.'

'I agree. It is a surprise.'

'But the Soviets were the first to use armour in big units. Fifty in Esquivas. Zhukov used 500 in Kholkhin Gol just a few months ago. That was their greatest victory. Why?'

'I wish I could answer the question. Our generals are as surprised as you are,' von Dolnitz said.

Krugov sat down heavily, almost breaking the tiny chair.

'The Soviets might have some new armour,' von Dolnitz suggested.

'I don't see the logic. No matter how good and powerful the tank, to be effective in a mobile war it must be used in huge formations. You know it.'

'I still believe that even Stalin could not have made such a move without some new development in tanks.'

Some voices and laughter were heard behind the doors of the lounge.

'So that is why you came here, Herr von Dolnitz, to inquire about my garden?'

'I would like to fertilise some of your seedlings, Herr Krugov.' Von Dolnitz pushed the pearl-headed pin deeper into his tie.

'I am pleased to note your concern for the plants in my garden. Any special one?'

'Have you planted any in the Kobryn Pruzhany area?'

Krugov took a cigarette out of a cardboard packet, realised that smoking was prohibited and put it back.

'Yes, I did,' Krugov said.

'May I see one?'

'The seedlings don't like to be disturbed,' Krugov said. 'The roots may get damaged.'

'In this case some cross pollination might be crucial.'

'I am pleased at your knowledge of gardening terms, Herr von Dolnitz. However, the plants don't pollinate until they blossom.'

'The seedling would be replanted in the same soil.'

'Replanting in the same soil cannot guarantee a seedling's survival. Some roots are very vulnerable to light.'

The gong sounded once. The second act would begin in a few minutes.

'They are building proving grounds,' von Dolnitz said. 'They are doing it between Kobryn and Pruzhany. They have collected there some of our PKW-2 and PKW-3 tanks – the debris of our

Polish campaign. It is conceivable that they will test their new tanks there.'

Krugov took out his blue handkerchief and wiped his forehead.

'There are thousands of persons still crossing the new border,' von Dolnitz continued. 'Refugees are moving in both directions.'

'I am aware of the situation on that border,' Krugov said.

'A short absence of your agent won't be noticed, Herr Krugov. People travel for many reasons.'

'The agent in question is not experienced.'

'Immaterial, Herr Krugov. After a few hours of instructions he would be able to spot – '

'Our agreement, Herr von Dolnitz. You are not supposed – '

'I will give you my word of honour as a German officer. Only I will know his assumed name. I won't keep any records.'

'I could transfer another agent.'

'No, Herr Krugov. An agent coming there now would be very vulnerable.'

'You still seem to be well informed, Herr von Dolnitz, without our assistance.'

The gong sounded twice.

'Believe me, I hate to admit it, Herr Krugov, but we need your help in this case. Our research group has analysed the area. The most famous military commander in Russian history, General Suvorov, later on Generalissimo Suvorov, won his first major battle near Kobryn. He was awarded an estate there with 6922 male serfs.'

'That is German Grundlichkeit, 6922! Some dead souls too?'

'Stalin is known to worship Suvorov; he is a sentimentalist.'

'Murderer,' Krugov interjected.

'Stalin, his name meaning "man of steel", is obsessed with steel tanks. He might want to test a new one there.'

The gong sounded three times.

Von Dolnitz rose to his feet. 'We will meet your agent in a private place,' von Dolnitz said. 'A former Polish estate just inside the new borders of the Reich. It is located nineteen kilometres from Czestochowa. When the agent calls your number in Vienna, one of our operators will give him his travel directions. We will be waiting for him there. It is crucial to detain him as short a time as possible for his safety.'

The music began the overture to the second act of *La Bohème*.

'I will expect your call, Herr Krugov, in the next few days,' von Dolnitz whispered. 'I hope you will enjoy the remaining acts and the Russian voice of Cebotari. *Gruss Gott.*'

Krugov returned to his seat and stayed till the end of the performance. He left the Opera House with the crowd of ladies in long evening dresses, gentlemen in tuxedos, and officers in their gala uniforms. He hurried to his artist studio and home in one, seized his telephone and dialled the operator. After a long wait he was connected with a number in Lublin, a town formerly located in the centre of Poland, but now in the eastern part of General Government, only a few kilometres from the Soviet border. The telephone was answered by a familiar young voice. Krugov gave him instructions in code. The young man in Lublin understood them. After he put down the receiver, he put on the uniform of a German soldier, mounted his motor cycle, and rode east. The streets and roads were deserted. The curfew for the Poles was on. Half an hour later he arrived at the village of Zarzece. The last house overlooked the River Bug. He did not have to knock. An old man with a white beard heard the sound of the motor and came to open the door and to take the message.

At five in the morning, long after the cyclist had gone, the old man lighted a kerosene lamp, extinguished it after three minutes, lighted it again. Then he lighted a lamp in the attic for one minute. He lighted other lamps too. From outside it might look as if in the house of the white-bearded man, someone was getting dressed, washing and eating breakfast. After seven in the morning the old man walked on his side of the river. He saw from the other side of the River Bug, black smoke rising from one of the houses. He smiled. He knew that his message had been received. Someone over there in Soviet territory would get an order. He might do something good. Something that might contribute to the liberation of Russia from the Soviets. Then the old man would be free to return to Russia and die in his homeland.

Chapter 9
Anton's Story

Pruzhany, November 27, 1939

In the second part of November, there was a renewed movement of tanks and I was skipping my classes to watch and count them. For the first time I was able to see the newest T-28M model that I had recognised by the hanging baskets from the subsidiary turrets. Encouraged by this discovery I decided to try a visit to the library. I chose a time shortly before closing, at a quarter to nine, hoping that there would be only a few persons there. My hunch was right; there were only two soldiers there, both in the process of filling out some forms that would enable them to take out books. Masha smiled on seeing me, and she motioned to me to come in. It was stuffy inside and it smelled of glue and tobacco. All Soviet books, as I had noticed a long time ago, had the special smell of their book-binding glue, a smell that was different from those books produced in Tsarist Russia or elsewhere. There were a lot of wooden shelves, most of them only half-full. On the table were stacks of magazines. As I approached it one series of magazines immediately caught my eyes: '*Avto Bronetankovoy Zhurnal*' (Armoured Tanks Magazine).

I looked at Masha. She had just finished processing a book for one of the soldiers. As he left she began to work with the other. The most recent available issue of the magazine was number seven, dated July 1939. I picked it up and began reading it. First I glanced through an article by Benderchuk entitled 'Cooperation of Tanks Artillery and Infantry in Offensive Combat,' but the article did not appear to contain any useful facts. Another article by Bibergan, 'History of Tank Construction in our Fatherland,' did not appear to promise any new information. I started to skim it: not unexpectedly it began with a statement about the Tsarist regime's lack of foresight in planning for the building of tanks.

I heard the deep voice of the soldier speaking to Masha; 'I want ... book about love.'

'All the novels are about love, or almost all,' I heard Masha's cheerful voice. 'You should be more specific. Love at first sight, first love, married man and single woman ... '

Skipping several paragraphs, I went on reading: 'The forerunners of the armoured tanks forces were the armoured trains and cars ... '

'My favourite novel about love is Dostoyevsky's *Idiot*,' Masha's voice continued. 'A prince loves two women, one out of pity and the other one out of deep sensual feelings.'

I looked at Masha who was also looking at me. Our eyes met for a moment.

'You must decide whether you like to read about happy or unhappy love,' Masha went on. 'Most of the books are about the unhappy kind. Maybe that's what love is all about.'

Skipping some more I read on about the French tank strategy of supporting infantry with tanks, mostly small ones, a strategy that had been accepted at the time by the Soviet command. The author of the article quoted a foreign authority with regard to speed: 'One should consider the question of Achilles and the Tortoise. A superior tank with the slow speed of twenty kilometres per hour is sufficient.'

'So let it be,' the deep voice said, 'about a sad love.'

'One of the most beautiful short stories on the subject is by Chekhov, *On Love*. You will never forget it.'

'I read that one many times. I would like a poem to read to, hm, Tamara.'

'Lermontov's *Damon*. It is a perfect poem for your purpose: it is the most beautiful declaration of love.'

I went on reading. 'It appears strange now when our tanks travel at speeds of 45 to 50 kilometres per hour through the Red Square ... ' and the author continued to make fun of the foreigners who had failed to design tanks capable of a higher speed. The article taught me one thing: the Soviets would be emphasising speed in any future design of their tanks.

The soldier was leaving when Masha said to him, while looking again at me: '*Liubov nye cartoshka, ne veebroshiz eez okoshka*' (Love is not a potato. You cannot throw it out of the window).

Masha was now quickly arranging pieces of paper.

'Welcome my favourite *Tsaplya,*' she said. 'It's good of you to visit me. You can see me at my exciting work.'

'And see the exciting librarian bestowing words of wisdom, gathered from books, on her customers.' Masha was putting on her cap and a long warm trench coat. If I could ever get a coat like that for Nadya, I thought.

'The books have more wisdom than their readers, and more than the librarians.'

Masha was turning off the lights, 'I am sorry that I don't have much time tonight. I am due for a meeting of the regional council for *Prosvieshtshnye* (Enlightenment), but you can walk me there.'

It was drizzling. Masha was late for her meeting so we strode along at a good pace. A series of huge tracked vehicles was passing by, spraying mud that we avoided only by jumping quickly aside. The trucks made so much noise that we had to shout to each other to be understood.

'Your favourite novel is *The Idiot*?' I shouted.

'Lots of truth in it.'

'You think my love for Nadya is like Myshkin's for Aglaya?'

Another truck was passing. We had to jump away. When it disappeared and was quiet again, Masha said, 'Often a chicken of love crawls out of an egg of pity.'

'I disagree,' I said.

We were approaching the canteen where Masha was going.

'You may not be in love at all,' Masha said. 'What I mean is that you may not be in love with any woman.'

'I don't understand.'

'The way you were reading the tank magazine, one might get the impression that a tank is your mistress. I must go.'

I did not like it that Masha had divined my interest in the tanks. 'What a perceptive girl that Masha is,' I said to myself. Even while processing books, she had noticed what I was reading.

I began to think of what Masha had said about my feelings for Nadya. 'Masha is wrong, completely wrong,' I kept telling myself, as I returned home. 'My love for Nadya is complete, and as in any Russian love, or for that matter any human love, there is an element in it of pity and compassion, but that is not all.'

After a few days I was still unable to free myself of the thoughts stirred up by that conversation. I wanted to talk it over with Nadya, but I did not have enough courage to do so.

Three days after my visit to the library, during the intermission Franek whispered to me to come that evening to the Catholic cemetery to give them my report on the communist election meeting. He told me that Krystyna, who had been absent from the school the last few days, had heard about the death of her father.

When I met Krystyna and Franek in the cemetery and expressed my sympathy, she said, 'My father died on the foreign soil of Russia. All of us should be ready to die here to fight for our independence.'

'We will fight them to avenge his death,' Franek said. 'He died for a cause.'

It was drizzling and so dark that I could hardly distinguish Franek from Krystyna. I was freezing and I wanted to present my report to them as quickly as possible.

'We will win. We must,' Krystyna said.

'I want to give you the report,' I said.

'I hope you did not vomit hearing that garbage,' Frank said. 'It was your patriotic duty to accept the task and we thank you.'

I began to give them a brief account of the proceedings, but it was not brief enough for Krystyna.

'I cannot, just cannot, stomach it any longer,' she said.

'Any names of the participants, the commissars?' Franek said.

'Yes, the conference chairman and keynote speaker was a Commissar Lobin,' I said.

'Did you notice his face?' Krystyna asked. 'Would you be able to recognise him?'

'Yes, I would.'

'We may want to get rid of such a son of a bitch,' Franek said. 'Would you volunteer?'

I was surprised by the turn the conversation had taken.

'No, I could not,' I said. 'I could not kill a man or a woman. I could never do it.'

'You may have to learn one day,' Franek said. 'It may come in handy in time of war.'

'I don't think so,' I said.

After some more talk about the war and the future victories of

England and France, we parted at the gate of the cemetery. My topcoat was wet from the drizzle and I wanted to reach my home and bed as soon as the deep mud of the country road would let me. But after I had passed the first few houses of Pruzhany I realised that I was being followed. I slowed down my walk and was ready to turn when I heard a voice saying: 'Stop three, the king is coming.' I turned round.

In the darkness I was hardly able to see his face. He was of medium size. 'The trump three takes the king,' I whispered.

'Take this,' the man said, 'and deliver it in the General Government as soon as possible.'

'The message was to be oral, not written.'

'Don't worry!' The man changed to Polish. 'You can read it. It is just about family.'

'But ... I don't know.'

'Well, goodbye, and I guess, good luck.'

Without pausing for even a handshake the man turned and disappeared into the dense fog of the late November evening. I wanted to talk to him, ask him some questions, have him share my anxiety and fear. But he was gone. I would not recognise him even if I should see him in daylight.

I walked home slowly, hoping that nobody had seen this brief encounter. Before undressing I sat on my bed and read the letter. It was written in Polish and, as the man had said, it was innocuous. It described in detail the life of a family, their health, their habits and dress. I could easily have received such a letter from one of my relatives if I had any who were living in Eastern Poland.

The only train that left Pruzhany was at noon, so I had plenty of time to make my preparations. Not being able to sleep, I packed a few things in my little valise and took my money. I decided to leave the rucksack in my room. I still could not fall asleep for hours after that. I was thinking of Nadya. Would I ever see her again? In some way I felt relieved that the mission was on. The uncertainty of the last few weeks had been almost unbearable. Maybe this new development would help me to clarify my situation. I thought of telling Krugov that I was not good at the business and I would resign and come back here. I wouldn't do that, though, I supposed. Then I remembered the letter. I became concerned about how I could hide it. After considering a few alternatives I decided to sew it into the lining of my uniform jacket. That task took me quite a while, but it relieved some of my tension.

It must have been almost morning when I finally fell asleep. I woke up early, paid Avram one month's rent in advance, and told him that I had to go to Bialystok to visit my sick uncle. I also told him to inform the school of my absence and that I would probably be back in a week.

The narrow-gauge train left on time. There were only a few passengers. The train went as far as Warki, where one changed to a regular train going to Brest.

Since this was an important route, the Soviets had converted the line to their gauge, which was a few centimetres broader than the Polish. For the first time I had an opportunity to observe the Soviet trains and the Soviet passengers, some of them in civilian clothing. The ladies wore only one kind of cover for their head, a beret. The colours, however, varied and from the way they were worn one could conclude whether the wearer was a coquette or a serious minded Soviet woman. I tried to avoid any conversation, fearing that someone might guess the purpose of my trip, even after a short exchange of words.

My plan was to arrive in Brest, a town on the river Bug. The river was about 60 metres broad, a distance I knew I could easily swim. I was used to swimming in cold water, so that should not be a problem. It seemed to me possible to find an unguarded spot and swim to the German side of the river.

The station at Brest was crowded with thousands of people, most of whom I assumed had the same purpose as I – to escape to the West. As I was leaving the station someone tapped me from behind on the shoulder. Frightened, I turned around.

'Excuse, please, Panie. I want to talk to you.' The man who had spoken was dressed in a shiny black overcoat, with a black yarmulke on his head, He wore his hair long in the typical fashion of the Orthodox Jews, and his white beard reached almost to his belt.

'What do you want?'

'Just to talk to you, that's all.'

'About what?'

'About this and that.' He smiled and bowed.

We were standing among hundreds of people, coming to and

going from the station, but nobody paid any attention to us.

'Well go ahead,' I said.

'Oh, not here. Come?'

He turned around and indicated by a gesture for me to follow him. For a moment I wondered whether I should. Then I thought that he might know something of my plan or that I might be under suspicion. I decided to go with him.

We walked through some narrow streets. It was well after eleven o'clock, but the streets were still crowded. I did not pay much attention to where we were going. We turned left or right many times, and finally we mounted some stairs, and passed along a corridor dark and with a strong smell of onions and urine. Then we turned into a room. There were a few young men wearing the yarmulke sitting at a table. The walls were decorated with portraits of people wearing old-fashioned clothing, all men, probably relatives of my new acquaintance. At least the faces seemed to resemble his. The men at the table stood up, bowed, and left the room without any words. My guide closed the doors.

'What do you want to talk to me about?'

'Something you will benefit from.'

He spoke Polish with a heavy accent. The sound of voices came from behind the thin walls. I was not sure whether I could believe him, and I would not have been surprised if a Soviet Commissar had come in and arrested me. 'Well, tell me about it,' I said.

'Well, I would like to buy your coat, among other things.'

'Oh, damn it, you should have told me that before. I don't want to sell anything.' I was angry with him, but relieved to know that this was his only reason for getting me here.

'Why not? I will pay you a good deal of money. Is it wool?'

'I need it.'

The man touched the skirt of my overcoat. 'It is wool,' he said, nodding his head with pleasure.

'Goodbye,' I said moving towards the door.

The man ran in front of me, blocking it. 'For the money I will pay you, you could buy four, maybe five, overcoats like this one.'

'Please, please, let me go. I don't need four or five overcoats.' I moved closer to the door.

'I will give you 300 zloty. Your mother may need one, maybe

your fiancée, your little sister, brother –' He almost shouted, holding fast the door. 'On the German side they are cheap.'

'How do you know where I am going?'

'Everyone coming to the station is going there.' The man seemed relieved that I hesitated. The image of Nadya wearing her short coat appeared in my mind. Then I thought of little Magda, covered with a rag, because she did not have any warm clothing. Noticing my hesitation, the man smiled broadly, knowing that he had won his argument.

'Will you sit down, please? Now we can talk reasonably. Right?'

I sat down, setting my valise close beside my feet. I started to calculate. 300 zlotys would be 150 marks. Indeed I could buy three new coats to replace mine, or maybe two very good ones; one for Nadya and one for my mother, and a sweater for the little girl. But I still needed a coat for myself.

'Your train for Bialystok leaves at five in the morning. You have time.'

'I am not leaving for Bialystok.'

'So how are you going to go there? You know what I mean.'

'I was planning to swim.'

'My God, they will shoot you. The Russians. It was possible before. Not now.' The idea of swimming under the guns made him nervous. He stood up and started to pace back and forth. 'I hear that near Bialystok it is easier. There is no river to cross. Here on the river the soldiers stand and shoot.'

He may be right, I thought. I was glad to get this information. He told me also that the villages to the west of Bialystok were the places where one might get help. The villagers made money guiding people across. There was still plenty of traffic in both directions. When I took off my coat he inspected it in the light of the bare electric bulb shining from the ceiling.

'It is not as good as I thought,' he said, 'but I will still pay you the 300 zlotys. You should also sell this uniform. The Germans do not allow them. They may kill you if you wear it.'

So after some more discussions I sold him the uniform in exchange for 250 zlotys and an old suit which he threw in into the bargain. It was too big for me, but my new friend was also a tailor, and he quickly shortened the trousers. The suit was shabby, but it would do until I could buy a new one.

When I left it was well after midnight. I felt tired, and I hoped that I could get some sleep in the station, if only on the floor. But that turned out to be impossible. There were hundreds of people in the station, and every square inch was occupied. Eventually I was able to find a spot near a wall, not big enough to sit down in, just large enough to let me stand. I was pleased with my transactions. I now had 550 zlotys. I knew I would be able to replace the things I had sold and buy presents for Nadya, Magda, and my mother. I decided that I would send my mother 75 or 100 marks. For Nadya I would buy a long, warm overcoat. I would tell her I got it from my uncle in Bialystok. Then I would buy a warm sweater for little Magda. She would enjoy it. My only worry was what Krugov would think of my shabby clothing.

Krugov. I suddenly remembered. My God! The damn letter was sewn into the jacket I had sold. I started to shake. What would Krugov say when I arrived without the letter. That letter was the sole purpose of my trip and the purpose of my assignment.

I must get it back. I pushed through the crowds and ran in the direction I thought we had taken the previous evening. It was dark and all the streets looked alike. So did the houses. After a few hours of frantic searching, I knew that I would never be able to find the house, not even in broad daylight.

I cursed my own greed and the man who had talked me into the deal. I no longer believed in my ability to carry on with the assignment. For a moment I decided to go back to Pruzhany and start a new life. Maybe I could go to Moscow or Kiev to study. I could get a scholarship, perhaps. So could Nadya. But these thoughts made me feel guilty of betraying Krugov. Could I face life with the thought of this failure? No, I must face reality and recover my coat. After all, the man might be at the station again in search of other potential sellers.

Consequently, I did not take the train to Bialystok. After its departure the station almost emptied, and I found a seat on which I was able to catch a little sleep. It was not to be for long. A uniformed Soviet policeman woke me. Everyone must leave the station – it was time for cleaning up. I tried to retrace my path to the house again, but my efforts were futile.

While walking around I was thinking about my assignment. I knew now that I was not suited for it. What concerned me even more, though, was the doubt I began to feel about the purpose of the whole project. It is true that my father had been killed by Bolsheviks. But that happened during the revolution when lots of people got killed. Besides, the vast majority of the people I knew now had not been born or were children at the time of the revolution. Could they be responsible for the atrocities? And of course both sides in the revolution had been responsible for horrors.

I returned to the station in the early afternoon, and after a few more hours of waiting and searching, came upon the man who had bought my belongings. He was surprised to see me still in Brest.

'How come you are still here? Did you miss the train?'

'No, I am here because I wanted to see you again.'

'But our deal was completed.'

'I forgot that I had a letter for a relative in my jacket.'

'There was nothing in the pockets. I checked them myself.'

'The letter was sewn into the lining. I will pay you –'

'Impossible. I just sold your suit to a Soviet man. He was leaving town. I wouldn't know where to look for him.'

So that was that. The letter was gone. But had my jacket been bought by someone who needed one or by someone who was on my trail? Someone who would discover the letter and decipher the message. He would learn the truth about me and possibly set in motion the persecution of my friends.

When I took the train, despite my fatigue, the thought of my failure continued to plague me. Maybe the failure had been caused by something deep within my own character, by forces over which I had no control. Possibly that failure was what fate had in store for me. I could not rid myself of a feeling of despair. I paid little attention to my fellow passengers, seeing them through the mist of my thoughts as the superfluous background for my bitterness.

The train station in Bialystok had a depressingly familiar look. There were hundreds of people milling around, men, women, and children, eating, sleeping, laughing and crying. All of them were here for the sole purpose of escaping to the West. Despite the presence of uniformed Soviets these people carried on conversations about their escape plans. There were no more trains going west. Since the border was 30 kilometres away it was necessary to arrange for transportation of some other kind. That meant hiring a local peasant with his horse and cart. Such a trip involved a considerable risk for the peasant; that was why he usually charged outrageous prices.

'It will cost us 200 zlotys, and we don't have that much. All we have is 80 zlotys.' I turned around. The speaker was in his thirties. He was facing his wife sitting with her three children on the floor. Behind her sat an older woman, probably her mother.

'I will pay the difference,' I said. 'I am going there too.'

After studying me for a few seconds the man nodded, then smiled: 'Welcome aboard. We can use not only the money but a pair of strong hands too.'

The cart was waiting for us only a short distance away. It was not covered. Its wheels were shod with iron. The passengers sat on straw. On the way I became acquainted with the family. The man's name was Kielecki. He was an assistant professor in the Law faculty of Warsaw University. His wife, Felicja, a beautiful woman, had been an actress in the Warsaw theatre.

In the late afternoon, we arrived at our destination, a village called Olszany. It was the last village in the part of Poland that was occupied by the Soviets.

On the way we met many uniformed men, many on horses with rifles. If they chose to do so they could probably mow us all down in seconds, but they looked at us with indifference, and without incident we came to a hut where we all got down from the cart.

It was only seven o'clock in the evening – eight hours before our group was to leave. I wished I could sleep but there was no room in the hut, not even on the wooden floor. The place was like an overcrowded railroad car, and I was lucky to get a standing place near a wall so that I could lean against it. As the hour of our departure approached all of us began to talk, mostly about why and where we were going, a few were returning to rejoin their families, but the majority were escaping in the hope that it might be better on the other side.

Around midnight, more people squeezed into the hut. This was the group that had just crossed the border from the other side, the German side. We began to question them about life there and why they had come here.

'My husband, a Professor of archeology,' a lady in a fur coat said, 'hopes to teach in Lwow. The Germans closed all the universities and even the high schools.'

'I don't think it will be possible,' Kielecki said.

'But the Germans are arresting and deporting professors,' the lady said.

'The same here,' said Kielecki.

'It is only a matter of choice,' said an old bearded man with pince-nez, 'whether you prefer to meet your saviour via the German or the Soviet concentration camp. At least some of us here are making that choice.'

During most of the conversations I remained silent. The purpose of my trip was clear, and I did not have to make a choice. That realisation made me an outsider. I was sorry not to share their fears and anxieties, not to be one of them; in the overcrowded room I began to feel lonely. My thoughts were interrupted at that point by the arrival of our guide.

The peasant who drove us introduced us to a friend or relative of his called Wieloch, an unusually tall fellow with a heavy moustache. He invited us into his house, where we found another group of refugees. There would be two crossings that night, Wieloch told us, patting his moustache. We would be leaving at three o'clock in the morning, but in the meantime we must stay inside the house. We were packed like sardines. But I managed to find a spot on the floor where I slept for a few hours. When I woke, it was already two o'clock, and the Kielecki family was up and about. The price of the crossing was 100 zlotys a person. Since the Kieleckis did not have any more money they paid with a watch and a gold ring. Wieloch explained that at the moment there was no danger for the refugees. In the worst case they would be turned back. But the guide would be arrested and executed.

Our guide, Bolek, was introduced to us, a tall boy of about my age with cornflower blue eyes. Before our expedition began he told us how to behave. We were not supposed to ask any questions or to speak at all. He taught us a few elementary signals – one to stop, two to go ahead, and three to lie down.

Before our departure Bolek knelt down in front of a small print of the Black Madonna of Czestochowa and prayed for at least twenty minutes. It was a cold November night; the ground was frozen. The small children, all girls aged five to nine, must have sensed the danger of the situation and they neither spoke nor cried. In the night I heard a dog barking, then the meow of a cat. We had to lie down a few times. In one place we waited for about half an hour. Eventually we reached the house of Wieloch's cousin, which was on the German side.

There we met the same people we had seen on the preceding evening, and many others. The Kielecki family was overjoyed to have reached its destination. They kissed one another. Even I got a few kisses from the girls. Some people began to leave the hut, but Kielecki decided to stay for a few hours and let the girls sleep.

We were awakened by the sound of rifle butts hitting the doors. I heard the shouting of voices: '*Aufamachen*! Open the door!'

The door was opened. Two uniformed men entered the room with their flashlights shining on our faces.

'*Mensch, siehst Du wie viele da sind?*' (Do you see how many there are in here?) The speaker was the older of the two soldiers. He was a heavy, round man. His companion was taller.

'*Sind Juden dabei?*' (Any Jews here?) the younger German asked. There was a silence. I thought I could hear the heartbeats of every refugee in that room. The beam of the flashlight passed again over our faces.

'*Ja.*' Two beams of light focused on the face of the speaker Kielecki.

'*Komm*!' the younger soldier said. Kielecki got up. One of his daughters seized his hand and began to cry.

'*Lass ihn! Er hat kinder.* (Let him go! He has kids).' The soldiers turned around and left.

Later on, as I was walking with Kielecki to the nearest station, I asked him, 'Why did you come here? Wouldn't it have been better for you and your family to remain in the Soviet-occupied zone?'

'No. They've already begun to arrest the intelligentsia. A few of my colleagues have been deported to Siberia. In most cases that means a verdict of death. The Germans will put us in the ghettos, but they have no plans for deportation.

'Germany is a land of western culture. Maybe one day they will recognise how foolish the whole business is.'

When I reached Warsaw, I was appalled by the evidence of destruction in the city. Most of the houses seemed to be in ruins. In the post office I placed a call to Vienna. The Polish telephone operator was shocked at my appearance, and she hesitated before accepting my request.

The voice which answered my call was not Krugov's. I was surprised to hear a man who spoke German with a Berlin accent. When I told him that I was calling from Warsaw, he gave me another number in Czestochowa. 'Herr Krugov is living there now,' the voice said. When I reached him Krugov told me to take the next train to Czestochowa, which would be leaving Warsaw at 11:30 A.M. He told me to come to a hotel near the railroad station called Hotel Kupiecki, where he was registered.

The train was overflowing with passengers, men and women, carrying huge bundles. I had to stand for the whole journey, which took about five hours. Most of the time I was thinking of Nadya, and missing her. Oblivious to the crowd around me, I was imagining what she might be doing at every moment, and in my thoughts I accompanied her to school, brought her home, sat with her at the table. I wondered which of the Chekhov stories Carl would read this evening. In my mind I was telling her my experiences on this trip, my strange encounters and my adventure with Szmulka. That reminded me of the lost letter. I was thinking bitterly of that as the train pulled into the station in Czestochowa.

Striding down the platform to the exit, I spied Krugov, partly hidden behind a group of people. He was accompanied by a man who was standing very straight, about Krugov's size but only half his weight. I did not like that surprise. I had wanted to tell Krugov about the missing letter at the very first moment of our meeting.

Krugov smiled, opening his arms, but then, probably thinking about the reaction of the other man, just shook my hand.

'Nice to see you again, Herr Anton.' Krugov spoke both German and French with a Russian accent. What's more, he spoke these languages in the Russian manner. Even when uttering banalities, he sounded like an actor performing *Uncle Vanya*, and not like a member of a spy ring greeting his colleague. 'This is, ah, Herr von Dolnitz, our, eh.'

That gentleman shook my hand.

'Herr von Dolnitz will drive us to his home.' Krugov waded through the crowds of men, women, and children carrying valises, baskets and rucksacks full of food from the country.

Passing the waiting room I glanced at a poster: *Bekanntmachung – Obwieszczenie* – an announcement both in German and Polish. The black letters proclaimed that ten Polish prostitutes had been sentenced and executed for engaging in sexual intercourse with German soldiers; the said prostitutes having been aware that they had a venereal disease. The terror of the German occupation had begun. I was sorry for the poor girls and wondered whether they really had known that they were sick.

An Opel Kapitän stood in front of the entrance to the railway station. I sat in the back. Von Dolnitz drove and Krugov sat next to him. There was no chance to tell Krugov about the letter. I started to mumble the information in Russian, but Krugov must have guessed my intention, and he mentioned that Herr von Dolnitz knew Russian. We drove through a street lined with Lombardy poplars, now without their leaves, past the Jasna Gora, a Polish monastery, with most of its buildings dating from the 17th century, and the site of Catholic pilgrimages to the Byzantine Ikon of the Black Madonna.

Just a few kilometres farther on there was a stop at the new border between the part of Poland annexed to the Reich and the other part which had become the General Government. The sentry must have recognised the car and its driver, since we were waved on without any inspection of our papers.

I couldn't wait any longer to tell Krugov about the letter. 'Herr Krugov, you know the letter –?'

'Anton Illich, not now. We will have plenty of time.'

'But I must tell you, I don't have it. I mean I did not bring the letter.' I felt terrible. If Krugov had pulled out a revolver to shoot me through the head, I shouldn't have minded.

There was a moment of silence, I wished that I could see Krugov's face.

'What letter?'

'The man gave me a letter. I don't have it.'

'He was not supposed to give you anything,' Krugov said.

'He gave me a letter and I don't have it any more.'

'That's all right,' Krugov said.

Von Dolnitz, who had not shown any emotion during the exchange, said, '*Gut*, Herr Slavski, *sehr gut*, fine Mr Slavski, that's quite all right.'

I wanted to tell them how I had sold the jacket. 'But –' Krugov interrupted me. 'Your instructions were very clear: bring verbal information. I told you that I am the one issuing your instructions. You disobeyed my orders.'

A few minutes later, as I saw from the road sign, we went through a small town named Klobucko. It was a ghost town, with no one in sight. Not like Pruzhany where hundreds of young people would be singing in the streets, even late at night.

Von Dolnitz noticed that I was looking around. 'This is newly annexed territory,' he said. 'The Jews and Poles are in the process of being expelled. Now they have to maintain a curfew.'

My thoughts were still on that letter. All my fears had been for nothing! I was relieved of my anxiety, but not pleased with myself. I knew I was being praised for something I did not deserve. I wanted to tell the truth to Krugov. But I decided to wait. My story might embarrass him with von Dolnitz.

After Klobucko the road narrowed. We drove along between fields. Then we turned into a fenced-in property, a place belonging to some Polish family, now banished, I thought. I was right, as I learned later.

The house stood two hundred metres from the road. It was painted white, and it had a large porch that one could reach by stairs on both ends. The room in which we held our meeting still had traces of its former inhabitants. There were no longer any pictures on the walls, but the places where the pictures had once hung were visible on the wallpaper. The furniture, well-worn rococo pieces, had been left behind.

Von Dolnitz pulled out a large notebook. 'I congratulate you on your appearance,' he said. 'It must not have been easy to travel and to cross the border.'

'I told you, Herr von Dolnitz,' Krugov said, 'Slavski is extremely intelligent.'

Von Dolnitz did not like to be interrupted, as I gathered from the movement of the muscles around his mouth. He tried to control his displeasure, and lighted a cigarette. 'We have a limited time,' he continued. 'First I will ask questions. Then I will give you your next assignment. You will leave on the train the day after tomorrow. The train to Warsaw leaves at three in the morning. Your absence from Pruzhany should be as short as possible.'

So it would be Pruzhany again! I was relieved to hear it. If my next assignment had been in some other place what would I have done then? Return to Pruzhany on my own, forgetting the role I had to play? Then I could be with Nadya as much as I wanted. The image of my first evening with her crossed my mind – the young girl painting an ikon.

'Tell us about your stay in Pruzhany with all the details you remember – whom you met and all the conversations you had. Then everything you observed.'

I summarised my experiences in Pruzhany, minimising my personal contacts. I hardly mentioned Nadya and I called her a girl as if she did not have a name. I did not tell him about my meeting Boris and Gleb. Von Dolnitz took a few notes. He did not interrupt the flow of my presentation. He sat bolt-upright in his chair. His civilian clothes were tailor-made, I assumed. Somehow they did not seem to be appropriate, given his martial bearing. That must have been the first civilian suit he had worn in a long time. His navy blue tie was fastened to his white shirt with a pearl pin and his starched collar reflected the light. Von Dolnitz made sure that the pin was properly adjusted. Although I could not see under his jacket and vest, I was sure that he must be wearing braces and a belt.

'Will you look at these, Herr Slavski? Tell me which ones you saw in Pruzhany?' With his manicured hands, von Dolnitz took out of a portfolio a number of enlarged photos. All of them were of tanks.

I looked at the photographs. There was more than one photograph of each model.

'Look at this illustration,' von Dolnitz said, handing me one of the photographs. 'This is the model T-28M, the most advanced Soviet tank. This tank was used in the Soviet campaign, if we can call it that, in Poland.' Von Dolnitz showed me a number of photographs, taken from all angles.

I was ravenously hungry and tried to guess what would be served for dinner. As yet any sign of a meal being prepared had failed to materialise. I could not even detect any smells of dinner being cooked.

'Your assignment will be to inform us if you spot any new model in the medium-size class of tanks. In other words, a tank similar in size, and probably in design to the T-28M. You understand?' Von Dolnitz looked for the first time at Krugov.

I was surprised that Krugov had not informed him that I had seen them.

'Yes, I have seen a number of these tanks,' I said. 'I recognise them by the baskets hanging from the turrets.'

'You are very observant, Herr Slavski,' von Dolnitz said, and he smiled. 'I summoned you here so that I might define our objectives more precisely. From other sources I know that the Soviets are working on a new medium tank. It is essential to us to find out the characteristics of this new tank as soon as possible, so as to enable our own engineers to create effective weapons to use against it. It will take us several months to create such a weapon system.'

'Yes, Anton Illich. We know the Soviets are working on a new tank in this class,' Krugov said. The 'we' used by Krugov and the 'I' by von Dolnitz did not escape me. I also noticed that Krugov avoided his French now. 'We also know that the Bolsheviks have established in Pruzhany . . .'

Krugov glanced at von Dolnitz, as if he wanted to get his permission to continue, and seeing no change in his expression, Krugov went on. 'They have there a research centre, or in plain language, an espionage centre, concerned with tanks. You know they collected some German tanks.'

Von Dolnitz leaned back, but then immediately sat up straight again as if the back of his chair did not exist. 'It is likely that when the new tank is ready they will have it in Pruzhany. They may want to test it against our models.'

Outside the rain blown by the wind was hitting the glass of the windows. I wondered what Nadya was doing at that moment. Was she walking in her short coat and getting wet? Wasn't my preoccupation with a better overcoat for her justified? After all, Gogol made the overcoat not only a garment but a symbol, a legitimate preoccupation.

'I know it will be difficult for you to concentrate,' von Dolnitz said, possibly guessing that I was far away in my thoughts, 'particularly after such a long trip. But you will have to since it is essential for me to teach you the basic material.' Von Dolnitz looked at his wrist watch. 'We still have about an hour before dinner and I would like to start right now.'

I was tired and hungry but at least there was a firm time set for the meal.

Von Dolnitz had his course well prepared, with large sheets which he pinned on the walls. Showing designs of tanks. '*Der Panzerkampfwagen*, the tank,' Von Dolnitz began, 'has three essential characteristics: armour, armament, and mobility. For your benefit I must simplify, even over-simplify, because of the time limitations.' Von Dolnitz moved to the first sheet on the wall.

'This is an outline of a typical tank,' Krugov said. Von Dolnitz did not respond to that, but he began to lecture.

'The armour of a typical tank takes up about forty-five to fifty per cent of its weight. The whole science of tank design consists in placing the armourplate in such a way as to assure the tank's maximum protection. There are two basic ways of achieving that: one can vary the thickness of the steel plates, depending on their location on the tank. In other words, one can put the heavier armour in the areas of highest vulnerability. I will talk about that in just a moment. The second way is to place the plates not precisely in a vertical position, but to slope them. Let's assume that a bullet strikes such a plate, while moving parallel to the horizon and that the plate is fifty millimetres thick. If that plate is vertical, the thickness such a bullet will have to pierce is fifty millimetres. But when the same plate is placed at a slope of say, forty-five degrees, the same bullet would have to pierce a distance of sixty-five millimetres.'

'Herr Slavski, as an engineering student, knows that principle,' Krugov said

Von Dolnitz did not turn to look at him 'Or, at forty-five degrees, a required penetration of thirty per cent more. That is why the designers try to slope the armour plates around the turret and in front of the tank's hull.'

I wanted Nadya to have the overcoat as her defence and armour against the cold. In that way I would be able to give her warmth. I am only repaying a debt to her; since I am in love with her, I live as if in a cloud of happiness that shields me like armour from the disappointments and hardships of my life.

'... Ergo Herr Slavski,' von Dolnitz said. 'The tendency of future tank design must be the lowering of its height, thus increasing the available weight to be spread in the form of armour plates for protection, or possibly lowering the total weight, allowing higher speed and mobility.' Von Dolnitz checked his watch. 'We will break now for supper.'

Von Dolnitz led the way to the dining room, furnished in rococo style, with a huge crystal chandelier, and a scattering of brass and crystal sconces on the wall instead of pictures. A rug must have graced the parquet floor, I imagined, since there was a lighter section of oblong shape. The table bore plates filled with cold cuts and a few bottles of wine.

All three of us appeared ill at ease in this situation.

'There will be no service at the table so as to maintain security,' von Dolnitz said. 'Further, Herr Slavski, you are requested not to go outside the house.'

Von Dolnitz was a rather formal host, but he made a visible effort to make us comfortable, and he seemed to feel that one does not discuss business at dinner. But while no mention was made of tanks, we did talk about the war: the stalemate at the Western front where no battles had been fought since the beginning of the war, or the Finnish-Soviet War where the Red Army did not seem to make any progress despite their thirty-fold superiority in manpower. Seeing how exhausted I was, von Dolnitz suggested that I should go to bed early, have breakfast at seven and listen to his further presentation starting at eight the next morning.

As soon as Krugov and I were left alone in the room, Krugov looked around and moved towards me on tip-toe.

'The letter,' he whispered.

'What about it? You said that it was the right thing –'

'That was in the presence of von Dolnitz.'

'But my instructions –'

'Forget them now. If your contact man disregarded them, he must have had a reason, a very good reason.'

'I read the letter. There was nothing significant in it.'

'It was in code. What did you do with it?'

'I sold it to a tailor. I mean the jacket in which the letter was sewn. When I realised the mistake it was too late.'

'Why? Why too late?' Krugov asked, his face turning red.

'Because the tailor had sold it to a Soviet.' Krugov hearing this, appeared to have difficulty in catching his breath. Krugov let his face sink into his hands, a gesture I had seen only in the silent movies. But I knew what it meant. He was in despair.

After a minute of silence Krugov said, 'The Soviets have rewards for anyone reporting anything out of the ordinary. If the letter were in the pocket, the purchaser would probably dispose of it, but a letter sewn in the jacket would no doubt arouse suspicion.'

'But you just told me it was coded.'

'Once the Soviets learned that it had been sewn in, they would have no trouble decoding it. Besides they would arrest the tailor and question him.'

'The buyer of the jacket may not discover the letter, not for a long time.'

'Let's hope so,' Krugov said sighing. I was sure that he was exaggerating the importance of the whole business.

Despite the excitement of that conversation, I slept well and felt rested for the next lecture.

Von Dolnitz was an indefatigable man. He told me all I might ever need to know about the tank gun. The tank is designed around the gun, its accuracy and lethal power.

I learned that achieving accurate gunfire from a moving tank depended mainly on the suspension system: the smoother the ride, the more accurate the fire. Von Dolnitz also told me that the Russians were using standardised diesel engines in their tanks instead of the gasoline engines used in other countries, including Germany.

'The diesel engine increases the cruising range of action by about a third over. that of the standard gasoline-powered tank. The risk of fire in tanks equipped with diesel engines is also significantly reduced.'

As the day progressed, my respect for von Dolnitz rose. I began to admire his knowledge and his enthusiasm for tanks, but at the same time I also began to realise that my mission was primarily for the benefit of the Germans and of Herr von Dolnitz. My initial vision of a free Russia, and von Dolnitz's concern to achieve a military advantage, represented two different objectives, that were difficult for me to connect.

The presentation lasted until late afternoon.

When von Dolnitz had collected all his papers including his notebook, and packed them up, I concluded that the meeting had come to an end. Von Dolnitz stood up; so did Krugov and I.

This time before dinner we had Sekt, the German version of champagne. Von Dolnitz proposed a toast to my success and to the freedom of my country. He did not join us for dinner, though, excusing himself on the plea that he had too much work to do. Krugov and I ate in silence – ham, and a variety of sausages and cheeses. Later that evening Krugov drove me to the station. When we were alone in the car, I said to Krugov, 'I never imagined that I would be working so closely with the Germans.'

'It just turned out that they needed that information in Pruzhany, you know, *mon cher*. I am annoyed myself.' He coughed. 'You must be very careful. Watch out for your own safety and that of the other.' At that moment we were stopped at the new Polish border.

When we resumed our drive, Krugov said, 'There was the case of one of our agents in Grodno. He was caught. They arrested everyone he had had any contact with. None of those people was ever heard of again. None.' Then he asked me about the expense money,and I told him I still had over 300 zlotys. He gave me an additional 2,000. 'We may not be able to reach you for some time.'

'May I call my mother?' I asked him.

'No, better not. She is fine, as I told you, but she may ask some questions. They could be embarrassing. I will call her and tell her that I have seen you.'

The whole meeting left me with a somewhat unpleasant taste. I had started to work as an agent for the Russian émigré group, and now I was becoming a real spy – a spy for the Third Reich. Did I really want that?

It was difficult for me to keep my eyes open but I listened to Krugov's talk.

'After the war of 1914-18, the Germans were the first ones to establish relations with the Soviets. They even operated a tank school there. They taught the Soviets, but one day they will regret it. They may be regretting it now.'

'Their pupils do not seem much skilled at tank warfare in Finland.'

'It's too early to say,' Krugov said. 'What is significant is that the German press is quite sympathetic to the Finns and not to their friends the Soviets. I am telling you, Anton Illich, there will be a war between the Soviets and the Third Reich much sooner than we imagine.'

'The Germans would not wage another war with two fronts.'

'They will finish France in a matter of a few months,' Krugov said, stopping the car at an intersection. 'The French have no desire to fight; you know, I lived there for years.'

'But for the time being the two adversaries are locked in a *sitzkreig*, a phoney war. There is no action on the Western Front, only in the Atlantic, where a few ships are being sunk from time to time.'

'The Germans are waiting for the right weather and then, believe me, they will attack France. After they win that war it will be the turn of the Soviets. Their defeat may take several months, but it will come. And that is why your mission is so important. The more the Germans know about the Soviet tanks the sooner they can win. You will see that the Russian people are tired of the bloody Red regime. Millions of soldiers will surrender to the Germans; the Russian people will welcome them as liberators.'

Krugov drove in silence for a while.

'You must be careful, Anton Illich. We have already had some losses as I told you. Don't bother to send us reports unless you learn about the new tank. Then I would prefer that you return as soon as possible. Since that might be most difficult in the future.'

'It was all right this time,' I said.

'In a few months they will make the border almost impassable. It will take quite a lot of ingenuity to cross it. But I have faith in you.'

'People have always succeeded in escaping from the Soviet Union,' I said.

'That is true,' Krugov said. 'But those were the exceptions, and practically none of those who succeeded had been suspects. Once they would suspect you to be a spy, or even if they knew it for a certainty, they would take their time before arresting you.

'They would want to catch all of your possible contacts. Once you notice that you are being trailed, your chances of running away are nil. At that point, don't try to get in touch with anyone! It often happens that even after the arrest the Soviets have released the prisoner in the hope that he might lead them to his contacts. But let's hope that you will never be in that situation.'

It was difficult for me to keep my eyes open, and I must have fallen asleep for a moment, to be awakened by the car hitting a bump on the road, and to hear Krugov's voice going on with the same litany: 'The Germans know that the future war will be a tank war. Tanks will be decisive. The Polish war showed it very,

very clearly, Anton Illich. They are afraid that one day the pupils will be stronger than the masters. Quite possible, too. That would serve them right for their stupidity in working with such monsters as the Soviets.'

I yawned, but the trip was coming to an end. We were passing the Monastery in Czestochowa, and then we were at the station.

Krugov deposited me in front of the building. 'You had better go alone into the station. Now listen to me, Anton Illich. Take good care!' Then in a whisper: 'There will be war between the Germans and the Soviets. It is in our interest to help the Germans. They are strong now. They can win and put an end to the Bolshevik killers. That's our only hope, Anton Illich. That's why your assignment is so crucial.'

I was glad to be on the train again. Now I could catch some sleep. When I arrived in Warsaw, I checked for the next train to Biala Podlaska. It did not leave until afternoon, so I would have time to buy the presents I had planned to take back to Pruzhany.

It was not an easy task, since all the stores were closed. However, I soon found a sign, 'Kraviec Meski, Tailor,' and I went into the shop. I bought a long, heavy, woollen overcoat for Nadya, and a small overcoat made of white wool with a little fur collar for Magda. For myself I bought an old sports jacket, a pair of used trousers, and a used but warm overcoat. I packed my purchases into a bundle. My remaining money I converted into German marks at the same tailor's. Later I bought an envelope and a stamp and mailed it to my mother without a note. It came to 105 marks.

On the train to Biala Podlaska were many refugees going east. A majority of them were Jews. At a small station before Biala Podlaska the train stopped for half an hour. Everyone wondered what would happen. Then came the Germans in uniform. There were many of them. '*Juden Manner raus*!' 'The Jewish men out' they shouted. Several men left the train and the Germans formed them into a column. Other soldiers were still checking inside of the train. A soldier looked at me. '*Jude*?'

I said, '*Nein*.'

For a second I felt happy not to be a Jew, not to have to suffer. Then immediately I blamed myself for being so inhuman as to think that way. Others were suffering, and I was happy that I would not have to suffer with them. I did not have much chance to think about it further. The same soldier was still facing me. *'Er wäre kein Jude,'* he said to his companion. At that moment a pair of hands grabbed me from behind. The soldier facing me then pulled at my waistband with all his strength. The buttons fell on the floor of the compartment. Then with his gloved hands he lowered my underpants. At that moment I wanted to shout. I saw a woman standing only a few metres from me. She was looking away and crying.

The soldier looked at my bare penis. *'Er ist kein Jude.'* He turned around and his companion loosened his grip. They walked away.

I dressed, fastening my pants with an English pin. I was disgusted. During the rest of the trip to Biala Podlaska, I could think of nothing but that incident.

Crossing from west to east was much easier than the other way around. The Germans did not care who left their territory. Anyway, I crossed the border with a large group. When we met the first Soviet soldiers, they assumed that we were fleeing and directed us back, meaning eastward, where we wanted to go anyway. At the first opportunity I took the train to Bialystok, and later on a train to Brest where I had to wait a few hours for a train in the direction of Pruzhany. In the station I met my friend the tailor again, and was happy to see him. He eyed my bundle of clothing and wanted to buy it, but I refused.

The rest of the trip I thought only of Nadya. Anticipating her reaction to the overcoat, I was impatient to see her.

Chapter 10

Moscow, December 5, 1939

It was only eight in the morning when the door opened to Vashin's office and Brodilo's broad figure appeared in it.

'*Guten morgen,* Kamerad Brodilo,' Vashin said.

'You are not up to date in your German, Oleg. That greeting has changed to "Heil Hitler" in the Third Reich.'

Looking exhausted, Brodilo sat down. The whiskers on his face contrasted with the baldness of his head. The strong smell of stale tobacco coming from his rumpled clothing filled the small office.

'I brought you those reports from Berlin.'

'I was waiting . . .'

'I've not had much time to study them.'

'I understand,' Vashin said. 'The Finnish front. The war will be over there in a couple of weeks.'

'Hard to say, Tovarich Vashin. It's only the third day. We are encountering heavy resistance.'

Brodilo lit a cigarette. 'Now, to change the subject, I repeat it is Tovarich Stalin's personal wish that you wipe out the spy ring in Eastern Poland. I came here to tell you that. Read the reports and inform me about the measures you propose to undertake. The sooner the better!'

Brodilo stood up and left the room.

Vashin knew that the reports had arrived with some of the members of the military and commercial delegations that had visited Berlin. He knew too that the translators had had to work all night to finish their job.

He opened the top folder. Each individual report was typed on a separate sheet of paper and placed in a grey folder containing information already on file in N.K.V.D. headquarters.

As requested, the names were of the members of the Freedom for Russia organisation who had moved from their domiciles since August 1, 1939, and who could not be located in the Reich. There were fifty-three folders on his desk. The reports from the secret agents varied considerably in precision and the amount of information given. Each of them contained the name, patronymic, address, and age of the subject. Some reports were quite detailed and included the description of the person, his family status, rank in the Tsarist army, and rank and activity during the Russian Civil War.

The report from Berlin was the most detailed. It included even the drinking and eating habits of the potential spies, their hobbies, speech mannerisms, knowledge of other languages and their degree of fluency in those languages.

The reports from Munich and Vienna were least informative. Sometimes they included no additional information beyond the basic facts of name, patronymic, etc. Fortunately, thought Vashin, the N.K.V.D. had files on 41 of the 53.

Vashin made a note on a separate piece of paper to draw up complaints about the work of the agents in Munich and Vienna.

After completing the general survey of the reports and files, he began to immerse himself in each folder, writing notes on a separate piece of paper. He used a pen which he had to dip often into the ink. Since the paper was of poor quality, it bled. He had to wait until the ink dried before starting a new sheet. He recorded the important facts about each person which would help him to locate the spies.

Vashin knew that of the fifty-three persons, forty-seven men and six women, a number would have moved for reasons other than spying in the Soviet Union. He also realised that there could be non-members working for the organisation. It was also possible that the organisation recruited agents from other countries, besides Germany.

But anyway, this was what he had to work with. He began to segregate the folders according to the degree of probability that the persons whose dossiers were before him were now working as spies. First he eliminated the folders of those the N.K.V.D. listed as dead. He also eliminated seven more whose files indicated chronic illnesses or senility. They probably had been moved to hospitals. Of the remaining forty-one, seventeen did not speak Polish. He knew it was not likely they would be used in the area, for their lack of knowledge of Polish would betray them.

There remained twenty-two men and two women.

There was a knock at his door. It was a messenger, a young man with a shaved head who told him that Tovarich Brodilo was ready to see him.

He picked up the folders and his sheets and strode along the narrow corridor to the office of his superior. It was already one o'clock in the morning, yet the lights in most offices were still on.

Brodilo looked even more tired than he had that morning. His face was covered by three days' growth of whiskers. The circles under his eyes had deepened.

As soon as Vashin entered the office, filled with the blue smoke of Kertch cigarettes, and sat down in front of his boss's desk, Brodilo said, 'Our men have identified one of the men in the "Operation Parterre." They are holding him in Pinsk.'

'Why did they not let him remain free?'

Brodilo picked up an ashtray full of cigarette stubs and emptied it into a waste basket.

'They picked him up as a Pole, in the current process of "resettling" the undesirable Polish elements. One of our men was familiar with his dossier and recognised him as a former lieutenant of the Tsarist infantry, Alexey Nikolayevich Lepin.'

'Did he confess?' Vashin asked.

'He did not deny it. He is a reluctant talker.'

'Maybe I can help there,' Vashin said, smiling.

'What did you conclude from reading the reports?' Brodilo asked. Vashin, referring to his note, told him his findings.

'You will have more trouble identifying the younger members, Olenin, Gorski and Nizov. Also the women,' Brodilo said. 'You should take the train to Pinsk and try to get something out of Lepin.' Brodilo stood up. 'You can start your hunt for the others. You may use all our resources, thousands of men to hunt down all of these Parterre people. I will get in touch with Vienna and try to obtain more information on the younger fellows, Nizov and Gorski. I will recheck the deaths and try to trace the sick ones. I will also try to locate the non-Polish speaking members. But you must catch them soon, Tovarich Vashin.'

Seated in the train, Vashin was still thinking about the last words: 'Catch them soon.' The train was leaving Moscow and the lights grew dimmer and dimmer.

As soon as he had arrived in Pinsk, he began to interrogate Lepin, who answered all questions, 'I don't know.' Lepin, fifty-one years old, a tall, slim man, a former cavalry lieutenant in the Tsarist army, had shown his disdain for Vashin from the start of the interrogation. He knew that he would be executed in any case.

A week later Vashin decided to give up.

It was twenty after midnight and Vashin had talked to Lepin for several hours. Both were hungry and exhausted.

'You still do not know who your contact is?' Vashin asked.

Lepin nodded, his grey hair unkempt, his face covered by whiskers.

'You refuse to answer all my questions,' Vashin continued.

'You will be executed tonight.' Lepin did not react.

It was cold in the small office in the prison building. One bulb glared, hurting their eyes. Vashin sat in his overcoat and cap; the prisoner shivered in his torn jacket. Vashin knew that Lepin was a bachelor and had lived in Berlin before this assignment. Had Lepin been married or had he any family Vashin could have promised not to kill them if the prisoner cooperated. But in this case there was no lever; nothing that Vashin could say or do would matter.

Vashin stood up and opened the door.

'Vozov, come here!'

The boots echoed outside. The sentry, armed with a rifle, entered. Vashin motioned with his hand towards the prisoner.

'It is raining,' Vozov grumbled.

'Who else is on duty?' Vashin asked.

'Galkin.'

'Good, the two of you,' Vashin said.

The prisoner stood up. Vashin walked first, followed by Lepin, then the sentry. At the door they were joined by the sentry Galkin. They entered a small court. It was pouring. The floodlight was focused on the wall across the court from the door.

'Take off your shoes!' Vashin shouted to the prisoner. 'And your rags!'

Lepin took off his jacket and his shirt and threw off his shoes. In the light Vashin noticed a scar on Lepin's left arm.

'Where did you get it?' he asked the prisoner.

'Battle of Tannenberg,' Lepin answered. Vashin knew that name well. His own father had died in that battle of September, 1914.

Vozov and Galkin raised their rifles. Vashin wanted to ask the prisoner some questions about the war of 1914. He wanted to ask what battalion he had fought in or whether he had known Vashin's father.

'To the wall!' Vozov shouted at the prisoner.

Lepin walked slowly, his socks sinking into the mud up to his ankles. Two shots rang. Lepin, hit from behind, fell to the ground. Galkin went over to the fallen figure and fired again. Blood mixed with water covered the body.

'Take it inside,' Vashin said.

'It can wait until morning,' Vozov said, holding up the shoes and inspecting them in the light.

Vashin turned up the collar of his overcoat and walked towards the body lying face down. With the help of Galkin he turned it around. The three holes where the bullets had left the body were visible. The open eyes stared at Vashin. With his fingers Vashin pressed on the eyes. That was the regulation. There was no reaction. The man was dead.

Vashin walked back through the doors to his office. He carefully poured water into a wash basin, took a piece of soap out of a drawer in his desk, and began to wash his hands. After he had finished he picked up from his desk a list of people the dead prisoner had known. They included the Polish landlady from whom Lepin rented his room, her twenty-year-old daughter and her husband; the local Jewish baker, a widower living alone, from whom the prisoner used to buy his bread; Dr Garfinkel, his wife and fifteen-year-old son. Vashin knew that the prisoner had consulted the doctor for a severe cold. They were the only people Vashin had been able to unearth with whom the prisoner had had any contact. The only result of his investigations.

As a matter of procedure Vashin had requested a list of people who entered and left Pinsk, and the local N.K.V.D. was compiling it. The list already had hundreds of names. Vashin knew that he had to wait until some pattern emerged. For one thing it was reasonable to expect that someone was bound to appear to collect information supplied by a spy.

The people on the list of seven who had had contact with the spy must be arrested tonight. Vashin called Vozov.

'You will come with me!' Vashin told him.

'The truck will get mired in the damn mud,' Vozov said.

'Tell the driver to go to Dr Garfinkel's house. I will wait in front of it. He knows where it is.'

Not looking at Vozov, Vashin left the room, his overcoat collar still turned up. He walked through the court. The half-naked body of the prisoner was still lying there. The rain had washed away the blood. The floodlight made the old scar visible. Vashin turned his head.

The streets of Pinsk were muddy. The pavements were covered with wooden planks, partly rotted. Between the planks the mud was ankle deep.

When Vashin arrived at the Doctor's house, he waited. It was quiet. There was no light inside. Only when he heard the sound of the truck's motor did he knock at the door. After a moment he saw a light in one of the rooms. The doctor must be used to being awakened at night. Vashin knocked again, but it was not necessary, someone was opening the door.

Chapter 11

Anton's Story

Pruzhany, December 9, 1939
I was tapping hard with my fingers against the window of the car as the train was pulling into the Pruzhany station. I felt nervous about seeing Nadya and wondered whether she would be in school or at home. It was already dark. Most of the other passengers were met by relatives who were waiting for them in the station. I did not expect to be met by anyone, so I rushed through the crowd to the exit. When I turned the corner of the first block beyond the station, I saw Nadya. She was standing there in her short coat, shivering.

'Thank God you are back, Anton Illich.'

'Oh, Nadienka, you're here! How did you know I would be coming? I mean today?'

'I've been worrying ever since you left. You never told me about your uncle. I was afraid you would never come back.'

It was freezing. We began to walk in the direction of Avram's house.

'I came here every evening hoping to see you. I was lucky today.'

We slowed our pace. 'But you knew all the time that I would come back.'

'You left in such a hurry. I was worried. It would be only natural for you to return home and stay away from all these Russians.'

'You think that I dislike Russians. Then you must hate Poles.'

'You know how I feel about you, Anton.'

'But Nadienka ...' I could not finish the sentence. The tears gathered in my eyes. I knew if I continued to talk, my voice would break.

We were passing a dark street. I took off my glove and took Nadya's hand. We walked for a while in silence.

Avram was happy to see us. He mentioned that Boris and Gleb had come by twice; they wanted to see me. Then Nadya and I walked into my room. An ikon of St Anton, my patron saint, was hanging in the corner of the room.

'You see, in your absence I was here a few times to inquire from Avram. I saw your room. It was so empty.'

We were still standing in the middle of the room in our overcoats. I took her in my arms and started to cry. Nadya kissed me many times on my cheeks. 'It is so good to have you back.'

Then I unpacked my bundle. When I gave her the overcoat, for some time she could not believe that it was for her.

In her new overcoat, caressing the fabric, she approached the window in which she could see herself. She tried the pockets, raised and lowered the collar, buttoned and unbuttoned her coat. Nadya behaved like a happy child who had hoped for but never expected a new toy for Christmas, and then found it under the Christmas tree.

I was ready to take her home, but she took off her coat, hung it carefully on a hook, and sat down on my bed.

'It is so cosy in your room, Anton. Without you the room looked so empty.'

She moved her legs rhythmically; her knees were partly uncovered. For a moment I thought how nice it would be to touch them, to move the palms of my hands over the silk of her stockings, but immediately I became ashamed of myself, blushed, and poured myself a glass of water that I gulped down.

'You seem to be tired, Anton. Sit down next to me.'

'Oh no, not at all, Nadya. Your mother will worry. We must go.'

We left together in a very happy mood. Nadya, in her new overcoat, repeated how warm it felt. I carried her light, short coat over my arm.

Nadya took my hand and said, 'When you were away I realised

how much you mean to me. I never dreamed that this could happen to me, and besides that I would find myself in love with a Pole.'

'It's the same for me too.'

'And of course I understand that you could never marry me, Anton.'

'Why not?'

'Our nationalities. Your mother would not approve,' Nadya said.

Fortunately we had reached Nadya's house.

'We can talk about it some other time.'

'But we still could –'

Carl opened the door.

Olga and Carl were very pleased to see me again. They were also surprised to see Nadya's new overcoat.

'We just cannot accept that, Anton Kazimirovich,' Olga said. 'It is so generous. But on the other hand Nadya needs it so badly.' With that the matter was settled. Olga prepared a good dinner for us, emptying her pantry. We also had vodka and tea. I felt happy and at home.

After dinner Carl read from Chekhov, as usual. This time, it was the short story called *The Bath,* his funniest story, about the conversation of merchants discussing the sad state of eligible bachelors for their daughters. At one point I saw Nadya glance at me. When I caught her eye, she blushed.

But I was not listening to the story, which I had read many times. I began to think that I would find a way of staying here forever. Maybe I could find work, marry Nadya. I began to think about how nice it was here. The Soviets are Russians. They speak my native tongue. I could feel at home here.

That night Nadya and I took a long walk. We spoke about the Russian soldiers.

'They really behave nicely here,' Nadya said. 'There was not a single robbery. They are helpful to women, carrying water or anything heavy. Anyone who needs to move a piece of furniture can ask any soldier on the street to help. They will do it.'

'You must feel all right then?' I asked.

'The soldiers are good people,' she answered. 'Any time someone needs a smoke, he can approach a soldier and ask for a cigarette. They'll take out their tobacco. They'll provide the necessary piece of paper. That will be a piece of *Pravda* which they don't read, just smoke.'

When, after our long walk, we were standing in front of Nadya's house again it was painful for me to say goodbye. I just could not part from her. When I was on my way home, I began to realise that it would be harder and harder as time passed.

I walked along, thinking how I might manage to establish myself here and give up my mission. I began to feel guilty thinking about it. Krugov put so much faith in me. I was using the expense money he had furnished, and which I would not earn. Maybe there would be a way for me to return it somehow.

Anyway I decided to explore the possibility of staying here permanently. The first step would be a conversation with Magda's mother. The next morning, when I called on her, she was alone. I was surprised.

'Where is Magda?' I asked. 'I brought her this.' I handed the small overcoat to Wanda.

'Oh, that's . . . How very . . . Too bad, Magda is asleep. She will enjoy it so much. She will thank you tomorrow.'

'Is anything wrong?'

'We did not sleep much last night. They came to arrest my father.'

'What? Why?'

'He was a member of the Polish Administration.'

'But, my God! He has done no harm to anyone. Licensing bicycles, filing. He himself joked about being a kind of porter.'

'He still represented the Polish Government.'

'But Pani Wanda, how . . . you even seem to approve.'

'I love my father. We are very close but – I do understand the authorities. The old system must be destroyed, uprooted, before the new proletarian . . .'

'But he is your father. He tried to make a living in order to feed you both.'

'Anton, I know, I know it is hard for you to understand.'

She began to wash the dishes. She must have been doing it before my arrival. Her hair was unkempt. She had black rings under her eyes. I wondered whether I should bring up the subject I had come to discuss with her.

'I want to understand the . . . system. I want to live here. I don't mean in Pruzhany, but in the Soviet Union.'

Wanda nodded. 'You could find a place here,' she said. 'Work in the factory, work hard, and contribute to production.'

'But I would want to study and become a teacher.'

She smiled. The empty walls appeared grey and depressing.

'Our proletarian society would have no use for a teacher with your bourgeois background. You could not even be admitted to a university. You are lucky to be in the Gymnasium, because in future people like you will not be admitted there. There are quotas - one percent for children whose parents are not proletarians. Besides, you are a Pole.'

The idea of going to work in a factory, forever living in one room with Nadya, where she would find it hard to breathe, was too painful to accept.

'But, perhaps if I joined the Communist Party I would be allowed to study.'

Wanda laughed. 'I can see that you don't understand,' she said. 'The Communist Party is for the best of the proletarian class, for people who have worked for the cause of the proletarian revolution. It is like a religion. It calls for sacrifice.'

'I would work for the -'

'You would question everything.'

The whole conversation was becoming theoretical. I knew very well that I could not work for the revolution, as Wanda expressed it, nor would I be able to stop questioning everything, but still I said, 'I could stop questioning everything.'

'What you are saying sounds naive. You would be unacceptable because you would have the potential for differing. No, no, the Communist Party is not for you. But you could certainly work here. Possibly you could become a good proletarian after ten years or so. You must do it anyway, because we shall carry the revolution everywhere.'

I began to regret coming here. Surely, I thought, she must be wrong. As an activist she had the wrong ideas. I still could find a place here.

Maybe I could join the army, become a soldier first, then a commander later. Maybe I could still join the Communist Party. I should ask a Soviet citizen about it.

Wanda, finishing her dishes, began a tirade against the bourgeois system, but I lost interest in her talk. Besides I could not understand most of what she said. 'Means of production in the hands of the working classes ... the end of capitalist exploitation.' She spoke as if she were reading slogans from the walls of the Pruzhany city hall.

I got tired. Magda was apparently still asleep. I thanked Wanda for her advice, and I left with a bad taste in my mouth.

It was raining outside. I had to walk carefully in order not to step into the mud, which in some places was knee-deep. To avoid that I had to jump from one stone to another - the stones had been put there, apparently, by people living nearby. The autumn rains had turned Pruzhany into a sea of soft, black mud and the surrounding swamps into a huge black puddle.

The cobblestones, which were supposed to make the roads usable for motor vehicles, had been scattered by the Soviet tracked cars, trucks and tanks.

My conversation with Magda's mother had been a great disappointment. But after a few days I began to explain it to myself. Wanda had never lived in the Soviet Union, and she might not be as well informed as some Soviet people. Besides, I thought, life is always changing, and Wanda's information might be out of date. I decided to consult someone who ought to know, the new teacher in the school who had arrived from the Soviet Union to give a course in the history of the Communist Party. His name was Leonid Ivanovich Zevin. He was a small man with a narrow face and narrow, somewhat slanting dark eyes.

He always wore the same black, crumpled suit. When lecturing he followed one book, which he recited by heart. He disliked any questions, and when they were asked he referred to the book for answers. When the class ended he seemed to try hard to conceal his relief.

I decided to catch Leonid Ivanovich after school and discuss with him how I might live in the Soviet Union.

One evening I waited for him until I saw him leaving the building.

'Pardon me, Leonid Ivanovich,' I said approaching him from behind. It was a cool, clear day. 'May I talk to you for a minute?'

He seemed to shrink even more into his cheap-looking overcoat, which was worn out at the sleeves.

'Can it not wait until tomorrow?' he stammered. 'Questions should be asked in class.' He looked frightened.

'It is a private matter,' I said. Leonid Ivanovich speeded up his pace as if he wanted to run away from me.

'I cannot discuss any private matters. I am just –'

'It is information that I want,' I said.

He stopped. His face turned the colour of ashes.

'I don't have any in ... info ... information.' To confirm his statement he waved his small fists. I noticed that they shook.

I was ready to abandon the whole project. What I really expected was that we would sit down somewhere and talk about my opportunities for living in Soviet Russia. I knew now that it would not be possible. So I decided to ask him a question he ought to be pleased to discuss. In Nazi Germany millions were encouraged to join the Nazi Party, including Germans in Czechoslovakia and Poland. They immediately received citizenship and rights equal to those of the Germans in the Reich.

'I just wanted to ask you, Leonid Ivanovich, how I could become a member of the Communist Party.'

If the colour of his face had resembled ashes, after my last question it was the colour of white ashes.

'But why?' His body shook. 'Oh, yes, yes, I understand. I am not the pro ... proper authority to discuss the matter.'

'But, surely you are a member of the Party,' I said.

'Not me. I am not.' He turned around and ran as fast as his short legs, and his long overcoat, touching the mud, would allow.

That evening Nadya and I were planning to go to a school dance. Wanting to reciprocate, we invited Boris and Gleb to join us for the party. When I arrived, Boris was alone, reading aloud.

'It is the poet Marshak's poem about an American millionaire,' Boris said. 'Do you want to listen?'

'I came to invite you,' I said. 'Tonight we are having a party.'

'Of course I'll come.' Boris got up. 'Too bad you don't seem to be in the mood for this poem. The American comes to Leningrad with his wife, his daughter, and a monkey. He refuses to stay in a hotel because there are coloured people there and –'

I said, 'We must pick up Nadya in about an hour.'

'Then we have time,' Boris said, opening the book.

I hesitated. Boris was searching for the right page in his book.

'I would like to have a private talk with you,' I said.

Boris put the book away.

'Are you sure?'

'Yes, you are my friend, I feel. I would like to marry Nadya.'

'That is no secret,' Boris smiled. 'That hardly requires a private talk.'

'But you see, Boris, I am really a Russian.'

'That's not a secret either. I guessed it the first time we met.'

'I am telling you that because I want to ask your advice. I would like to live with Nadya in the Soviet Union, in Russia.'

Boris walked over to the window. His room, like all the rooms in Pruzhany, was on the ground floor. I could see the white branches of the birch trees through the window. He turned around. His face wore an expression of gloom.

'Do I have a chance?' I asked.

He sat down, and took his face in his hands. 'No, my friend, none.'

We remained silent. His wrist watch was lying on the table. I could hear it ticking. The wind moved the white branches of the birch trees. Boris looked up.

'You and Nadya must leave as soon as possible. There are people still crossing the borders to the west. I know that in the present state of confusion it can still be done. In a few weeks it will be very dangerous, in a few months impossible.'

The watch was still ticking.

'You know foreign languages. You will be able to live there,' Boris said. 'I am locked in. I would escape myself, but I have my family in Russia. They would persecute everyone, even my nephews and nieces. They would deport them. They would be barred forever from all the opportunities of decent work, even if they survived the deportations.'

Boris stood up and began pacing the floor.

'We are treated here as pieces of machinery. Any time we can be discarded and replaced by others. Somebody in my father's office might tell an innocent joke that could be interpreted as being against the regime. My father, who could be just sitting there, might be arrested and imprisoned for the rest of his life. My own career would be over. I would be considered the son of a political prisoner.'

Boris was telling me nothing that I had not known before. But somehow, hearing my native tongue, seeing the Russian faces around me, I had been ready to forget the reality. I had been under an illusion. Boris dispelled it, but it did hurt.

'You could never work anywhere except in a factory ... in menial jobs ... provided that you would not be deported to Siberia.'

'I could become a citizen.'

'You would be a second-class citizen. You could not serve in the army.'

Boris started to put his boots on. 'You must forget this conversation,' he said.

'I will, but I am sorry, so sorry,' I said.

'Maybe one day everything will change.' Boris went on. 'We will have a war against Germany. Who knows what will happen? They might win, liberate us from our regime. In the meantime Gleb and I will be leaving, for the Finnish front.'

We left his room both feeling depressed. Even Nadya's chatter could not lift up our spirits. At the first opportunity, Boris and I left the party, went to the lavatory, and shared his bottle of vodka. I danced with Nadya, but still could not recover my cheerfulness. After my second visit with Boris to the lavatory, I ran into Masha.

'I have not seen you for a while,' she said, smiling. 'Where have you been hiding?' We began to dance.

'You mean now? In a very special place.'

'Oh, yes. I can smell your breath. And before that?'

'In far away lands.'

'Tell me about them.'

'There are kings there. Milk and honey flows there.'

'And in our country too one can live well,' Masha said. 'I wish you could visit my home one day.'

'Live well?' I asked.

'We live well,' Masha said.

Turning around I saw Nadya looking at us. After the dance ended, I said good night to Masha and returned to Nadya.

'You seem to be having a wonderful time,' she said.

'Yes. And you?'

'I would rather go away.'

'Then let's go,' I said.

I had turned in the direction of Nadya's house when Nadya said, 'Could we go to your place first, Anton?'

'But, Nadienka, it is so late. Olga Carlovna will ...'

'Maman is asleep.'

Holding my hand, Nadya was leading me in the direction of Avram's house, my home.

'But what will Avram say if he wakes up and sees you coming up to my room so late at night?'

Nadya kissed me on my cheek.

I went on, 'He would imagine the worst possible thing.'

'Then we should live up to his imagination of the "worst possible thing" Anton.'

I stopped. My heart sank down to my knees. I felt weak.

'You cannot possibly ...'

'Sh ... There is no need to wake up the whole town.'

I was shaking. We walked up on tiptoe the few steps from the door of Avram's house to my room. We entered it, but I did not turn on the light. The contours of my bed, table and chair were all outlined by the moonlight. Nadya took off her overcoat and put it on one of the chairs. She had never looked as beautiful as in this light. Her delicate features acquired a new dimension of beauty. I could understand what Goethe had in mind about the 'eternal feminine'.

I took her in my arms and we kissed.

'We had better leave now,' I said.

But Nadya kissed me again.

'Shouldn't we sit down?' Nadya said, sitting down on my bed and taking off her shoes.

I sat down next to her. I still had my overcoat on. I took her hand.

'They will gossip. Pruzhany is such a small town. Everyone will know.'

'They will gossip anyway,' Nadya said, leaning back on the pillow.

My heart was pounding. We kissed.

'Anton, will you please take off your overcoat? The buttons are hurting me.'

'I am sorry,' I said. And I took off my overcoat and my jacket. We kissed again.

'You look so beautiful,' I said.

'You may unbutton my blouse,' Nadya said.

I jumped up from the bed. My head was spinning. I had to lean on the table so as not to fall.

'I love you,' I said. 'You, Nadya, are the only woman I would want to marry, but I cannot. I have no right . . . If only I could marry you.'

'I know,' Nadya said. 'But it's sometimes done when people are not married.'

'But you are a girl from such a good family,' I said, pacing the floor. 'It is out of the question.'

I stumbled over a chair and hurt my shin.

'I may never be able to marry you,' I said, rubbing the sore place.

'I am not asking you to marry me. You don't need to make any promises.'

'I wish I could.'

'I tried to borrow a book about it,' Nadya said. 'I couldn't find one.'

'So you thought about it before?'

'Yes, I thought about it.'

'Why didn't you tell me about it?'

'I simply did not know how, Anton.'

'Then why did you select this night?' I could see her smile in the moonlight.

'You don't want me because I am Russian.'

'That's not true . . . absolutely wrong.'

'Why not, then?'

'I like Russians. I speak Russian.'

'But you are Polish.'

'I swear to you, my God, your being Russian has nothing to do with it. I respect you.'

'Come here,' Nadya said. I sat down on the edge of the bed. 'Give me your hand!'

My hand shook. We kissed holding hands. Her body had a faint aroma of roses. I tried to unbutton her blouse, but my fingers could not do it. They shook too much. Nadya helped me.

'It may hurt you,' I said.

'I won't think about being hurt, Anton.' I looked at her eyes, the colour of the sky at noon, reflecting the moonlight. We kissed. Nadya closed her eyes.

Later on I was lying on the beach by the Black Sea; the sun was shining and the wind brought the aroma of roses from the neighbouring gardens. But I woke up soon, realising that I was in Pruzhany and in my bed with Nadya. I was frightened.

'We must go now,' I said.

'Will you please hold me tight, Anton. Just for a moment.'

I still felt her body burning, her cheeks hot. We got up, collected our scattered clothing. We dressed in the moonlight. We walked to her house holding hands.

'So now I am your mistress,' Nadya said.

'We don't have to talk about it.'

'Why not? I love you. I am happy to be your mistress.'

'You must regret it,' I said.

'Why should I? Of course not.'

We walked in silence. The bare trees threw long shadows in the moonlight.

'Does a mistress have some rights?' Nadya asked.

'I don't know what you mean, darling.'

'May she expect that her lover will be faithful to her?'

'Nadienka. That's nonsense.'

'I am jealous, Anton, Masha is so good looking, and so healthy.'

'You know I love you ... That's why, tonight.'

'But jealousy is a normal feeling when one loves, Anton. Isn't it?'

'Oh, darling, my Nadienka, I feel so close to you.'

After she entered her house, I wandered around the streets, got lost and managed to get back home at dawn. My bed still had the warmth of her body and the scent of roses.

As soon as I had covered myself with a blanket, there was a knock at my door. It was Avram.

'I just heard that they'll be selling something. The waiting line is forming in front of the warehouse.' I dressed, and in a few minutes I was rushing to the warehouse with Avram. There were other people hurrying in the same direction. A long queue was forming. People were discussing what would be sold. No one knew for sure. Somebody mentioned vodka. An old woman in a babushka said, 'Shoes.' I was shivering. The doors opened two hours later. One person at a time was admitted.

When the first purchasers came out we learned that they were selling Crimean apples, two kilos per person, and two packages of Mahorka tobacco. When my turn came, I was handed twelve apples and two packages of Mahorka by a buxom girl. I paid two roubles.

I had not brought any paper, so I had to take off my overcoat to carry the apples in. I was pleased with my purchase. I would be able to exchange the tobacco for food.

On my way back I stopped at Nadya's house. She was up, I handed her the apples.

'This is what I should have done last night. Given you an apple as a symbol,' Nadya said. She looked fresh. She blushed a little.

'I am offering you this like Paris. You are my choice,' I said.

'In that case I will eat it, with delight.' Nadya said, smiling. 'Come inside. Your apple tastes so good.'

PART III

The Winter

Chapter 12

Anton's Story

Pruzhany, December 24, 1939

I woke up with such a feeling of love that I decided to stay in bed a little longer. Nadya had spent the preceding evening with me. The scent of roses was still around me. We both had fallen asleep last night. I awakened at four in the morning, and I woke Nadya. We had to dress in a hurry, and now in the light of this Christmas Eve morning I saw her scarf on the floor.

Through the windows I could see heavy snow flakes falling. December 24 was the Christmas Eve of the Catholic Christmas. Some of the Russians celebrated their Christmas on that date also, but not Nadya and her family. They followed the Julian Calendar strictly and observed Christmas on January 7. I was used to the two Christmases all my life, and today felt like celebrating more than ever.

I decided that the best way for me to honour that day would be to visit Magda. Since her mother was an atheist, Magda would not celebrate anything, so I decided to share my feeling of joy with her.

I went out into the morning. The streets were covered with snow and the town of Pruzhany looked to me to be the most beautiful place in the world. Most of the morning I spent trying to find a present for Magda, but to my regret I did not succeed.

In the afternoon I went to school, walked Nadya home, and spent a few hours drinking tea in her home. It was late when I began walking to Magda's home.

When I arrived in front of Magda's house, at nine o'clock in the evening, I was surprised to see the windows dark. The doors were locked. I knocked a few times and waited, but there was no one inside to open them.

A grey-haired woman came out of the door of the neighbour's

house. 'Pani Kuper is not here,' she said. 'What do you want?'

'I am a friend,' I said. She must have been hard of hearing. She did not react to my statement, but came towards me supporting herself on a cane.

'Who are you?' she asked.

'I am a friend of the family,' I shouted.

The woman looked at me. A gust of moist wind was hitting the windows of the Kuper house.

'Pani Kuper was taken away last night.'

'Arrested?' I asked.

The woman nodded.

'It must be a mistake,' I said.

She shrugged her shoulders.

'And Magda, the little girl?'

'They left her behind. The women from the Jewish orphanage picked her up this morning.'

In front of the house I saw the little carriage Magda used to play with. There must be some misunderstanding, I thought. The Soviets must have made a mistake. Pani Kuper was a communist, and the matter would be cleared up in a few hours.

'Do you know where they took her?'

She shrugged her shoulders again.

'Pani Kuper did not come back?' I asked.

'No,' the woman said.

I thanked her for her information and rushed to the Jewish orphanage. On the way I was anticipating how I would tell Magda that her mother would come back very soon. I knew the house, I had seen it on the main street many times. I could hardly miss it since it was the noisiest place in Pruzhany.

It had a large sign in Hebrew and in Polish. Recently a Russian sign had replaced the one in Polish. As I approached the orphanage I saw a number of children still milling around outdoors. I entered through a porch. The air was bad; it smelled of onion and garlic. But it was warm inside; and noisy. Some children were crying. Others were eating, talking, shouting and screaming. A middle-aged woman in a black satin dress was serving soup.

'I came to see Magda Kuper, the little ...'

'I know,' she said pouring the soup into aluminium plates. 'Are you a relative?'

'No, just a good friend,' I said. 'How is she?'

'What do you expect?'

'May I see her?'

'Why not?' she said.

I followed her through a narrow passage. The doors of the rooms on both sides were open. There were children everywhere. Two or three slept in one bed; some slept on mattresses placed on the floor. In one of the rooms I recognised Magda. She was lying on a bare mattress and she was crying.

'Magda, it's me,' I said.

She jumped up, raised her hands, waiting to be picked up. As I carried her out of the room, she put her arms around my neck, holding me with all her strength. I felt her little body shaking.

'Take me away, away from here. Take me away. Please.'

I carried her to the porch, found an empty spot on a bench, and sat down. I wanted to place Magda on my knee, but she would not loosen her grip.

'Your Mama will be back, very soon.'

'Take me away, please.'

'You see Magda, I would take you, but I live alone. Your Mama will be looking for you here. You will be playing with other children here. The lady here is nice. They have hot food.'

Magda strengthened her hold on me.

'We could play here for a while. Or should I tell you a nice story – maybe about Puss-in-Boots?'

But Magda would not play with me. She did not appear to listen to the tale of 'Puss-in-Boots'. She would not release her tight grip around my neck.

The lady in the black dress passed.

'I will come here tomorrow to visit,' I said. 'I hope it will be all right.'

'Why not?'

At that moment, Magda began to cry.

'Don't go! Don't ... don't!'

I tried to free myself, but I couldn't. The lady came to my help.

'Come, darling, the nice gentleman will come tomorrow.'

Magda, like a wild animal, began to fight, and she scratched the lady. She even tried to bite her.

'I will come. I'll stay with you. Your mama will come too.'

But Magda continued to cry. Tears rolled down her cheeks.

She shouted, 'Take me away! Take me away!'

I heard her screams when I was on the street, and even when I had reached the corner of the block. I was shaken by the visit. I went back to Magda's house, but there was no sign of life there. Her mother had not returned. Not yet.

I went home, still hearing Magda's voice: 'Take me away! Take me away!'

I went to bed, but I could not sleep. I covered myself with the blanket and pulled it over my head. But Magda's cries sounded even louder in my ears.

Poor child, she had lost her father just a few months ago, and now her mother was arrested. That was a shock for her, but I could not help her. Her mother would be back. Magda could stay a day or so with me, I thought, until her mother returned. I would do it tomorrow, I promised myself. But her screams in my ears became unbearable. I got up, dressed, and went back to the orphanage. The lights were still on, and as I entered, some of the children were still up. I saw the lady trying to put the last ones to bed. Some other adults were busy helping her.

'Is Magda asleep?' I asked.

'Why should she be, after such a tragedy?'

'Is she still crying?'

'Wouldn't you in her place?'

'Could I take her? I want to help. Just until her mother –'

'So ... why not?'

She took me to Magda who was lying on her mattress, just as she had been. Again she stopped crying, grasped my hand, and did not want to loosen her grip.

'I am taking you to my place,' I said.

'Thank you, thank you.'

I was moved, and tears came to my eyes.

'She has not eaten anything,' the lady said, 'Do you have anything to feed her.'

I nodded. She handed me a little valise with Magda's belongings. Magda and I walked through the deserted streets.

As soon as we arrived, I fed her some bread with Olga Carlovna's preserves, and warmed some tea for her and for myself. Eventually I found a flannel nightgown in the valise, dressed Magda in it, and put her to bed.

As soon as I turned off the light, I heard Magda jump up and climb into my bed. She pushed herself under my blanket and took my hand.

'I want to sleep here.'

In a few minutes I heard the regular breathing of a sleeping child.

Next morning, I awoke early. When Magda woke up, she wanted to be held in my arms for a while. Later on at breakfast she said, 'I'll cook for you.'

'You know how to cook?'

'Yes, I'll cook, and clean, and work, and I'll be a good girl . . . and –'

I just did not have the heart to bring up the subject of the orphanage.

'What will you cook?'

'Oh, kasha, borscht, and meat, and everything.'

After we finished breakfast, she ran to my wash basin, poured the water and started to wash the dishes.

I had already decided to take her back to the orphanage when one of the glasses she was carrying fell and broke into small pieces. I saw Magda become frightened and start to cry.

'Don't send me away, please! I didn't mean to break it.'

I did not have the heart to take her back to the orphanage then.

I went out alone, telling Avram about my visitor and asking him to watch her. I went to Magda's house once more and I knocked at the door but there was no response. I attached a note to the door advising Pani Kuper that she could find Magda at my house and I returned home. Magda was sweeping the floor.

'You need me,' she said, pushing back one of her pigtails. 'You have lots of dirt. I'll clean everything up.' Her black eyes were shining with the pleasure of accomplishment.

Later we ate again. She was enjoying the role of my helper. She beamed with delight after I had praised her efforts. I wanted to take her for a walk, but she would not hear of it. She lay down on the floor and held onto the leg of my bed with both hands. Eventually I had to abandon the project.

Nadya came in the evening, bringing along a pot of kidney and pickle soup that we shared. During the meal Magda watched Nadya with anguish.

'Do you like staying here?' Nadya asked, looking at Magda.

'Yes, I like it. I can cook, and clean, and wash.'

'And if I wanted to cook, clean and wash, would you let me?' Nadya asked smiling.

Magda hesitated. I could see how she searched in her mind for what she considered the right answer.

'There is enough dirt here for both of us,' Magda said. 'We can both clean and wash . . .'

Nadya and I burst out laughing. Nadya took Magda in her arms and kissed her.

In the next few weeks I got used to the idea of Magda's presence in my room. I even began to think how much I would miss her when her mother returned. On most evenings, Nadya came to eat with us, or we ate at the Gromovs' house. Magda liked to go shopping with us, and sometimes when the weather allowed it, the three of us took long walks.

In the afternoons I had to leave Magda alone in my room, but she never cried any more. She always waited for my return sitting by the door.

One evening Nadya was sitting with me after we had put Magda to bed. When the child was sound asleep, Nadya said, 'I am afraid that Magda's mother won't come back – at least not for a long time.'

'I am beginning to think so, too,' I said.

'Rumours are circulating in town that Pani Kuper was deported to a labour camp in Siberia.'

'What should I do?' I asked. I felt Nadya's warmth.

'We – you must keep her.'

The light in the kerosene lamp was flickering. I stood up and blew it out.

Nadya lay down on the bed and I came to lie next to her.

'I want to marry you one day,' I said. 'I love you, if only I could do that now.'

'I want to be your wife,' Nadya whispered. 'I think I could be a mother to Magda. I love her too. I was attracted to you the first time I met you. Then I loved you, but now, since you have taken Magda, I also admire you. I could not love anyone else.'

It was quiet in the room. Through the window I could see large flakes of snow falling.

'An adopted child would be a burden for a young woman of twenty-two,' I said.

'I've thought about it a lot,' Nadya whispered. 'At first I was even jealous of Magda. I didn't want to share your feelings, your love with her. Then I felt guilty for everything that had happened to her. There were the Russians who arrested her grandfather. Soldiers or policemen speaking Russian came to take her mother away. Whenever these arrests take place, I suffer as if I were responsible.'

'But those were communists, Red Russians,' I said.

'They are still Russians. After thinking about it a lot I know now that I would want to be your wife and keep Magda with us. It would make our lives richer, more worthwhile. We would be a family right away. In these times we don't know how much time we have to live, to be happy.'

'But that is just the point, Nadya,' I whispered. 'I cannot possibly. I have a dreadful secret. I am forbidden to reveal it.'

'You can confide in me,' Nadya said. 'No matter what your secret, I would still love you, Anton.'

'I am a spy,' I said, expecting that Nadya would faint.

'A spy?' In the flickering light of the kerosene lamp I could see her smile. There was something enigmatic about the expression on her face. 'Don't look guilty about it, Anton. There are lots of spies around. How do you know I am not one myself?'

I dismissed her remark with a wave of my hand. 'Nadya, darling, don't talk such nonsense!'

'Oh, Anton,' Nadya said, with the same cryptic smile hovering about her lips. 'I understand. The Poles are patriots. I respect you. I feel it is your duty. Although I don't believe in some of these Polish things, I will stand by and help you.'

'I would not want you risking your life,' I said.

'I am not afraid to risk my life.' The smile disappeared from her face. 'Do you know what it was like living here? My life filled with the daily talk of my parents, my grandfather and their friends about the splendid and glamorous life of the past compared to the grim reality of our existence in Pruzhany. Being a spy is - would be exciting.'

'You are still talking nonsense. You should stay away, Nadya.'

'As a spy I could use some of my talents. I could draw planes, tanks, guns. I have the eye of a painter. Or I could reveal some of my hidden talents and obtain secret information from a general or a commissar. I could flirt like Greta Garbo in the *Mata Hari* movie.'

'Spying is a dangerous business. The risks are very real. The chances of success are minimal.'

'I still would want to be on your side, work with you, share the danger.'

'The organisation would not want –'

'What organisation?'

'Freedom for Russia.'

'What?' Nadya sat up on the bed. 'They accepted a Pole?'

'I am Russian.'

'My God!' Nadya jumped off the bed. 'Then, really, there is no problem. Everything is wonderful. We can get married in three weeks.' She was pacing the floor. 'Actually during a time of war we could – I mean Father Yacov could dispense with the required announcements. We could get married in the next few days.' She stopped for a moment and paced the floor in silence. 'By the way, are you Russian Orthodox?'

'Yes.'

'Oh, Anton.' She came to me and embraced me. 'There is no problem. None.'

'There is, Nadya. I am a spy and –'

'That's very exciting. I believe I could be a good spy. I want to participate in your mission.'

'But your health ...'

'An asthmatic girl could be an asset. She would not be suspected as easily as a young Pole who speaks fluent Russian and knows all about ikons.'

'No, Nadya. Please forget what I told you. In case I am caught, I will tell them that you never have known about my role.'

Nadya came close to me.

'You know why I want to help you. I believe that we must help anyone who fights them. The Soviet regime consists of murderers who are afraid of losing their power. They use the label of Communism because that gives them a better opportunity to terrorise and kill. That way they even get support from abroad.'

'Nadya, you can't! I don't want you to.'

'But you must promise that if you need me –'

'We can talk about it when the time comes.'

That night we didn't make love. We spent a few more hours

talking about the horrors of the regime and the arrangements for the marriage ceremony.

When I came to visit Nadya the next day, Olga embraced me and Magda. 'We welcome both of you into our family. Nadya told me that she has already discussed the matter with Father Yacov and that the ceremony will take place in three days.'

The ceremony was a small private affair. After returning from the church we had a dinner prepared by Olga with a few toasts by Carl. That evening Nadya moved into my room with a valise and a small bag, her dowry, as she called it. In the next few days our life settled into a routine. We went on attending school. Nadya cooked in the evenings, and I watched her playing with Magda, who tried to help her with cooking. In all my life I never felt as happy as during those evenings.

One morning when we were still asleep, there was a knock at the door. It was still dark. Before we had the chance to say come in, the door opened, and Avram appeared.

'A terrible thing has happened,' he cried, sitting down on the chair. 'Your mother, your grandfather – arrested.'

I took Nadya into my arms. I felt her body quivering, I was shaking myself. Nadya did not cry.

'There were others,' Avram continued, 'Dr Cynfeld, Professor Czapski. Both of them were arrested with their families.'

'Where did they take them?' Nadya asked, sitting up in bed.

'It was after midnight. The trucks stopped in front of their houses. They were taken away with their personal belongings. The houses are sealed. Nobody knows where they took them.'

Nadya's face turned white. Magda began to cry.

'Such good people,' Avram went on.

'If only we could help. If only we could do something,' Nadya said, taking the crying Magda on her lap.

After Avram left, we dressed quickly and went to see Dr Cynfeld's sister, who was married to a lawyer named Zwajgman. It was before seven in the morning and still dark.

When we arrived at Zwajgman's house, the house was full of people, relatives or friends of those arrested last night. Berta, a stout middle-aged lady dressed in a red morning coat, embraced Nadya, wiping the tears from her eyes.

'People say that the trucks went to Kobryn,' Berta said. 'Nothing else is known.'

Berta and Nadya sat down on a sofa. 'When the previous arrests were made,' Berta continued, 'the Soviets would not give any information. "That is none of your business," they would say. None of your business when your mother, son or brother are carted away – who knows why and where.'

We did not expect to learn much there, but it was easier for us to be with other people who were living through the same tragedy.

After a while Berta served us some tea. I was not thinking anymore about Olga or Carl. I began to contemplate the discovery of a secret Soviet tank, a plan of which I would take to Krugov and the Germans. I recalled from the lectures on the military history of the Byzantine empire, how Andromacus, a Syrian, stole the secret of the magic fire, later known as 'Greek Fire'. A combination of sulphur, saltpetre, and quick lime. In the hands of the Byzantines this weapon changed the course of history for centuries, giving them superiority in naval warfare and enabling them to lift the Arab siege of Constantinople which had almost succumbed to the enemy. If only I could get information about the secret tank, and take it to the Germans who would vanquish the Reds.

That afternoon we did not go to school. Avram joined us in our room, trying to console us.

'The transport has not left yet,' Avram said.

'But they would not let us see them,' I said.

'As long as they are alive, there is hope,' Avram said.

'There is nothing, nothing we can do now.'

Avram began pacing the floor, squeezing a lock of his grey hair in his fingers. Magda, sitting on Nadya's lap, kissed her.

'We, the Jewish people,' Avram said, still pacing, 'when we are in trouble we can go to see our Rabbi. He is a learned man. He can always help us.'

'I'm afraid,' I said, ' that in this case no one can help us.'

'One never knows until one tries.'

'But we are not Jewish,' I said.

'He still would help you, I am sure.' We sat in silence.

'You have nothing to lose, so why shouldn't you go to see him?'

I looked at Nadya, but she was looking out of the window absorbed in her grief. Maybe a visit to a Rabbi would take her mind off her thoughts. I hesitated.

'I will run and ask him whether he can see you now,' Avram said, and without waiting for a comment he hurried out of the room.

He came back several minutes later, trying to catch his breath.

'He will see you now,' Avram said. 'He is such a clever man. I will stay with the child. Go now.'

We put our coats on. Avram stayed in our room, pleased with himself. When we were leaving the room he smiled. 'You will come back happy. I know it. I do.'

Nadya, who knew every house in Pruzhany, showed me the way. The Rabbi's house had the same kind of thatched straw roof as the other houses in Pruzhany. However, it was bigger and the walls were painted.

On the porch of the Rabbi's house stood three Jews discussing something and gesticulating with their hands. As we entered the porch they stopped talking and looked at us in surprise.

The Rabbi was sitting at a large table dressed in a black top coat and a black, wide-brimmed hat. Seeing us he stood up.

'Avram told me about your visit.' The Rabbi spoke fluent Russian. 'I learned about the unfortunate events this morning. I am sorry.'

With a gesture he invited us to sit down. He was a man in his late forties. His black eyes switched from one to the other of us. The windows were covered by thick curtains. The conversation of the three men on the porch went on. I could hear their agitated voices and was able to picture their gestures and facial expressions.

'Yesterday we tried to learn where they were taken,' I said. 'Nobody seems to know.'

'The people arrested during the last two nights,' the Rabbi said, 'are on a train some 20 kilometres away.' The Rabbi focused his eyes for an instant on me. 'But the area is well guarded by the Soviet Police, and no one would be able to get near it. There are six Jewish families in that transport.'

The room was stuffy and warm. Not being used to the heat, I began to perspire.

'So there is nothing that can be done?' I asked.

'Some people tried to use doctors' certificates to get out. Not even those seriously ill were released.'

'Escape perhaps?' Nadya asked.

'Do you want them killed by the N.K.V.D.'s bullets?' the Rabbi asked.

'My mother will manage in this situation,' Nadya said. 'She will adapt, but not Carl Vasilievich, my grandfather. He would –'

'Carl, Carl Vasilievich,' the Rabbi interrupted. I could see his lively eyes shifting. 'Yes, I know your grandfather's first name is Carl. I almost forgot it.'

'He does not seem to like it,' I commented.

'Carl is not a Russian name,' the Rabbi said.

'Of course it is as German as sauerkraut,' Nadya said. 'My grandfather hates it.'

'I can testify to that,' I said.

'Is your grandfather a German?' the Rabbi asked. 'I mean of German origin.'

'No, my great-grandmother was taking a vacation in Carlsbad, Czechoslovakia, when he was born. That's the reason.'

'But Carlsbad has been part of the German Third Reich since 1938,' the Rabbi said.

'But my grandfather is pure Russian,' Nadya said.

'He might claim German origin with a name like Carl and with a place of birth like Carlsbad,' the Rabbi suggested.

'Both his parents were Russians. They had Russian names,' I said. 'He hasn't a drop of German blood in his veins. He himself is very insistent about it.'

'But the Soviets might not believe him,' the Rabbi said.

Nadya and I exchanged a glance. We both knew that Carl would not claim German origin even to safe his life.

'The Soviet Union and the Third Reich concluded an agreement,' the Rabbi continued, 'specifying the return of all German nationals to their fatherland. A German mission is functioning in Lvov.'

'I am sure that my grandfather would not cooperate,' Nadya said.

The Rabbi's glance shifted from me to Nadya a few times. 'That might be quite fortunate,' the Rabbi said. 'He might have, despite some of my previous statements, considerable difficulty proving in a straightforward fashion his German nationality. His military record, his known anti-communist sympathies.

The fact that he was a hero of the Russian Civil War on the side of the White Guards.'

The Rabbi stood up, and he walked towards a door that he did not open but only knocked at nervously. Apparently the other people living there must have been used to that habit of his, since no one hurried to open the door from the other side. Suddenly he turned back and stood in front of us.

'The Soviets have a very peculiar system of justice. One must operate within it,' the Rabbi said. 'Now, I will tell you what you should do: write an anonymous letter to the Pruzhany N.K.V.D. informing them a German Carl von Utapoff is trying to pass as a Russian. He is now in the transport leaving for the Soviet Union. No one knows the purpose of this masquerade and deceit. Mark on the original that you are also informing the German mission. You don't have to bother to send them the copy. There are two possibilities. Either someone will burn the letter, and then our scheme will not work, or – Soviets are bureaucrats and as such hate any possible complications, involving reports or apologies. I think that there is a good chance that they would want to send Carl and his daughter as soon as possible to the German repatriation centre, and that is quite a different thing from a camp in Siberia.'

When we were leaving, the Rabbi said, 'You don't have much choice, do you?'

We were grateful to him and returned full of hope and resolution. Nadya wrote the letter in capital letters and we mailed it the same day.

That night, despite the flicker of hope that our anonymous letter had given us, Nadya and I could not sleep. It was well after midnight and I could still hear Nadya's irregular breathing, her frequent tossing and turning. Feeling that I was not asleep, Nadya whispered, 'Do you think that there is some hope?'

'Oh, certainly. That letter –'

'I didn't mean that, your mission.'

'With some luck, lots of luck.'

'If we both work, we could double our chances, Anton.'

'No, no, Nadya I told, you could not –'

'But I even have some experience.'

'What!' I almost jumped out of the bed.

'You will wake up Magda, Anton. I don't mean that I have

been a spy, no. But before the war I helped a few refugees from the Soviet Union, who were given asylum by the Polish authorities.'

'That's different,' I said with a sigh of relief.

'The Poles kept files of these refugees, and during the interregnum, while the mob was in charge, I managed to go to the City Hall and destroy the file.'

I remembered having seen Nadya, then an unknown slim girl, leaving a crowd and disappearing. So that was where she had gone, I thought. I knew that the file in the hands of the Soviet Police would mean death to everyone whose name appeared on it. 'There was another file of Communist sympathisers that I picked up. I could not carry it too far and left it with the storekeeper. You even helped me carry the file to Krystyna's.

'I thought a Soviet soldier might help me. The file is invaluable to inform them whom not to include in the Polish Underground.'

'You risked a lot.'

'A risk is worth taking if it can save many lives. That is what you are doing, isn't it?'

'But that's different. I am like a soldier. My assignment is military.'

'You must report on Soviet planes?'

'Why planes?'

'Boris and Gleb are pilots.'

'Oh, no: they are my friends. Tanks are my . . .'

'Tanks, tanks. I will help you.'

'We'll talk about it tomorrow.'

For a long time Nadya did not sleep, and the next morning as soon as we let Magda go out by herself, Nadya began to ask me about the details of my assignment. I told her everything I knew, starting with the first meeting with Krugov, our other meetings, my observations and my meeting with von Dolnitz. The same afternoon she went out with Magda looking for tanks, but she did not see a new model. That evening she drew a beautiful picture of a T-28, its crew, resembling the devils of her ikons, sitting on top.

In the next few days she spent lots of time outdoors without making any progress. She found only the same old tanks that were familiar to me. On the fifth day she returned quite excited.

'*Des bonnes nouvelles*?' I asked in French not wanting Magda to understand.

'Not exactly what you might expect,' Nadya answered in French, catching her breath. 'But there are a number of tank commanders who arrived recently in Pruzhany. One of them is billeted in Father Yacov's house.'

'I cannot possibly go to Father Yacov's house, meet the tank man, and tell him to give us information about a new tank.'

'There is *une petite difference* in this case. The fellow likes to drink a lot.'

'I see your point, but I don't drink.' I knew that the best way to get on friendly terms quickly is to drink together. A drunk man would say things he would not say when sober.

'You could learn the art,' Nadya said.

Chapter 13

Pinsk, December 20, 1939

Vashin, sitting in his temporary office in Pinsk, looked out of the window for a moment, and his thoughts wandered to his native village and his mother.

Ever since he had become a commissar he had not written any letter to her or for that matter to anyone. Knowing that written words, both sent and received, were always subject to a malicious interpretation, he had also asked her not to write to him. The simplest sentences concerning some domestic problems could be twisted around and used as a proof of treason or other crimes against the regime. He was aware of these methods since he had used them with people he had arrested. The only way for Vashin to find out how his mother was, and how the other members of his family were, was to visit his native village. But that was impossible for the next several weeks. He was too involved in the operation 'Parterre.'

There were daily developments in his work. First there was additional information coming from the Third Reich, supplied by Communist agents there. A new detail, thus obtained, like the description of the scar on the forehead of one of the spies, enabled Vashin's people to identify the man and arrest him. After Vashin had flown to Bialystok he interrogated the prisoner and executed him there.

The N.K.V.D. officers in various towns were able to spot and arrest some of the other Parterre members. One Parterre agent in Brest told his secret to his girl friend, who after a quarrel with him, betrayed him to the N.K.V.D. Another agent in Grodno got drunk and told his drinking companion about his work while finishing a bottle of vodka in a restaurant. An N.K.V.D. man masquerading as a waiter in that inn had overheard the talk and reported it. The agent was caught. Vashin personally questioned all of the arrested spies and spent days and nights interrogating them, but he did not learn much from them. The spies, even those who were willing to talk, did not know the names of their contacts.

Vashin was pleased, however, with the progress made in his own scheme, checking the movements of all people arriving for a short visit to towns where the spies were caught. This required a large staff of agents. The experienced ones were able to spot and eliminate the local people, and thus concentrate on suspects travelling on some pretext who might be members of the Parterre group.

One such suspect, a woman spotted in Pinsk selling ikons near the Orthodox church there, travelled on to Brest, then to Pruzhany. Her income from those sales could not justify such travels and efforts. Vashin wondered whether she would cover six different places on her trips, and proceed according to the scheme he had learned from solitaire: the work of the spy ring based on groups of six people. He ordered her surveillance to be discreet and used several agents to follow her.

He also requested that a snapshot of her be taken. He sent it through diplomatic channels to Berlin, to be forwarded to Hamburg, where an agent named Nina Zaverin had lived. Nina's description approximated the features of the ikon saleswoman, but Vashin wanted to be sure.

The ringing of the telephone interrupted Vashin's thoughts. Vashin picked up the receiver. 'That you, Tovarich Vashin?' Brodilo's voice said.

'Yes, Tovarich Brodilo. I can hear you quite well.'

'Vashin, I want you to come to Moscow right away. I will have a plane at the military airport in a few hours. I will wait for you.' Without waiting for Vashin's answer Brodilo hung up. Vashin was not surprised at the curtness of Brodilo's message. Both of them knew that all telephone conversations were recorded and filed. Consequently, the shorter the record the better.

Vashin stood up, walked to the wash basin in his office, and washed his hands. It was already 10 o'clock. It was a windy, cold December night.

Fortunately the frost froze the mud on the streets and made walking possible. Vashin was now passing Dr Garfinkel's house, the doctor who had treated the executed spy Lepin. For a moment Vashin recalled how, when he had told the doctor, his wife, and his fifteen-year-old son to dress, they went to the bedroom and never came back. A few minutes later Vashin, walking into the room, saw their dead bodies lying on the bed.

But soon Vashin forgot about that incident and wondered only why Brodilo had summoned him to Moscow, and why by plane. It must be a very urgent matter, Vashin thought as he hurried to the airport. He was already expected there, but his plane had not arrived yet.

The local commander in charge of flights invited him into a barracks. It was a hastily constructed wooden hut with low ceilings. In the small area three pilots sat drinking tea. The commander, a small fat man in his thirties, offered Vashin a glass of tea that he declined. The room was filled with tobacco smoke so dense that Vashin had difficulty seeing the pilots' faces. He could hear voices without being able to tell who was speaking.

'What a damned place this Polesie!' a thin voice said. 'Nothing but moors for hundred of miles.'

'You're damn lucky to be in Pinsk,' another voice with a Ukrainian accent said. 'I am stationed in Pruzhany, a kind of island among the miles of water and mud. Only a few thousand people live there sinking in mud. You go crazy there. It rains all the time making the mud deeper.'

'Thanks for the frost. At least one can get around by tanks,' the first voice said.

'The other day, a few kilometres away from Pruzhany,' the man with the Ukrainian accent said, 'I stopped with a car in a settlement in those moors. Some people came to greet us. They thought we were Poles. They did not even know that the war had started.'

'So you don't mind going to the Finnish front?' the thin voice said.

'I prefer anything to this mud. Even hell.'

'Wasn't the war against the Finns supposed to be over?' a third voice, deep and hoarse, asked.

'Drink your tea, Vasilly,' the first voice said.

But Vashin was no longer listening to their conversation. He was wondering now whether his recall to Moscow had anything to do with the Finnish war. He might even be recalled from the Parterre group and assigned a new task.

Two hours later Vashin's plane arrived. After refuelling was completed Vashin boarded the plane for his flight to Moscow. The first light of a new day broke on the horizon when Vashin's plane landed at Moscow's military airport. The airfield was covered by snow, dry and fresh. Vashin had walked only a few steps when he recognised Brodilo waiting for him, smoking a cigarette. Brodilo's face, covered by a two days' growth of whiskers, looked greyer than usual; the rings under his eyes were darker and deeper. A heavy fur cap covered his bald head.

'I summoned you here,' Brodilo said after a few words of greeting, 'to brief you on some new developments. After you have heard my orders, you will return at once to Pinsk.'

A cold wind was blowing tiny snowflakes into their faces. The planes around them were taking off and landing. The roar of the motors made hearing Brodilo's words difficult. Vashin, exhausted after a sleepless night in a cold plane, shivered. He wanted to wash up and eat, but he knew that Brodilo would conduct the conversation outside so that no one could hear them.

On the horizon the outlines of hangars became visible against the reddish-grey sky.

'Listen carefully,' Brodilo said. 'The day before yesterday Tovarich Stalin gave the go-ahead to build the new T-34 tanks. There will be two prototypes of this tank constructed in the Kharkov Locomotive Plant.'

The two of them were ambling on snow at the edge of the airfield.

'The new tank will be superior to anything the Germans have,'

Brodilo continued, lighting another cigarette. 'It will be able to hit and destroy the German tanks from a distance of 2000 metres, against the German tanks being able to do the same only from 500 metres. It will also manoeuvre.' The sound of the motor of a landing plane made the rest of the sentence inaudible. Vashin did not ask Brodilo to repeat it. He shivered and his hands felt numb from cold.

'... ready by the end of February.' Vashin could hear again Brodilo's words. 'Tovarich Stalin decided to make the test in Minsk first, and then again in Pruzhany against the German tanks. The proving grounds are just about –'

They reached the end of the path and turned back.

'I want you, Tovarich Vashin, to clean up that Parterre group, most specifically in the Pruzhany area ...' Vashin could not understand the rest of the sentence.

'I can do it, if –'

'No ifs,' Brodilo shouted. 'I promised Tovarich Stalin, that I would answer for the safety of our tank research in Pruzhany. The safety ... Another matter: an army lieutenant bought a jacket from a tailor in Brest; there was a letter sewn into the jacket.' Brodilo looked around to make sure that no one could overhear their conversation. 'The letter in Polish was in code; every second letter made up the message: "Recall bearer at once. Involved Poles. Also a girl." '

'So probably that spy is gone; they must communicate again.'

'The fellow who sold the letter reappeared again here, after a probable visit to the West. We got the tailor.'

'But that could be an agent for ...'

'The author of the letter must have been a Russian: there were a number of Russianisms in the text. Also our calligraphy experts are certain that whoever wrote the letter learned to write the cyrillic alphabet first.'

'The tailor could recognise the fellow.'

'But where?' Brodilo asked. 'The man is between twenty-two and twenty-eight, tall, slim, long hands and long legs. The tailor gave us a good description of his body but does not remember much about his face.'

'We will find him.'

'There is a deadline. I already checked with the tailor all the photographs in the dossiers. The results were negative. Another plane landing close by stopped their conversation. Brodilo lighted another cigarette, and Vashin, feeling the cold penetrating deep into his bones, began moving his hands. The first few rays of reddish light coloured the snow.

'The man must be important,' Vashin shouted. 'The only one who crossed the border and back.'

'I know. I will find his trail.'

'But how, Tovarich Brodilo?'

'If you want to find the fox, you must find his trace at the foxhole. I will visit Berlin soon again ... some friends there ...'

'I understand,' Vashin said.

'Your plane has refuelled,' Brodilo said. 'I want you to leave without delay. I don't want you to be seen here. Remember! I promised.'

They shook hands. Vashin strode towards the plane, looking at the buildings and hangars around the airport, now more recognisable in the light of the dawn. He moved on the snow without a sound.

Chapter 14

Anton's Story

Pruzhany, February 15, 1940

February was the coldest month in Pruzhany and it snowed a lot. One morning I went out to buy food and vodka: only a light snow was falling and it was relatively mild. I liked this sort of weather when one could enjoy the beauty of snow covering everything with a thick layer. Even Pruzhany on such a day looked enchanting and the people seemed attractive.

To buy food I usually had to stand in line for hours, but that time it turned out to be my lucky day. After only half an hour I was able to purchase five eggs, the first we had seen in a few months, and a kilo of buckwheat. To buy vodka it was not necessary to stand in queues: it was not available in stores and the only way to get it was to barter for it on the black market. That morning I exchanged Nadya's short coat for two litres of Polish vodka, Wyborows with the red cap and fifty-five percent alcoholic content. The other Polish vodka, at forty-five percent alcohol, could be bought at half the price, but the Soviets did not like to drink it, it was too weak for them. As I was returning with a smile of triumph, anticipating the joy on Nadya's face at the news of my acquisitions, I heard the steps of someone running after me.

'*Ah ato ty, tsaplya,* that's you, crane.' It was Masha's cheerful voice. Her uniformed fur coat was open, her face glowing with joy.

'Oh, Masha, it's been a long time.'

'I recognised you immediately, looking at the back of you, by your *tsaplya*-like way of walking', she laughed. Her face was reddened by the cold and she blushed on top of it, as we shook hands. 'It is a most serious way of walking, careful ...'

'I am not so serious. I am overjoyed to see you.'

'Let's see, *Tsaplya*, whether we can test your unseriousness. Let's play *snyezhki,*' Masha said, forming a snowball in her bare hands and running to the other side of the street. There was nothing else for me to do but put aside my newspaper-wrapped packages and make a snowball. We both laughed a lot while hitting each other with soft snowballs that did not hold together too well.

Two colonels, both big and heavy, were passing in the middle of the street. Masha aimed and hit one on his fur cap, roaring with laughter. Encouraged by her success, she threw another snowball and got another perfect hit.

'I'll spank you, Tovarich Boyets,' the colonel said, looking at Masha and smiling, 'and in front of your boyfriend.'

'A good looking couple,' the other officer said as they went out of the range of our snowy missiles.

'And in love,' the first one said, lighting a cigarette. 'Love is everything there is in life.'

We continued our game for a little while. At one point I remembered the packages and turned around to check them. They were still there, but right behind me was Masha trying to put some snow down my collar, a standard manoeuvre in snowball fights. I tried to reciprocate, and in the process tore a button from Masha's tunic that opened a bit to show the stretched cotton undershirt over the braless breasts.

'Oh you *Tsaplya*, tearing my clothing in public,' Masha said laughing, 'I need that button.'

The warmth and the aroma of the ordinary soap mixed with that of her body I found most pleasant. We both knelt down to look for the button. Our faces touched and I felt how hers was burning. I found the button and both of us stood up.

'What a marvellous *tsaplya* you are.' Masha smiled, half closing one of her slanting eyes. 'I was transferred three months ago to Smolensk, a big, good town. Still, knowing that there is Pruzhany among the swamps, where a lonely *tsaplya* lives, with great difficulty I managed to be reassigned here.'

'Masha, Masha, but I am married now.'

She did not try to conceal her disappointment. The expression of joy disappeared to be replaced by sadness.

'I should have known that a *tsaplya* like you does not stay alone for long,' she said in a different voice.

'When we met,' I said picking up my packages, 'I was with Nadya.'

'I know Anton, I know. It's me who is such a fool, feeding myself with false hopes, building in my dreams the image of happiness that never could be a reality. Are you happy, Anton?'

'Yes, very happy Masha, and we have adopted a five-year old girl Magda.

'That's nice. You have a family now,' Masha said with a faint smile as we walked along the side of the street a metre apart from each other. 'From the bottom of my heart I wish all of you a happy life.'

'And for you Masha, and for you.'

'I will try. Yes a happy life,' she said as we reached a corner and were shaking hands. Her usually smiling eyes were filling with tears.

A moment later I turned. Masha was walking in a very uncharacteristic way, with her head down, at a slow pace, and without any of her customary exuberance.

For a while I remembered her smell, her warmth, and I was sorry not to be able to accompany her and to stay with her. A beautiful girl and so lonely. The thought that I would not be able to see her again hurt me. I felt pity for her because of her loneliness, a feeling I had experienced during so many years, and I began to think that Masha, an attractive and intelligent girl, should easily find the right man for herself but I did not like the image of another man with Masha.

Entering Avram's house I continued to think about Masha, and hearing Nadya's voice as she spoke to Magda I decided not to mention anything about my recent encounter.

When I reached our room I was surprised to see Nadya setting the table for two. In the middle of the table was *zakooska* (food one eats after drinking vodka) consisting of pieces of bread with sliced pickles and apples.

'But why two glasses?' I said, taking off my topcoat and shaking the snow from it.

'Your drinking situation must be realistic,' Nadya said. 'I think you need a drinking companion.'

'But you never drink, Nadya.'

'We could train together in the art of drinking vodka.'

I opened the bottle and filled the two small glasses.

'Let's get this thing over as soon as possible,' I said picking up a glass.

'Oh, darling, don't rush. We want to prepare you for the new role of a vodka aficionado ready to outdrink the captain *et apprendre ses secrets*.' Nadya switched to French since Magda had stopped playing and was following our conversation with curiosity.

'How are you going to accomplish it?' I asked.

'Let's see. Imagine I am the captain coming in from the cold carrying a bottle of vodka. You are sitting in Father Yacov's living room. Here I come.' Nadya walked to the door, and ostentatiously switching the weight of her frail body from one leg to another walked towards me. 'Boom, boom, boom. Here he sees you, Anton, and grumbles. "Weather, Devil's mother's weather," in his basso.' Nadya tried with a great effort to imitate the captain's voice.

'What do you say then?'

'Welcome Captain, it's warm and pleasant here.'

'Oh my God, Anton,' Nadya laughed. 'He will run away from you if he hears that. He will think you're one of those Polish gentlemen whose caricatures he sees daily on all the posters. You are not sitting in Versailles and greeting a count or a

Marquis de Tortoni: "Welcome, your highness, to the chambers of your palace".'

I started to laugh and Magda joined in.

'Is Papa a Polish gentleman?' Magda asked.

'He is, darling. He is. Now back to our captain. What do you say to him, Anton, after he has damned the weather?'

'I would say to him, "it's always devilish weather here", and I would look sad and dejected.'

'A shade better, but not perfect. And not particularly catching or original.'

Nadya returned to the door and walked towards me again. 'Boom, boom, boom. It's devil's mother's weather, and then, Anton, you say, "It's always wet here, either rain or snow - but I am dry, very dry, my throat is dry." You see, this way you arouse his compassion. A fellow agrees with him about the weather and suffers from the same dryness of the throat that can only be cured by a generous flow of vodka.'

'My throat is very dry,' I repeated looking at the glass of vodka.

Nadya sat down at the table. 'Something is wrong, my darling, very wrong. You claimed to have a dry throat; you entered the room with the captain who took off his coat, searched for the bottle, opened it, put it on the table, filled your glass and his . . . and all that time you were burning with impatience to wet that throat of yours; and now you are looking at that glass as if it were filled with poison, like a child looking at a bottle of cod liver oil. You must look at it as if it were your sole source of joy. Of course you don't need to be too obvious with that feeling, but the desire must be there.'

'All right. I love you, vodka,' I said, gulping it down. Nadya did the same, but in the midst of it she started to cough. After she had her coughing under control she finished the glass.

'Now we must eat, right away,' she said, serving me the little canape. 'A man who drinks in our house eats after gulping down his vodka.'

Nadya refilled my glass and put only a few drops into hers.

'Anton, again that expression of grief on your face while you are contemplating the vodka. You should look at it the way you used to ogle Masha while dancing with her.'

'Oh, Nadya, I was thinking of you then, talking only about you,' I said, wondering whether Nadya had seen me playing snowballs with Masha.

'Fine, Anton. Your diplomatic explanation of that special spark in your eyes is accepted. Now look at the vodka the way you looked at Masha while dancing with her and thinking only of me.'

'Nadienka, I thought I would be learning to drink vodka and not be reminded of some old jealousies.'

'Jealousy is a twin of love, my dear,' Nadya said. 'Which reminds me that while drinking with your captain you should talk to him about the reason you like to drink.'

'Sure, I'll tell him that I drink because my wife is jealous.'

'What does jealous mean, Papa?' Magda, who had returned to her dolls, asked.

'One wants to keep all the feelings of the loved person,' I said.

'So, Papa, you are jealous when Nadya plays with me and with the dolls?' Since our marriage Nadya played with Magda with enthusiasm, trying to catch up on her own lost childhood.

'Oh, no, I like it when Nadya plays with you.'

'I can feel the effects of these drinks now,' Nadya said. 'The bright colours, the world in flowers. Why don't you tell your captain that you drink, because your wife loves you too much. You like to solve chess problems with the queen sacrifice and others, and she disturbs you because she loves you too much.'

I drank the vodka.

'He wouldn't believe it. There is no such thing.'

'Why not?'

'Love is an absolute. There are no degrees and no comparisons. It is a total commitment. I love you Nadya and when I say it –'

'It is so beautiful to hear it. You haven't said it in weeks; don't say anything else. I still hear those words, those heavenly sounds. Oh, I feel very sentimental now. Please sit down next to me on the bed, and you, Magda, on the other side.' Nadya moved towards the bed, picking up Magda.

'I was supposed to –'

'Please forget it for a moment. I just would like to hold your hand . . . I need to.'

Nadya's hand felt warm. We remained silent for a while. The only sound came from the wind blowing hard against the glass of the windows. I wished that this moment might last forever.

Later on Nadya fell asleep. I took away the bottle and did not drink any more that day.

Next day I drank much more and ended up feeling sick. On the third day my session went better: I consumed half-a-bottle in a couple of hours, and while I was drinking, I was able to function and I knew what was happening around me. Encouraged by these results, I ventured to visit Father Yacov. I got there at eight in the evening, having learned from Nadya that the captain usually arrived about that time.

I felt guilty telling Father Yacov that I wanted to meet his tenant in order to exchange a bottle of vodka for sugar, having heard that the captain liked to drink.

A few minutes after eight the captain arrived, wearing heavy boots, a cap of leather and fur, and a fur trenchcoat. He was a well-built man of about thirty, at least a head taller than I and double my weight, all of it probably muscle. I wondered how he could fit his large body into a tank. Without looking at us he walked towards the door of his room, pulled out a key and started to unlock it. He did not mention the weather, giving me little opportunity to demonstrate how well I had learned Nadya's lesson. He opened the door and was about to disappear behind it when, after having gathered all my courage, I said, 'I have a bottle of Polish vodka.'

For a moment he stood there, and I was afraid that he might slam the door and that would be the end of my project. But he turned around and said, 'Let's see it.' I pulled out the bottle and brought it to him. He looked at it curiously, observed the letters in Latin script, then turned the bottle upside down and looked through it against the light.

'Come!' he said, carrying the bottle with him and placing it on the table. The room smelled of stale tobacco; the bed was unmade, a plate serving as an ashtray was full of cigarette stubs. Without taking off his cap or coat, he went to a cabinet, took out two glasses, and with a quick movement of his fingernails removed the seal. Then he hit the bottom of the bottle hard, and the cork popped out. He smelled the open bottle for a moment, then filled one glass. 'Drink it!' he said. Facing the glass I was reminded of Nadya's advice to look at it as if it were Masha. It struck me as ridiculous, and I smiled. I drank it at a gulp. He observed me for a while after I had finished it. I realised that he was wondering whether or not I was trying to sell him some poisoned vodka.

He filled his glass and gulped it down. 'Not bad,' he said. 'How much?'

'I don't know,' I said. 'How much are you willing to give me for that bottle?'

He shrugged his shoulders.

'I need sugar,' I said. He nodded. Verbosity was not one of his weaknesses. Encouraged by his nod, I added, 'Three kilos perhaps?' He nodded again. Taking off his coat but not the fur cap, he refilled the glasses. For a moment he appeared to hesitate. Then he went to the bed, pulled a bag from under it and brought out a can. After he had opened it, I saw that it contained sprats.

Sitting down on his bed, he motioned me to sit on the one wooden chair.

'I am Vadim. And you?'

'Anton.'

'Well Anton, you see, a man walks on two feet,' Vadim said. 'We have to have the second drink.'

As soon as Vadim had gulped down his vodka, he pulled a sprat from the can with his fingers, put it in his mouth and ate it, encouraging me to do the same.

'And you know a good reason to have a third one?' Vadim asked.

'No.'

'My grandfather used to say, "God loves the Trinity." I'm not quite sure that I know what it means, but that's as good a reason as any.'

We gulped down the vodkas again, and I began to feel drunk. I wished to bring up the subject of tanks in one way or another, but I had sworn to Nadya that I would not do so the first evening, and I was still sober enough to remember my promise. As we continued with other rounds (the horse is running on four legs, the red star has five corners, half a dozen is six, the lucky number is seven), my host became more talkative. He told me that he came from Novosibirsk, a town in Siberia, that he was married, had two boys, one of them a year old whom he had never seen yet.

Vadim asked me about my wife, and he was sorry to hear that she suffered from asthma.

When we finished the bottle, I felt dizzy and had trouble getting up from my chair. I did not know what was going on, but I knew one thing, my host was still quite sober.

As I was leaving, he said, 'Your sugar.'

'Never mind,' I said. 'I don't care.'

'But it's yours.'

'I drank half of your vodka.'

'That doesn't matter,' he said, handing me a package.

I don't remember how I reached home. I do know that I woke up late the next morning, saw Nadya sitting at the edge of our bed, and had a terrible headache.

After swallowing Kogutek, a Polish medicine against headaches, I drank three cups of tea and began to feel better. I told Nadya whatever I still remembered of my conversation with the captain the previous evening. And while at that moment I was ready to swear never to touch a glass of vodka again, I called on the captain three days later. Again we finished a bottle of vodka without either one of us mentioning the word tank. He brought up the subject himself during our fifth drinking bout. At that time we had already finished the seventh round and were talking about the depth of snow in Pruzhany after a recent snow storm.

'Our boys in Finland,' Vadim said, 'had to fight in snow deeper than this. And even the tanks were not of much use there.'

'What! The tanks could not handle the snow?'

'Of course they could, ha, ha. The depth is not a problem, but the cold is. We have plenty of experience in treating our fuel to run the tanks at minus 30 degrees, but when the damn cold reaches minus sixty, it's tough. You need a special fuel that we did not have in December. That is why we were so slow then. We are learning a lot in Finland.'

Despite the seven drinks I had gulped already, I became alert.

'The Finns don't seem to have many tanks,' I said, 'but the Germans have a lot.'

'Sure, but so do the French and the English.'

'Which of these countries has the best tank?'

Vadim laughed again.

'There are so many categories, manufacturers, production models. The French build tanks with heavier armour than the Germans, but the German tanks are faster.'

'How fast are they?'

'Here again it depends on the category of tanks. Their medium tanks, the Panzer III, for example, about thirty-eight kilometres per hour. All the tanks are getting faster. During the war of 1914-18 the faster tanks could only run at twelve kilometres per hour and now our tanks can go up to almost sixty.'

Vadim raised his glass and we drank. He forgot even to

mention a reason why we should start the eighth round.

'What is more important, speed or armour?' I asked trying to keep the conversation going.

'Both are important, but you know what the most important thing is?'

I shrugged my shoulders.

'The gun is the most important,' he said looking hard at me. 'The gun that can hit any enemy tank at a distance of fifteen hundred metres, two thousand metres, and mind you with precision, that is the tank to beat.'

'And the German tanks can do that?'

'Oh, no, no, maybe at three hundred - five hundred tops.'

'So there is no such tank now?' I asked.

'Not yet, not yet Anton. But if there is someone who would get it first, it would be us.'

'It would be good to have such a tank,' I said. 'How could this be achieved technically?'

'Accuracy of a hit depends on many elements,' Vadim said refilling the glasses. 'Since a good tank in action must shoot on the move, the quality of the suspension system must be improved. Then the matter of trajectory is essential for the accuracy. The flatter the trajectory, the higher the probability of a hit, but even the flattest trajectory would not ensure a hit. The trunnion cant might reduce it significantly; for instance the deflection in reaching the target with trunnion left, impact point high left, cant right, impact point low right.'

He lost me. I could not possibly follow him. He continued to talk about tanks standing at twelve o'clock, turret at six o'clock, and again about trunnion cant. My inability to understand him worried me. I consoled myself by thinking that what he was saying must have little to do with a new tank and must be known to any artillery officer.

Vadim interrupted his speech and raised his glass, inviting me with a gesture to drink another round.

'The form of a trajectory depends on the muzzle velocity and the wind factor,' Vadim continued after we had emptied our glasses. He was out of sprats, so we had used small pickles called *kornishony* for our *zakooska*, picking them from a large glass jar with our fingers. Vadim apparently did not own or like spoons or forks.

'But the ability to hit an enemy tank is not the only problem. You must not only hit the damn tank, but -' he looked at me, checking whether I was still listening, 'you must penetrate the tank - penetrate. The hit to be effective must be lethal, you understand? This depends on the muzzle velocity and the weight of the missile. Or to say it in other words: velocity times weight equals power of penetration. And we will have such a tank. Our new T-34 will do it, I am sure.'

The statement naming the tank came so unexpectedly that I had to concentrate so as not to show any special interest or excitement. For the first time in all these long months I had heard something that might be of value. There was a new model of a Soviet tank. Its name was T-34, and it might have a gun that would penetrate the enemy armour of longer ranges than the current tanks. All those drinks had paid off. Would I be able to convey this information to anyone? Would I learn more?

'We Russians have geniuses, engineering geniuses, that no other nation can match. We were the first ones to develop a method of carrying the tanks by aircraft. I saw them myself, how the bombers were carrying the T-38 and the T-27 slung beneath their fuselage. Our engineers were the first to use the cosine principle in the design of our tanks. The sloping increased the protection without the burden of weight.'

Vadim spoke with enthusiasm and pride reminding me of a dialogue in Dostoyevsky's *Adolescent*, a scene that stuck deep in my memory although I could not remember even the name of those who had participated in that emotional, almost tearful assertion of the superiority of everything that is Russian. I had heard such stories repeated in every meeting of Russian émigré officers, but this was the first time I had heard it from a Red Army captain.

Looking now at Vadim I found him most *sympatico*; I found him sincere and honest. His own deeply felt emotion was contagious, and I began to feel the same way he did, or perhaps I always had believed what Vadim now was saying. I wished I could participate in this dialogue, mention the victories of Suvorov, Kutozov, speak about Russian geniuses in medicine, the sciences, the arts. But then I reminded myself that I was here as a spy to steal Vadim's secrets and deliver them to his enemies. I began to feel ashamed of myself and to hate myself for my role. A strong urge to tell him about my secret took hold of me.

'And we were the first to power tanks with diesel engines,' I said.

'First ones to standardise them,' Vadim said. 'Many advantages: less danger of fire, substantially longer range of travel. But a drawback is that the tanks powered by diesels give off smoke visible to the enemy. More smoke than the gasoline engine. The tank soldiers must be prepared to die like all other soldiers, but I hope that the war with Germany will not start right away. I still would like to see my child before I die. Now I have only a photograph.'

With his fingers he opened a pocket in his tunic and pulled out a folded sheet of newspaper. From it he took a small snapshot of a child, perhaps a few months old. The paper of the photograph was yellowish, but one could still see that the baby was smiling.

'Alyosha has eleven teeth now,' Vadim said, looking at the picture of his child. I was moved to see the little photograph in the huge hand. After admiring it for a while, he showed it once more to me, then folded it carefully in the newspaper and put it back into his pocket.

'There is a war now with Finland,' Vadim said. 'I don't know, I might be assigned there.' The thought of his child, the war, his life made Vadim taciturn. I was moved, I couldn't stand it any longer, and I left.

Another evening I came early to wait for Vadim, but he was already in his room. As I had entered I saw that he had already been drinking. He was sitting with his cap on as usual, but this time he had not taken off his trenchcoat. The room smelled of unwashed bed linen, and of the pickles lying in the middle of the table on a wet piece of newspaper.

'You did not wait for me,' I said, sitting down. And from the half-empty bottle I poured myself a glass.

He shrugged his shoulders and without looking at me drank down another vodka.

'What's the matter?' I asked, seeing how different he was from my several previous visits with him.

He did not answer. He was gazing out of the window and possibly looking far beyond it, seeing his family in his native town in Siberia. It struck me suddenly that he must have been ordered to the Finnish front, where a major tank offensive by the Soviet Union was under way.

'You are leaving?' I asked.

He nodded, I did not have to ask him where he was going. Something told me that I would never see this man again, and that upset me. I felt guilty about my role and sorry for him and for myself.

For a while we drank in silence.

'Pickles are the best form of *zakooska,*' he said, eating one. 'But it is too bad that they keep you sober, and I want to get drunk.'

'The war will be over soon,' I said.

'It doesn't matter to me. The war is my duty. I don't think about it. It just hurts somewhere deep in my soul, and that is why I am drinking and why I want to get drunk.'

He lit a cigarette and offered one to me.

'I expected to see my former teacher, from the Academy,' Vadim said. 'He is coming here in a few days – and now this *komandeerovka,* "this assignment". I have not seen him for seven years. He was like a father to me.'

Vadim emptied another glass.

'Khomikov was a good teacher, methodical. He knew everything there was to know about tanks. Although he never trusted his own memory, took everything down, kept a perfect file on everything. He always had a big black bag with him where all of his notes were arranged in the most orderly way. I used to carry his bag for him. It had a big initial X on it. He always lectures sitting down, and since he is a small man one could see only his small head over the lectern, and sometimes his pince-nez would fall down and he could not find it. He spoke with a nasal accent like the people from Leningrad where he studied before the war of 1914. When he used to refer to his studies, he would often say, "in our St Petersburg," and then he would correct himself, blushing, "our Leningrad Academy." '

Vadim was getting drunker and drunker, as he continued to talk about his life in the Frunze Military Academy, and I kept feeling sorrier for him with each drink I gulped down. It hurt me when I thought about my reason for being here and drinking with this man. I felt guilty about stealing Vadim's secrets that one day could be used against him, and others. Against Masha, who loved her country, who had abandoned her good job in Smolensk to come back to Pruzhany for my sake.

An urge came over me to see her and apologise to her for her loneliness, for everything I was doing to her, for my guilt.

With that thought in mind I left Vadim and began walking towards Masha's house. It was very windy and it snowed. I remembered the house where she had lived before, and hoped that she might be living there again. Despite my drunkenness I found it. A light shone in the window of her room. I knocked. Masha opened the door; she was barefoot and she had a towel wrapped over her head.

'Oh, Anton.'

'Do I disturb you?'

'You? Never. Come in!'

In the middle of her room on the table was a wash basin; a piece of common soap was lying next to it. The room smelled of soap. The bed was made and on the wall were pinned several yellowish snapshots.

'I came, Masha, I came to ask your forgiveness,' I said reaching for the back of a chair and trying to support myself against it. 'You will forgive me Masha, will you?'

'There is nothing that you should feel guilty about,' Masha said taking away the wash basin from the table.

'There is Masha, there is,' I said sitting down in my overcoat and looking at Masha's healthy feet.

Noticing how I looked at them, Masha blushed and put on her *valenky*, high woollen shoes.

'You drank, Anton, you did,' she said, seeing me shaking my head. 'But that's all right. A man must get drunk once in a while. I will make tea for us.'

The wind was blowing hard against the windows.

'Outside is *vyooga*, "the howling wind", and here it is nice. It is good to be here Masha. And yet there is a heavy weight on my soul, *menya khandreet*, "I am overcome by the feeling of spleen." '

'I have the feeling so often, Anton. I understand.'

'You have no reason, Masha, none. I feel so bad, I need to ask you to forgive me. You are so pure, and I am such an evil monster. I always wanted to be good. That's what my father wished for me, but I am not, Masha, I am not.' The tears began to stream from my eyes.

'Anton, that's not true. You are an exceptional human being, with a good, loving heart. You have adopted an orphan. You have done many things from the goodness of your heart.'

Masha poured a glass of tea for me and one for herself.

'But towards you, Masha? I feel so guilty! I want to kneel in front of you and ask your forgiveness, kissing your hands.'

'Please Anton, I am touched by your words, deeply moved, but I don't deserve it.'

'You sacrificed Smolensk to come back here.'

Masha took my hand.

'Oh Anton, you should not feel guilty about it. I returned to Pruzhany because I wanted to see you again. I did it knowing that you were in love with Nadya. I am the guilty person. I was the one who was unable to control my feelings.'

Masha had tears in her eyes.

'You talk about sacrifices,' she said, wiping her tears with her sleeve. 'An act of giving up, of sacrifice, enriches the person making it more than the one who benefits from it. The deeper the feeling the greater the sacrifice. Oh, there is happiness in sacrifice.'

The towel fell, her thick brown hair that was still wet and her tears evoked in me a feeling of deep compassion.

'You look so desirable, Masha,' I said. I wanted to tell her that I would love to kiss her.

'Anton, don't say anything more. You are not sober now, but later on you will regret it. You will feel guilty again. You will feel permanently guilty.' Masha smiled.

'I like your face when you are sad but it is more beautiful when you smile.'

'That's better. Continue in this vein and I will not only smile, I will melt.'

'That would be nice in this weather, indicating that the spring is around the corner.'

'The spring is my favourite season, when the lilacs are in bloom.'

'That reminds me that now we have a veritable *myetelitsa*, a snowstorm, and that I should go home.'

I finished my tea and stood up. So did Masha, putting on her fur coat.

'Where are you going?' I asked.

'To bring my favourite *tsaplya* to his nest, otherwise it might be swept away.'

The wind increased in violence and it was so strong that we

were unable to talk as we walked towards my home. As we were only a few steps away from my house, Masha took me in her arms and kissed me on the cheek. I had no chance to kiss her because she ran away and disappeared in a cloud of snow.

Nadya was asleep, when I entered our room. I did not light the lamp, and for a long time I sat in the room thinking about Masha, Vadim, my guilt. Later on in my bed I was still thinking about my life, regretting to have spied on Vadim's secrets and feeling sadness because of Masha.

A few days later Nadya came back from a walk very excited. She put her arms around me and kissed me several times. Before I had the chance to ask her the reason, she exclaimed, 'Maman and Grandpapa are saved! I got word from a cousin of Pani Maicka, a storekeeper. They are in Warsaw, with my father. You see, everything will be all right. For us, too.'

'We have a different problem.'

'Don't worry. We will get the facts about the tank and we will escape. I am sure about that but we must get the information first.'

I was not as sure about our chances as Nadya was, but I was happy for her and her family.

Chapter 15

Berlin, February 23, 1940

In the beginning of February the Soviets mounted a major attack on the Finnish front. Fifteen hundred Soviet tanks were used and their numerical superiority began to gain ground after three months of stalemate. These developments kept Captain von Dolnitz at his desk for long hours, long after his colleagues had left the office. At home he would continue to read reports, magazine articles, and books about tanks. That evening he was re-reading Reynaud's *Le Problème Militaire Français,* when the telephone rang. Von Dolnitz checked his wrist watch: it was a quarter to midnight. He set down the open book on his bedside table and picked up the receiver. It was Wurmlein's voice that said, 'Hello, is that you, Captain?' After von Dolnitz replied 'Yes,' Wurmlein informed him that it was an emergency and that he would pick up the Captain in a few minutes in front of his apartment house.

Von Dolnitz did not have to wait long for the arrival of his superior, whose car stopped abruptly beside the young officer.

Wurmlein, sitting at the wheel, motioned him in.

'The Soviet N.K.V.D. man,' Wurmlein said speeding away, 'is in town. He wants to see us. It is an emergency. He is waiting for us in his room in the Hotel Aiglon.'

'I hoped never to see that man again, Major.'

'It was a vain hope.'

'The Soviets, despite their big effort,' von Dolnitz said, 'have not made much progress on the Finnish front. Maybe Herr Brodilo is looking for our assistance because he may be, as he said, "in a desperate situation." '

Wurmlein said, 'While the Soviets have not shown much skill in operating their tanks, or their new models, thus proving your concern somewhat groundless, I doubt that Herr Brodilo has come to discuss the Finnish war with us. To motivate me getting up from my bed, he mentioned a problem we might have with our neighbour in the West.'

'He obviously means France,' von Dolnitz said, looking at a convoy of military vehicles passing them. 'Does he know about the invasion plans?'

Von Dolnitz was referring to the complete set of the plans for the invasion of France that had fallen into the hands of the Allies on February 5 when a German plane carrying them had crashed in Belgium.

'I don't think so,' Wurmlein said, stepping harder on the gas pedal. 'That would be no news to us. He might suspect as we do that the Allies doubt the authenticity of those documents.'

'The Allies would seek to find out about it,' von Dolnitz said. 'I wonder what Brodilo wants in exchange for the information he might have for us.'

'Not much use to speculate now,' Wurmlein said parking the car at the entrance of the hotel. 'Soon enough we'll find out how the hare runs.'

They traversed the lobby in silence and began to walk up the stairs. Von Dolnitz wondered why he, too, had been invited by

Brodilo. Usually such meetings took place with only one intelligence man from each side. He wanted to ask Wurmlein that question, but it was too late. They were standing at the door of room twenty-three, and Wurmlein was knocking.

Brodilo opened the door. Von Dolnitz noticed that his host wore the same striped double-breasted suit, was freshly shaven and had applied an aromatic after-shave lotion to his face, its pungent aroma filled the room. Brodilo invited them to sit down at a small round table with an oversized ashtray in the middle.

'It is good to have friends,' Brodilo said, smiling at his guests. 'Very good friends. And how does one know how good his friends are? Oh, because they are ready to do things for one – favours.'

Von Dolnitz was annoyed at Brodilo's self-assured manner.

'As soon as I met you,' Brodilo continued, 'I said to myself, I am living at the shore so I talk about ships. These friends live at the shore too, and they must talk about ships, too. So we can talk together ... about our ships.' Speaking in German tired Brodilo, and he paused, trying to express a new thought. Not finding the words he wanted, he said, 'I was impressed by how good and understanding you were.'

'Herr Brodilo,' Wurmlein said, 'enough of this smearing of your honey around our beards. Tell us straight out what you want from us.'

'You see, Herr Major,' Brodilo said, 'I have a boss and you have a boss. I can help you to do what your boss wants, and you can help me too. So you have an advantage and I have an advantage.'

'Sure, Herr Brodilo,' Wurmlein said, 'I don't mind myself to put the sausage in the frying pan on the side where there is more lard. Now tell me what you want to give and for what.'

Brodilo thought for a minute.

'Ha, ha. I got it.' Brodilo laughed. 'It tastes better if it is cooked on the lard side. I like the German language. It is logical, precise, and it allows for some colourful expressions. But it has one deficiency. It is not too imaginative.'

'Why would it be less imaginative than Russian?' von Dolnitz asked surprised.

'I don't know how to say it, Herr von Dolnitz. You see in Russian there is a verb that originally described a sexual relation and now –'

'We have such a verb in German,' von Dolnitz said.

'Yes you do, but you use it only to describe the act of sex, while we use it for all possible purposes. By the way, other languages have the same capacity to use that verb, like French and English, for instance, but not German. That verb allows us to express certain nuances.'

'What nuance do you want to express Herr Brodilo?' von Dolnitz said. 'You can say it in Russian and I will translate it into our language for the Major.'

'It is not so much the nuance – ' Brodilo hesitated, 'but a kind of icebreaker is needed. Talking in Russian with you I would say ta, ta, ta, you guys, ta, ta, ta the world, and we could begin to talk straight as the Major has suggested.'

'I understand you,' von Dolnitz said smiling. 'The ice is broken. All of us are equally ta, ta, ta, guys.'

'Although I don't quite get it,' Wurmlein said, 'go ahead, Herr Brodilo.'

'Then I will,' Brodilo said lighting another cigarette and watching the smoke as he exhaled it. 'Spy for spy.'

'That much I gathered,' Wurmlein said. 'A ship for a ship.'

'You have here in Berlin a small leakage, Herr Wurmlein. The French are very interested. They are about to find out but they don't know it yet.'

Wurmlein and von Dolnitz watched the Russian with great interest. The German attack on France was about to begin, and any leakage of the German plans would cost lives and delays.

'You have a certain plan,' Brodilo said, 'and, mind you, I don't know anything about it. A plan that was prepared by your general ... von Manstein.'

Oh God, von Dolnitz thought, the worst possible leakage. Von Manstein was the author of the new strategy plan of attacking France by first moving the German forces through Holland and Belgium, diverting the enemy, and moving the main force through the Ardennes towards Dunkirk.

'I am interested,' Wurmlein said.

'How much interested?' Brodilo asked screwing up his eyes.

'I am very much interested, Herr Brodilo,' Wurmlein said. Von Dolnitz noticed how Wurmlein had stretched his neck in his eagerness to hear the rest of the deal.

'Good, good,' Brodilo nodded. Then he leaned back. 'In our country we make tea in samovars. By doing that we learned a good lesson. It is not the fire that makes our samovars dirty but the smoke.' Brodilo studied Wurmlein's face. Not being sure that Wurmlein completely understood what he wanted to communicate, he continued: 'The fire is important to heat the water but the smoke is not; the smoke is just a nuisance.'

'So you would like to eliminate some of the smoke with our help, Herr Brodilo,' Wurmlein said.

'Perfect, perfect,' Brodilo said. 'The smoke is visible from afar. Everybody notices it and it stinks. It does not even heat your water for your tea, ha, ha, ha.'

'Let's see,' Wurmlein said, 'whether we could help you get rid of the smoke.'

Brodilo reflected for a moment. 'Well, let me tell you the story,' he said. 'There is a young man who at a certain date crosses the border from our country to your side – and we know the date – and about the same time Herr von Dolnitz leaves Berlin and another gentleman leaves Vienna. That gentleman from Vienna is a good friend.' Brodilo turned to von Dolnitz. 'And a few days later our young man comes back.'

Von Dolnitz's face turned the colour of ashes. There was no doubt that Brodilo was talking about Anton and it was clear now that what Brodilo wanted in exchange for the spy in Germany, was Anton's name and whereabouts. The atmosphere of that room became unbearable to von Dolnitz. He wanted to shout, 'Never, I will not give you that name. I promised.' But he took hold of himself.

'So that is my story,' Brodilo said, smiling.

'Quite a lot of smoke, Herr Brodilo. Let's see how we can clear it out,' said Wurmlein.

'You see, Herr Wurmlein,' Brodilo said, lighting a cigarette, 'you have your boss or bosses, so have I my bosses. And when my bosses know of such a man, they tell me, "Brodilo you must get rid of him soon." And everyone knows about it. So I think and think and say to myself, "I will tell my friends about their hole and they will tell me about mine." It is not good to have even a small hole in one's ship. It might sink it.'

Von Dolnitz stood up and began to pace the room. 'I will not do it,' he said quietly.

Wurmlein and Brodilo exchanged glances.

'I just can't do it,' von Dolnitz repeated.

'We had signed with your country a friendship agreement.' Brodilo was getting tough. 'Your own bosses would not be too happy if they learned about your part in the spying activities, Herr von Dolnitz.'

'You have fabricated the leakage in our country so that you could get that man,' von Dolnitz said. 'The fabricating of false evidence is one of your specialities.'

'I am a professional man,' Brodilo said, 'and I am prepared to give you evidence. If you are not satisfied you can arrest me. After all I am now in your country.'

'What kind of evidence can you give us?' Wurmlein asked.

'There is an X here in Berlin,' Brodilo said, 'who gives facts to Y and Y in turn communicates them to Paris. I am prepared to name both X and Y, and I know that you will find at Y's apartment proof of the leakage.'

Von Dolnitz continued to pace up and down.

'There is always a limit,' he said, 'to what one is prepared to sacrifice, and that limit has been reached.'

Brodilo sat back, and seemed to enjoy the proceedings, like a man who has come to cash his winning ticket and is sure that he will be paid despite the reluctance of the cashier.

'Von Manstein was born here in Berlin as Lewinski,' Brodilo said. 'Then he was adopted by von Manstein. He must be a very smart general to make such an interesting plan of invasion.'

'There are values,' von Dolnitz said, 'above plans. Eternal values that are not negotiable.' Von Dolnitz's pace quickened and he started to shake.

'I am not sure that I understand you, Captain,' Brodilo said, exhaling smoke rings. 'When one decides to walk in a swamp, one has to be ready to get his feet wet.'

The word 'swamp' alerted von Dolnitz. Did Brodilo know that Anton was in Pruzhany?

'Excuse me, Herr Brodilo,' Wurmlein said, standing up. 'If you would not mind, I would like to discuss this matter with Captain von Dolnitz alone.'

'You can use my room,' Brodilo said. 'It is a good idea for you, Major, to have a word in private with the Captain.'

'I am sure that we will sort this thing out among ourselves in a few minutes,' Wurmlein said. 'Drink a glass of beer downstairs, Herr Brodilo, and be sure it's Bavarian beer. I will be ready for you in fifteen minutes.'

Brodilo rose and said, 'It is good to deal with a professional who knows that no matter how excellent a horse, it is still not worth diamond studded horseshoes.'

As soon as Brodilo left, von Dolnitz sat down at the table and opened his collar button.

'It is all a communist plot to catch our spy,' he said. 'And you, Major, are falling for it. They just heard about von Manstein's plan – learned the name, but they don't know any facts. It is more important for us to find out about the Soviet tanks, a new tank, than the whole matter of von Manstein's plan. We can easily win in the West, but the Soviet Union is going to be our main adversary one day. We have a spy in the right spot to get us the facts. Brodilo and his bosses are so concerned because something is going on there with a new tank.'

It was difficult for von Dolnitz to control his emotions; at times he had to stop to gasp for air. Wurmlein sat down facing the captain, and listened with the air of a father hearing his young son telling him in a series of irrational arguments the reasons for not doing his school work.

'And the most important reason of all,' von Dolnitz continued, 'I gave Krugov my German officer's word of honour and I will keep it. There is no other way. We must send Brodilo to hell, to his red hell.'

Wurmlein leaned back, and taking his time lit a cigar. After being satisfied that it was well lit, he said, 'Let me review the matter with you point by point Captain. First, I am your superior officer, and if I give you an order you must execute it. If you disregard it, you will be shot. Let's understand that.'

'There are times – ' von Dolnitz said.

'Don't interrupt me, Captain. Second, we are in a war with France now, and not with the Soviet Union. I agree that it is our duty to be alert and to study the Soviet progress in tanks, but there is a matter of priorities and I am the one to determine these. Any investigation of a leakage of von Manstein's plan must be followed through. The danger of such leakage is too great – as you know, we might be using von Manstein's plan of attack very soon. Third, the Soviets know already about the comings and goings of your spy; somebody must have seen that *dummkopf*; thus his value to us as an agent is limited or nil. As we both know, the Soviets have captured a number of the "Operation Parterre" spies, and it is a matter of a few weeks or even days before they would catch that one anyway.'

'All that you are saying doesn't matter, Herr Major. I was the one to have given – '

'It is *Unfug*, nonsense.'

'We could give Brodilo false information.'

'More nonsense,' Wurmlein said, shaking ashes from his cigar onto the rug. 'Brodilo did not tell us everything he knows. He is keeping a few facts to himself. He would know right away that we are lying. It is childish.'

'We could give him the information and then arrest him,' von Dolnitz said. 'After we had learned about – '

'Captain, you are losing your mind.' Wurmlein said impatiently. 'We had a directive not to send out any new spying missions. You met with the spy, which is all right, but the Soviets know about your meeting, and that is terrible. The sooner the Soviets get your favourite spy the better. That would finish the whole problem for us.'

'I told you, Major, "no". And that stands.'

'You must cooperate.'

'No and it's – '

'I order you to do so.'

'I officially inform you that I am disobeying your order.'

Von Dolnitz picked up his hat and overcoat, and ran towards the door as if he wanted to avoid being stopped by Wurmlein, but the Major did not make any effort to get up and continued to smoke his cigar.

'*Du bist ein Arsch, ein Arsch mit Ohren,*' (You are an arse, an arse with ears), von Dolnitz heard the Major shouting after him as he shut the door. Then he ran down the stairs and into the cold of the February night. Oblivious to the freezing east wind, von Dolnitz went on running, still holding his coat and hat in his hands. He was not cold; on the contrary, he was burning with the rage of somebody cheated of everything that he had ever valued. To be an officer was for von Dolnitz not just a job; for him it was a way of behaving, acting, thinking, a way of life. There were sacred and inviolable rules that had determined for generations what is wrong and what is right, and the only way von Dolnitz could live was according to those rules. He would never break them for anything in this world.

Von Dolnitz did not remember how he reached his apartment.

The open book was still lying on his bedside table. He recalled how a few months ago he was teaching the young Russian émigré the basics of tank designs, and now he was being forced to betray this man, breaking the tradition of the German officer's code of honour.

As he sat down, he asked himself the question, why is no one here to arrest me? Why did Wurmlein not even try to stop me? Now it began to dawn on von Dolnitz that Wurmlein did not really need any facts from him. Wurmlein knew that the spy was located in Pruzhany, and that knowledge would enable him to negotiate with Brodilo. Once Brodilo learned the name of the town where Slavski was located, knowing how he looked, Brodilo could catch him.

'*Schnell*, right away,' von Dolnitz thought. 'I must call Krugov and tell him that his spy in Pruzhany is about to be arrested.' He seized the receiver, a sleepy operator answered, and ten minutes later he learned that Krugov's telephone did not answer. 'Does it really matter?' von Dolnitz asked himself. It would take Krugov several days to communicate with Slavski, much too long to interfere with Brodilo, who had at his disposal all the modern means of communications in his embassy. All Brodilo had to do was to cable a coded message to Moscow 'Pruzhany' and the N.K.V.D. men would start the hunt.

Von Dolnitz went to the window. He wanted to open it, but the blackout regulations required that the light inside must be turned off before opening windows at night. So he switched off the light and opened the window and sat on its sill. The cold wind struck his face. All that he could see was darkness.

How would he be able to face Krugov again? Would it matter that somebody else had betrayed Slavski? It was still a German officer who had done it. How would Captain von Dolnitz be ever able to live with himself, without self respect and without honour?

There was only one answer. Von Dolnitz strode to the bookshelf. His hand picked up the revolver. The sensation of the cold steel in his hand was reassuring.

Von Dolnitz stood in the middle of the room facing the open window. For a split second he had an urge to close it, but he said to himself that it did not matter. Then he pulled the trigger.

Chapter 16
Anton's Story

Pruzhany, February 20, 1940
After Vadim left, I tried to find another commander with whom I would be able to drink vodka and talk about tanks. From Vadim I had learned about the existence of the T-34 tank and about the arrival of General Khomikov in Pruzhany, in late February, possibly indicating a test here. It was, in my opinion, a considerable achievement, but at the same time I knew that it was of limited value. All the nations of the world test new weapons that often appear defective during the test and the engineers are sent back to their drawing boards. It often happens that the deficiency cannot be corrected and the projects are abandoned. Would that happen to the T-34? In that case my efforts would have been worthless. From my talks with Vadim, I had concluded that the T-34 might be a dramatic departure in tank design, but I was not sure. So, in spite of the snow I kept trying to learn where another tank officer might live so that I could get acquainted with him.

Walking around the town, I tried to stop a few tankers, asking them for a light or a cigarette, but to my disappointment, none of them was eager to start a conversation in a heavy snowfall and a freezing wind. After two hours of this fruitless effort, feeling numbness in my fingers and toes, I decided to go home. It was getting dark. As I was approaching my house I recognised Franek, standing several metres away from it.

'I thought you would never come home,' he said.

His cap was covered with snow and he was shivering. 'Tomorrow night at eight,' he continued. 'There will be an important meeting.'

'Could we handle it in some other way,' I asked looking around. 'I don't like these meetings – they are too dangerous.'

'This time we must. In Krystyna's house. There will be only seven of us.'

I knew that some of the members had been deported with their families, arrests that had nothing to do with their underground activities. Some had left Pruzhany, either to escape to the western part of Poland occupied by the Germans, or to areas occupied by the Soviets.

'I thought that there were Soviets billeted in her house.'

'They will be away.'

'I'll come, then,' I said, shaking Franek's hand.

Nadya was upset to learn about the meeting of the Polish underground.

'The timing is very bad. But I'm going to the meeting with you.'

'But they consider you –'

'Oh, no, I'm your wife now. I can come.'

I was not happy about her decision, but I knew I would not be able to change her mind. So we arranged to have Avram watch Magda and we went together to the meeting.

Krystyna greeted us. If she was upset about Nadya's arrival, she didn't show it. Everybody else was most polite to Nadya. While we waited for Stach, we talked about the Soviet occupation and its horrors. Everyone regretted the absence of Halinka, who had been deported with her father a month ago.

As soon as Stach arrived, Franek began. 'I am pleased to greet Nadya Slavska, who had the foresight and the courage to remove the files of Poles who were politically active before the war. Her act has saved many lives, and helped us to avoid enrolling suspect members.'

Everyone looked at Nadya, who was blushing.

'We are meeting tonight for a most important reason. As all of you know, for the last three months Finland, a country of four million people, has been bravely resisting the attack of the Soviets who are thirty times stronger in numbers. General Sikorski, the head of our Polish armed forces in England, has decided to help the Finns. At the very outbreak of hostilities Sikorski offered to take our navy from the French harbours and send the ships to defend Finland, but the French refused to let them leave. But now the English are ready to send an expeditionary force to defend the Finns, and our brothers in England will join them.'

Everyone was listening. No one interrupted Franek's speech with questions or comments. I was curious to find out the real purpose of the meeting. Franek could not possibly have summoned us to tell us about the Poles defending the Finns.

'Polish blood shed on the snow of Finland will help free our country. In the past we fought for the freedom of other countries and regained our own independence. Now we have another opportunity to do so. Polish blood shed in the battle for Finland's freedom will help us to win our own.' Franek looked at us for a moment. 'It is important that we who have stayed behind in occupied Poland join that fight for freedom. We must try to go to Finland to fight on the side of the Polish forces there.'

'But how can we go there?' Stach asked. 'We would have to go hundreds of kilometres through enemy territory.'

'Well, then we must make our way through enemy territory. For instance, we could try to make our way through the Soviet Union and then cross the front. But that would be practically impossible, I admit. The other way would be to cross the border to the German side of Poland, make our way to the Baltic, seize a boat and reach Finland.'

'You think that's possible?' Stach asked.

'There might be casualties, but it could be done.'

The whole idea was unrealistic. Recent articles in the Soviet press reported that Sweden and Norway were refusing passage to Finland. Besides, the Soviet offensive was gathering momentum and the war in Finland might be finished before we could arrive there, not to speak of our chances of surviving such a journey. I exchanged a glance with Nadya who appeared quite interested in the proceedings.

'Have you received a directive for us to move?' Andrzej, a student of medicine, asked.

'No, not yet,' Franek said. 'It is our own local initiative. We have the responsibility to initiate.'

Nadya said to Franek, 'Have you worked out the details of such an expedition?'

'I have, up to the point of reaching the West. I assume that there we would get in touch with the local underground for further assistance.'

'Can you tell us those details?' Nadya asked.

'But we have not yet decided to do it,' I said.

'It is important to hear them,' Nadya said, tugging at my sleeve. 'Before we decide, we should evaluate the difficulties.'

'I'll tell you,' said Franek. 'I've talked to a few guys who crossed recently. First take the train to Brest and change there for Bialystok. Change again and go as far west as you can go. I say that because usually the border guards chase you from that train a few kilometres after Bialystok. Make your way to a village, kilometres through fields, the last four or five kilometres are kilometress through fields, the last four or five kilometres are difficult: kilometre five, four and three before the border is all thicket – dwarf pines, juniper, that kind of stuff. That's why this crossing area is recommended. Those bushes provide good cover.'

'For romance?' Nadya asked.

'And the last two kilometres,' Stach said, 'you provide targets for the Soviet border police.'

'If you decide to walk through swamps,' Nadya said, 'don't be afraid to get your feet wet.'

'Sometimes you do,' Franek said. 'There is one kilometre and a half of open fields. There are towers every 500 metres with floodlights making a full circle every minute and covering approximately a radius of 250 metres.'

Nadya said, 'All possible comforts. The Soviets provide the light.'

Stach said, 'That's when you make yourself invisible.'

'Even with the floodlights they might not see you. The human attention span isn't so great that those guys can watch effectively all the time. When the floodlight is approaching you freeze. After the fields you reach the woods, about 400 metres in breadth. Then there is a zone of fifty to a hundred metres, where the police patrol with dogs. You cross it when there is no one around, preferably at a run. Finally there's a barbed wire fence, about five metres high, and if you can climb it, you are on the other side.'

'Where you are greeted by a friendly Gestapo officer who shoots you down!' said Andrzej.

'They don't seem to bother the escapees,' Franek said.

'Not right away,' Stach said.

'The recommended time for crossing the last zone is four o'clock in the morning. That's all I know.'

I thought the situation on the border has changed a lot since my last crossing. It was clever of Nadya to ask about it. Soon I would have enough facts about the tanks and then we would be ready to leave. But could I do it with Nadya? And Magda?

'As I see it,' Andrzej said, 'crossing the border, with all these problems, is just a small part of the journey. I don't mind participating in a dangerous mission, but an effort of this scope should be ordered by headquarters. I don't think it should be made on local initiative.'

Andrzej seemed to express the feeling of the majority.

'Are there any contacts on the way?' I asked. Franek frowned. 'What if we should get in trouble on the way – need money, information, anything?'

'There is a restaurant in Brest, "Pod Debem". If you want help, you can go there and order vodka with a piece of *kobanos* (a thin dry sausage), which is not available. Someone might approach you if you ask a few times for it, and if – '

'And if a Soviet commissar does not appear to arrest you,' Nadya said, 'you might be lucky.'

All of us laughed.

'Anyway we will fight against *Sowieckie czolgi* in Finland,' Franek said, 'and we will win.'

I had heard the Polish word for tank, *czolg*, often, but never thought about its real meaning: "crawler" quite a fitting name, I said to myself.

The formal part of the meeting was over. Krystyna served us tea with hard, homemade cookies. Andrzej was telling us about his friend, a doctor from Grodno, who had been deported with his family three months ago, got ill, and was able to escape with the help of a Soviet doctor.

'You know what they did to him? They took him and other Poles, doctors, lawyers, teachers, and their families and they displayed them like wild animals in an arena, where N.K.V.D. men were telling the assembled people, "Here are the bloodsuckers of the proletariat. Our victorious Red Army liberated the working people from their yoke." They travelled in a cattle train from place to place. Later on they were sent to labour camps.'

'Please don't say Russians, Andrzej,' Nadya interrupted. 'The name is Soviets, a clique and ideology foreign to Russia, subjugating and exploiting the Russian people.'

'But still,' Stach said, 'the majority of them are Russians.'

'There are Poles among them, too,' Nadya said. 'The first two heads of the Soviet secret police were Poles, Dzierzynski and Mierzynski.'

'Nadya is right,' Franek said. 'Our hope of liberation lies in the Poles and the Russians uniting to destroy the Soviet regime.'

'Even with the help of the Germans?' I asked.

'Yes, even with the help of the Germans. Then we would have only one enemy to deal with.'

I knew that we could spend all night discussing these things, but I felt that it would be wise to leave as soon as possible. So, after I had kissed the hands of all the girls and all the men had kissed Nadya's, we left.

As soon as we were outside, in the cold wind of a clear winter night, Nadya said, 'An instructive meeting. I wouldn't mind going to Finland.'

'But you know it is unrealistic.'

'We could cover part of the way.'

I was about to answer when I noticed two men standing a few metres ahead of us. As we approached them, I recognised one of them as the commissar, Lobin, the keynote speaker at the election gathering. He looked straight at us. 'Pani Slavski,' he said, with a strong dose of irony.

After we had walked far enough not to be overheard, Nadya asked who he was and I told her.

'That's no coincidence,' Nadya said. 'Even for a Soviet commissar it's too cold to be standing in this wind just for a breath of fresh air.'

I agreed and did not like it. I knew that our time was limited, and that we must run soon.

The next day I was out again, trying to find another tank officer, but my efforts turned out to be fruitless. Disappointed with my lack of success I decided to go home. Passing the former City Hall, to my surprise I saw the tailor who had once bought my clothing in Brest.

'What are you doing here?' I asked, approaching him.

In the light of the gas lamp I could see that he looked emaciated and sick. On seeing me he began to shake. He seemed to be trying to say something, but no words came out.

'I am sorry,' I said. 'You look frozen. May I help you to a warm place?' He shook his head. 'You could come with me and share a hot meal with us.'

'No, no,' he said. 'Go, go.' He appeared to be suffering terribly.

Since he didn't want to come with me I continued on my way home. I turned around a few moments later, but he was no longer there. His presence in Pruzhany began to worry me. Why was he here? Was it possible that the Soviets had discovered my letter? But how would they know that I was in Pruzhany? As I remembered there was nothing in the letter about Pruzhany. On the other hand he had looked so strange. I decided to share my anxiety with Nadya.

As I entered our room, Nadya and Magda were busy preparing the Lenten borscht, without cream or meat. Nadya was shredding cabbage and Magda was throwing it into a steaming pot. The room smelled of cooked buckwheat, beets and cabbage. Both of them seemed to enjoy their work, and they were so cheerful that I did not have the heart to spoil their joy by talking about the tailor.

First I had a glass of hot tea. Later on we enjoyed the dinner that Magda served us, even without the meat it tasted so good that each of us had three helpings.

After Magda had fallen asleep, I told Nadya about my recent encounter. My story startled her. Seeing her reaction, I said, 'We should run now.'

'If what you are assuming is true, then it's too late,' she said.

'By running right away we might – '

' – kill our chances,' Nadya finished the sentence. 'We would all be arrested right away. If you are a suspect, they will want to watch you and try to discover other spies through you. If we use our brains we could take advantage of that time to find a way out.'

I knew that Nadya was right. To quieten myself I began to re-read *The Possessed*. Reading it now in a Communist land I admired Dostoyevsky's genius in being able to anticipate the hell created by the revolutionaries. Nadya, who had begun to mend Magda's dress, asked me to read aloud.

As I was finishing the second chapter, there was a knock at our door. As a violinist can distinguish the slightest differences of tone in his strings, I could differentiate among the knocks at our door. This time the knock was unfamiliar. We exchanged glances.

'Come in,' I said.

The door opened and a squarish man in his early thirties walked in. He had bushy brown hair and was of medium height. His face was broad with slanting eyes – that of a typical Soviet man, of peasant stock.

'I came to ask you if you have any hot water.' As he spoke he showed two upper front teeth capped with white metal. 'I saw the light. Avram is asleep. I'm a new tenant here. I have the alcove assigned by the Komandantura. My name is Oleg Akimovich Vashin.'

I was looking at Nadya. She appeared to recognise him.

'I am Nadya, and this is Anton, my husband. You are welcome to have tea with us.'

'Thank you, Nadya.'

She motioned him the chair at the table, but Vashin hesitated.

'If it is not too much bother,' he said, 'I would like to wash my hands before I sit down at the table.'

'It will be my special pleasure to give you a fresh towel, Oleg Akimovich.' Nadya handed him our best linen towel. 'Here is our best soap, or whatever is left of it.'

Vashin slowly applied the soap to his hands. 'What excellent soap you have here!'

'That's almond soap, the last we have,' Nadya said. 'Would you like to have some hot water to wash in?'

'Hot water would waste too much of this soap. Cold water will do.'

He took his time drying his hands.

'I hope you will acept this.' Vashin pulled out of a box from his side pocket a fist-sized lump of sugar, and set it down in the middle of the table.

'You must be new in Pruzhany,' Nadya said. 'I have never seen you before.'

'Yes, I arrived only yesterday.'

'From where?' Nadya asked, sitting down next to Vashin.

'From Moscow,' Vashin said. He seemed to be surprised by Nadya's question and appeared to regret his answer.

'From our capital city!' Nadya exclaimed. 'How vey interesting. It is so nice to have a neighbour a *Moskvich* (inhabitant of Moscow). We seldom meet such interesting people here. Pruzhany must be quite disappointing to you.'

'I am not a native of Moscow. I was born in a place even smaller than Pruzhany.'

'Are you employed here?' I entered the conversation with that question. Vashin hesitated.

'Yes, the Post Office, a sort of inspector,' he said.

'Will you stay here for long?' I asked.

Nadya seemed to be displeased with my participation in the talk and she interrupted me. 'Although our town is dreary, I hope your stay here will be most enjoyable.'

'As I told you, I like small places,' Vashin said, gulping the tea.

'Tell us everything about Moscow!' Nadya said. 'For us, the inhabitants of God-forsaken Pruzhany, a visitor from Moscow is heaven-sent, unique and a visitor who knows the finer things in life too, even good soap.'

Vashin looked at Nadya. He seemed to feel uneasy. I thought his cheeks reddened.

'And so you like our Pruzhany?' Nadya asked, smiling at Vashin.

'It is a town,' Vashin mumbled.

'A *Moskvich* calls Pruzhany a town, ha, ha, ha,' Nadya said. 'How funny! What a sense of humour! We are very, very honoured.'

I did not find his remark funny and was surprised at Nadya's reaction. Vashin appeared embarrassed and did not seem to know what to say next.

'So when I visit you in Moscow,' she said, 'and you will invite me of course, Oleg Akimovich, then I will feel after having been in this town, as if I were in Paradise. Right?'

Two hours later, after the three of us had drunk five glasses of tea each, with Nadya talking most of the time and laughing and smiling a lot, Vashin left, but only after he had solemnly promised Nadya to call on us the next evening.

I could hear Vashin beyond the wall, walking around where a bed had been prepared for him.

'You seem to like our new neighbour, Nadya,' I said in a whisper.

She was washing up the tea glasses.

'I know I have met one of the most important men in my life,' she said.

'You are trying to get even for my friendship with Masha. That's childish.' I was annoyed with her for flirting with the newcomer.

'I am serious about what I just said. He will be the most important man in your life, too, Anton.'

'That kind of talk is not even dignified.'

'He would be one of the most important men in your life if you had never met me.'

'Nadya, I'm tired. That boor kept me from going to bed early, but you enjoyed his company, and now you are playing games. I want to sleep.'

'If I tell you the truth, Anton, you won't be able to sleep all night.'

'And you, Nadya? Will you be able to fall asleep? Perhaps you will, and then you can dream of the *Moskvich*.'

'I am pleased to note that you are also jealous, except that the timing and the reason are wrong. He is . . . ' Nadya lowered her voice, 'an N.K.V.D. agent.'

'What? Are you sure? How can you?'

'The night we were returning from the Polish meeting, there was a man standing with Lobin. It was Vashin.'

'Oh God. You and Magda must run away at once. You would have a few days' start. It's too late for me.'

I could not stand. I had to sit down. Would Nadya be able to escape with Magda? Would Vashin arrest me right away? How soon would I be executed? When I took the assignment I was ready to die any time; that is the risk a spy takes. But then I did not have Nadya and Magda. I looked at Nadya, who was preparing our bed. She seemed to be in a good humour.

'I worry, Nadya, I worry so much and you are so calm.'

I stood up and poured myself a glass of water, gulping it down.

'Worrying is not going to solve anything, Anton. We must fight back.'

'And you recognised him from the moment he crossed the threshold. You greeted him.'

'Even the chicken fights back when the falcon comes to the chicken coop. That was my way of defending us. Had I shown fear, he would have known that I recognised him. This way we might have a chance to delay.'

'What for?'

Nadya turned down the lamp and began to undress.

'You must think and make a plan, an original, terrific plan that will save all of us. You know how to think. You have had good training with all those chess problems.'

'The best plan is for you and Magda to run away right now, tomorrow morning. And I'll stay here.'

'That's not a good plan. It's king's sacrifice, the end of the game, and a loss. It won't do. I think that the most important element of your plan should be getting hold of the plans of the T-34 tank.'

'Oh, Nadya! We must forget them now. Our problem is to escape, to survive,' I whispered. But Nadya looked very disappointed.

'We must get the plans, Anton, and take them to the Germans. It is crucial for our flight and the freedom of our fatherland. We are on the right track now and we mustn't give up. Imagine our country free, people living without fear, and us living among them no longer the despised refugees. Stealing those plans is our only hope.'

'But it's too late.'

'It's never too late. I will help you, Anton. You can count on me. I could set fire to a building where those officers would be meeting, and steal that bag for you. Or dress in a Soviet uniform, getting entry into their meeting.'

'That's not very realistic. It's impossible,' I said.

'Try to sleep now. The morning will bring cleverer thoughts than the night. Then you'll figure it out.'

For a long time I kept turning in bed, imagining Nadya and Magda exhibited as bloodsuckers of the people, or working in snow and cold in a Siberian labour camp. I thought of Krugov's words: 'They shoot well, they've had a lot of experience.' Would I be facing an execution squad or would Vashin shoot me down? Alone?

A dream of Nadya and Magda escaping through snow and ice, while I was trying to catch up with them, awoke me. Nadya was up already, but Magda was still asleep.

'I heard Vashin leaving,' Nadya said. 'We can talk the whole thing over reasonably now.'

I said, 'We have a few days left because they want to find out who our friends are. We must warn them secretly.'

'Lobin must know about the Poles,' Nadya said. 'I told

Krystyna about our meeting him after the evening in her house, but Franek felt it might still be a false alarm.'

'You must tell Krystyna right away that all those who were at her house that night must leave Pruzhany today. If they can't they shouldn't sleep at home tonight and they should get out of Pruzhany as soon as possible. I think they anticipated an emergency like this. And Boris and Gleb were transferred a few months ago. Possibly they're fighting somewhere in Finland. I think they'll be safe, at least from their own authorities. No one saw me with Vadim. I went often to Father Yacov's house, but so did hundreds of parishioners. That leaves Avram, who could move in with some member of his family in another town, and Masha –'

At hearing Masha's name, Nadya made a face as if she had swallowed a glass of lemon juice.

'But why her? No one knows about your special friendship with her. By seeing her, you might even endanger her.'

'I still think I should tell Masha. I'll see.'

I felt it would be essential for me to see Masha; she might be able to give me information about Khomikov. Nadya looked sad, and she began to wheeze. She grew pale, and for a moment the image of her carrying a heavy load in a Siberian labour camp crossed my mind.

'I will get those tanks plans for you, for us, Nadya. We'll escape with them. Everything will be all right.'

'The fact that you say "all right" shows that you doubt it, but I don't Anton. I know for sure that we'll make it. *Omnia vincit amor*, might be an old Latin cliché but I firmly believe it. Do you?'

'I do Nadya, I do.'

'Then I am reassured. And now I must return to more prosaic matters, like fixing breakfast.'

It was cosy in our room warmed by the fire Nadya had started in the stove. She wore a woollen sweater, and she was moving around in her house shoes, which made her appear smaller and weaker. I noticed that she had covered the table with a fresh linen cloth that she reserved for festive occasions. Usually my breakfast was two slices of bread with prune butter or apple preserves, but this morning there was a piece of sausage added to the menu, a rare luxury.

I didn't have to ask why. Without words, both of us knew that from now on every meal we ate might be our last one together. The same might be true of every hour together, every moment. That added another dimension to everything I saw, smelled, heard, touched, felt. Every detail became significant. I saw Nadya placing an empty tea glass on a saucer, a gesture she had made hundreds of times before, but now I noticed her fingers around the glass, long, graceful, holding it in a way that struck me to the heart.

I went over to her to embrace her. I loved to do that. But this time the joy of it was magnified thousands of times, as if this one touch of her lips must stand for the millions of kisses that would not happen. There was no need for me to tell her that I loved her or for her to say so. She knew I did. I knew she did. I felt as if our two souls experienced in their depths a resonance that made words superfluous.

We sat in silence. But from our innermost selves we shouted to each other: 'It cannot be: we must live on, together. Anton will find a plan to save us, all of us, that's the only thing that counts. A plan, Anton's plan will save us from the Red Hell.'

But what plan? What chance did I have now that Vashin, an N.K.V.D. commissar, was about to arrest me? Pruzhany, a town in the midst of nowhere, with one narrow gauge train once a day, connecting with the regular train several kilometres away, the two roads out of town both snowed in and impassable except for tanks or heavy-tracked vehicles. We could hide perhaps one or two days with someone who would himself run the risk of death for giving us shelter. And that was it.

A number of fantastic ideas crossed my mind; confessing to Vashin that I was a spy, and telling him the truth, in every detail. But of course that would not work. I would be interrogated for months and eventually executed, while Nadya would be deported. Or we could run away tonight together. But that would not work either. Provided we could survive a night outdoors, particularly Nadya, we would be captured at dawn. Another idea, to force a pilot at gunpoint to fly us out of the country, was even more ridiculous.

Deep in my thoughts as if in a thick cloud, I was aware that in the meantime we had finished breakfast. Magda had awakened and got up. She had had breakfast and left with Nadya.

Pacing the floor, I was still thinking when Nadya returned, alone.

'I left Magda to play at Avram's. Then I warned Krystyna, and she will spread the word to the others. Any progress?'

'Only some vague beginnings.'

'Did you re-study all your mental chess games with the queen sacrifice?' Nadya asked, taking off her overcoat.

'No, I didn't. Our problem isn't like a game of chess. We have a double objective: to get the tank specifications and to escape. In chess you win by getting the king. Most of the time I was thinking of ways to flee. But none of them would work.'

Nadya began to unpack some purchases. I resumed pacing up and down.

'Perhaps I should consider the two aspects of our problem as one,' I said, looking at Nadya who had started to shred some cabbage. 'I must tie our escape plans to the tank documents – benefit in some way from our eventual possession of these documents in our escape. It's like using the wind blowing against you. If you're a good sailor you can do it.'

'I would like to suggest that the fresh air might help you in your mental exercise. Take a walk! It's nice outside.'

I agreed with her. It would be interesting to see if anyone followed me. But there was nobody standing in front of our house, and later on, while walking for two or three hours, I could not see anybody following me. Being cold and hungry, and, having made no progress in my plans, I decided to return home.

As I entered my room it was so changed in decor that I hardly recognised it. On the wall were large, newly-painted posters showing couples dancing in Tyrolean hats. In style it was an interesting combination of early Byzantine with Art Nouveau. The faces of the men looked like those of saints, and the women had faces more like the women on the posters of Alphonse Mucha than like those of Austrian mountaineers. The table had been moved to the corner, the beds were by the walls, and the light of our kerosene lamp was shaded with a band of red, transparent paper. On one of the beds was a hand-operated victrola. The greatest change was in Nadya's and Magda's clothing. They wore long skirts, but in the skimpy light I could not tell what material they were made of.

'I'm stunned. What's going on here?'

'You are now in the Café des Artistes in Vienna, 1941,' Nadya said to me. Then turning to Magda, '*Fraulein Magda, Musik, bitte.*'

Magda turned the victrola crank, and the screechy sound of the Polish tango, '*Jest Jedna Jedyna*,' filled the room.

'Aren't you going to invite me to dance?' Nadya asked.

'Yes, yes,' I said throwing my coat on the bed and taking Nadya into my arms. 'What's the reason for the celebration?'

Nadya smiled, I was sure that she had arranged it because she had wanted to go with me to such a Viennese *Kaffeehaus*, and now she didn't know if we would ever make it.

'Can you guess, Anton?'

'I think so.'

'I think you are wrong, Anton.'

'Why?'

'Because you looked sad.'

'Should I have looked happy, Nadya?'

'Of course, darling, very happy,' Nadya said as we went on dancing. 'I had a reason. I wanted to show you how magnificent our life will be.'

The music stopped. Much moved, I kissed Nadya. And holding hands, we went to the table by the wall.

'Fraulein Magda,' Nadya said, '*Bitte, zwei Vodka Zakooska.*'

'*Ja, Ja*,' Magda said cheerfully, bringing the two filled glasses and a plate of small canapes.

'Thank you, Magda,' I said.

'You are very welcome, most distin ... distinger ... ' Magda said, 'Nadya told me to tell you that Papa, distinger ... what is that?'

'Distinguished, Magda,' I said. 'A man who has done many important things, or who looks as if he has.'

'Have you done important things?' Magda asked.

'In this scenario you did, Anton. You are an author, a novelist.'

'I couldn't possibly be a novelist now that I'm no longer lonely. I'm happy.'

'Do novelists have to be lonely?' Nadya asked.

'Writing a novel is a way, I think, to overcome one's loneliness, or to be with a person one loves when that's impossible in real life.'

'And you have no urge to write, Anton?' Nadya asked, smiling, and with a touch of irony in her voice.

'No. What kind of books would I write?'

'That's for the author to decide. What kind would you like to write?'

'Fables, I guess,' I said, looking at Magda, who was watching the proceedings with curiosity. 'About a man who meets a little princess, takes her to his castle where she cooks for him, cleans his castle, makes it into a nice home – but something very important is missing in their life.'

'What is missing?' Magda asked, her wide eyes fixed upon me. 'Tell us, Papa, what is missing?'

'Let's drink a toast to "what was missing in this man's life."' I raised my glass, looking at Nadya.

'I drink to the author,' she said, raising hers.

'The Fairy Queen was missing, but –'

'What is a Fairy Queen?' Magda asked.

'A beautiful woman who has magical powers. Anyway she comes to the castle, the man married her.'

'One thing more is needed in this fable,' Nadya said. 'You forgot to mention love. The Fairy Queen must have been very much in love with the man to come and marry him.'

The birch wood in the stove was crackling and making the room warm and cosy while the wind was buffeting the windows.

'I wanted to tell a happy story. Most of the books about love are sad.'

'That is the challenge for you, Anton, to write about happy love. You are too much influenced by the Russian literature of the nineteenth century.'

'But that would be boring to the reader. Happy love is static.'

'Oh, no Anton, on the contrary,' Nadya said. 'Love is finding out about each other, each act of discovery more exciting and beautiful than the last one. It is growing up and sharing together in learning about the world around. It is dynamic; there is nothing static about happy love.'

'I want to hear more about the Fairy Queen,' Magda said.

'You will,' I said. 'My fable is all about her. But first I must ask if they serve any food in the Café des Artistes?'

'We have a menu,' Nadya said handing me a painted sheet in the Byzantine-Art Nouveau style:

'La soupe: Borshtshok Russe à la Karobochka, aux legumes variés et aux herbes fines qu'a pu acheter à Pruzhany.

'L'entrée: la viande de boeuf bouillie à la Pushkin, à la sauce de radis noir? Fort, obtenue en échange: changée contre les bas soie de Nadya.

'Le dessert: Confitures de Cérises à la Sobakevich obtenue

pour les dits bas du vendeur ressemblant beaucoup à M. Sobakevich.

'Les Boisson: le thè Chichikov.'

'What an excellent menu,' I exclaimed. 'How wonderful to be in the Café des Artistes! But why all these dishes dedicated to the characters of *Dead Souls*?'

'So that we should be reminded of Gogol's message: "Be the living souls, and not the dead ones." Do you agree, Anton?'

'And the Fairy Queen?' Magda asked. 'I want to hear about her. More about her, please, please!'

'I promise to tell you the end of the story after dinner,' I said.

I kept my promise. After dinner we sat down on our bed, Magda on my lap, and Nadya leaning against me, her hair against my cheek.

The fire in the stove had burned out, but the wind was rattling the windows even harder.

'The man was happy living with his Queen and his Princess. They loved each other very much. Whenever he looked at the Queen, she appeared to him to be still more beautiful. Whenever he talked to her, she surprised him anew with the brilliance of her mind. Whenever he held her hand he felt anew how noble her heart was and how deep her soul. So they lived happily, but one day the bad wolves surrounded the castle: they wanted to eat the man, his Queen and the Princess. The man feared for the safety of the Queen and the Princess.'

'What did he do to save them?' Magda asked.

'The Queen inspired the man to do the impossible. He threw out of the window a piece of meat drenched in a sleeping potion. The wolves ate the meat and fell asleep.'

As the author of that story, I was not quite sure how to finish it happily.

'While the wolves were asleep, the man went out and stole a lamb. The wolves wanted that lamb very much. So the man and his Queen and his Princess packed up their things and left the castle and started to run away.'

'And what then?' Magda asked.

'They were running through the storm, a snowstorm, holding the lamb, and the wolves, the entire pack, were chasing them. They came so close that the three of them could hear the wolves' paws striking on the ice as they ran, and could smell their breath.

And then the man threw the lamb to them. And all the wolves jumped on the lamb, and forgot the man, his Queen and his Princess, who escaped far, far away into the Café des Artistes. That is the end of the story.'

'Poor little lamb, alone among the wolves,' Magda said. 'What happened to it?'

'It's late, and I'll tell you that story some other time,' I said, knowing that I had exhausted my literary imagination.

'Café des Artistes reminds me,' Nadya said, 'that we do not want Vashin there. I must change the decor of our castle.'

After re-arranging our room and putting Magda to bed, Nadya and I settled at the table with our books. I went on reading *The Possessed,* and I noticed that Nadya had a copy of Gogol's *The Inspector General.*

It was so nice for the two of us to be together that I hated the idea of Vashin coming tonight.

'Why Vashin?' I said aloud. 'What am I going to talk about to him?'

'You don't need to talk to him,' Nadya said.

'You will, then?'

'Yes. But you could play a game of chess with him. While decorating our room as the Café des Artistes I modernised your chess set.'

'I am sure that some of the pieces will look like Byzantine Saints and others –'

'I said *modernised,* Anton.'

'May I see them?'

'At the right moment,' Nadya said, going back to her book.

It was much later than we had expected, almost 11 o'clock at night when Vashin arrived.

After an exchange of greetings and some more talk about Pruzhany, Nadya asked him, 'Are all those letters keeping you late?'

'What letters?' Vashin asked.

'You are the postal inspector,' Nadya said. 'Thanks to your job we can get all the news.'

Vashin nodded. He was even in a less talkative mood than last night. I was wishing that he would go when Nadya asked him, 'Will you play a game of chess, Oleg Akimovich? Anton is a good player.'

'*Mozhno*,' Vashin said nodding, 'that's possible.'

'We have only a homemade set,' I said.

'That will be all right,' Vashin said. 'I'm used to playing with homemade chess sets.'

Nadya brought the box with a mysterious smile on her face that I could not fathom. But when she opened the box I understood. She had repainted the black chessmen red. As we were setting up the game, I also noticed that she had sculptured a new design for the red pieces.

'Chess is one of the oldest games of conflict,' Nadya said when I looked at her in surprise. 'I thought it might help to make it more realistic. It is ridiculous, these days to have a red king so I replaced it with the Secretary of the Communist party.' I looked at Vashin who appeared embarrassed but tried to control himself. 'Similarly the *dama* "the queen", the most effective piece on the board, is an anachronism in the new proletarian reality, so she is replaced by an N.K.V.D. man.'

Vashin moved his chair but still did not say anything. He looked at the board, and seemed not to have heard Nadya's words.

'Please, Nadya,' I said, 'we are now ready to play. We should draw for which side we'll play.'

'Just draw lots for who will begin,' Nadya said. 'I made the set so Tovarich Vashin would feel more at home with the red pieces.'

Vashin began. He was a conservative player and started out with the knight opening. I did the same. Vashin took a long time to deliberate on each of his moves, but his moves were good. He did not hesitate to exchange pieces. In the middle game I was able to exchange my bishop for two of his pawns.

It was an excellent idea for me to play chess with Vashin; in that way you learn a lot about how your adversary's mind works. I found that Vashin was a player who minimised his risks. All his pieces at all times were disposed so as to protect one another. He thought out his moves well in advance. Despite my many years of experience with chess, we seemed evenly matched.

Nadya was silent, reading a book. Since she often skipped pages and looked our way, I knew that she was bored and would rather have participated in the game. After a while she could not stand it any longer, and putting the book away she came over to us.

'Who is winning?'

'The game is undecided as yet,' I said.

'Oh, I can see that all your tanks are still on the board.'

'What tanks?' Vashin asked.

'Of course the rooks are the tanks. Originally they were moving towers built of wood and pushed by manpower. That technique has made progress – the modern version is a tank of steel propelled by engines.' Vashin glanced at her.

'The next time I will try to make the pieces look like the real tanks, like your T-28s or, even more modern, your T-32, T-33, T-34.'

Vashin's body jerked as if he had been struck by lightning. Drops of sweat appeared on his forehead.

'Or T-35, T-36 or whatever other numbers you have. It should be your choice.'

'Nadya, you are making it difficult for Oleg to concentrate.'

'I apologise and withdraw.' She returned to sit on our bed and resume her reading.

The game went on. We exchanged queens (his N.K.V.D. man for my queen) and one rook each. I was able to make some little progress on the right side of my board, moving two pawns protected by my king. Vashin had to commit his remaining rook to stop them. That enabled me to make progress with a single pawn protected by my rook, and he was left to defend the position with his bishop. As the game neared the end Vashin was taking more time to make his moves.

I knew I had the strategy to win the game, but still I did not know how to solve the problem of our own escape, how to save Nadya, Magda, and myself. Looking at the board, I found a light beginning to dawn: as on this board, when there were two separate actions I ought to separate from Nadya. Vashin was concentrating on me. I was the chief suspect, a spy for 'Operation Parterre'. All his energies would be devoted to me, but the pawn on the other side that I could exchange for a queen was the winning piece. In order to stop that pawn he must free the pawns on the right side and leave the king unprotected. If I could in reality switch the main attraction to Nadya, I would be tied down for a while, but I would escape since his attention would be transferred to Nadya. But only something very important would make him do that, something vital. Such as? Such as the plans for the new tank, such as General Khomikov's papers!

I got so excited about the idea that I paid little attention to the game. I was beginning to shape the scenario. I steal the papers in the briefcase, and give the documents to Nadya. Vashin assumes that the papers are in my possession and arrests me. In the meantime Nadya escapes with the documents. The only chance Vashin has to recover the papers then is to release me, hoping I'll lead him to Nadya and the stolen secrets. Of course there were dangers – the key problem was that Vashin was going to watch me and follow me with a number of agents whom I would have to elude. But at least we would switch the action to another location, to other towns and places away from the locked-in situation in Pruzhany.

I was so pleased with myself that I was not shocked when I heard Vashin saying, '*Shakh ee mutt*!' I had lost the chess game, but I might win the game for our survival.

Vashin did not want to stay for the tea that Nadya offered to make for us. As soon as he left, I said, 'I love you Nadya, although you were playing a dangerous game yourself with all this chess commissar business.'

'It doesn't help the mouse to say meow when she is in the cat's clutches. Despite my diversionary tactics, you lost.'

'But darling, I think I have the plan.'

Lying in bed together, I told it to Nadya. We talked about it for a long time. Nadya did not like the idea that as part of the plan I would be caught and arrested. But I told her that would hardly be different from the situation now. For all practical purposes I was already caught, and the key to the situation was to move the action away from Pruzhany. The great problem would be to get possession of the papers. We decided to work on that part of the plan the next morning.

In the bright light of morning, when I began to review the business in my mind, it seemed much less possible than the night before. I knew now what it was to fear not just for myself but also for my loved ones.

In the first place, how was I to get hold of the bag? (Even to myself I was ashamed to say 'steal' and preferred to use a euphemism.) I realised that I must learn whether Khomikov had arrived. Then I could try to devise a plan for getting the bag. After thinking it over reviewing all possibilities, I decided that the only person who could help me was Masha. I had not seen her for a while.

I did not think that she would be arrested because of me, but still I ought to warn her, and that would give me the opportunity to talk about my plan for escaping. I knew that it would be dangerous to reveal that to anyone, but I felt that I could trust Masha.

I hoped that I might be able to ask her about Khomikov during our conversation. And that I might have an opening for asking her to help me. In any case, I thought it probable that Khomikov would be dining regularly in Stolovka, and perhaps I could in some way get access to that place and to the bag.

The talk with Masha would be helpful, since, as a girl raised in the Soviet Union, she would know better than I whether my plan had any chance of success. And since most people in her country were daily faced with the danger of arrests, she might also know how some of them escaped such dangers.

I tried to arrive unobserved at the library just before closing. When I arrived Masha was alone, arranging books on a shelf.

'Too late!' she shouted before she saw me. 'We are closed.'

'I came here just –'

'Oh, is that you?' Masha said, dropping a couple of books. 'I did not expect you, but it is nice of you to have come,' she said, bending down to pick up her books from the floor. The library was filled with the smell of glue and tobacco smoke. Since the supply of electric current was not regular, the few bulbs flickered like candles in the open space.

'I had to see you, Masha, I am sorry.'

'No apologies necessary.' She came forwards with her hand outstretched. She was wearing a different cotton tunic that was too tight for her. She blushed as we were shaking hands.

'I am leaving. I mean we are leaving Pruzhany.'

'For long?'

'I think forever.'

Masha moved towards the window and stood there a while, looking at the snow lighted by a lonely gaslamp.

'I did not expect that,' she said almost in a whisper.

'I came here, Masha, to tell you why.' I was ready to warn her about my forthcoming arrest.

'It does not matter why. Nothing matters,' she said, turning to face me. 'I will miss you.'

Both of us had realised that we were seeing each other for the last time. There was sadness in her eyes, the colour of oak leaves after the first frost with the touch of green still remaining.

'My leaving shouldn't make much difference. We haven't seen each other.'

'It still was nice for me to know that you were living here. I saw you a few times with Nadya. Both of you with that special glow in your faces that is so unmistakable and means love for each other. And at the bottom of my heart I felt joy, knowing how happy both of you were.'

'I am very fond of you, Masha, and I wish I could make you happy.'

'You gave me moments of happiness and moments of despair. Since I met you, I no longer feel lonely.'

We were standing very close to each other, I could hear her heart beating.

'I know the meaning of that word so well, Masha. For many years I suffered from loneliness. Oh, how much I desired to feel a hand.'

'I felt that, your need, and that is why I had wanted to stretch out my hand, touch yours.'

Knowing that I would never see Masha again hurt me and I wished I could take her hand in mine and amble with her along some lonely road and tell her about my life and listen to her telling me about hers.

'Will you feel lonely, Masha?'

'No, I don't think so. The opposite of "being lonely" is "being in love" and I love you Anton.'

'But from the very start it was impossible,' I said.

A group of soldiers were passing on the street, singing in loud, cheerful voices the *Katiusha* song.

'The word love has as many meanings as there are people,' Masha said. 'And each person experiences that feeling in a different way. And when I met you I knew that it would be hopeless and impossible for us.'

'And you still wanted to love me?'

'I could not chase it away like a stray dog. Although I must confess I tried for a while, but the more I struggled against it the stronger it became.' Masha smiled, but I saw that tears were beginning to form in her eyes. She did not want me to see them and she moved away, and paced about for a moment, and then, as if she were exhausted from chasing that stray dog, she sat down.

'Every morning, when there is mist or when it drizzles or snows, I think of you, of your happiness, of Nadya's happiness, and I think I share in your happiness with an element of suffering that makes that feeling beautiful. And I think that my feeling of love has more depth that way.'

'Oh Masha, I wish you would meet a wonderful man who would love you and whom you would love.'

'I thought about that, Anton, I thought about that. And now I know: one has no choice in love; one gets what is rationed out, but it is better to have that than nothing. It is like when one walks in the spring dawn and one is stroked by a branch of lilacs in bloom in the neighbour's garden, wet with the morning dew. And one cannot have the lilac, and that touch of the bloom is better than not to have seen and touched it ever. So even the gentlest stroke of love makes a much better life than a life without love.' Masha was speaking with a sadness that also had overcome me, and the tears gathered in my eyes. The supply of electric current had steadied and the flickering stopped. We both remained silent for a while.

'I must tell you, Masha, since we are seeing each other for the last time that when we met you attracted me very much. It was a very strong attraction and I had a dream about you. I must confess it was physical desire, very strong, Masha, and I am ashamed of it.'

'Oh, Anton, that is nothing to be ashamed of. It is like Chekhov's story, *The Lady with a Lap Dog*. First physical love and then that is transformed into a total love, hopeless and impossible, with no possible resolution. There is a difference here though. I am not a lady, and I don't own a *sobatshka* (lap dog), there is only a stray *sobaka* in my life.' She laughed, 'An imaginary stray dog to boot.'

'And I am not a successful merchant like Ghurov, living in a mansion. I live in one room at Avram's.'

'But with a beautiful lady who loves you, and you love her and that ends the similarity.'

'I might become sometime a successful - something or other.'

'You, *Tsaplya*?' she asked, laughing.

'Why not? I could become a *Pavlleen*, a "Peacock"? Walking around with dignity and self-assurance, perhaps even smoking cigars.'

'I just cannot imagine you like that, Anton,' Masha said, roaring with laughter. 'You as a fat man with a cigar. It's so funny.'

'Of course you would be a distinguished lady then, you are a lady already. All you need is a lap dog.'

'I still prefer my stray dog, Anton; it is closer to my heart; it is more like me. A lap dog sits around, well groomed and well behaved, eats a little, drinks a little, loves a little. The stray dog does everything in excess, and when in love, loses its head and howls at the moon. I prefer to remain in your memory as a simple provincial Red Army librarian.'

'And for me you will always remain a good and beautiful woman, Masha.'

She looked at me for a moment and again tears gathered in her eyes.

'And maybe one morning, after a spring storm we might meet, Anton, on a lonely road with birch trees on both sides, and there would still be wet lilacs in the gardens, in my garden ...'

'I don't know whether we ever will meet again,' I said, 'or whether I will ever see the lilacs.'

'Why is that, Anton? People meet most unexpectedly. And where are you going to?'

'It is not really a matter of going that is why I came to see you. I must escape – we must escape.'

'But why, Anton, why?'

I did not know how to tell her the truth about me. Some young men and young women were passing by, and we both could hear the sound of their cheerful young voices.

'I'm in trouble, Masha, in great trouble. I am being followed by the N.K.V.D. and my arrest is imminent.'

'*Akh, batyushki* (Of, fathers). That is because they know that you are a *Byelogvardyeyetz* (a White Guard).'

'Much worse, much worse. It's because I am a spy, a White Guard spy.'

Even in the yellow light of the bulbs that was flickering again, I could see Masha's face turning the colour of ashes.

'Is there anything I can do to help you?' she said after a while.

'I don't think so. I came here to warn you that my arrest might create the danger of deportation for you.'

'Don't worry about me, but you and Nadya –'

'It looks bad for us, but I am planning something. I still hope that I may be able to get away with Nadya and Magda.'

'You are like a herring among great sharks, Anton.'

'I still have some teeth left, and I have a plan.'

'Even a small shark isn't safe among those big ones.'

'I hope to be able to manoeuvre better than they can, because of my size.'

'Sit down, then, and tell me your plan.'

I brought a bench from the corner of the library and placed it next to Masha. Looking at the thousands of books arranged neatly on the pinewood shelves, I told Masha my design for escape. She looked at me as if she wanted not only to hear my words but to read every nuance of the thought accompanying each of the words. When I finished, Masha was silent.

'What do you think?' I asked.

'It's not bad. It's original, I must say. They would not suspect any one of deliberately trying to get arrested. But it is dangerous. They might not care about these papers, and then you'd be finished. They would have to catch Nadya and want to recover the papers very badly in order for them to release you. I don't think that a local N.K.V.D. man could decide on his own to release a dangerous spy. He would have to clear it through Moscow. Another difficulty would be to elude your pursuers, once you were released. These men are specialists who know their jobs well. They would anticipate every single move you make.'

'Do I have a choice?' I asked.

Masha thought for a while.

'No. I don't think so,' she said. 'You might be giving Nadya a small chance to escape by temporarily drawing their attention to yourself. I admire you for that, and I want to help you, both of you, and of course the little girl.'

'How can you help me? I came here to warn you of the danger you might be in. And I don't want you to take any further risk.'

'First, I don't think that they know that we know each other. Otherwise I think I would have had some indication that I am a suspect. Perhaps we were seen a few months ago on election night, but then all of us had been told to invite as many local people as possible. I don't think that Lobin even noticed me. When did this Vashin appear for the first time in your home?'

'Monday night,'

'That's good. It means that they will still give you some leeway. Their purpose is to learn all they can about you and your organisation. That is why they will give you freedom of action. They don't want to scare you. In the beginning they usually follow a suspect only at a distance, and sometimes not even follow him at all. They would want to find out about your important contacts – people coming from out of town for instance. And for that I am pretty sure that they have their net already spread. I mention that because if they knew about us, I would be useless to you, I would not be able to help you, Anton.'

'But, I really –'

'I heard Khomikov's name today. An officer mentioned that he is coming. I'll let you know when he arrives. It is better for us not to communicate directly. Let me think. I could put something on the window sill for a signal. It would still be visible from outside even when the lights were out. I know, I'll put my cap on the sill of the centre window. You'll see it when you go by.'

'Splendid, Masha. Would you be likely to meet him? He would probably take his meals at the Stolovka where all the Red Army officers eat.'

'I eat there too, and I would recognise him by his bag and the pince-nez. But you will still have one great problem – how are you going to get hold of that bag?'

'I am not sure yet. Maybe I could try to find out where he will be staying, or possibly I would try to enter the Stolovka. He would have to hang up his overcoat and perhaps leave the bag beside it. Is there a coatroom?'

I was not proud of myself to be in the process of making Masha my accomplice, but it occurred to me that the best way to enter the coatroom would be through a window. For all practical purposes, the Stolovka in Pruzhany was a kind of officers' club, and it would be *de rigueur* for them to leave their trenchcoats and briefcases and bags there.

'Yes, there is. It's in the back of the building. It would be – let me see – the large room on that side has two windows. Yes, it would be the third window. But it's a double one, locked on the inside.'

I could see that Masha was debating a decision. She stood up, walked to her desk, sat down behind it, then rose again. Looking outside she said in an almost inaudible voice, 'I'll open the lock. And I should be able to put the bag on the window sill.'

'That would be risking a great deal.'

'It would be much less risk for me than for you.'

'But why should you?'

'When loves comes naked to you, then you must give it your best dress. I want to do everything for you. I hate the thought of stealing my country's secrets. I love my country, but I will do it for you. The evening that Khomikov is expected, I'll put my scarf next to my cap. Then you come to the Stolovka, to the third window in the rear of the building. And it will be open, Anton.'

We stood a long time in silence. I took her hand, it quivered.

'I wish you, Masha, many lilacs on the road of your life.'

'You too, you too,' Masha said.

I moved slowly to the door. Masha remained standing in the centre of the room.

As I was going through the door, I still heard her saying, 'You too, Anton.'

There was a freezing wind outside, but I walked with my overcoat open, not feeling the cold. Masha's words were still in my ears as I made my way home.

Vashin was not there, but Nadya was still up. I told her that I was too tired to discuss anything now, and we went to bed. For a long time I could not fall asleep, thinking of Masha, the lilacs and her love for me.

Next morning, after Magda went outdoors to play and Vashin left for his so-called post office, I told Nadya about my plan for getting hold of the bag and the gist of my conversation with Masha. Nadya listened with interest, and I was surprised that she did not interrupt me with any questions or make any comments when I had finished. When I asked her whether she liked the plan, she only nodded.

'Masha thinks that the plan will work,' I said, trying to get Nadya's reaction, 'if he needs the documents enough to find you.'

'Last night Vashin was here for a while. I think that he hates me much more than you. He suspects that I am making fun of him, and of course you were away last night. I felt lonely without you here, and I must confess a little bitter, so I took it out on Vashin.'

'Oh, my God, what did you tell him?'

'I really let him have it. Don't ask me what I told him.'

'But what was it?'

'I told him what I thought about the N.K.V.D.'s murdering ten thousand people a day, innocent people. About the treatment of Poles here and their deportations. About Stalin being at one time an informer for the Tsarist police – '

'But Nadya, he could kill you.'

'Don't worry. He could not possibly put those things in his report. He would be finished. But that's not what made him most angry. Of course I spoke to him as if he were the postal inspector he wants us to believe he is, and I told him that the really important spies are roaming freely here and laughing at the N.K.V.D. And when he asked me where you were, I said that you had an appointment with a friend from Berlin or Vienna. You should have seen his face turning the colour of a beet. I asked whether there was anything wrong with that, since after all the Germans are such good friends of the Soviet Union. But he didn't say anything, and a few minutes later he left.'

'Oh, Nadya, he will try to get even with you.'

'I'm sure he will, but it doesn't matter. If we're caught nothing matters.'

'I must try to arrange your getting away. I'll talk to Avram. I think it would be best if he could leave with you. If he were to remain here, he'd be arrested because of us.'

Taking advantage of Vashin's absence, I went to see Avram. He was sitting at the kitchen table grating a horseradish root. He wore his black yarmulke and a satin frock coat.

'I am crying,' he said, wiping away his tears with his coat sleeves, the tears caused by the pungent horseradish. 'Shouldn't I cry, with everything that is going on here?'

'I am afraid that when I tell you my reason for coming to see you, you'll cry some more. And I will cry with you.'

The room smelled of horseradish, cooked beets and onions.

'A few tears more or less,' he said, 'don't make much difference.'

'We must leave soon.'

'Young people shouldn't stay forever in a place like Pruzhany. Where are you going?'

'You should ask where we are going, including yourself,' I said. Avram merely nodded. 'Aren't you surprised?'

'Why should I be? Even through tears I can see what is going on.'

A series of bearded men in yarmulkes were looking at me.

'Good, I can be frank with you now. As you know, when the Soviets arrest someone, they take all the other people living in the house for good measure. I know I'll be arrested in a few days, and I'd like you to get away with Nadya and Magda.'

'And you?' Avram asked.

'I am a man alone, I'll have better chances to escape later on. Since I am afraid I'll be watched, it would be hopeless to try to escape with all of you.'

Avram nodded.

'You must have relations someplace. Don't even tell me where. Try to find out whether there are some Soviet trucks leaving Pruzhany at night. We have money for that purpose; I'll be glad to pay for your and Nadya's trip.'

Avram nodded. 'I'll try.'

'You should be able to return here after a few months. They won't bother you then.'

I wasn't sure whether Avram had heard my last words, since he had gone back to grating the horseradish.

In the afternoon of that same day I strolled through the streets of Pruzhany with Magda. At one point we went by the library. Masha's cap was on the window sill: Khomikov was here. Once we were home again, I arranged in my mind the further details of Nadya's flight with Magda and Avram. Before we went to bed, I told Nadya about it.

'Now that Khomikov is here,' I whispered, 'anyday I might find that Masha has placed the bag on the windowsill.'

'Of course you would prefer to have Masha in the bag rather than the documents.'

'Oh, please, Nadya, for once. That night I'll pretend to be arguing with you about my wanting to drink vodka – in a loud voice, so that Vashin will hear it. Then, while you are giving me hell, I'll quietly slip out the window, pick up the bag, take out the documents and bring them here, hiding the bag somewhere out of the house. I'll argue with you some more and then leave by the door. Vashin will probably follow me, but I will go to one of those Soviet dances.'

'To have that last tango with Masha.'

'Please, Nadya. And you'll take advantage of Vashin's absence to slip away with Magda and Avram. He will arrest me on my return from the dance hall, and by that time you will be far away.'

'You still haven't told me the details of your meeting with Masha.'

'Some other time. Do you like my plan?'

'You are the master schemer. You really know how to do those things,' Nadya said, turning out the lamp and getting into bed.

'I don't even want to know where you'll be hiding. The Soviets have ways of getting that kind of information out of a prisoner. As soon as I am released I will try to get to Brest.'

'Don't worry, Anton, I will find you anywhere in the world,' Nadya said, kissing me goodnight.

Next morning Avram told me that there was a regular service of trucks going out of Pruzhany, leaving a quarter before midnight. They picked up food in Brest and returned in the afternoon. The drivers were strictly prohibited from picking up civilians, but five or six litres of vodka was the going price to get them to overlook such restrictive orders. I gave Avram the money to buy the vodka, and I walked out to check on the library window, but there was no message. A day later, however, as I strolled by again with Magda, I saw both the cap and the scarf.

I had an immediate urge to go into the library and give Masha a kiss of gratitude, but I knew that I would never be able to do that, and the thought pained me.

Once we were back home, I told Avram to be ready that night, and Nadya started packing her things. That evening both of us were silent most of the time; we knew the danger ahead, and it was better not to talk about it. Fortunately, since Nadya's last meeting with Vashin, he had stopped honouring us with his presence, so there was little likelihood of his visiting us tonight and ruining my plan. I hoped that he would not come home too late.

He did come later than I expected. But we still had enough time to go ahead as we had decided to do.

'You hid that vodka from me again,' I shouted, hearing Vashin moving on the other side of the wall.

Nadya nodded with a smile. 'You're a drunkard, and now you want to get drunk again,' she cried. 'But I won't let you.'

'Give it to me!'

'A father, a husband! Shame on you, buying vodka with our last kopeks while we starve,' she went on. 'Hit the table hard with your fist,' she whispered.

I did.

'Hitting the table! Oh, God, you will ruin everything we have. Why did I have to marry such a man? Why, why why?'

'I want vodka. My throat is dry. Please, Nadya, please!'

'You need a good sleep and not vodka, Anton,' Nadya said aloud. 'I love you,' she whispered.

'Good, good, sit there, sit there – the bed is the right place for you.'

'I need vodka, vodka, please.'

'I think that will do it,' Nadya whispered approaching me. I took her in my arms; our cheeks touched; our lips quivered as we kissed.

'I want to discover you again, and again,' I whispered.

Nadya nodded, still embracing me.

Noiselessly she helped me with my coat.

'Vodka, vodka!' I cried, opening the window.

'Sleep, sleep, Anton! It is much better for you,' I heard her voice as I jumped from the window sill into the snow.

For a moment I stood looking around, but there was no one there. I turned and in the dim light of the lamp I could see Nadya's face. For a moment our eyes met. Then I went away through the snow-covered streets. There was no wind. It was a clear night with the moon and the stars shining brightly. My heart pounded as I hurried towards the Stolovka. On the way I met only two soldiers. They were talking in loud voices about a girl named Vera.

In front of the main entrance to the Stolovka a sentry stood guard in a long fur trenchcoat and a heavy fur cap. He looked at me without any interest. I turned the corner. There was another sentry guarding the kitchen door. But he too paid no attention to me. I turned another corner. I counted the windows. Approaching slowly, I came to the third one. I looked around. Two civilians passing on the street were speaking Polish.

I waited. As soon as they had gone by I pushed the right side of the window. It moved. I reached out, my fingers touched leather, it was the bag. Pulling at the window sill I raised myself, seized the bag, and jumped down. I looked around. There was no one in sight. The bag was heavy. By the light of the moon I could make out the large letter 'X' upon it.

For a while I moved slowly along in the rear of the houses, and then I turned into the streets once more. A truck came along, but it did not stop. Finally I reached the house where Nadya used to live. There was no light there; the new tenants must have been asleep or away. In the little garden, where I had once buried and dug up again the relics of the Tsarist past of Nadya's family, I sat down and opened the bag. On reaching inside, the first thing I touched was an apple. There were others there. But there were also folders, three folders. I pulled them out, put them inside my jacket. I ran towards our house, leaving the bag in the snow. I slowed my pace as I came near it. There was no one in the street. In the window I saw Nadya's face again. As I approached she opened the door. 'Success,' I whispered in her ear. 'Vodka, vodka, I must have it,' I said aloud.

I looked at my watch. It was ten thirty-seven: the whole operation had taken thirty minutes.

'No vodka for you,' Nadya said, helping me with my coat. 'Go back to bed.'

I pulled out the folders and rushed to the lamp, I opened the first one. Several pages were covered with small writing, the letters were almost illegible. After I got used to them I was able to decipher some of it. It appeared to be a lecture on firing tank guns when the tank is on an incline. There did not seem to be any reference in it to the new tank. I opened the second folder. On the first page was a tank design with an inscription: T-34. The tank gun had a note – 76.2 mm L/30.5 Model 1938 (L-11). On the second page was a plan showing the disposition of the armour plate with the various degrees of slope given in a list. The third folder contained more technical data on the T-34.

'We've got it,' I said in a whisper that it was difficult for me to keep low.

'Go to your bed, Anton,' Nadya said smiling.

'With a wife like you,' I said aloud, 'a man takes to drink.'

'That's your excuse,' Nadya said. 'What's wrong with your wife?'

'Too strict, too strict.'

'Where are you going?' Nadya asked handing me my coat.

'I want to drink,' I said.

We were standing close to the door facing each other.

'Antosha,' she whispered. I touched her hand. She closed her eyes for a moment.

'I must, I must,' I said opening the door.

Without turning I ran outdoors, hearing Nadya cry out, 'Come back, Antosha, come back!'

Would Vashin run after me right away? I would be able to elude him for a while, since I had a headstart.

What if he decided not to leave at all? Or not for a few hours? Nadya had to catch the truck at a quarter to midnight.

What would she do if he were still there? And what if someone had come upon the bag and taken it away?

My last question was soon answered. I found the bag in the same place I had left it. Stuffing it under my coat I hurried towards the school building.

On entering I heard the band playing a familiar tango, 'The Heart.' Hundreds of couples were dancing to it. Many of the dancers were singing too and some were calling out to other couples or to the people looking on. It was warm inside, but the air stank of tobacco, cheap perfumes and sweat.

Fighting my way through the crowd I reached the far wall and found a chair. The tango was followed by a foxtrot. The Soviet fighters and commanders danced to it with such vigour that for a moment the floor seemed about to collapse under their boots.

The dance hall, the music, and the crowd reminded me of my first party here, and of Masha, the girl who had risked so much tonight to help us to flee from the fatherland that she loved so much, that all of us loved.

I placed the bag next to my chair and dropped my coat over it. I looked at my watch. It was eleven thirty. In only fifteen minutes Nadya might be boarding that truck.

A couple both in uniform, stopped near my chair.

'My little brother, Kolya, is good at trigonometry,' said a round faced girl with slanting eyes.

'My brother is in the seventh grade,' said a tall soldier with short hair on his round head. 'He is not a mathematician, but he likes music. He plays the piano. My mother thinks that he might pass the entrance exam for the conservatory.'

'It's very hard to get into the conservatory.'

'It is,' he said. 'It is, but he has talent.'

'He must play a lot. Practice is essential for a piano student.'

'It is, it's very important.'

They looked at each other for a moment in silence.

'And you'll write to me, Sonya?'

'Yes.'

They stood in silence again, oblivious to the noise and the crowd.

'You won't forget me?' Sonya said, looking at the floor.

'No. And you?'

'Never, Misha, never.'

The band began another song, and they disappeared into the dancing crowd.

I looked at my watch again: it was still eight minutes before Nadya was to leave. I was watching the crowd, hoping to see Vashin. He should be here by now circling around me. Perhaps he was, and as a trained policeman he could watch me without my noticing him.

Other people came near me. Someone asked me for a light, somebody else for a cigarette. Midnight had passed, but Vashin still did not appear.

It was twelve-fifteen when I saw him. He was accompanied by Lobin. Both of them were in uniform and they strode towards me.

'Come,' Vashin said quietly.

I stood up and put on my overcoat. Both of them fastened their eyes on the bag.

'You have it with you,' Vashin said almost inaudibly, taking hold of it. 'That simplifies things.'

I was scared, now that the arrest had occurred so early. If they opened the bag right away they would see that the plans were missing and Nadya had not reached her destination. They might guess that she was travelling by the military truck and alert police at the other end.

Nobody in the crowd seemed to have noticed our encounter. The music continued, and the people were dancing as we made our way to the door. The street was empty and a light snow was falling. Suddenly Vashin put a whistle in his mouth and blew a piercing blast that I'll never forget. A few moments later, a large tracked vehicle arrived.

The three of us climbed in the back of the truck. Five soldiers were sitting inside with their rifles grounded between their legs. Without looking at us they moved to give us room to sit. The truck began to move.

We stopped at the former Polish municipal building, the place where Kruper and Bendarski had been killed. Maybe it was my destiny to die there too, I thought.

Vashin jumped down first. He waited by the truck until I climbed down.

'Follow me!'

Lobin walked so close behind me that I could smell alcohol and garlic on his breath.

We went up two flights. Vashin stopped in front of the door marked 'Lobin.' The fat commissar took out the key to his office, opened the door and let us in. Without taking off his cap or his topcoat, Lobin sat down behind the desk and placed the black bag upon it. The desk was littered with the remains of food, greasy papers, cigarette butts, and a dirty shirt. As Lobin took off his gloves I saw black dirt under his fingernails.

'Sit down!' he ordered. I obeyed. Vashin remained standing next to the desk, while Lobin lighted a cigarette. He looked pleased with himself.

'Do you know the contents of this bag?' Lobin asked. He inhaled deeply and held the smoke in his lungs for a long moment.

I hesitated.

Vashin moved to the window sill where he sat down. All the time he did not lose sight of me. Lobin's self-satisfied expression did not vanish from his face, even though I had not answered his question. The room was filled with tobacco and I began to cough. I knew that I could not achieve much for myself. I hoped only to be able to prolong the interrogation so as to give Nadya and Magda a better chance of getting far away from here. I remembered Krugov's advice to talk a lot. Since the members of the 'Parterre' group had been recalled, it was doubtful, no matter what I told these two now, that what I said would have any bearing on their safety.

'You don't want to tell us what is in the bag?' Lobin spat out the cigarette into a spittoon. 'All right. What is your name?'

'Anton Kazimirovich Slavski.'

'That is your cover name,' Lobin said. 'Don't you lie to me any more, you son of a bitch.' His face expressed disgust and hatred. 'What is your real name?'

'Anton Nizov,' I said. 'Anton Illich Nizov.'

'Why did you change your name?' Lobin asked, pouring himself a glass of vodka and drinking it.

'I preferred the name Slavski. It is a Polish name. Poland was at war. It is true that originally it was at war with Germany only. As you know, Polish people do not adore Russians, and during the war it would be better to be a Pole. So I took the name of Slavski. Also I took a different patronymic: Kazimirovich. That sounds really Polish.' I looked at their faces. Both of them did not seem to be interested in what I said. But they observed me intently, their eyes never leaving my face.

'What were you doing in Vienna in the summer of 1939?' Vashin asked.

'I was studying at the University of Vienna. I was a student of medicine. Anatomy course by Professor Pernkopf, given in the Anatomy Institute, Wahringerstrasse, from nine to ten, Monday through Friday. Later in the day, Histology, Physics, Chemistry, Zoology and Botany. All courses for the first year of study,' I lied.

'So you wanted to become a doctor?'

'Yes, I wanted to become a doctor, but it would have been difficult for me to practise, because I was stateless, a citizen of no country. All Russian émigrés had such problems.'

Hearing about the life of the émigrés and their problems appeared to interest them. I was surprised that they had not interrupted me. I told them about the attic I lived in, my lonely life. I even told them about my date with the French girl, Yvonne, and what her mother had said to her about me.

As I was talking I remembered how a certain lady, whose name I could not recall, saved her life by telling the tale of 1,001 nights.

Lobin must have noticed the amusement in my eyes.

'Why in hell didn't you stay there?'

'Vienna is a beautiful town, with large boulevards, avenues and streets. I did not like my medical studies that much. I preferred to study art, Byzantine art. Professor Otto Demus gave a course called "Byzantine Art since The Iconoclasts" on Tuesdays from four to five in the afternoons.'

'Who were the iconoclasts?' Vashin asked.

'People who stopped believing in pictures of God and Saints.

They started to destroy them – something like people pulling down the portraits of your –'

'Why did you become a spy?' Lobin interrupted.

'The iconoclasts succeeded, at least for a while,' I went on. 'They trampled what they considered false images with their feet.'

'Stop it!' Lobin was getting red in the face. He spat towards his spittoon but missed.

I did not know just when the truck would reach Brest. I guessed it would be about three or four o'clock in the morning, and should my interrogators open the bag before that time they would suspect that she might have caught the truck and they would telephone the authorities in Brest and ask them to arrest her. Both Vashin and Lobin kept watching me so closely that I did not dare to glance at my wrist watch and make them suspect that I was anxious about the time.

I tried desperately to find a subject that would keep them interested. Recalling how Boris and Gleb had been taken by the tale of my encounter with a member of the oldest profession, I decided to repeat the story and perhaps add some things that had never happened.

'I admit that I lied to you.'

'We know you are a liar,' Lobin said.

'I was not a student in Vienna. I had a job there.'

They did not seem to be interested in this corrected statement about my life in Vienna. Lobin yawned, showing a row of large teeth, and Vashin was ready to interrupt me.

'I worked there in a house of love, or bordello, where you can buy favours from ladies.' Vashin took another cigarette from Lobin's pack and Lobin leaned forwards.

'I am afraid you may not be familiar with such institutions. They have been banned since the Revolution.'

'Are there many such places in the West?' Vashin asked.

'In Vienna alone there are several. You can recognise them by the red lanterns over their doors. When you enter these places you can see hundreds of girls, some dressed in evening dresses, with long skirts and even with fur jackets; others are nude, and some are half-dressed with bare breasts or in dresses made of net or transparent materials or just very skimpy ones.'

I had reached the limit of my personal knowledge of such

things. It was obvious that my audience was curious to hear more details.

'To get in, do you have to have State tickets for good work like Stakhanovites,' Lobin asked.

'No, you have to pay your own money.'

'I knew it. The West is rotten to the core,' Vashin said. I was not sure whether he was referring to the mere existence of such establishments in the West or to the system of monetary compensation.

'How much do you pay,' Lobin asked, 'if you want a good piece?'

'It depends what kind of girl you choose.'

'They are not allocated to you by the management?' Vashin asked, surprised.

'Oh, no. You have your pick.'

'And the girl has to do it?' Lobin asked, licking his lips.

'Sure she must do it, but it's expensive.' It was impossible for me to quote a price because I did not know what it might be but even had I known it they would not have understood me. 'You must give her a pair of shoes or the equivalent.'

'That's impossible,' both of them said in unison.

'That would be once every two years that you could go there,' Lobin said, disappointed. I had in fact heard that in the Soviet Union, if you were lucky, you might get a pair of shoes every two years.

'This thing is only for criminals and speculators,' Vashin said.

'No. In Vienna if you work you can earn the price of a pair of shoes in a week.'

'That's a lie. Don't give us that propaganda,' Vashin said, getting impatient and looking at the bag.

I was afraid that my presentation, which had been going well, might be prematurely ended.

'It is a lot of money, but whatever it is it's worth it. You get the best looking girls in the world and in very interesting surroundings: there is a room decorated like a beach with a quartz lamp making everything warm, and instead of the floor there is sand; another room has fresh grass instead of a floor, and still another moss.'

'So there are no beds there?' Lobin asked.

'Sure there are,' I said.

'Why in hell would anyone want to fuck on the grass if there are beds?' Lobin asked.

'Rotten people, disgusting,' Vashin said.

'Some people who do it in bed all the time want to have a change,' I said, noticing that Vashin was becoming impatient again. 'There is one room on the top floor filled with mercury that is covered with a silk rug and on that there's a layer of rosebuds five centimetres thick – fresh rosebuds every day and there is the most beautiful girl, the queen of the house of love, all dressed up.'

'What do you have to pay for her, a whole suit, an overcoat or even more?' Lobin asked.

'You have to give her everything you've got.'

'And if you don't have much?'

'It does not matter how much you have. She is an exception to the rule. She has to like you, but then –'

'And if she doesn't like you, what then?' Vashin asked ironically.

'You are lost forever. You cannot live without her; you would die without her.'

'That's damn nonsense. Just a bunch of lies and fables,' Vashin said.

Lobin was clearly disappointed that Vashin had interrupted my stories, but having realised that the fun had been spoiled irretrievably, he decided to join Vashin in attacking me.

'How did you come here you damn liar?'

'I was escaping from the Germans, but –'

'And you selected shitty Pruzhany as your favourite spot?' Lobin looked at me with a smile of superiority.

'This was the first town –'

'That Krugov assigned you to spy in,' Vashin finished the sentence. He jumped down from the window sill and stood in front of the door as if he wanted to stop me if I had decided to run.

'Cut out the damn nonsense,' Vashin continued. 'You were working until tonight on "Operation Parterre," and just a few hours ago you carried out the assignment to steal that.' Vashin motioned to the bag. I had lost track of time. Vashin had said, 'a few hours ago.' I looked at my watch. It was already three in the morning.

'I know a lot about you and the Parterre group,' Vashin said.

He took still another cigarette from Lobin's pack on the desk and lit it. I was surprised since I had never seen Vashin smoking before. 'I've been listening to your nonsense to learn more about the mentality of the White Guard spies. Did they tell you what happens to you when you are caught?'

I nodded.

'Our laws specify the death penalty by firing squad for traitors and spies,' Vashin said. 'I cannot change that. But I can make the few hours or days before your execution less painful – if you cooperate with us.'

'We could keep our hands off your wife,' Lobin said. 'I mean not arrest her, if you work with us.'

'What kind of guarantee for her safety would I get?' I asked the question simply to delay them. I knew that all their promises and guarantees would be worthless.

'Do you know about the various traitors and spies we have executed? We did not persecute their families if they confessed,' Lobin said, spreading his fat, greasy fingers.

'So if I don't cooperate, you will torture my wife. Is that a Soviet law?'

'You fucking bastard!' Lobin shouted. 'How did you find out about this bag? There were several bags, briefcases and valises in the Stolovka. You selected this particular –'

'It looked better,' I said.

'Better in what way?' Vashin asked.

'It was thicker.'

'The bags in the place were even bulkier, you fucking liar!' Lobin screamed. 'Who told you to pick this one? I want to know!' Lobin was shouting so loud that the glass in the window shook. My eardrums ached.

'Nobody told me anything,' I whispered. 'I took one at random.'

Lobin's face was the colour of meat. His eyes were bloodshot.

'Fuck your mother and your taking at random.' Lobin stood up and opened the bag with his greasy hands. 'I will show you what you stole, you whore's son.'

He turned the bag upside down, emptying its contents on the desk. Apples, many of them, hit the desk and fell on the floor.

Lobin's face turned ashen. He fell back into his chair. I thought he had fainted. Vashin's face was pale too. I saw his hands shaking.

I burst out laughing madly. I had never laughed so long and so loud in all my life. I was roaring with laughter. The tears came to my eyes.

The apples, large and yellow, were scattered on the floor.

Vashin came to me and grabbed my neck. It hurt badly. I thought that he was going to choke me to death. 'Where is she, where –' he yelled. Then he ran out. I could hear the echo of his boots, striking the floor outside.

Lobin grabbed me, yelling, 'Where is she?' He struck me again and again. I fainted.

When I came to I felt sick. I could hear someone talking on the telephone. People were rushing about. Then a soldier with a rifle appeared. He ordered me to stand up, and to walk ahead of him. In this way we reached a cell in the basement. I looked through a small opening at the sky. It must have been the beginning of the new day, for the sky was grey. I was weak and I sat down. Then I stretched out on the floor. I did not think about anything: my mind was blank. I fell asleep.

After that, I lost track of time. In the next several days, as it seemed, Vashin and Lobin interrogated me for many hours, both in day time and at night. They tried to discover whether I had had an accomplice. They asked me about 'Operation Parterre', about the Polish Underground, about details of my private life. Most of all they questioned me about Nadya's whereabouts, but I think eventually they started to believe my denials that I knew where she was.

I was happy that Nadya and Magda had succeeded in escaping, but still I worried that they might be caught. As time passed my hope that I would be released dimmed, particularly since the interrogations became less frequent, and both Vashin and Lobin seemed less eager to grill me than before.

PART IV

The Spring

Chapter 17
Anton's Story

Pruzhany, March 22, 1940
It was my fourth week in prison, and I had reached the stage when nothing mattered to me. I did not care whether I was interrogated or left alone. I did not even care whether there was anything to eat or not. The one thought that kept me going was the certainty that Nadya had escaped. She might possibly be abroad and in the process of delivering the Khomikov file to Krugov.

On the morning of the first day of spring the sentry arrived, and I was marched into Lobin's office. To my surprise there was a new interrogator behind Lobin's desk, a heavy man in his fifties with a bald head. Vashin was standing near the window and leaning against the sill. The room was filled with cigarette smoke.

'I am Gregory Phillipovich Brodilo,' the stranger introduced himself, emphasising his first name and his patronymic as if he wanted from the start to create an atmosphere of familiarity. 'I came from Moscow to interview you. Of course, Oleg Akimovich has fully informed me about his talking with you and I will try to avoid asking the same questions.' While talking he looked at me intently, and I was sure that even my smallest reaction would not go unobserved. Knowing that Brodilo must be one of the top interrogators, I tried to be especially alert.

'You are a Russian patriot, Anton Illich,' he said exhaling a cloud of bluish smoke. 'That is why you are here.'

I nodded, looking at the wall and noticing a new and larger portrait of Stalin hanging in place of the old one. 'I love Russia,' I said. I was surprised at this approach to questioning me.

'I love Russia too, Anton Illich. The only difference between us is that we have opposite notions about how to express our love for our country.' Brodilo pushed his chair closer to the desk.

'You believe that the return of the Tsarist regime would be best for our country, and I know that our government is best for our people.'

I was ready to tell him that I did not believe a Tsarist regime was best for Russia, but I was certain that the Soviet tyranny was the worst possible form of government, but that would be pointless. So I shrugged my shoulders.

'But frankly it does not matter to me what you believe, Anton Illich. I know that we would not be able to change each other's view in this matter. What is important to me is to recover the Khomikov notes. And that is the subject I came to discuss. There is another that is even more important for me,' Brodilo added. He lit a cigarette.

'First of all let me say to you, Anton Illich, that your egg is boiled. What I mean is that no chicken can come from a boiled egg. That can serve as a good beginning for our talk.' He looked at me for a moment, then smiled at a new thought of his. 'Your egg is boiled but not eaten. I came from Moscow to see you and I don't make such trips except in very rare cases.'

'Quite an honour. But it doesn't matter. To the hanged man it makes no difference how high the gallows are.'

'Perfect, perfect,' he said and a broad smile appeared on his face. 'We seem to understand each other. I mean that I like your use of Russian ways of speaking. Except that you are playing the wrong chord on the wrong kind of instrument.'

'Tovarich Vashin told me the penalty for spying.'

Hearing his name, Vashin jerked his head up.

'Oleg Akimovich correctly stated the law but he lacked the necessary facts to make a correct judgment about the application of the law.' Vashin did not seem to like what was said, but Brodilo did not care.

'You mean that you are ready to reward me with Stakhanovite honours for my high achievement in the field of spying?'

'I must confess I was not thinking in those terms. But that could be considered – though in my book not every hero must display his medals.'

'So you'd give me a medal! That's interesting, Gregory Phillipovich.'

'Of course. In our country we are just. We reward everyone according to his accomplishment – on our behalf.'

I could not believe my ears, and I looked over at Vashin. He did not appear surprised. Brodilo must have discussed the subject with him before.

'Do you really expect me to become a spy for you? For the Soviet Union?'

'I know that this turn in our talk surprises you. As a spy you have shown great talent and extremely good results. A talent, I might add, well recognised by my German colleagues, since you were the only spy recalled for consultation. And I envy them their good judgment. The spying talent is found very seldom. I, for example, have seen more spies in my life than you have seen snowflakes in Pruzhany: none of them measured up to your abilities and potential. An untried spy is like an uncracked nut. You never know what you'll find inside, and unfortunately for us most of the spy nuts are empty.'

'Do you really think that I would sacrifice my honour, my self-respect, my ideals?' I said angrily.

'You mentioned three abstract nouns, and I will be glad to discuss them with you. In regard to honour, I will just say: it is better to be without a plate than without the buckwheat. On self-respect: the hunter who brings in lots of partridges is respected by his fellows no matter where he got them. And ideals: all the best spies do not believe in the ideals of their employers, often professing opposite ones. An idealist makes the worst spy and is easily caught. The best spies are the most ordinary characters, human beings who are afraid, who feel panic even, but who have superior motivation to succeed and can use their brains.'

'Gregory Phillipovich is right,' Vashin said, showing his two capped teeth in a broad smile. 'I can confirm the wisdom of his words. You succeeded because you are in love with your wife. Nadiezhda Petrovna.' In saying Nadya's name he almost choked as if he were trying to swallow a lemon.

'All of this is nonsense,' I said. 'It is a naive trap. I will give you back the papers; you will kill me and my wife and that will be the end of your politeness.'

'We are not underestimating you,' Brodilo said. 'We know that you are a professional and that you will not bite at a rusted hook. We could offer you terms after you cross the border, perhaps with our help.' Brodilo smiled, showing the full range of his yellowed teeth. 'Then you could start on your assignment, leaving your family behind as a guarantee. They would be accorded the full luxury of a resort life, somewhere in the mountains.'

Brodilo knew how to interest me, and of course he was fully aware of Nadya's asthma and how much the mountain air would have done to cure her. It was an enticing proposal, and I hesitated.

'You don't seem to realise that I have a duty to people for whom I have been working.'

'I am glad that you've brought the subject up. Your former German boss, Captain von Dolnitz, is dead by suicide. He did not like the fact that his boss revealed your whereabouts to me in an exchange for a little favour.'

'I don't believe it,' I said, jumping up.

'I expected you not to. Here is the *Berliner Zeitung*, February 25. Read it.'

He gave me the paper folded so that I could immediately notice a circled item that reported the untimely death of Captain Otto von Dolnitz of the Third Panzer Corps, formerly with the Seventh Cavalry Division. I unfolded the newspaper. Brodilo was right: it was the *Berliner Zeitung* of the date he had mentioned.

Brodilo knew that he had won the battle.

'All that comes as a shock to you,' he said, a benevolent tone in his voice. 'I don't expect you to be able to give me your answer right away. It takes time to think such a thing over. You may go to your room now if you choose. We will return your money to you. You are now free, a future member of our spy mission. In a few days we may discuss the details with you in Moscow.' Brodilo stood up, offering me a cigarette and lighting one up himself. 'Of course you might choose to consult Nadiezhda Petrovna, and that is your privilege. On the other hand, as an experienced spy you should know that you would be followed, and in that way you would reveal her whereabouts. Which is all right too. It would even simplify our future talks.'

Everything had come so suddenly that I felt dizzy. I collected my belongings and went out into the street. The icy wind hit my face, but at that moment I did not feel the cold. The streets of

Pruzhany appeared bright and beautiful, superior to all the famous avenues in the world. But that feeling did not last long. I began to worry about Nadya and Magda. The doors of Avram's house were locked. I entered our room. Somebody must have been searching it. Everything was upside down. The pillows had been cut open and the floor was covered with feathers. The contents of the tin boxes in which we had stored buckwheat, sugar, and salt had been emptied on the floor. The mattresses had been cut open too, and the straw stuffing was piled in a corner of the room. Even the wooden legs of the table and chairs were split.

My first reaction was to run away. Through the windows the rays of the afternoon sun entered the room. I noticed the ikon of my patron saint lying on the floor. I picked it up. I also found my rucksack.

By my arrangement with Nadya I was to travel to Brest where she would find a way to get in touch with me. Would she be able to do that? I hoped that she might be helped by some organisation – possibly the Polish Underground. Anyway there was no use staying here. The sooner I left here for Brest, the sooner I might see her again. I knew from Brodilo's words that I would be tailed, but I hoped that I might be able to elude the Soviets.

I began to pack whatever I could find that might be useful on my trip and that could still be salvaged from the mess on the floor and the table. I collected some of my underwear and enough food to last me for a couple of days. I knew that the train would be leaving at four, so I had to hurry.

As I was leaving the house I looked around to see if anyone was following me. I saw nobody, though that did not mean that I would not be watched and followed. I realised that the reason I was free was that Vashin wanted to find Nadya. I represented his only chance to locate her.

The station was crowded with travellers carrying large bags and parcels. Pruzhany was a terminal, but the train was not there yet. I joined the crowds waiting on the platform. There were a number of uniformed Soviets travelling, which was not unusual. None of them seemed to pay any attention to me.

As soon as the train arrived the crowd moved forwards. I also pushed my way through the doors into one of the three cars.

Someone behind me grabbed me by the elbow. I heard a whisper in Polish: 'Brest, men's room.' I did not turn. The crowd went on pushing through the car.

Standing in front of a window and looking at the platform, I wondered who the stranger might be. Anyway I decided to take his advice.

During my trip I watched my fellow passengers. None of them appeared to be interested in me. In Kobryn we had to wait for a connection. Here again no one seemed to follow me. The train to Brest was not as crowded as the train from Pruzhany. I was able to fall asleep. I awakened when the train was on the point of entering the station in Brest.

I saw the lights of the station. I looked at the passengers in my compartment. Everyone was preparing to leave the train. Nobody seemed to be observing me.

As the train stopped I rushed into the station building. I did not see anyone directly following me.

I remembered the station well. Last December it had been crowded, but now it seemed empty by comparison. Only a few travellers had arrived with me. As soon as I found myself in the central hall, I went towards the men's room. At the door stood a tall man with a blond moustache. 'Camel?' he asked seeing me.

'*Tak* (yes),' I answered in Polish.

He pushed me inside the door which he closed after we were inside. He put a padlock, the size of a pear, on the door and snapped it shut.

Someone began to bang on the door from outside. There were three men in the room with us.

'What in hell is going on here?' said a man who was standing and urinating.

'Open up!' someone shouted from outside. 'I'll break the door.'

The moustached man showed me a small window. 'Climb through it,' he said.

I grabbed the frame, and with the man helping me I pulled myself up and pressed through the window. Outside, the ground was about seven metres below me. In front of the window was a ladder with a small platform on top of it. I stepped onto it and clambered down as fast as I could, followed by the moustached man.

As soon as he reached the ground, he pulled the ladder down, and said, 'Follow me!'

We ran some twenty metres to the left. I heard shouts from the lavatory, then shots. We entered an old building through an opened door which my companion closed and bolted. It was dark inside. It must have been an old warehouse. My guide used a flashlight. Some packages were scattered about at random.

After a few seconds we reached a narrow stairway. My companion ran down. I followed him. I heard voices. The area downstairs was well lighted. Two men were loading crates on a truck. One crate stood open. 'Get in,' the moustached man said, and walked away swiftly. From upstairs I heard voices. Immediately the cover of the crate was nailed down and I felt the crate being lifted. Seconds later other crates were placed over mine.

The crate was much shorter than my body, and I was inside it in a sitting posture. It hurt badly.

All the other crates on the truck were much smaller than mine. Placing smaller crates around mine must have made it appear that only crates of that size were on the truck.

There was a small hole in the crate through which I could breathe, and I could hear what was going on.

'Have you seen two men?' a voice asked in Russian.

'*Nie rozumiem po rosyjsku* (I don't understand Russian)' someone answered.

'Did ... you ... two men?' Another voice asked in broken Polish.

'Yes, we did!'

'Where did they go?'

'One to the left, the other to the right.'

'Check the truck!'

Someone jumped on the truck. I also heard the door to the driver's compartment being opened.

'Nobody here.' I heard the shout over my crate.

'Let's go!'

I heard boots hitting the pavement, more shouts. Then these noises died down. The engine's ignition was turned on. The truck began to move.

I was suffering in my cube. I thought I would choke to death. I don't know how long it took the truck to reach its destination because I was semi-conscious from lack of air and from the pain.

Finally the truck stopped. Some men began to unload it. They carried down my crate. They opened it. Some strong hands pulled me out.

'Hey there, are you all right?' a man asked me.

'*Tak, tak,*' (Yes, yes,) I said.

My limbs felt numb, but the unknown men massaged me quickly.

'Breathe, breathe deeply!' one man said.

'Dangerous trick, the crate. We opened one up once, and it was too late. You're lucky,' another said.

For the first time I looked around. The truck stood in the middle of a courtyard, enclosed by buildings and a high concrete wall. A large gate was closed.

'We must hurry,' the first man said. He was tall and broad shouldered.

They put what looked like a motor into the crate that I had occupied, nailed on the cover, and loaded it onto the truck. They jumped into it. Another man appeared from what looked like an office at the gate, and opened the huge doors. A few seconds later the truck was gone.

The man, wearing a night watchman's uniform, approached me.

'Welcome to relative freedom, Camel,' he said, offering his hand.

'I'm very grateful,' I mumbled. 'You saved my life.'

'Not yet,' he said, 'but I will try. Incidentally, my code name is Las.'

Las was a middle-aged, short, muscular man with a bald head and black, somewhat slanting eyes.

'I thank you for – '

'Never mind,' Las said, smiling. 'You saved many lives in Pruzhany by warning the people in time.'

He took a cigarette case out of his pocket and offered me a cigarette.

'What is my next step?' I asked him. 'Do you know where my wife and daughter are?'

'Everything in due time, Camel. Let's go into the office first. We'll be able to chat about those things there.'

I followed him into a cubicle that only someone with a great deal of imagination could call an office. It had a small desk, one chair and an iron stove. That was overheating the place.

Las sat on the desk and he motioned to me to sit on the chair.

'First, we must hide you for tonight, or possibly for the next few days. That is all arranged. Then we'll reveal the whereabouts of your spouse ... in due course.'

Las spoke educated Polish, the language spoken by Poles who attended universities, by officers, by those with a good family background. I noticed that he observed me with a great deal of curiosity.

'Is she all right? Do you know her?'

Las appeared surprised by my question.

'Of course I know her,' he said. 'She was my liaison to the Pruzhany group, from the very beginning.'

'What?' I asked not believing my ears. 'Nadya née Gromov, your liaison, your spy?'

'Yes, her father and I fought the Bolsheviks in 1920, in the same regiment. I knew her as a child. I knew she was someone I could trust to be anti-Soviet. So she didn't tell you. Bravo for her.'

'But the Polish group there did not want to invite her to their first meeting.'

Las put out his cigarette and threw the butt into the stove.

'The famous meeting,' he said with a broad smile on his face. 'I know all about it. Nadya was sure you would try to take her along. At least she was sure that you would make an attempt, but Krystyna won. It doesn't matter. She was not supposed to attend it anyway – my orders.'

Las stood up and took some clothing from a hook.

'This is your new outfit, my dear Camel,' he said, handing me a black hat with a wide brim, a long shiny overcoat, and a reddish toupee.

'You will now be a Jewish Orthodox youth. There are hundreds of them walking around dressed like this. You will go to Ulica (street) Czarna number 39, apartment 3. It's on the second floor. At the door you will identify yourself as Camel. You'll be admitted. They'll keep you there for a day or two.'

I wondered whether Las also knew about my role as a spy for 'Freedom for Russia'.

'Can you tell me where I could find them, Nadya and Magda?'

'Not yet. You will learn about it when the time comes. In the meantime you have to concentrate on reaching the address I gave you. It might not be easy, even with your disguise. The Russians are quite determined to catch you.'

'But she is all right?' I asked.

'Yes, fine. Nadya will feel even better when she learns how our plan worked so well for you.'

'What plan?'

'Your escape of course,' Las said. 'When you leave here, walk to your left for three blocks, then turn right for two blocks. The cross street will be Czarna. You'll find the number easily.'

I put on the toupee, the topcoat and the wide brimmed hat. There was no mirror in the place so I could not see myself.

'You look all right,' Las said. 'In the darkness outside you will not be recognisable. Now, you must not take the rucksack with you. That would be a giveaway. Here is an old bag you can put your things in.'

After I had put the contents of the rucksack into the bag and shaken hands with Las, he said: 'Take this along.' He handed me a large book in Hebrew.

'Part of your and Nadya's plan?' I asked.

'She is brilliant. But I helped her, too, I must admit. Good luck to all of you!'

It was strange to be walking through the streets in that attire. I was afraid that I might be stopped by someone and asked for directions, but the streets were empty except for an occasional passer-by. At one of the street corners a Soviet truck passed me without stopping. I reached number 39 of Czarna street without difficulty. The house was old; the stairway had a damp, musty smell. The name on the door to apartment number 3 read Cwibelman. I knocked.

'Who's there?' a woman's voice asked.

'Camel,' I answered.

The door opened. 'Come in, Pani Camel,' an old woman in a red wig said. 'You are late.'

The door opened into a room with red plush furniture, the fabric worn out. Most of the space in the centre was taken by a large table and six chairs around it. On the walls hung portraits of old men with beards. I took off my hat, toupee, and topcoat.

'You don't have to do that,' she said and smiled. 'You looked good in that outfit. But you must be hungry.'

The room smelled of onions and urine. She served me a plate of hot soup with plenty of bread.

After I had eaten she motioned to the couch.

'This is where you will sleep. The toilets are in the court. You are not supposed to use them. The chamber pot is under the couch.'

In the morning a young Jew came and took my photograph. He handed me a document and asked me to sign the name Moyshe Fajn. That evening the same man returned with my document, which had my photograph attached and a stamp over it. He also told me that he would come at four the next morning to pick me up. He was not talkative and did not want to answer any questions about what would happen then.

It was dark and cold when we strode through the streets the following morning. We stopped in front of a house by a cart loaded with sacks. A few minutes later three men, dressed in black hats and shiny black topcoats, arrived. They spoke Yiddish for a while with my companion. Their agitated conversation continued even after all of us had boarded the cart, drawn by two horses.

Chapter 18

Moscow, March 27, 1940

Brodilo's office was as usual filled with the smell of stale cigarette smoke that formed a permanent blue cloud, enveloping the general and his visitor Vashin.

'Even a perfect house,' Brodilo said, 'might collapse because of one rotted beam. You must admit yourself that you have lost this time, Tovarich Vashin; Anton outsmarted you and won the game.'

Vashin's face reddened. It was the very first time in his career that he had been criticised about his work.

'It is our standard procedure to delay the arrest of an important spy – '

'The delay is justified if we learn the spy's contacts, but not if we allow him to get at crucial information.' Brodilo looked at Vashin ironically.

'If you'll allow me, Tovarich Brodilo, nothing – '

'Not nothing,' Brodilo interrupted with a smile. 'Anton played his part well, using all the resources available to him; his wife, his landlord, the Polish conspirators, and time. It was a virtuoso performance both in planning and in execution. Finally, he fooled you and Lobin by delaying with his lengthy, skilful testimony your discovery that the bag did not contain the documents.'

Vashin lowered his head and was about to protest, but Brodilo stopped him with a motion of his hand.

'As one of the *cognoscenti* of the art of spying, I believe he did a good job, one that qualifies him for service on our behalf.'

Vashin shuddered. The idea that someone had outsmarted him, even for a short while, hurt him. Especially as Anton would not be punished for his act but rewarded instead with a spying assignment for the Soviet Union.

'He still can't be trusted,' Vashin said.

'With his wife in our hands, a wife that he loves so much, he will do even better.'

At the reference to Nadya, Vashin's face turned red with hatred. When Vashin had met her for the first time he was stunned by her delicacy, her manners and her beauty. She reminded him of the Barski girls whom he had so much admired, and he hoped that after Anton's arrest and execution he might one day win her for himself. But that was only a daydream. Even in her desperate situation, Nadya had been laughing at him; despite his power, for her he was a proletarian, a nonentity, and for that he could not forgive her. And now in Brodilo's scheme, Nadya, the wife of a spy who at best should be toiling in a labour camp, would live like a queen as an important hostage, accorded superior treatment equal to that given members of the party.

'I had a message from our commercial delegation, now in Berlin, with the special assignment to buy tanks from the Germans. It said that the Germans must be hiding some new developments in tank design. The only tanks the delegates have seen were the familiar models. A good tank spy, or as he would be called in German, a Panzer spy, could be an asset.'

'But he is not so smart, Tovarich Brodilo,' Vashin said wiping the tears from his eyes, a result of the cigarette smoke. 'After all, we were able to anticipate all his moves, and tail him with such success that he did not notice anything. We traced Nadya before he could reach Grodno – he was not smart enough to elude us.'

'We could give him a few lessons in the art of escaping, Tovarich Vashin. When do you think they might meet?'

'In a few hours, I suppose.'

'All right. Then you will give orders that they are to be brought here, Tovarich Vashin. We must get the documents back. It is crucial for us to keep the T-34 tank a secret.'

'It is important to discover whether they will contact or be contacted by German spies who would want to help them. I will get those papers back. I swear it.'

'Do you have any evidence?'

'They cannot be so naive as to try escaping without outside help. We observed Nadya: she went around the town. We are investigating all her contacts.'

'Keep watching them, but as soon as they begin to move, stop them and bring them here.'

That is exactly what Vashin did not want to do. No one would go unpunished who had made fun of Vashin, who had made a fool of him. Vashin had lied to Brodilo. There was no doubt in his mind that Anton would try to cross the border on his own. Vashin did not want Anton to be brought to Moscow, nor did he want to let him escape. He had another plan, a much better plan for handling the matter.

'When are you leaving?'

'In two hours. I will be in charge.'

'Remember one thing, Tovarich Vashin,' Brodilo said standing up. 'It is either a fox's shrewdness or his fur.'

Vashin did not like Brodilo's last words. He knew that he would have to pay a high price for what he had planned for Anton. But that did not matter. Brodilo was wrong in saying that Vashin had lost the game. It was not true. Anton and he were still only in the middle of the game, and as when Anton and he had been playing chess and Anton had an advantage Vashin had won in the end, just so this time he would show Anton who was going to checkmate whom.

As Vashin was walking down the staircase he looked out. The

sun shone over the roofs of the houses. The spring was here. Vashin smiled, not at the thought of the beauty of spring, but in anticipation of letting Anton and Nadya travel a little farther towards the border than his boss had in mind. He could justify his conduct by claiming possible discoveries of spy networks that would be helping in the actual crossing of the border.

But there on the border, just a few metres away from their freedom from Soviet persecution, he would kill Anton in his escape, right in front of Nadya. That would be the right punishment for that bitch. Then he would get Brodilo the stolen documents from a weeping, suffering Nadya.

Chapter 19

Anton's Story

Grodno, March 27, 1940

I was getting more impatient with every hour of our journey. It was difficult for me to sit immobilised on the skimpy cart, knowing that in a few hours I would be seeing Nadya and Magda. I longed to see their smiles, hear their laughter.

Finally, after some fourteen hours, the journey was over. We had stopped at what had appeared to me to be the centre of a town. One of my companions took me aside and whispered, 'the church of The Holy Cross.' Then he turned around and disappeared in the crowd.

After walking for a few minutes I stopped a young man and asked him how to get to the church of The Holy Cross. He seemed stunned by my question, but he pointed to a church tower only a few hundred metres away. I quickly realised the reason for his surprise: I was still dressed as an orthodox Jew. And in this outfit, upon entering a Catholic church I would draw the attention of the whole congregation immediately.

I turned into the door of an apartment building, found the staircase, took off my hat, coat and wig and put them into my bag. I did not feel secure walking towards the church, in my regular clothing, but no one seemed to follow me.

The church was full of people. It was difficult to spot Nadya in this crowd. And during the liturgy it was impossible to move through the packed aisles to look for her. Would Nadya be here today? 'She must,' I said to myself, my heart pounding in anticipation of seeing her.

I was looking at all the women, staring at their backs as I tried to recognise Nadya among them. Oh, God, I thought, I hope that nothing has happened to her. Not being familiar with the Catholic liturgy I felt strange in the church. I was afraid that an unfamiliar gesture would reveal that I was not a Catholic. People began to kneel down, allowing me a better view – and then I saw her. She was on the other side of the nave, a few rows ahead of me.

As if I were propelled by an irresistible force I moved towards her. Nothing could stop me. Disregarding everything, stumbling over the kneeling people, I rushed to Nadya. '*Tss, prosze kleknac* (please kneel down)' I kept hearing voices. '*To grzech* (It's a sin),' some unknown man said.

I was near her. She saw me and smiled; her body began to quiver. Kneeling down next to her, and putting my arm around her I said, 'Nadya, Na – ' I could not go on since I was choking up. I don't know for how long we remained like that.

Later on people began to get up and Nadya and I slowly made our way towards the door. Holding hands we walked down the steps to the street. The March sun warmed us; they were the first rays of sun I had seen in many long months. I wanted to tell Nadya so much but I could not find the right words. Suddenly Nadya stopped.

'Hold me, Anton, hold me tight.'

I felt her warmth, as I was holding her in my arms oblivious to the people passing by, the blue sky, the sunshine.

'Magda is waiting,' Nadya said as we resumed our walk. 'Each time I went out to meet you she waited for me to come back with you. "You must bring Papa back," she said, "bring Papa back." It will be a great joy for her to see you.'

'And where are we going?'

'Through Las I arranged to get a room for us. You must be hungry.'

'No, not right now. And you? Have you had enough to eat?'

'It did not matter, nothing mattered except your return.'

We continued our walk in silence until we reached an old two-storey brick building. In a few minutes I was holding Magda in my arms. We celebrated our reunion with a meal of bread and hard-boiled eggs. Later on, sitting on the bed with Nadya while Magda played with pieces of wood painted by Nadya to represent dolls, I told Nadya about my incarceration and my escape from my pursuers. She told me how she had reached Brest with Magda and how Avram contacted the Polish Underground in the Pod Debem restaurant, and asked Las to help me elude the Soviets.

I noticed that Nadya seemed somehow distant, as if something were not fully cleared up. Also she did not show much enthusiasm about our tank documents.

'Where do you keep them?' I asked.

'The usual place, under the mattress, Anton. You must be tired, darling.'

'We have to hide them in a better place,' I said. 'Perhaps the best thing would be to sew them into Magda's coat. That would be the last place they would check.'

Nadya nodded. I asked her for a needle and thread, and I began to sew the papers into the coat, while Nadya looked on, not volunteering to help me.

'I can see that you have had experience sewing things into clothing, Anton. By the way, have you seen Masha again?'

'Of course not,' I said surprised by her question. 'Why do you ask?'

'Ever since you visited Masha in her library you haven't been the same.'

'What do you mean?'

'You are still keeping a secret from me. You never told me what happened between the two of you.'

'I'll tell you, then,' I said. And I told her with all the details, the smiles, and the tears of all my meetings with Masha.

'It is much worse than I imagined,' Nadya said when I concluded my story.

'What is worse, Nadya? After all, nothing happened.'

'Everything happened.'

'But I did not even kiss her on the cheek – just a handshake. Don't you believe me?'

'I believe you. But that's exactly what is terrible. A man easily forgets, *une petite affaire,* but such a deep involvement with lilacs, the dawn dew and the *byeryozkas* lingers on for years. It is like a bomb that has not yet gone off.'

'So *une petite affaire* is all right with you.'

'Don't you dare, Anton! It is just by way of comparison.'

Both of us were silent for a while, staring at the blue chrysanthemums of the beaded wallpaper in our room.

'I certainly would never tell you that I am happy because you and Masha are happy. I hate it, I hate it,' she said, jumping up from the bed and pacing the floor like a tigress in a cage.

'What do you want me to do about it? You know that I will never see Masha again, that I love you and only you.'

'You will keep memories,' Nadya said, sitting down next to me and putting her arms around me. 'But I will fight them,' she said, and she kissed me.

'We should not be talking about that now. The problem is to escape to survive. The Soviets are on our heels and you – '

'Isn't our love the most important thing?' Nadya asked. 'With our love, a total and undivided love for each other, we will survive everything, including the Soviet pursuit.'

She was so convinced of the truth of her own words that the feeling was contagious, and I began to believe in them myself.

'Did you miss me?' Nadya asked me again.

'Yes, of course, darling.'

'Then say it.'

'I missed you every instant more than I have ever missed anything before in my entire life,' I said kissing Nadya, but I was not sure that she heard my answers. She had closed her eyes, responding to my kisses.

Later on, for a long time I could not sleep for thinking about our escape. I concluded that the best way would be again to persuade some soldiers to drive us as far west as possible in their truck, and in that way avoid the usual route that Franek had described, including travelling by train.

The next day, as soon as it was dark, I went out in search of such a means of transport. I stopped a few soldiers standing around their trucks, but they were either not interested in helping me or did not plan to travel west. After two hours of these unsuccessful efforts, I decided to try looking in restaurants.

In the first one I visited there were no Soviets, but at my next stop I saw a group of three soldiers drinking vodka. It was a small room with only six round bare wooden tables, three of which were occupied. In addition to the soldiers, two couples sat at separate tables and carried on conversations in Polish. I sat down at the table closest to the Soviets and ordered a small carafe of vodka. One of the soldiers, a tall man of about my age wearing a leather jacket, a frequent article of dress with truckers, was describing amorous adventures that made his companions roar with laughter. He happened to notice me, and he said to his companions, 'Look at that guy. He must have love troubles to be drinking alone.'

'Worse than that,' I said, raising my glass. 'My wife is sick and I have to go to the village of Bielisko tomorrow.'

'*Ty Nash*?' (are you one of us, literally 'ours', a Soviet) the man in the leather jacket asked, hearing me speak Russian.

'I was born here,' I said, bringing my chair and my vodka to their table. We drank a number of rounds. They were curious to hear about life in Poland before the war and they asked me many questions. Around midnight, when they were paying the bill, the man with the leather jacket told me about a friend of his who would take us, indicating that it would be wise to get him a five-litre bottle of vodka for his trouble, and that he would pick us up at six in the morning in front of this place.

Following his instructions I bought a five-litre bottle of vodka from the restaurateur. Later on in our room we packed, and a little before six in the morning wearing our costumes, we appeared in front of the restaurant.

As we waited for the arrival of the truck I began to wonder if my drinking companion had remembered his promise, but to my surprise the truck appeared. A very tall man in uniform jumped down. When he saw how I was dressed he was ready to climb back into the truck.

'I'm the same guy who drank vodka with your friend.' I handed him the bottle, but he hesitated. Finally he said, '*A tshort poberee* (the devil with it), I am *Starshina* (Sergeant) Volodya. Jump into the truck!'

We obeyed.

After we had driven for an hour, the truck was stopped by a sentry. One of the soldiers jumped up on the back of the truck and looked at us. 'Who are these people?'

'Don't you see?' Volodya answered. 'A Jewish family.'

'Don't you know, you son of a bitch,' the sentry said, 'that you are not supposed to transport any fucking civilians.'

'Fuck your mother,' Volodya said, without raising his voice and smiling at the sentry. 'Don't you see that the woman is sick?'

'Fuck yours,' the sentry responded with a friendly smile. 'Sick or not, you fucking bastards aren't supposed to do it.'

'You whore's son, you better shut up. Have you some tobacco on you? Fuck the world, we've run out of it.'

'Fuck. Here's your fucking tobacco,' the sentry said reaching in his pocket and giving a fistful to Volodya, who tore a piece of newspaper and made a cigarette. The sentry gave him a light. Volodya waved at the sentry, who watched us with a satisfied smile as we drove away. We went another hour without any interruption. Then the truck stopped in the middle of a country road.

Volodya appeared at the back of the truck and told us that we had reached our destination. We stepped down. Volodya took me aside, walking several metres from the truck. There were patches of snow on the road, but the recent rains had melted most of it, turning the road into a sea of mud.

'It's none of my business,' he said as we were walking on the side of the road, 'but I would not use this disguise anymore. The Jews are not running away to the Germans.' I did not dare say anything. I only nodded. 'Stay away from villages. I know what you are planning to do. I'll give the vodka back to you. You may need it.'

'We couldn't carry it,' I said.

'Then I'll give you food – a loaf of bread and a sausage. You can carry that.'

We returned to the truck. He gave me the things he had mentioned and shook my hand. 'It is straight west from here, some ten kilometres.' He turned the truck around and drove off in the opposite direction. Smiling, he waved to us.

We followed his advice. First I discarded all the items of my masquerade: the toupee, the hat, and the silky topcoat. The March sun was melting the remaining snow and the earth was soggy in the fields. Yet we were able to make a few kilometres per hour. Every now and then we saw a village, which we tried to avoid. We calculated our route by the sun since there were no other signs to guide us. I carried Nadya's rucksack with all that we possessed. We stopped at one point on a small elevation, ate a few slices of bread and sausage, and then continued our journey. It was noon and the sun felt warm and pleasant. I was planning to travel to within a few kilometres of the border, and to wait there until dark. I had heard that the best time to cross the border was three or four o'clock in the morning. Few sentries were on duty then, and those on duty were less alert.

As we began walking again, a truck appeared on the horizon. About three hundred metres in front of us it stopped. Two uniformed men stepped down from it and watched us. I knew it meant trouble but it was too late to do anything. We decided to walk straight towards the truck. As we approached the two men, I noticed from the stars on their sleeves that they were N.K.V.D. commissars. Without any word of greeting or any questions, one motioned to us to board the vehicle. We drove only a few hundred metres. The truck stopped in front of a house in a village. Again without wasting any words, one of the two, a tall broad-shouldered man, waved us into the house. The other, also broad-shouldered, but shorter than his colleague, followed us.

The interior was typical of Polish farmhouses, with handmade furniture, pictures, and a statue of the Madonna, a few faded photographs on the wall, and red geraniums on the window sills. I wondered where the owners of this house could be. Evicted to Siberia?

As soon as all of us were inside, the tall commissar asked me to hand him over my rucksack.

'Your passport?' the commissar asked, addressing me.

I handed over to him my recently acquired document.

'Moyshe Fajn,' he read. 'Are you a Jew?'

I nodded.

'He does not look Jewish to me,' the other commissar said.

'The kid does,' said the tall man sitting across the table from us. Nadya and Magda were sitting on a bench against the wall. I could see Magda's eyes getting bigger and darker. Nadya did not appear to be concerned.

'The wife does not,' said the smaller of the two.

'Who the hell knows?' the tall commissar said, taking a cigarette and lighting it. 'The devil himself wouldn't be able to settle the matter. Some Jews look like Easterners, some others look like the Slavs. What are you doing here with your wife and your kid?'

I hesitated.

'Answer my question!'

'My mother is on the other side,' I mumbled. 'Her parents too.'

'Do you know,' the smaller commissar asked while pacing the room, 'that escaping from the Soviet Union, crossing the border illegally, is a crime punishable by death?'

I did not say anything.

'You are now in the border zone,' the taller commissar said, inhaling deeply. 'That already constitutes a crime.'

'Oh, ho, ho! Look who's talking!' Nadya said. 'The world's greatest criminals are preaching laws. The world is coming to an end. That's like the devil preaching the Bible.'

The two commissars exchanged glances.

'Stay out of it,' the taller one said. 'I'm talking to him.'

'Let's see what they've got,' the smaller one said. He went to the table, opened the rucksack, and emptied it. The Jewish prayer book caught my eye at once. I had discarded my masquerade costume but had forgotten about the book.

Both of the commissars saw me glance at the book. They must have been experienced at this sort of thing.

'That's it,' the smaller one said, taking the prayer book in his hands. 'You are spies. The book contains some of your secrets.'

'Don't touch it with your dirty hands,' Nadya said. 'That is our holy book. Put it back!'

'Stay away, you bitch,' the smaller man said to Nadya, who stood up and moved towards the table.

The commissar opened the book and leafed through the pages. He seemed to be disappointed to find the writing in Hebrew lettering. The taller man looked at him, threw his cigarette on the floor and put it out with his boot. 'I told you they were Jewish.'

The smaller commissar took a knife out of his pocket and began to cut the book apart, slicing the binding into small pieces.

'Let's take them to the *Komandatura* (Police Station) for questioning,' the tall man said.

'We will check them here,' the other man said. 'We will bring them to the *Komandatura* as spies. Take off your shoes! All of you!'

We obeyed. The commissars looked at our shoes. Both were experienced. Seeing that the shoes had been soled a long time ago, they did not bother to cut them apart. Just a few probes with their knives on the inside of the shoes satisfied them. Then came the turn of the overcoats and jackets. The smaller commissar cut the bread apart and made a few cuts into the fabric of the rucksack. Magda's eyes showed her fear. Nadya appeared quite unconcerned. They cut through the lining of the other clothing, and found nothing. The taller commissar looked at his colleague.

'Well, shall we take them?' he said.

'Take off your pants and shirt!' the smaller man said.

I obeyed.

'Shame on you!' Nadya cried out. 'This in front of a child.' Magda began crying. The short man checked my pants and shirt quickly. I was standing in my shorts, but he did not touch me. 'You dress now!' the tall man said.

The smaller man approached Nadya. 'Take off your blouse!'

Magda ran to me crying. I took her in my arms. She was shaking. 'Don't be afraid!' I whispered. 'They are not going to hurt you.'

'Stay away from me, you fucking son of a bitch!' Nadya said. He tried to grab her blouse, but she slapped him in the face. I was surprised that Nadya knew such language. I was sure that she could not be aware of the meanings of words of that kind. Or was she?

He grabbed her blouse from behind and tore it.

'You whore's son!' Nadya snarled. 'Take your dirty hands away!'

With his short fingers he quickly touched her breasts.

'You are like your boss Beria,' Nadya shouted, 'abusing females.'

At the sound of the name Beria the man stopped as if struck by lightning.

'You will regret that,' he said. 'I'll make a report. You will be shot for it.'

'Oh, be my guest,' Nadya said, readjusting her brassiere. 'Everybody knows Beria and his cohorts are grabbing young girls from the streets and abusing them sexually. Beria abuses the wives of arrested men.'

The two commissars were stunned.

'Make the report!' Nadya continued. 'Maybe Tovarich Stalin will read it. Then the greatest whore's son will be shot.' Nadya put her sweater on. 'Hundreds of thousands, millions should read this report. The whole world should read it.'

The two commissars seemed not to know what to do next. The three of us dressed. Nadya collected into the rucksack the things that were still usable. She helped me slip into the straps of the rucksack. Without looking at the commissars she marched out of the hut, holding Magda by the hand. As I started to follow, I glanced at the commissars. They sat there with their heads down, not uttering a word.

We walked west. When we had been waiting for several minutes, we heard the truck's engine. I looked back, but the truck was moving in the opposite direction.

'I was so scared,' I said. 'You didn't have to abuse them. They let us go in the end.'

'You don't understand the Soviets, Anton,' Nadya said, trying to catch her breath. 'The only way to deal with them is to hit them hard. The harder the better. If you are polite, they'll hit you. Squeeze you like a lemon, take full advantage of you, and they won't respect you.' Nadya halted.

'If I had been polite with them by now we'd be at their station, being processed for a camp. Your identity would be discovered and they would shoot you. This way, what I said about Beria it would be too embarrassing for them to bring us in and make out a report that they would have to sign their names to. Right now they're hoping that we make it to the other side and the whole matter can be forgotten.'

The sunny morning was over. The sky was now covered, overcast and a few drops of rain began to fall. As we pressed forwards the few drops turned into rain. Here and there in the distance a Soviet soldier appeared. We knew we were approaching the border. In front of us was a space covered by bushes.

'We are only three kilometres from the border,' Nadya said.

Beyond that thicket there were fields, I had been told. There were watch-towers on those fields, projecting floodlights. Beyond the fields was a clear zone, fifty metres long, ending at a barbed-wire fence. Beyond the fence – freedom in the German occupied zone.

When we were only a few metres from the patch of thicket, a soldier with a dog on a leash appeared. He walked towards us. We ran until we reached the thicket, which turned out to be growing in patches of water and mud. We heard the barking of the dog and the soldier's shouts. We were completely hidden by the dwarf pines and the juniper bushes. I tore my overcoat. Nadya breathed with difficulty. We could not run any more. We stopped and sat down. The noises faded. We were lucky. The soldier must have decided not to pursue us any longer, or perhaps he had caught sight of someone else. He might have been reluctant to enter the thicket and risk getting shot, or sinking into the mud up to his knees. Besides it was raining hard.

There was now nothing else to do but to sit there, waiting, and getting wetter.

The rain had been going on for six hours and the big cold drops were hitting us ceaselessly. It did not matter very much since our clothing had got soaked in a short time and weighed a ton. More rain would not get us any wetter.

Nadya took out the bread from the rucksack, our last bit of food. It was wet, but we were hungry and we ate it in silence.

With the rain the soggy ground turned to puddles and we were literally sitting in water. All of us were very cold, but none of us mentioned cold, hunger or wetness. We knew it would not change.

'Still six hours until midnight,' Nadya said.

'Yes.'

'Papa, when we get there ... ' Magda said, 'the Germans are good, aren't they?'

'Yes, they are good. Some are good.'

'And the Russians are bad?'

'Yes, some of the Russians are bad,' I answered.

'Papa, but you and Nadya are Russian.'

'Yes, we are.'

'But you and Nadya are good.'

'We try to be,' I said.

'But if you are Russian, why do you want to go to the Germans?'

'We must. They would arrest us if we stayed here.'

'Like they killed Mama?'

'Yes.'

'Will the Germans arrest us?'

'No, I don't think so,' I said.

Nadya said, 'We will have a good home in the mountains. We'll live there. There'll be many flowers! It will be warm.'

'And I'll have a doll?'

'Yes, we'll get you a doll,' Nadya said, 'and a ball and many other toys.'

Nadya wrapped the remains of the uneaten bread in pieces of newspaper, but the sodden paper fell apart. Our last bit of bread was being destroyed. I did not have the energy to do anything about it.

'We must sleep a little,' Nadya told Magda, who was sitting in her lap. A few minutes later Magda was breathing evenly. Nadya seemed to doze off too.

It grew dark. The rain stopped, but the sky was overcast.

'A good night to make the crossing,' I thought.

I tried to fall asleep but I could not. I was thinking about Vienna and the Rosengarten. The roses would not be in bloom yet, there were still some weeks to go. But the buds must be forming already. The horse-chestnut trees were probably beginning to blossom. The new season was starting.

Nadya woke up, shivering in her wet clothing.

'Did you sleep?' I asked her.

'Sort of. I was thinking of the mountains.'

'Why?'

'Are there many flowers? I have never been in the mountains. I have not even seen any hills.'

'Yes, there are many flowers, this time of year particularly.'

'And the air?'

'Yes, the air is full of the scent of the pines.' I saw that she was finding it hard to breathe. 'The best thing in the mountains is the views. As you go up and down they're always changing. You can see villages in the valleys. The sky is different too. It is blue and not grey as it is here.'

'And the people,' she said, 'will they hate us?'

'A few. Some of them will but not all.'

'But nobody will want us?'

'Yes, I'm afraid that's so. Everywhere we will be the unwanted refugees. Of course the Germans should be grateful to us for our achievement, but they consider Slavs and Jews as inferior races, so even there despite our success we'll be second class at best.'

'I don't mind,' Nadya said smiling. 'We'll make up for that by respecting and loving each other more. We'll start a life with a new deeper meaning, trying to forget the past with its horror.'

'It's not easy to erase the past, Nadya.'

'We will try. We must, Anton. For a happy life there we must.'

I looked at my watch. It was approaching midnight.

'We'd better start walking.'

Nadya had to wake Magda. We stood up. Our overcoats were terribly heavy. All of us shivered. We began to walk forwards in a westerly direction. I went first, carrying the rucksack that seemed to weigh a ton. Nadya followed holding Magda's hand. We walked some two hundred metres. Fear and exertion warmed us up. Each of us stopped shivering.

We made slow progress through the thicket. Some parts of it were so dense that we had to walk around them before we could resume our westerly course.

It took us about an hour to reach the thicket's edge. According to our information plan the field was three kilometres long. The towers stood about two kilometres away, each projecting a floodlight that circled around.

I looked at the sky. It was dark and overcast. Unless we encountered a horse patrol we should be safe until we were near the towers.

We started to walk across the field, Magda between us, Nadya and I holding hands. The soil of the field was soaked and in places Nadya and I sank nearly knee-deep. We made very slow progress. We heard shots in the distance.

'What is that, Papa?' Magda asked.

'Someone is shooting.'

'Are they shooting at us?'

'No, I don't think so.'

'Will they shoot at us?'

'They might. But they won't hit us. You must be very quiet. When we are close to the towers, no matter what happens, you mustn't cry or speak.'

'Yes, Papa.'

I was wondering whether they were shooting at other people who were trying to escape or if they were firing on principle to scare people. We were coming closer and closer to the towers. They were placed some five hundred metres apart. The floodlights spanned a radius of 250 metres. It took approximately one minute for each floodlight to complete its circle. As we approached I saw that all the area covered by the floodlights was well lit. 'Do the guards on each tower watch all the time?' I asked myself.

'We must crawl now,' I said. We began to slither along on the ground. I chose a route midway between two towers.

'When I touch you once, it means stop. Two touches mean go.' The ground was soaked and in a few minutes we were covered with mud.

'Put the mud on your faces,' I whispered. We were still beyond the 250 metre radius. When the lights were turned in our direction, they would be able to see our movements. I figured that when we lay still we could not be seen. Since we were crawling, we had to stop more often. Our progress was very slow. Now we had reached the very centre. We stopped moving and the lights covered us. We were silent. I could hear the beating of my heart through the thick wet clothing, and Nadya's wheezing. As soon as the lights passed we struggled on. Our stops became less frequent, and I could see the edge of the wood.

When we reached the area beyond the field I decided that we could stand up. The intermittent sound of shooting continued. Sometimes the shots seemed to be so near that I thought they were aimed at us.

The mud clinging to our clothing made them still heavier. When I turned around I saw in the floodlight several uniformed men running. They had lights and were shouting. We fell to the ground and crawled until we reached the trees. The shouts came closer. In the woods we threw off our coats and began to run. Now we could not be seen from the field. After a few metres of running, Nadya stopped. She was breathing heavily.

'I just can't,' she said. 'You must, you must escape - with Magda. Go on alone, I'll stay ... behind.'

'Nadya, you must,' I whispered. 'You must! We have no choice.'

She sat down, trying to catch her breath. The shouting from

the field went on. They were nearer now. I took Nadya in my arms and Magda, forlorn, held on to my jacket. I realised that I would never be able to carry her over the rough ground.

Nadya noticed. 'I'll try,' she said.

The shouts grew no louder – the search patrols remained in the field. We were walking now, and we came to the edge of the woods. Fifty metres away was the barbed-wire fence.

I looked at the sky. It was no longer overcast. There were broken clouds. I checked my watch. It was four o'clock in the morning.

'We will have to run the last stretch,' I said. We waited a few minutes in order to catch our breath. In that time the moon came out and flooded the space around us with light. Beyond the fence I could see a farmhouse. People slept there quietly. It was just seventy metres away. 'Oh, God,' I thought, 'if only we can make it.'

Nadya was breathing more easily now. The moon still shone brightly. It was a three-quarter moon, but by its light one could see well even at a distance.

We began to run. Suddenly I heard the voices. I pushed Nadya and Magda down. Along the strip of land between the wood and the fence a patrol was advancing. We were only a few metres from the woodline. Slowly we crawled back and hid behind the trees. There were two border guards walking with a dog. They carried rifles and they were talking in loud voices.

'In our country,' one said in Ukrainian, 'the cherry trees will be blooming, and here there's nothing but fucking mud.'

'Why in hell this fucking look around?' another voice said. Suddenly their dog stopped and began to bark.

My heart froze. 'This is the end,' I thought.

The guards stopped, too. The dog pulled in our direction.

'There's someone there,' the second guard said. 'Oh, fuck it. The damn dog smells a fox or a hare. I've had enough running for one night.' He kicked the dog. 'Come on, you stupid bitch. And then I would climb the flowering cherry trees.' Their voices died away.

We let some time pass. The clouds had disappeared. We would have to run in the full light. Except for the shots, which were still going on, there were no sounds. A distance of about 50 metres separated us from the fence. A good runner could cover it in six seconds, but not us. The ground here was firm and covered in grass. I looked at the farmhouse again. It was some twelve metres from the fence. The dark shadows reflected the light of the moon. There were other dark stretches around the house. Between the house and the fence lay a pile of wood planks. I stepped forwards alone. I could not see anyone. I heard no voices. The shooting went on.

As I came back to Nadya I saw that her breathing was very irregular. She was sitting erect with her eyes closed, using the trunk of a tree for support. I took her hand, and she pressed mine with all her strength.

'I'll carry you first. Then I'll return and get Magda.'

She shook her head.

'But we must. We must run now darling. I'll carry you.'

In the moonlight I could see her features well; despite the cold there were drops of perspiration on her forehead. She tried to say something – her lips moved, but I could not hear the words. I felt desperate and sat down next to Nadya on the wet ground. The air was filled with the smell of rotted leaves, the smell of death.

Nadya made another attempt to say something. This time, reading her lips, I understood: 'Magda.'

'Yes, darling,' I whispered, 'I'll carry you first, and then Magda. I cannot carry both of you, and Magda might get lost.'

She shook her head.

'Carry Magda first.' I could hear her almost inaudible whisper.

'All right, and then I'll come back for you.'

Nadya shook her head again.

'Too risky. Stay there Anton.'

'I won't go without you, Nadya.'

I knew that Nadya had been right. Running once, we had a chance to make it; running back and forth we had none. But there was no point in my going alone – a life without Nadya would not be worth living. I looked again at the farmhouse on the other side, that I could see clearly through the barbed wire. We could not make it. It was so close, and yet too far for us.

The sound of a whistle cut the air, a sound that I had heard before.

'Nadya, it's Vashin. We must try once more.'

'I can't.'

'Vashin's last move, and he's won again,' I thought. I knew

that he might reach us in a few minutes or even a few seconds, and that it would mean the end of 'Operation Parterre', the end of us. My thoughts raced on: what did Krugov mean when he named our mission 'Operation Parterre'? By Parterre did he mean on the ground, through the ground, across or close to the ground? Did he know the Polish word for tank: *czolg*, a crawler?

We could not run the fifty metres, but I could crawl. I could do that even with Nadya and Magda on my back. But that would take a few minutes ... too much time. Vashin would catch up with us. I must find a way to stall him for a few crucial moments, but how? The thought of Khomikov's papers came to me. I could scatter a few pages – the ones on top, they were not vital; yet Vashin seeing them would want to collect them. Only a few seconds had passed since I began to think about that decision; with trembling fingers I tore open the lining of Magda's coat, pulled out several sheets, ran back and scattered them.

'I got rid of some of the documents to delay Vashin. Now put your hands around my neck,' I whispered to Nadya as I lay next to her. 'I will crawl with you and with Magda.'

She nodded, but did not move.

'Nadya, we must hurry! Please!'

'Do ... you ... love ... love me?' Nadya whispered, struggling with her breathing.

'This is not the right –'

'The time ... is always right to ... say ... I love.'

'Of course I do,' I whispered. 'Please Nadya, please!'

'Then say it!'

'I love you Nadya. Let's rush!'

The sound of shouts came from the woods, but Nadya still did not move.

'The tank stuff –' she whispered, 'throw away all of it!'

I was shocked.

'Darling, but why? We struggled so much.'

'You mean you and Masha did.'

Oh, God. Nadya's jealousy. She did not want to carry the documents across the border. They would remind me of Masha, and if they contributed to the liberation of Russia, my gratitude to her would last forever. But that was insane.

'We must help the Germans.'

'Let ... them ... find out for themselves.'

The sound of voices drew nearer. I seized the rest of the sheets of paper and threw them away. Nadya placed Magda, half-asleep, on my neck and lay on top of me herself. Despite the sound of shots and voices I could still hear Nadya's whisper: 'And do you promise to forget?'

'I promise to forget,' I whispered, moving forwards with my load, oblivious to everything that was happening behind me. I slithered forwards like a giant tortoise until I reached the fence, feverishly raised the lowest barbed wire with my bare hands, pushed Magda and then Nadya through the opening. Nadya held the wire for me; I felt it cutting into my back but I made it through. The three of us crawled behind the stack of boards. I heard voices and shots quite near to us.

The shots went on as we found shelter behind the pile of wood, and intensified as we crawled behind the house. We were saved from the horrors of our own country to become again the unwelcome and unwanted refugees on a foreign land.

Later on, after our clothes had dried a little and we had eaten a few pieces of bread bought from a Polish farmer, we started to walk towards the nearest railroad station. I put my arms around Nadya and Magda, relishing their closeness. It was cold and misty as we stumbled through the mud of that lonely country road. Soon the large drops of the March rain began to fall on us again, but none of us cared that we were going to get wet.